T0368769

Wings

Of

Time

ROBERT H. LALONDE

Order this book online at www.trafford.com
or email orders@trafford.com

Most Trafford titles are also available at major online book retailers.

Printed in the United States of America.

ISBN: 978-1-4269-6121-2 (sc)
ISBN: 978-1-4269-6122-9 (e)

Trafford rev. 06/27/2011

 www.trafford.com

North America & International
toll-free: 1 888 232 4444 (USA & Canada)
phone: 250 383 6864 ✦ fax: 812 355 4082

Word & Abbreviation Meanings

-Abode-
Home/House/Apt.

-Adioso- Goodbye

-AML- Automatic
Mechanical Lift

-ASAP- As Soon As
Possible

-Centrics- Centimeters

-Centritton- Century

-Chamber- Room

-Cinematic- Video- Vid

-Clandestine-Secret

-Consociate- Friend

-Dectrittons- Decades

-Digits- Numbers

-E.M.V-Emergency
Medical Vehicle

-Enigmatic- Mystery

-Epock- Hour

-Gribbit- Coin

-Inkling- Thinking

-Jotter- Writing Pad

-Jotting- Writing

-Kilom- Kilometer

- K. B. N. S.-Kor
Bissal Nautical Ship

-K.B.M.Co. – Kor
Bissal Military
Coalition

-KPS- Knots per Sec

-Metrics- Meters

-Mites- Minutes

-N.Z.C.M.Co-
Northern ZarCedra
Military Coalition

-Octapar- Week

-P.A.R- Planetary Axis
Revolution=Day

-Parchment- Paper

-PAT- Prototype
Advancements in
Technology

-PCD- Public
Conversing Device

-S.B.M.Co.- Sol Bissal
Military Coalition

-Seminary- School

-S.H.Z.C.A- Secret
Humanarian ZarCedra
Alliance

-Swill- Drink

-Times Elapsed- Past

-Times Yet To Come-
Future

-Thrawl- Fish

-Transporters- Carriers

-Twilight- Night

-Trints- Months

-Tritton- Year

-ZCSD- ZarCedra Solar
Department

Introduction

In a solar system in the far reaches of the Dalnary Galaxy, on the Planet ZarCedra there is a dilemma that must be faced. For the fate of a free Planet depends on the actions of one citizen, his prototype aircraft, and his cybernetic and on-board super computers.

"On the planet I call my abode; this planetary axis revolution/p.a.r date is 07.06.2115. I have been ordered by Sr. Commodore Boone to dictate a detailed account of my time and all the things I have done in the 21st Centritton. He is unaware of the life we had in the 22nd Centritton before my step back in time to fix what had gone terribly wrong long ago. I told him of the alien dictatorship we were under for near a centritton before I made my wish to change times gone by so our times yet to come would be worth wanting. Before I start recording my detailed report allow me to explain a few things about the brutal aliens that took over our planet and the calmer, gentler alien race that in the end assisted us to reclaim it.

Protreria and Antreria are twin planets in a twelve-planet solar system, in the Currecuse Sector of the Dalnary Galaxy. The only differences of the inhabitants of these two Planets are the contrast of skin coloration and the formation of forehead structure. Antrerian skin color is a lighter shade of blue-green than the Protrerian because Antreria is 150, 000 kiloms closer to their sun. The bones of their foreheads protrude in opposite directions as the Protrerian.

Instead of embracing friendship these two Planets opted for war and they have been at war with each other for more than twenty centrittons, even though the reason for this altercation died along with their ancestors.

But in the tritton 2015, the Protrerian High Command, a race of beings that wasted all their planet's natural resources and know their sun is going to extinguish and go nova in about a centritton. So the Protrerian High Command sets their sights on the vast array of habitable planets for a Planet to concur and take over, and alas they find one.

Protrerian long-range sensors had discovered such a planet, which met their demands, a planet of citizens who haven't yet stopped fighting wars amongst themselves. This planet of mostly salt water, this planet called ZarCedra.

Protreria has sent its attack, energy extractor and personnel crafts to gather information about this planet, and to take it over at any cost. They decide on our planet, not only because it is the closest M-class planet to them but also because the citizens of our planet have discovered a way of preserving the purity of the breathable air around our world even with the quickly deterioration of the ozone layer.

On the planet of Antreria, this race of beings thinks it odd that a race of beings so intent on destroying them, just one p.a.r suddenly stops their attacks and wants peace. It isn't long until the Antrerian Armada discovers what the Protrerian High Command are up to and think the actions of the Protrerian's are despicable and come to the aide of the citizens of ZarCedra. But the advancements made by the Protrerian allowed them to become the victors. ZarCedra was now a planet that belonged to the Protrerian High Command, and the Antrerian Armada was barely able to escape but banished for the assistance they gave the Humanarian Race.

Life has been very hard on ZarCedra for near a centritton, since 07.01.2015, the planetary axis revolution or p.a.r ZarCedra was attacked with no advanced warning, by the Alien Race known as the Protrerian High Command. The following seventy trittons our captors shunned Humanarian kind, making life as miserable as they could. Until one p.a.r a Humanarian lady fell in love with a Protrerian male. Although there were many differences between them, they mated, proving a life of mixed species can exist. Now thirty trittons later the Humanarian's and the Protrerian's have been mating and joining in matrimony.

Even though the skin coloring of the Protrerian's is a dark bluish-green color, and they have a strong body odor. The foreheads of these alien beings had thick bones, which rippled the appearance of their faces.

The male Protrerian grew to the height of three metrics and weighed up to 150 kiloms. Females of the species started applying color to the rippled ridges to make themselves more attractive to Humanarian males. The Protrerian female were also shorter than the Protrerian male, only standing a maximum height of two metrics and weighed up to a maximum of 65 kiloms, although the average female weighed about 45.5 kiloms until their first litter of off spring. They were perfect for the average Humanarian male, and the fact that a Protrerian female had four breasts nestled on their belly of thick very soft fur, which didn't hinder their appearance in the least.

But the Humanarian Race secretly hated the fact that their planet had been taken over by these aliens. Secret facilities were built around the planet by ZarCedra's all Humanarian military forces. It is now almost the one-centritton anniversary since the overtaking of our planet and the Antrerian Race has returned to ZarCedra because now their sun is about to go nova. So they come back to planet ZarCedra in hopes they can also reside here.

Enter myself, Jr. Commodore Jeroque Teldat, but at the beginning of my mission I was a Major; I am a test pilot, also a teacher in the field of Aero Dynamics. For this reason, the Secret Humanarian ZarCedra Alliance, a secret division of the North ZarCedra Military Coalition had ordered me to take up and use the newly constructed prototype Supersonic Dragon 228-D Spy Jet Stealth.

Which is equipped with technically advanced features, such as its size, design, ominous Stealth mode capabilities, it is equipped with an Omagon 2115 Star Drive Engine and Electronic Flux Inducer that gives it great speed, a Comodrone Electronics P-52 Hydrogenic Generator, and it also has advanced weaponry such as Sareden Quantum laser and XTR-9000 Plasma Pulse Cannons, Protonic Electromagnetic Cluster Missals and Neutronic Electromagnetic Cluster Torpedo's.

Accompanied on my journey is 'PAT', my on-board and cybernetic super computers, a consociate who offers insight and someone who reminds me that what I'm fighting for is worth all the sacrifices I must make in order to attain the times yet to come we of the Humanarian Race had lost long ago. The scientists decided to give the cybernetic super computer a female form to calm my nerves in times of distress, which I found very comforting on my journey.

As I start my mission of secretly settling the Antrerian's on ZarCedra, everything seems to be going according to plan then something happens to make my mission much tougher. From keeping a race of beings under surveillance and safe from their enemies to finding myself at the beginning of the original Grand War to try and save ZarCedra from being severely attacked and taken over, again! As I record this report, I had to surmise what my companions said or did in my absence but in detail, this is my 11-p.a.r in-depth report."

Planetary Axis Revolution or P.A.R 1

"My name is Major Jeroque Teldat and this p.a.r's date is 06.26.2115. I am at the Grinshaw Military Facility and ZarCedra Planet Force's Main Headquarters in Cangla City, in the Honorary Regime of Placaden, Tanglar; the time is 07 hundred epocks. On this p.a.r I am in the office of Sr. Commodore Boone, my Commanding officer and to the best of my knowledge this is my in-depth report."

*****

"Computer, activate security mode. "Security mode activated, you may now commence."

"Maj. Teldat, we have numerous Antrerian spacecraft cloaked and secretly positioned over Vertgren Isle, by the Antrerian Race being here on ZarCedra violates the peace accord between them and the Protrerian High Command and the way of life they set out."

"On another very important note, we have secretly finished construction of a new prototype aircraft, the Supersonic Dragon 228-D Spy Jet Stealth. Humanarian scientists constructed this spy jet aircraft on a secretive level below the Grinshaw Military Facility. I want you to take this aircraft up to observe the Antrerian's, making sure that the Protrerian members of ZarCedra's Forces don't discover their existence here on this planet, although this aircraft is fully armed you are not authorized to fire on anything living but you will be permitted to test them in the morrow if you so desire. The weapons on this aircraft are not always readily available; I will elaborate further in the morrow," Sr. Commodore Boone informed.

"You are to rendezvous at the secret all Humanarian, Eclipse Military Facility, Division Gaznor Ometga-North Western

Quadrant, based 500 kiloms West of Terbien, Vertgren Isle. You are to report to my office in the morrow at 11 hundred epocks, for this p.a.r, finish your morn duties, and find someone Humanarian you trust to cover your classes until you return, in an octapar or so. Then go to your abode and say grand-adioso to your lady consociate and remember this operation is strictly Top Secret, so keep everything about it confidential. See you in the morrow morn prior to your departure, dismissed," Sr. Commodore Boone said as he saluted. "Affirmative sir," I answered as I returned the salute, turned and vacated his office.

When I was standing in the hallway, I replaced my beret and smiled at the pretty Protrerian Corporal who was the secretary/ aide to Sr. Commodore Boone. I went down the hall then took the turbo-lift up to my office where I retrieved my electronic briefcase, which stored in memory the lesson plan for this p.a.r on Aero Dynamics I had planned for my recruits.

As I was leaving my office, I ran into Capt. Durrant. "Grand morn Captain; how is your schedule between 09 hundred and 16 hundred epocks for the next octapar or so? "I don't have anything too pressing to do, why? "Come into my office and I will elaborate in private." As we entered, the entry-way quietly slid closed behind us. "Illumination on; Computer, activate security mode," I sternly said. "Security mode activated, you may now commence. "Take a seat Captain," as he did, I began to elaborate further.

"I was just given orders to embark on a top-secret mission that would require me to be away from this military facility an octapar or so and I was ordered to find someone Humanarian, who I trust, enough to instruct my course in my absence. So I immediately thought of you; would you instruct my class in my absence?"

"Affirmative, when would you like me to start?" The surprised Captain asked. "This p.a.r after our mid-p.a.r banquets at 13 hundred epocks but if you could accompany me this morn, you will see what my young recruits are currently working on. I have two classes per p.a.r, one at 09 hundred-12 hundred epocks; at that time we break for one epock for sustenance replenishing then the second class comes in from 13 hundred-16 hundred epocks."

"Does Commodore Vixto of the Protrerian High Command know that you are going? "Negative; remember this mission is top-secret. "All right; what chamber will you be in? And I'll meet you there at 09 hundred epocks," he asked as he started to rise from his seat. "I'll be in chamber TL1722, see you there," I said as we both saluted. "Grand that's one thing out of the way," I said as I stood.

"We better get going or we'll be late for our morn banquets, as if we had a choice when we are on the premises," Capt. Durrant said with a sly grin as he looked at his antique digital pocket timepiece. "Right behind you buddy," I said with a grin as I grabbed my E26 briefcase and we both went towards the entry-way. "Illumination off, end privacy mode" I said as we both vacated my office as the entry-way slid open then closed behind us. We turned and headed towards the turbo-lift that would take us down to the 1st floor where the officer's lounge was located.

A few mites later we entered the lounge; we stood in line in single file and waited for our turn at the sustenance replenishers. We ordered our morn banquets and caffinated brew; we grabbed eating utensils then went and sat at a table.

"So it's a top-secret mission you are going on?" Capt. Drew Durrant asked as he fixed his tea. "Shh, lower your voice a few decibels, we don't want this to be known by everyone, especially the Protrerian High Command. "Affirmative, can I ask where you will be going or is that top secret also?" He asked whispering even quieter. "Everything about this mission is top secret, my apologies but there is nothing I am able to discuss further. "Affirmative, I apologize for asking," he said as we continued eating and talking.

A while later we finished our morn banquets, pushed our trays aside, as we brought our caffinated beverages closer to us. We continued to discuss things pertaining to the class for the next few mites; we finished our liquid refreshment then gathered our trays and rose as we deposited them on the dirty dish conveyor before departing the Officer's Lounge. "See you at 09 hundred epocks," I said as we went our separate ways.

I carried my electronic briefcase and walked back to the turbo-lift and went up to the 17th floor, the Technicalities Level of the structure where my class was located. I wanted to use my computer console to review the progress of my recruits before I left on my mission.

I walked down the hall to my class; next to the entry-way was the retina scanner. I placed my chin on the padded chin rest and let the facial scanner scan my identity. "Maj. Jeroque Teldat," I said. Only after it confirmed my identity and voice pattern, did the entry-way finally slide open and I walked in.

"Illumination on," I said as I entered and the overhead lights illuminated. "Grand morn and welcome Maj. Teldat," my computer said. "Grand morn and many thanks," I replied as I walked to my desk sat and removed my beret as I turned toward the computer console. I accessed and interfaced my electronic briefcase with the computer.

Opening the file to the reports, I first downloaded everything I had in my electronic briefcase to the main computer so Capt. Durrant could also review at his leisure. I started reviewing each recruit's progress, 25 mites later the recruits started entering the chamber.

"What's on the agenda this p.a.r Maj. Teldat; are we doing anything of interest?" Private Simmons asked. "You will find that out in a few mites," I told him as I closed the file I was reading. I rose from my seat, and went to get myself a sip of water from the water fountain at the back of the lecture chamber. After I had and returning to my desk I glanced at the timepiece on the wall, 08:57 epocks.

"Everyone take your seats, momentarily an officer will arrive, who I would like to introduce to you." After they were all seated, we heard a chime at the entry-way I pressed a button on my computer and the entry-way slid open. "Welcome to my class Capt. Durrant. Ladies and gentlefolk I would like to introduce you to Captain Durrant. "How do you all do?" The Captain inquired. "Grand," they all replied.

"I have just received orders that would require me to be away from this military facility for a while, and in my absence Capt. Durrant will instruct this course. "Where are you going sir?" A recruit asked. "The mission I was ordered to go on is top secret and I am not at liberty to discuss the matter in detail," I told the young recruit as I turned toward Capt. Durrant.

"I explained what and where my recruits are doing in their e-manuals on the main topic of Aero Dynamics," as I turned towards Capt. Durrant. "When would the Major be leaving?" I was asked. "In the morrow morn, which is the reason Capt. Durrant is here now because this is the only time I would be able to explain things to him."

"Everyone take out your e-manuals and access page 135." As everyone was doing that, I went to a back shelf to retrieve an electronic manual for Capt. Durrant. I started by stating, "the ways of how the different types of jet engines operated and the types of fuel that was required for top flying performance..."

"Do you have everything and will you be ready to take over this mid-p.a.r?" I asked Capt. Durrant at 11 hundred 15 epocks. "Affirmative sir, I'll have everything under control. "Grand, report here at 12 hundred 50 epocks. "Affirmative sir, I'll be here. "My class this mid-p.a.r is being taught the same material as my morn class, so there shouldn't be any problems between the two classes, as long as you remember everything. Now follow me out in the corridor?"

We went out into the hall and stopped in front of the retina scanner. "I'm sure you are used to this; scan your retina then state your rank and name so the scanner could record your identity and voice pattern then you could enter the class as often as you wish."

"All the information about the class is in the computer on my desk. One more thing, there is a file of every recruit in this course. It tells of the progress each is doing, if you have any problem locating this report ask the computer to locate it for you. If you have everything you're dismissed?" I told

Capt. Durrant after he completed. We both saluted then the Captain walked away as I reentered the class and returned to my desk.

I called recruits one by one to my desk and gave them a quick oral report of how they ranked so far in the course. After I finished, the buzzer sounded. "Everyone dismissed," I said as they gathered their things and started for the exit.

"We wish you a safe assignment" the recruits said then continued vacating the chamber. "Many thanks," I responded as I disconnected my electronic briefcase.

A young lady of Humanarian/Protrerian descent returned. "Does the Protrerian High Command know of your assignment?" I was flabbergasted, I didn't know what to say considering my assignment was top secret and against the Protrerian High Command itself. "Affirmative, they know and approve," I said obscuring the truth.

She was content with my answer to her question as she turned with her electronic manual and slate in hand and left the lecture chamber. "Whew that was close, I don't like telling falsities but this mission must remain Top Secret," I muttered quietly to myself after she had left.

I picked up my electronic briefcase and went toward the entry-way; I stopped just before exiting the chamber and replaced my beret upon my head. "Illumination off," I said. "Have a grand p.a.r and safe assignment Major Teldat," my computer said. "Many thanks," I replied then continued out of the chamber and the entry-way quietly slid closed and locked. I turned and marched to the turbo-lift and went down to the third floor and to my office.

As I walked by a window, I looked out and watched squads of cybernetic recruit replacements (the C-Double R's) go flying by. I had a few things yet to jot before I was done for this p.a.r so I continued to my office, I smiled as I walked by Corp. Cheny, who was my secretarial assistant.

I entered my office; "illumination on," I said then continued to my desk, sat at my computer and went to work. 40 mites later I saved everything on a micro disk then stretched. I got up to turn off the multi-colored holographic portrait of ZarCedra, with a rainbow across it and the glittering words: '**The times elapsed cannot be changed but the times yet to come is whatever you want it to be.**'

"I really wish there was a way of changing the times elapsed so the times yet to come would be worth wanting," I said aloud as I returned to my desk. I started to drape my overcoat over my arm then stopped and decided to give my huni buni a call.

So I put my overcoat down and punched my serial digits into my cinematic pcd and received a secure up-link then accessed my abode. A chirp or two later the screen illuminated and I was staring at my black haired, hazel eyed 29 tritton old exquisiteness who had multicolored ridges on her forehead.

"Greetings."

"Greetings huni buni."

"Greetings Jero," she said with a very cute smile.

"Greetings my love, I will be at our abode in a short while."

"Why?"

"I will explain that when I arrive"

"Affirmative."

"The reason I called is because I was wondering if you are getting famished?"

"A speck, why?"

"Because, I was wondering if I should stop at a Protrerian Shaksu Hut and pick up a dehydrated Shaksu for our mid-p.a.r banquet; how would you enjoy that?"

"That sounds scrumptious."

"All right my huni buni I will arrive at our abode shortly, adioso for now," I said as I blew a kiss towards the cinematic pcd screen then pressed the off button and the screen distinguished.

*****

'I'm a lucky citizen, to have such an exquisite lady as Tsarina Alexander in my life,' I thought as I put my beret on then walked out of my office. I left with my overcoat and electronic briefcase in hand and walked by Corp. Cheny. "I am going to my abode, so you have the rest of this p.a.r free; have a grand p.a.r!" I said with a smile. "Many thanks sir, you as well," she said with a cute smile of her own.

I went out, took the turbo-lift to the first floor, walked down the corridor then went through the elaborately decorated foyer and out the main entrance. I went to the gate abode, had my retina scanned. "Maj. J. Teldat off for the remainder of this p.a.r. Have a grand p.a.r," I told the MP as I went to catch the shuttle coach.

I took out my electronic credits card that held my spendable credits for the quarter tritton. I looked down and grimaced at the holographic image of President Orpht, the Protrerian Monarch of ZarCedra.

'Hopefully one p.a.r soon, the Humanarian's of ZarCedra will take back what is rightfully ours and drive away these alien tyrants,' I thought to myself as I waited for the ride. I spotted the shuttle coach and waited patiently for its arrival, then for it to stop and lower to the ground in front of me as hover and other boulevard commuter transportation whizzed by.

When the entry-way slid open I stepped on, inserted my credits card into the fare computerized debit system and it deducted the amount of the fare, I removed my card then went to find a seat. The entry-way closed, the shuttle rose then off it went as if it floated on a cloud. I closed my eyes as I rode the ways to Genevie Blvd, the stop by the Protrerian Shaksu Hut Bistro.

A kilom later, I pressed the shiny red buzzer on the front of my armrest. The shuttle coach came to a complete stop and lowered to the ground at the next shuttle coach stop. I arose then stepped off, holding on to my overcoat and electronic briefcase as I went to the Bistro.

Inside, I ordered the banquet then started talking to nearby patrons as I waited for its completion. A few mites later my order was completed and arrived, I paid for it, put on my overcoat and held onto my E26 briefcase in one hand and Shaksu in the other as I left the establishment. I went to the shuttle coach stop and waited for the next shuttle.

When it arrived, the shuttle coach stopped and lowered; I got on, inserted my credits card in the fare computerized debit system one more time, removed it then went and sat. The coach rose then traveled the next couple kiloms, as it neared Carrington Heights. A few mites later I pressed the buzzer and it stopped and lowered. I got off and walked the few hundred metrics to my drive and could see my huni buni Tsarina peering out a window looking as exquisite as ever.

I walked by my Kazaki 2700 hover bike and straight to the side entrance. The entry-way remained closed and locked until I said, "Jeroque Teldat;" an orange beam of illumination protruded and scanned my facial features. As soon as it identified my features and voice pattern, a burgundy illuminated security button changed to blue as the entry-way unlocked then slid open.

I entered and set the Shaksu & my E26-briefcase down then removed my overcoat, beret and boots; after I did Tsarina came up to me. "Welcome back to our abode my darling" she said then gave me a kiss.

When we were through, I took the small box of Shaksu into the sustenance replenishing area and handed it to Tsarina. She took the Shaksu out of the box and put it on a Shaksu plate then placed it in the Santino Sustenance Redehydrator. While she did that, I walked up behind her and put my arms around her, kissed the soft dark blue-green and pink splotchy skin on the back of her neck then rested my head on her shoulder.

"I do love you huni buni and I want you to know just how much," I said as I rubbed her back. "How much, my huni?" She asked as she turned to face me. She fluttered her eyelids and looked especially radiant as she and I melted in a quixotic kiss. I stopped kissing her and held out my arms as wide as they could stretch. "This much," I said as I wrapped my arms around Tsarina once again and continued to kiss her succulent lips.

"How sweet," she said after we concluded. "I love you too huni, but why have you returned so early? "I was given an order this morn for a mission that will commence in the morrow morn. The length of the mission will hopefully be an octapar or so. I am not at liberty to leak out the contents of the mission but I can say knowing you are here waiting for my return, I will try to finish as quick as possible."

"It is hard to believe I will be turning 33 trittons old in a couple p.a.r's," I said changing the subject "It's unfortunate you'll be away for your special p.a.r huni buni, I wanted it to be wonderful and most of all for us to be together. "I agree, it will be unfortunate but I'll do my best to try to make it back as soon as I can," I said as I squeezed her again.

"We have been mated for almost five trittons and I was wondering why you haven't asked me to join you in matrimony yet?" Tsarina asked, as she looked deep into my eyes. "I didn't think we were at that plateau in our relationship yet. But if you would be willing to join me in matrimony, I'd be more than honored to take you as my legitimate mate." I said squeezing her tightly. "That's wonderful, I most graciously accept with honor," she excitedly said as she kissed me passionately.

Just then the beeper went off on the Sustenance Redehydrator but that didn't matter just then we were both in bliss. A few secs later we forced ourselves apart; Tsarina turned and withdrew two plates for our mid-p.a.r banquet. "In the few p.a.rs after you return, take an extended leave of absence and we'll join in matrimony then honeymoon on ZarCedra's 2nd moon." Tsarina said as she batted her eyebrows. "You got it my love," I told her as I rubbed her back. "Hmm," she purred. "The Shaksu is ready for consumption; we'd better get to it before it gets frigid," I told Tsarina as I let her go and she took it from the redehydrator then brought it to the table.

While she was doing that, I went to our refrigeration unit and took out the last bottle of Casanthemum Ale. I had picked up a few bottles from the planet Casanthis for the holy p.a.r's last tritton. On my way back to the table, I stopped long enough to grab two flute glasses as I turned toward Tsarina and looked into her gorgeous eyes.

"How would you like to go out this mid-p.a.r, and see a game of Astroball? "Sure, sounds fun." I sat then opened the ale and poured us each a glass. I handed a glass to my exquisite betrothed then picked up my glass. "To our times yet to come, if our destinies are set may they be pleasant in each other's company for all time," I said as I kissed Tsarina's hand. I then replaced the lid on the bottle of ale and placed it at the center of the table. Tsarina and I pulled our plates of Shaksu towards us as we grabbed our eating utensils and started consuming our banquet.

Awhile later after we were both stuffed we sat back and were engulfed in quiet conversation. I sat forward in my seat and took a hold of Tsarina's hand and gently squeezed. "My apologies my darling that I have to leave in the morrow; but this is the life you chose when you agreed to move in with me.

"I know, and it's all right, just can you promise me you'll return to me unscaved?" She asked with concern. "All I can promise huni buni is that I'll try my best. "Many thanks, that's all anyone can promise any way," she said as she got up, kissed me then went to put the dirty dishes in the ultrasonic dish receptacle. I drank the last sip of my swill then got up to give Tsarina a hand.

"What time does the Astroball game start?" Tsarina asked as she put the remainder of the Shaksu in a refrigeration safe container, covered it then placed it in the refrigeration unit. "At 15 hundred epocks," I told her then went into the front chamber to turn on our computerized entertainment system. I put in a micro disk of Celeste Quantrig then went and sat on the lounger to listen to her melodic composition and to relax a bit.

I closed my eyes and when I opened them again I found the love of my life sitting beside me stroking my short-cropped hair. "Go get changed so we can depart soon," she said as she smooched the end of my nose. "Alright huni buni," I said as I got up, lovingly squeezed Tsarina's hand then went to our slumbering quarters.

Tsarina sat back and listened to the micro disk as she sipped what remained in her glass. A few mites later I walked out wearing a thin white sweater and a dark blue military jumper.

"You look wonderful huni," Tsarina said as she got up to put her glass in the ultrasonic dish receptacle. Then she too went to change.

When she was through, she went into the latrine to look in the huge mirror to apply facial colors and add moisturizer to her lips. I came in and faced my exquisite betrothed; she was dressed in yellow short pants and a yellow mini dress with soft blue and pink blossoms.

"You look pretty amazing," I said as I gently kissed her. "What was that for?" She asked with a sigh. "Nothing really my huni, it's just I'm happy you and I are together," I told her with a smile. "I'll be yours for as long as you want me," she said as she spritzed a bit of hair spray on her hair. "Forever if possible," I said as I bent a little to kiss the sweet smelling tri-colored skin on her neck.

When she finished we stepped from the latrine and went to put on our footwear and jackets then grabbed the helmets as we left our abode. When we were outside the entry-way, I made sure the entry-way was secure then I inserted my security card in the designated slot and activated the alarm, as the blue illuminated security button turned burgundy.

Tsarina and I walked hand in hand to my hover bike. I squeezed her hand then let go, uncovered the bike as we both put on our helmets. Tsarina and I both straddled the bike; I inserted its key then pressed the ignition button. The bike roared to life as it rose 1¼ metrics. Tsarina held on to me as we slowly left the drive and traveled the boulevards.

We were talking via the helmet's internal com-link as we stopped for a burgundy commuter transportation stop indicator. I loved the feeling of Tsarina's four breasts mashed against my back as I moved sideways a couple times to better feel them against me. Tsarina pushed her breasts closer against my back as she too enjoyed the feeling. I had to force myself to sit up straight, as the stop indicator was about to turn blue; after it did I kept going toward the Astroball stadium.

After traveling six kiloms further we arrived at the grand stadium. I pulled into the parking lot then onto a stall reserved for my mode of transportation. Once I parked, I turned the ignition off and the bike lowered to the platform, Tsarina and I stood then removed our helmets. I locked the helmets to the bike then we stepped to the tarmac below as we walked hand in hand following other citizens into the stadium.

At the ticket wicket, the credits were automatically deducted from my credits card for our admission by the admissions computerized debit system. We entered the huge coliseum then went to the concession stand.

"Tsarina would you like anything? "A cold swill," she said as she nuzzled my cheek. "May I be of service?" the lady citizen behind the counter asked. "You may," I said with a smile. "I will order a Solar Dog, a Crunch Stick and two cold canisters of cherry nectar," I said as she totaled my order.

"Many thanks that will be 12 credits?" I handed her my credits card and her minicomputer deducted the total. After paying, I was given back my credits card as I received my order. Tsarina and I started walking amongst the crowd of citizen's as we made our way out to our seats. Once we were seated I looked at my Timor 6500 solar timepiece, and seen that it was 14 hundred 45 epocks.

"The game will be starting in a few mites," I told Tsarina as I began munching my Solar Dog. "How could you still be famished considering we just consumed our mid-p.a.r banquet a short time ago?" Tsarina asked with annoyance. "I'm a growing gent," I told her then took a sip of my nectar.

"I am going to purchase some memorabilia," Tsarina said as she put her nectar down. "All right, get me a stat e-book while you are in there and don't dally too long the game will be starting shortly. "Agreed," she answered as she blew me a kiss then disappeared inside.

I sat back in my seat and finished my Solar Dog and downed half my nectar as my eyes diverted between the player's warming up and the grand looking Protrerian cheerleaders. 'Ah Astroball, a game of action, thrills and unorthodox maneuvers carried out by very tall Protrerian male players. Something like rugbitie was played by ZarCedrian teams in the late 20th centritton but with a Protrerian twist.'

As I watched my mind drifted and I started inkling of the situation on Vertgren Isle. 'I hope my time there would be short,' I thought as I began to munch my crunch stick.

A few mites later, the game was just starting when Tsarina returned with a bunch of stuff, including my stat e-book. "Here huni," she said as she handed me the e-book. "By the way who's playing this mid-p.a.r?" Tsarina asked as she sat.

"The Cangla City Sha Raider's and the Chig Town Rigto Giants," I said as my eyes once again drifted towards the grand looking Protrerian cheerleaders in their very short outfits. They wore a double halter and very short skirts, barely enough material to cover their curvy four breasted bodies. "Keep your eyes on the game rather than the females in their skimpy costumes," Tsarina said when she saw what I was looking at then elbowed me in the ribs.

"All right," I reluctantly said as my eyes left the cheerleaders and went back to watching the male citizens play the game. Tsarina sat there in a huff with her arms crossed and breathing heavy. I looked over at her and started running my fingers up her leg.

"Relax huni; if they didn't want citizens to look at the cheerleaders they wouldn't have them." I said as I rubbed her smooth, creamy soft legs. "I know but you are with me and you shouldn't have to, don't I excite you?" She asked as she looked at me with annoyance. "Of course you do huni buni, of course you do," I told her as I squeezed her leg again then went back to cheering for my team.

At half time, I asked Tsarina "Would you like anything from the concession stand while I am inside? "Negative many thanks, just don't be too long? "Affirmative huni I'll be back soon," I said as I disappeared among the crowd of citizens going inside.

After I had gone, Tsarina looked over at the cheerleaders who were performing their half time show. "Why was Jeroque so interested in them? I look better than most of them anyway," she thought to herself. "Jeroque should count himself a very lucky ZarCedrian to have me, I consider myself very lucky to have him," she giggled to herself.

A bit later I arrived with a bag of confection sweets and another Cherry nectar. "If you keep eating the way you have been you'll get fat. Then you'll have to look for someone else to join you in matrimony because I don't want a fat mate." Tsarina said with a sneer.

"Don't worry my huni, I've eaten this way all my life and I haven't gotten fat yet and besides you won't ever find anyone as good looking or charming as I anywhere, I'm one of a kind. When I was made they broke the mold," I said with a laugh "You are correct, arrogant but correct," Tsarina said with a smirk as she rested her head on my shoulder.

"Time for the second half of the game," I told her as I offered her a bit of my confection corn. "Negative many thanks, I'm watching my figure. "Don't worry huni buni, I'll watch it for you," I said as I winked at her then took another swill. "I bet you will," Tsarina said as she raised her head for a kiss. I kissed her tenderly then got into watching the game.

A while later when the game ended, the Cangla City Sha Raiders won with a score of 34 to 27. I tenderly kissed Tsarina then held her hand as we got up and along with the other fans, vacated the stadium.

Tsarina and I walked out to my hover bike; I turned towards her and asked. "Would you like to go out to have our twilight banquet, my love? "How about getting something to go so we can return to our abode and enjoy each other's company in seclusion?" She asked with a wink then she put the memorabilia she was carrying in the compartment under the seat of the bike. "Sounds like a plan huni," I told her as I embraced her lovingly.

We both put our helmets on then straddled the hover bike as I started it and it rose, we decided to go to a Hum-Pro, sustenance establishment. I put the bike in gear then pulled away.

Ten mites later we arrived at our destination; I pulled into a parking stall reserved for our mode of transportation and parked my hover bike. Tsarina and I removed our helmets and we locked them to the bike then walked to the bistro. We entered and went to the hostess.

"Greetings, would we be able to see menus so we can order something to go?" I asked the attractive hostess. "Of course," she replied with a smile as she grabbed two menus. "Would you both follow me?" She brought us into the dimly lit dining area of the fairly busy sustenance establishment and to a vacant table. "You may sit here as you decide what to order," she said as she handed us the menus.

We were left alone to look at the menus; I took Tsarina's hand and squeezed it softly. "My huni buni, I love you very much and many thanks for giving me the opportunity of trying to show you just how much," I said as I looked deep into her exquisite hazel eyes.

"Are you ready to order?" A Protrerian waitress asked as she stopped in front of our table. "I looked up at her and asked for a few more mites? "Of course, but in the interim would you both care for anything to quench your thirst?" She asked with a smile. "Affirmative," I said then looked at Tsarina. "Whatever you are having will be fine with me," Tsarina said as she looked at her menu. "Two caffinated caramella iced brews?" I asked as my gaze returned to the young waitress. "At once sir," she said with a smile then turned and walked away.

We both turned and continued talking as we looked at our menus, after a short time we both decided on a combination platter for two. The waitress returned with our beverages and served them then took our order. "Can we have that to go? "Many thanks, affirmative you may, your order will be a few mites," she said with a smile as she turned and walked away.

After we were left alone Tsarina and I both sipped our caramella iced beverages. "I love you and you are the only male, Humanarian or Protrerian, that means the most to me except my kin," Tsarina said as she squeezed my hand tightly. "I understand huni buni and the feelings would be mutual if I had kin," I said as I smiled then winked at her.

We switched the subject and were discussing our after sustenance plans. Tsarina and I both held hands as we gazed lovingly into each other's eyes.

"Would you like your beverages refreshed? The waitress asked when she returned a short while later with our order in a white parchment sack that had 'Pangua's Bistro', scrawled on the front. "Negative many thanks, and have a grand twilight," I said as she handed me the bill.

Tsarina and I drank what was left in our glasses; we got up and walked to the hostess station. "Add a few credits as a gratuity for the waitress," I said as the hostess totaled our order. I handed the young lady my credits card and she deducted the total. "Grand twilight," we both said after the bill was paid then walked out towards my parked hover bike.

We put our helmets on and as we did I started whispering quite lusty passages to Tsarina through our helmet com-link. By the illumination of ZarCedra's triple moons, I seen Tsarina blush as she got on the bike; one hand held onto our sustenance and the other clutched tightly to me. I started the hover bike and waited as it rose, after I pulled onto the boulevard heading for our abode.

A little while later I pulled off the freeway and drove along Carrington Heights then finally into our drive. I parked my Kazaki 2700 hover bike then Tsarina and I removed our helmets. Tsarina held on to our twilight banquet as she retrieved the memorabilia then kissed me on the lips. "Let's go. "Right behind you my exquisite one," I said as I covered the hover bike, picked up the helmets then followed her to our entry entry-way.

"Alarm off," I said as an orange beam of illumination protruded from the entry-way. "Jeroque Teldat," I stated and the illumination scanned my facial features and verified my voice pattern then the burgundy illuminated security button turned blue and the entry-way slid open.

Tsarina and I entered the dark entryway of our abode as the entry-way slid closed behind us then locked. "Illumination on," I said as Tsarina and I entered the sustenance replenishing area,

Tsarina handed me the memorabilia as she got the Hum-Pro banquet ready for consumption.

I took what I had into the front chamber, put it on the beverage table and switched on the Intervision flatscreen cinematic monitor. I located the remote and viewed the listing channel a moment; I decided to listen to the Fusion Jazz channel for a change. As I switched channels I heard the love of my life call me for sustenance. I walked into the sustenance replenishing area and inhaled deeply, smiled at Tsarina then went to sit at the table. I watched as Tsarina poured two swills and brought them to the table, set them down then sat next to me. We both gave thanks to the God's above for our bounty; after we picked up our eating utensils and started enjoying the banquet.

"Are you concerned about starting your mission in the morrow?" Tsarina asked in between bites. "A little but hopefully it will end without incident and I will return in a short while," I said in between bites of the delicious saucy semi-living banquet. "I hope so too," she said as she squeezed my knee. All through sustenance we were engulfed in quiet conversation.

When we were through, I assisted Tsarina clean the sustenance replenishing area. "Let's go upstairs, disrobe and take a shower together," I suggested as I embraced Tsarina. "Sounds like a plan," Tsarina said quite excitedly, she kissed me as we let go of one another then left the sustenance replenishing area. Upon leaving the chamber I tweaked her bottom, Tsarina jumped and smiled at me. "Illumination off," I said and we vacated the chamber.

While walking through the front chamber I turned off the Intervision flatscreen cinematic monitor. "Illumination off," Tsarina said as we were left in darkness then we both went upstairs. As we arrived at the top of the staircase; "Illumination on," I said as I went into the latrine and Tsarina went to retrieve towels, when she entered the latrine we both disrobed and immediately we were in each other's arms engrossed in a quixotic kiss as I messaged each then squeezed the nipples of Tsarina's quadruple breasts.

When we finished, I stepped back to admire Tsarina's multi-colored naked form from head to toe. "You are so exquisite my darling partner in matrimony to be. "Many thanks, you're not so bad yourself," she said then turned around as I tweaked her bottom once again. Tsarina jumped then flashed me a mischievous smiled as we both entered the shower.

As soon as the sensor detected our presence the warm water showered over us at the perfect temperature. While we were both getting clean in the small area of the shower, we both had trouble staying out of each other's grasp as we were directly drawn into one another's arms.

Once we were able to complete our shower we got out, dried off then brushed our teeth and hair. "Illumination off," I said after we finished then we both streaked to our slumbering quarters and hopped into our retiring unit. "Illumination off," Tsarina squealed as I tickled her.

Under the covers I pulled Tsarina's warm body closer to me as we both melted in a long quixotic kiss. As we kissed, my hands were all over Tsarina's silky soft furry belly as she rubbed my hairy chest. "I love you very much." Tsarina said as I pulled away then started nibbling her ear. "I love you too huni buni," I said as Tsarina scratched my muscular back with her long fingernails.

I nibbled her lips then rubbed her all over. Next, my head lowered and I enjoyed suckling each of the four nipples of Tsarina's breasts, she moaned loudly, as I rubbed the velvety softness of her furry stomach, once again. I then lowered my head and felt the moistness on my lips as I began to lick all over. A few mites later I forced myself away as I left little wet trails all over her gorgeous form. She was in sheer ecstasy as I pulled her on top of me.

For the next epock and a-half we made sweet passionate love. When Tsarina finally rolled off me, we were both covered in sweat and breathing heavy as we both embraced each other tightly. "Is it imperative that you leave in the morrow?" Tsarina asked, as she softened her embrace and looked deep into my eyes. "My condolences huni buni but affirmative it is," I said as

I wiped the wisps of hair from her eyes then kissed her rigid forehead. "Aughh," she moaned as she got out of our retiring unit and went to the latrine. "Illumination on," she said; then a few mites later I heard her say "illumination off." Secs later she crawled into our retiring unit and we cuddled our naked bodies together and we spooned, closed our eyes then drifted off into a deep slumber.

*****

Later that twilight as I slumbered, I found myself in another one of my many twilightmares that I've been having off and on for almost a tritton. I was flying my aircraft through a sudden wet snow storm, thunder crashing and lightening flashing all around me. It was dark out but with all the snow, flashes of lightning and the illumination of the triple moons I could see clearly as if it were a bright p.a.r.

Although in spite of the brightness I couldn't see anyone, but there was a voice emitting from across the cockpit warning me of the closeness of each lightning strike, secs later my aircraft was struck by a giant bolt of lightning as fire and sparks emitted from the starboard side of my craft as I entered a swirling pool of churning air. I then woke soaked in sweat; it took a few secs but I then realized it was just an unsettling dream. At that moment Tsarina turned over and put her arm over me and that's when it hit me, I was safe in my abode and in the arms of the lady I love.

"What on ZarCedra did that twilightmare mean," I quietly asked myself. I thought hard for the next few mites but was unable to come up with a solid scenario for the twilightmare. So I rolled over and closed my eyes again as I fell back into a slumber.

P.A.R 2

As I waited for the shuttle coach, I held onto my briefcase as I shifted my duffle bag and got excited inkling about the prototype Supersonic 228-D Spy Jet Stealth. Which was secretly constructed and I am supposed to test then use on my top-secret mission.

A few mites later the shuttle coach arrived and I got on, I inserted my credits card into the fare computer. It withdrew the cost of the fare then I went to find a seat as I put my credits card away. A while later I arrived at the stop by the Grinshaw Military Facility. I pressed the buzzer on the armrest of my seat and the shuttle coach stopped and lowered at the next stop and I went to the side entry-way then stepped off.

Once I departed the shuttle I stopped at the gate abode. "Grand morn to you Sergeant. "Grand p.a.r to you as well Major," the MP replied as I had my retina scanned. "Maj. Teldat reporting for duty at 08 hundred 54 epocks," I told the scanner as I looked at the Sergeant. "Have a grand p.a.r Sergeant," I said as I continued to main headquarters.

I entered the military structure then went straight up to my office in anticipation of soon seeing the advanced prototype spy jet.

"Grand morn Maj. Teldat sir," Corp. Cheny happily said as I arrived. "Grand morn Corporal," I replied as I returned her salute, smiled at her then disappeared into my office and the entry-way slid closed behind me.

"Illumination on," I said as I removed my beret and over coat. I put my E26 briefcase and duffel bag down then went to my desk and turned on my computer console. "Grand morn Maj. Teldat, I trust you had a pleasant twilight," my computer console said. "I did, it was most pleasurable," I replied as I went to work.

The next thing I knew it was time for caffinated Brew, I closed the file I was working in then turned my computer console off. "Illumination off," I said as I departed my office and the entry-way slid closed. "I'm going to the Officer's Mess Corp. Cheny," I said as I passed her desk.

I decided to take the long way around to the turbo-lift as I walked down the hall and around a corner past the physical education chamber with zero gravity. I stopped and watched through a window at the new recruits as they finished their training, floating around the inside of the padded chamber.

I walked further down the hall and watched a battalion train using the jet backpacks and paint ball laser rifles. I reminisced about the time I was a new recruit, when I first enlisted in the Military and was trained to use them. 'That was exciting,' I thought as I went the rest of the way to the turbo-lift then went down to the Officer's Mess.

A few mites later I entered the lounge and walked up to a sustenance replenisher and ordered my hot caffinated brew and nibbles. I went to a table and sat, as I started swilling my black brew, a consociate, Capt. Steve Gagnon walked in. As soon as he received his caffinated Brew and nibbles he came over to join me.

"Grand morn Major, may I join you? "Grand morn Captain be my guest. "Are you ready for this p.a.r? "I sure am, it should be an exciting p.a.r. "Did you do anything of interest last p.a.r? "My betrothed and I went to see an Astroball game during the mid-p.a.r. "Oh, who was victorious? "The Cangla City Sha Raiders of course, with the final score of 34 to 27."

As we were talking Sr. Commodore Boone walked in and came to us. "Grand morn gentlefolk. "Grand morn sir," we both replied with a salute. "Grand p.a.r isn't it?" The Sr. Commodore asked as he returned our salutes. "Affirmative sir," we both replied. "Remember our meeting at 11 hundred epocks Major," Sr. Commodore Boone said as he looked at me. "I haven't forgotten sir I'll be there. "Grand, have you found anyone to take over your schedule?" Sr. Com. Boone quietly inquired.

"Affirmative sir, I asked Capt. Durrant and he agreed to take over my schedule until my return."

At that instance Capt. Durrant walked in the Officer's Mess and received his tea and nibbles then came to our table where we were talking.

"Grand morn gentlefolk, might I join you?" He asked as he looked around. "Of course, have a seat. "I understand you will be taking over Maj. Teldat's class during his absence." Sr. Commodore Boone quietly said as the Captain sat.

"Affirmative sir, I started the p.a.r before this one at 13 hundred epocks and I will continue to instruct from 09 hundred epocks till 16 hundred epocks until the Major returns. "Wonderful, see you at 11 hundred epocks Major; gentlefolk have a grand p.a.r," the Senior Commodore said as he returned our salutes then walked away as the three of us continued talking and eating.

"I asked Tsarina to join me in matrimony," I told them then took a swill of my caffinated Brew. "That's wonderful," Steve said. "I was wondering when you would get the stones to ask her," Drew added with a chuckle then sipped his tea.

"I in fact didn't, it was Tsarina who asked me and I told her we would join in matrimony after my return," I said as Commodore Vixto of the Protrerian High Command walked by with his entourage of cohorts.

"Drew would you be my best citizen and Steve would you be one of the marshals on my special p.a.r? "I'd be honored to," they both replied in unison. After we finished our morn brew and nibbles, we all got up and put our dirty trays away then left the lounge. "Adioso," we said when we were in the hallway then went our separate ways.

I went back to my office to finish unfinished work. I worked on my computer console until 10 hundred 50 epocks; at that time I switched everything off, retrieved my duffel bag, put my beret on then left my office.

"Corp. Cheny I'm leaving on assignment for an octapar or so, so as of now you are relieved as my secretary. On my return I will request you once again as my secretarial assistant. "Affirmative sir, have a safe assignment," Corp. Cheny replied as I returned her salute and smile, turned and headed towards Sr. Commodore Boone's office.

Upon arriving I greeted the pretty female Protrerian Corporal and returned her salute. "I am to see Sr. Commodore Boone," I informed her. "Grand morn sir, just a moment while I contact him and advise him you are present." She pressed a button on her computer's cinematic cam and a microsec later the Commodore was on the screen.

"Can I be of assistance Corporal? "Sr. Commodore Boone, Maj. Teldat is here to see you. "Send him right in Corporal. "Affirmative sir, at once. "You may enter," she said as she switched the cinematic cam off. "Many thanks ma'am," I said as I swung my duffel bag over my shoulder and went to the Sr. Commodore's entry-way, I removed my beret and activated the chime. "Enter Major," the Sr. Commodore said as the entry-way slid open.

After I entered, the entry-way quietly closed behind me. "Greetings sir," I said as I stood at attention and saluted. "At ease Major. Computer, activate privacy mode. "Privacy mode engaged; you now may commence."

The Commodore started informing me more of my mission. "You will be flying the new prototype spy jet, the Supersonic Dragon 228-D Spy Jet Stealth Aircraft to Vertgren Isle. Now I say prototype because we just finished construction of this highly sophisticated computerized spy jet and this will be its maiden voyage."

"This craft is in the 228 line of Stealth aircraft but it is more than five times the size of all previous Stealth Aircraft in the times elapsed but with one major difference. It will have all the necessary stealth capabilities, radar jamming and whisper modes and that major difference is, when you tell your onboard computer to go into spy mode or press the appropriate touch pad; this aircraft will become invisible to the naked eye as well as radar. It will seem like the aircraft phases out of our plane of existence altogether."

"Even though of the grand size of this aircraft, we decided one pilot could handle this craft with the assistance of the cybernetic onboard super computer's counterpart who you'll meet later, if we are incorrect by all means bring it to my attention and I'll assign other pilots to assist you. This is a top-secret mission we are sending you on, that is the reason we wanted one Humanarian pilot for this excursion."

"For armament, this craft will have unlimited Sareden Quantum Laser Cannon capability and have Protonic EMC-Missals and Neutronic EMC-Torpedo's. Protonic EMC-Missals are positively charged electromagnetic highly explosive energy clusters that are combined with the perfect amount of gaseous Liquid Naprisyte[2] to give it that explosive punch but Neutronic EMC-Torpedo's are negatively charged energy clusters, which will be explained later. This craft has additional defensive weapons we'll also explain later when you see the aircraft in all its glory. Another modification we made is that this aircraft has the acceleration speed of up to Star Drive Acceleration Two, which is equivalent to Mach 200."

"Unbelievable sir, how were you able to figure out a way to acquire that firepower and allow the craft to reach that speed. "I consider myself a pretty smart citizen but unfortunately that was beyond my comprehension, my top two scientists and their E-tech team invented this engine. Again, they will explain all about this craft's armament and how it attains its airspeed a little later when we see the aircraft. "Understood sir."

"Like I conveyed the p.a.r before this one you are only to record images. This craft also has an XT-165 DigiCam which has a maximum 165 epocks of recordable imagery taken on a Dexter micro disk. The onboard super computer controls everything about this aircraft and everything will run by voice command or touch pad, if you prefer to activate things manually. After you change into your flight suit, I will show you this breakthrough in aerodynamic technology. When you are ready, I will be down in our secretive underground hangar."

"Here is a special keycard, when you are ready, enter the far port service turbo-lift, make sure you are alone and after the entry-way closes, insert this keycard in its slot below the carpet in the upper far-left corner. After you hear a beep, this keycard will bypass the system and bring you down to our secret hangar 350 metrics below the surface. When you are about to leave the turbo-lift, send it back up immediately. Take the cart and travel that hall two kiloms, where you will find me, my scientific heads who created our prototype craft, and of course the craft itself all ready for its unveiling, I will leave directly so I'll be there when you arrive."

"Affirmative sir," I acknowledged as I saluted, retrieved the keycard, grabbed my duffel bag, turned then vacated the office. "Many thanks again Corporal, and have a pleasant p.a.r," I said with a smile as I walked by her desk replacing my beret. "You as well," she said as she returned my smile.

I continued on my way to change into my flight suit. After I had, I carried my duffel bag to the very last of the three service turbo lifts. I made sure no one was around; as I looked around then entered. After the entry-way closed I located the slot, inserted the keycard and waited until I heard it beep, then the turbo-lift started descending down to the secret level at a great speed.

After a fast ride I arrived at the secret destination, I pressed the M button as I exited the turbo lift, so it would go back up to the main floor. I hopped on a cart and drove down the corridor until I arrived at the destination where I met Sr. Com. Boone and his two top scientists.

Sr. Commodore Boone, Doctors Armitage and Graham greeted me, upon my arrival. "Greetings again Major, these two scientists and their E-Tech team are the engineers of the Supersonic Dragon," Sr. Com. Boone said as he pressed a button on the remote hand held device, the side wall lowered to reveal a very large underground cavern, approximately the size of an astroball field. In it was the very sleek, gleaming massive black, grey, brown, orange and silver craft. On each side the wings were hydraulically contracted and the wing on the port side had been slid back to expose a hatchway.

It had 'N.Z.C.M.Co./S.H.Z.C.A SS Dragon SJ written on the side of the cockpit and beside it was a depiction of a ferocious looking dragon; the craft was about five times the size, if not larger than the Stealth Aircraft of this p.a.r or in the times elapsed. Though it did have the same familiar design. On the crown of the craft was a somewhat large piece of weaponry, about 10 centrics in diametric and 30 centrics in length.

"That weapon looks impressive, doesn't it? "It sure does," I said as I looked on. "Those double barrels rotate 360°and fires the Sareden Quantum Laser Cannons. The P-52 Hydrogenic Generator will keep it fully charged at all times so your aircraft will have unlimited protection."

"In addition to that, this aircraft is equipped with these," the Sr. Commodore said as he pressed a button on his hand held device. The wings extended outwards then he pressed another button and as he did, my eyes widened. I couldn't believe it but from the underside of each wing came a futuristic cannon weapon of considerable mass. "These two weapons will give the aircraft additional protection; they are the twin XTR-9000 Plasma Pulse Cannons. The ammunition for this weapon is also supplied by the generator and it also operates using Liquid Naprisyte[2] enriched gaseous ammunition."

"Underneath the nose of the craft you will notice a sliding metal plate, when it opens you will be able to fire the Protonic Electromagnetic Energy Cluster Missals and Neutronic Electromagnetic Pulse Energy Cluster Torpedo's. "You should know the destructive force of an Electromagnetic Missal is grand. You will have a total of fifteen missals after they are expelled you will have to wait ten mites before the next compliment can be supplied by the Comodrone Electronic P-52 Hydrogenic Generator."

"Unlike the devastating destructive force of its counterpart the torpedo's have no destructive force behind them. You launch a torpedo at a target with an operating electronic system and when the torpedo strikes it, on contact the torpedo will be absorbed by whatever it hits. Knocking out its operating electronic system, rendering that piece of equipment powerless and vulnerable to attack. The Supersonic Dragon will only be able to hold a maximum of ten of these EMC-Torpedo's in its weapons array; after they are expelled you will have to wait twenty mites for the next compliment of ten torpedo's. In my observation this craft is the only grand thing to happen from the combined technologies of the Humanarian and the Protrerian species. "Affirmative sir, I won't let you or the whole Humanarian Race down."

The Commodore patted my shoulder and said. "In that there is no doubt Major, that is one of the reasons you were selected for this assignment. The p.a.r before this one I told you there was something important you must do before your weapons will operate and that is, you must inform your copilot to activate battle mode before all your weapons will operate. You will need to know this if you want to do a speck of target practice before you leave on your assignment."

"Another contribution made to the defensive system is the installation of Inertial Dampeners- which are a replacement for motion compensators that uses graviton emitters to dampen the effect of quick acceleration." Dr. Graham jumped in and said.

"Unfortunately you won't be allowed any fly byes over the tower, considering this craft is our attempt to finally sever all ties with the Protrerian's. Just take the craft up making sure you are in Stealth Mode and leave the vicinity immediately."

"This Supersonic Dragon is a fair size larger than all the previous stealth aircraft because to power such a craft it uses two huge F405-F1D3 afterburning engines. "Which we'll show you later," Dr. Graham said.

"After you are up and away from this military facility you can take her on a trial run. By the way this craft isn't fueled on regular jet fuel alone, to accelerate the special Omagon 2115 Star Drive Engine it also uses a Liquid Naprisyte^2 supplement called Liquid Naprisyte^2 SDC, SDC stands for Star Drive Compound. The surplus vials of this compound is stored in the rear of the cockpit in a reinforced metal case marked Liquid Naprisyte^2 Star Drive Compound, Warning Radioactive," Dr. Armitage added.

"Before we go on there is something I want to show you. "What is that?" I asked. "This," the Commodore said as he activated another button on his hand held device and from the frame strategically placed golden modules appeared. On the nose of the craft a golden rod appeared about 2/3 of a metric long. "Wow what are they for?" I asked. "They are required for an experimental engine we'll show you momentarily."

"Now we will look in the cockpit to see all the modifications these fine scientific engineers made and you'll see just why this aircraft is called a prototype spy jet," Sr. Com. Boone said. "Affirmative sir," I answered. There is touch pads under a trap entry-way under the aircraft that will do everything this hand held device does, which Dr. Armitage will now demonstrate.

Dr. Armitage went and climbed the starboard wheel up to and opened a small trap entry-way, inside a few colored touch pads illuminated in the semi-darkness within. He activated a pale blue touch pad and the port wing contracted as a main hatch opened on the side of the craft and it slowly opened downward to expose the cockpit. When the main hatch was fully open it lowered about two metrics to the floor.

"In times when there isn't sufficient time, for one reason or another to open the cockpit's main hatch manually, later you will receive a set of platinum wings. Press the left wing and ask 'PAT', your co-pilot to open and lower the main hatch platform and she will open and lower it for you," Dr. Graham said with a smile.

"Now let's go view the cockpit. This lift is weight activated, when you stand on it motionless for five secs it will activate automatically," Dr. Armitage said as we stepped on then rose to the cockpit. Inside was like a scene from a science fiction digital cinematic-disk.

"Here is another specially designed electronic keycard, don't ever lose it or you won't be able to operate this craft efficiently until you get the spare keycard from us. If you need to access anything electronic in the aircraft, you will require that keycard. But if you ever need to dismantle anything electronic the keycard must be ejected from its port, if not it could result in severe electrocution," Dr. Graham informed me. She inserted the electronic keycard and activated the multicolored touch pads, monitors and illuminators of the instrument panels; I was in awe as I viewed the sights.

"What's your first impression?" Sr. Com. Boone asked. "I can't believe the advancements that were made and that you want me to test then use this exquisite piece of technology. "This isn't all, show him citizens," the Sr. Commodore said to the two scientific engineers as he chuckled.

"This aircraft is paneled with Ombient EM-Shield Resonating Panels; in the event this craft is ever under attack. This craft could sustain numerous direct hits as long as the shield holds. Before the shield resonator dwindles down to 0%, you must recharge. The aircraft is also Whipple Plated, which is a type of advanced armor. It uses multi-layered oxygenated atmospheric impact plating so the aircraft can take numerous hits before any real damage is sustained."

"As said before, this craft is equipped with an onboard super computer, named 'PAT'. 'PAT's image is available in your computerized system and if you prefer a physical representation, she is also back here as an artificial intelligent cybernetic being to act as a co-pilot," Dr. Graham said as he opened a closet entry-way exposing an alcove, turned her on and she walked out. "The letters P. A. T is an anagram which stands for Prototype Advancements in Technology," Dr. Graham also explained.

"Greetings 'PAT'. "Greetings Maj. Teldat, I would like to formally introduce myself. As you know I am named 'PAT', your onboard cybernetic co-pilot, my main function is to control and maneuver the Supersonic Dragon 228-D Stealth Aircraft. I have also been created to assist my pilot (you) in any way I can, cutting the need for additional co-pilots for an aircraft of this size and magnitude. "Many thanks 'PAT' that will be all for now," Sr. Com. Boone told her. "Affirmative sir," she said then went silent.

"This craft flies the same in respect as all the previous stealth aircraft except this craft is equipped with EM absorbent Panels for cloaking privileges; activate this touch pad here and the aircraft vanishes from sight as well as radar. Also, it doesn't require a runway. "What is your meaning? "This aircraft is hover inclined, when you are ready for liftoff. All you have to do is pull up on the hand contoured flight stick, and this craft will rise to your desired altitude. The wings will automatically level then push the flight stick in the direction you feel you want to advance, the nose of the craft will turn in that direction and that is the direction in which you will travel. When you desire to lower altitude or set down just press the flight stick straight down and the craft will descend. But heed caution for this craft is very sensitive, you only have to move the flight stick slightly, as it will immediately respond," Dr. Armitage reported. "Affirmative," I said as they continued.

"On top of the hand contoured flight stick is a teal colored button that will fire the SQ-laser cannons. Also, along the shaft of the flight stick you will notice a series of multicolored finger touch pads. Press the white one to lower the XTR-9000 Plasma Pulse Cannons, and then press the yellow finger touch pad to fire the port and pale blue one for the starboard Plasma Pulse Cannons. Press the magenta colored touch pad to activate the shield, the red one for the Protonic EMC-Missals, the dark blue one for the Neutronic EMC-Torpedo's and the green one for the XT-165 DigiCam. We don't anticipate you will be in many battles but you never know if you are discovered by the Protrerian's they will most likely attack," Dr. Graham explained.

"If ever you need to use this aircraft's weapons, the laser's and the cannons ammunition self rejuvenates as said earlier. The Protonic EMC-Missals will require ten mites time to recharge to its full complement and the Neutronic EMC-Torpedo's will require twenty mites. The reason it needs additional time is because they are larger charges that neutralizes a target of all electronic power, leaving that target vulnerable to your aircraft's weapons attack. Across from the two main engines is a Comodrone Electronics P-52 Hydrogenic Generator it is there to supply all the necessary electronic power this craft needs to operate efficiently. Plus for this reason you never need to reload ammunition. It creates the power that supplies you your ammunition and mixes in the correct amount of the Liquid Naprisyte[2] explosive."

"In addition, in the event you ever have to break ZarCedra's outer atmosphere, 'PAT' will automatically fill the cockpit with breathable oxygen. This craft has three oxygen tanks that have enough compressed oxygen to last a maximum 96 epocks. The cockpit is airtight and the tanks that supply the oxygen were filled with compressed oxygen the p.a.r before this one. If you are required to leave the atmosphere for any reason 'PAT' will keep you advised on the status of breathable oxygen that remains. When and if you break ZarCedra's atmosphere, the nose of this craft has to be pointed up. Ask 'PAT' to raise the golden rod and it will pierce the levels of the atmosphere being reinforced by the Energy Reactor Facilities here on ZarCedra. It is much easier when descending toward this planet, just locate where the thinnest location of the ozone layer is and that location is where you descend. There is something else very important about those tanks of oxygen, I'll explain in a bit."

"On another note, when you change vials of the Liquid Naprisyte[2] SDC you must wear a radioactive safe security suit and breathing apparatus. There is one of each located in the overhead compartment above the case of the chemical fuel in the rear of the cockpit," Dr. Graham said. "Understood."

"We supplied you with twice the amount of this chemical solution because it has to supply both the star drive engine and the Hydrogenic generator and we knew you would want to try out the Omagon 2115 Star Drive Engine before you go on your mission to Vertgren Isle." I was beaming with delight about everything I heard.

"The special com-link badge Sr. Commodore Boone mentioned earlier, here," he said as he opened a black case and handed me an oversized set of platinum wings. "All you have to do is pin this to your flight suit and press the right wing to talk to Sr. Commodore Boone," Dr. Graham told me. "Sr. Com. Boone, here is a technically advanced computerized gelatin covered receiver. Insert it as far as you can inside either ear cannel, leave it there and in five mites the gelatin will dissolve and the computerized chip will attach itself to your eardrum. Then you can talk directly to Maj. Teldat using mental telepathy."

"Major press the right wing to talk to the Senior Commodore, and you may talk normally and whatever you say will only be heard by Sr. Com. Boone through the computerized chip inside the Commodore's ear. Major press the left wing and you will have a direct link to 'PAT' whenever you're away from the aircraft."

"Here Sr. Commodore, if you'll insert the earpiece now, it will be in place during Maj. Teldat's initial test flight," Dr. Graham added. "Affirmative," Sr. Commodore Boone answered as he carefully took the gelatin covered computerized chip from a secured plastic case and inserted it as far as it would go inside his right ear. "Why am I permitted the opportunity to fly this magnificent, technically advanced craft when there are a lot of other Humanarian officer's with higher rankings than I?"

"Because, you are a test pilot, also a teacher in the field of Aero Dynamics, and because you have no living relatives, therefore, it is in my best judgment that you are the best candidate. And besides you are a pretty smart citizen, you would know how to handle certain predicaments if ever things went awry. Plus, when we were screening personnel reports for our test subject we noticed you have three trittons of astronaut training; that is mainly what made our decision that you were the right candidate for the job," Sr. Com. Boone said as he patted me on the shoulder.

"One more important thing this purple touch pad, over here on the port instrument panel is to activate the spy jet invisibility Stealth Mode and right next to it is a yellow touch pad. When pressed, it will hydraulically contract both wings so you can leave this and enter/disembark any other underground hangar; either activate it yourself or inform 'PAT' and she will activate them for you."

"When the port wing is contracted it will automatically slide back, out of the way of the main hatch. All the finger touch pads and monitors are labeled so you know which one to touch to activate when needed."

"Just one moment," Dr. Armitage said as he went to get the specially designed black helmet from the pilot's seat. "Here, this is a 'HUD' or Heads up Display helmet and it is a necessary part of flying this craft. This is a highly sophisticated piece of technology, very advanced in technology even for our standards. Before you turn the ignition on in the Supersonic Dragon, plug in this 'HUD' helmet where indicated. Either access the menu or ask 'PAT' for something and it will digitally appear on the bottom portion of the face shield (i.e. maps, ammunition levels, fuel levels, time etc.)."

"Another thing, if you press this touch pad here by the starboard ear position you will activate two-way communications. Whenever you want to talk to someone in particular you must activate two-way communications however if someone calls your name it will activate automatically. In addition, if you press it a second time in quick succession two-way communications will remain open until you press the finger touch pad a third time," he said as he handed the helmet over to me so I could inspect it.

"Affirmative understood," I said as I looked it over and noticed an array of finger touch pads jeweled along the side of the 'HUD' helmet. "Very impressive," I said as I handed it back.

"To view your radar when you have the 'HUD' helmet on, just say radar and a radar will be depicted on the lower portion of your visor. Or you can press this finger touch pad above the face shield and the visor will rise into the shell of the helmet, allowing you to view the radar or anything else, and then press it again to lower it. There is also an extra helmet in the back cloak compartment for passengers if you ever have any and go into Star Drive."

"Another important aspect, if you believe you are in imminent danger there is an ejection handle at the base of the pilot's seat, pull it and that handle will release the entire cockpit. The cockpit has a triple parachute attached to it and will open automatically. But pull it only in case of a life or death situation because when the ejection handle is pulled the cockpit will land safely but the body of the aircraft will fall away and crash," Dr. Graham said. "Understood," I answered.

"Now follow us, and we will show you everything pertaining to the engines," Dr. Graham said as she smiled. We lowered to the floor and Dr. Graham climbed up to the little trap entry-way and activated a black touch pad and the tail portion of the craft raised then slid forward. As that was being done, Dr. Armitage, the Sr. Commodore and I went to retrieve four hover-boards. We activated them, waited for Dr. Graham to join us at the rear of the craft then when she had; we stood on them and rose up to the rear of the craft.

When we were up, we stepped onto the metal walkway surrounding the inside tail portion of the engine galley. "On the upper portion of the craft, on the section that slides you will see two fuel intake caps, and there is where the craft is refueled. You have double fuel tanks for ordinary jet fuel, when one tank is depleted there is a touch pad on the instrument panel you or 'PAT' can activate and that will switch fuel tanks, a buzzer will sound when one tank is depleted." At that time we set our hover boards aside then walked over to a metal ladder and climbed down to the engine galley.

"These are the two huge F405-F1D3 afterburning engines; although they operate using the same type of jet fuel as all other aircraft. But instead of the acceleration of Mach six as all the other aircraft, these engines will propel you to a maximum regular air speed of Mach ten."

"Over here we have the Comodrone Electronics P-52 Hydrogenic Generator, which supplies the craft the power to create its own arsenal of various ammunition, power's the aircraft's stealth mode capabilities and full-bodied shield also it supplies power to the entire craft with the needed energy to operate efficiently."

"Right over here is the Omagon 2115 Star Drive Engine. This is the engine which when used will propel you from Mach ten to Star Drive one then if you choose to the maximum airspeed of Star Drive two. By the way, Star Drive one is equivalent to the speed of Mach ten * ten and Star Drive two is equivalent to

Mach ten * twenty. To attain those speeds we needed a powerful accelerant, which is the aforementioned Liquid Naprisyte[2] Star Drive Compound. That chemical compound is shared between both the Star Drive engine and the P-52 Hydrogenic generator to make the various weapon's ammunition."

"This highly volatile radioactive pale blue chemical solution is contained in 200 ml vials. The vials are very sensitive to movement and will explode if jostled roughly or dropped, so handle it with extreme caution. Star Drive two is almost too fast to fly within ZarCedra's circumference; therefore, we stopped at that speed and there is no Star Drive three at this time."

"Right here next to it, is the wondrous component which allows Star Drive speed within ZarCedra's oxygenated resistant atmosphere and gravitational pull. This is the Electronic Flux Inducer; it is also activated by the Star Drive Engine and powered by the Comodrone Electronics P-52 Hydrogenic Generator."

"When the Omagon 2115 Star Drive engine is activated, the chemical solution is mixed with electronic power within the Star Drive engine; which, flows into the EFI and in turn converts that saturated power to Ionic power. It flows through this insulated electronic cable to the rear of the craft. It will then encompass the craft electromagnetically running from those golden modules you were shown earlier. This Ionic power reaches the longer golden rod on the nose of the craft then it will spray out this Ionic mixture creating a swirling Humanarian-made wormhole. You fly into it and 'theoretically' you will be able to fly at Star Drive speed within the oxygenated resistant atmosphere and gravitation pull of our planet."

"Being oxygenated resistant means having no oxygen, the oxygen that is stored in your tanks I told you about earlier will automatically flood the cockpit and you will be able to breathe normally."

"I have a positive feeling that this craft will secretly revelutionize air travel as we know it; and if you give positive feedback of this craft's performance, we'll mass produce the Supersonic Dragon 228-D Spy Jet Stealth."

"One thing I must inform you of, in the compartment at the rear of the cockpit beside your radiation safe suit is a silver case which contains three extra golden modules and one extra rod just in case anything happens to the modules and rod equipped on this aircraft."

"Now if you are ready you can test this technically advanced marvel out?" Sr. Com. Boone said as he looked at me. "Affirmative, I'm more than ready," I replied with a smile then we all went back to the metal ladder, climbed up to the walkway, then went back to our hover-boards reactivated them and lowered to the floor.

"I know everything we have told you is a lot to remember that is why we have included an instructional e-manual inside the cockpit that will inform you of everything pertaining to this craft if you can't remember something. "Understood," I said as I saluted my senior officer then went up the couple metrics to the cockpit as Dr. Graham returned to the little trap entry-way and lowered the engine cover and the tail section closed as she climbed down.

"Many thanks for everything," I said as I stuck my head out the main hatch. "You're quite welcome," all three said as I raised then closed the main hatch platform as the hatch sealed air tight and locked. As the keycard was already engaged in its port, I walked over to and got in the cushioned pilot's seat, put on the 'HUD' helmet, plugged it into its designated port and connected my safety belts then touched the ignition touch pad.

As the engines started, the golden modules and rod automatically lowered into the shell of the craft. I couldn't believe the quietness of a craft this size. I touched the touch pad that activated stealth mode and the craft disappeared from sight so no Protrerian High Command official could detect my presence visibly or electronically.

After the engines warmed, I maneuvered to a secretive turbo lift. "'PAT', contract the wings. "Affirmative Major," 'PAT' acknowledged then I slowly pulled onto it. That turbo lift brought me up well behind the military facility as I looked around. "'PAT', you can now extend the wings," I said as I looked over at her. "Affirmative Major," she acknowledged as she did. I pulled slightly on the flight stick and the huge craft left the ground, I rose to 20, 000 metrics, raised the face shield and could barely make out the military facility below. I climbed even higher and stopped rising at 25, 000 metrics.

"Now time to see what this Dragon can do," I said to 'PAT' as I leveled the wings and started advancing at regular air speed; after a few mites I checked the radar and slowly started increasing air speed as I again lowered the face shield.

I advanced to the maximum normal air speed of Mach ten and literally flew through the clouds. I raised my face shield and glanced at the radar again to make sure my course was clear. Seeing it was, I disengaged Stealth mode, and my craft reappeared. I touched the touch pad, which activated the Omagon 2115 Star Drive Engine, as the golden modules and rod exited the frame of the craft as I lowered my face shield.

The Electronic Flux Inducer created the perfect Ionic charge, which electromagnetically encompassed the craft. The pale blue ionic charge shot out from the golden rod at the front of the craft. Immediately, a swirling wormhole formed in front of the craft as I guided the aircraft into it.

Immediately I went to Star Drive one then I advanced to Star Drive two, as breathable oxygen flooded the cockpit. The flight through the wormhole was very rough as the craft shook violently as it spiraled.

"The reason for this erratic flight is caused by external oxygen pockets within the wormhole, you will notice this whenever we fly at star drive speeds within ZarCedra's circumference but this should dissipate outside of ZarCedra's boundaries and go to star drive speeds, " 'PAT' stated. "Affirmative, many thanks 'PAT'," I said as I flew through this wormhole for forty-five secs.

After that time, which felt more like an eternity, I touched the touch pad again, which disengaged the 2115 Star Drive engine and I exited the wormhole. As I did the oxygen being pumped into the cockpit automatically ceased as I slowly decreased airspeed all the way down to Mach one.

'I wonder where we are?' I thought. "'PAT', produce a map of ZarCedra," I asked and a mini map appeared on the bottom portion of my visor. "What is our current location?" I inquired as scanned the mini map. A split sec later there was a red flashing illuminator over Zantara. "We are over the continent of Zantara, over the country of Zairet, over the city of Kishtanria," 'PAT' informed.

I reactivated Stealth mode and the craft vanished as I descended into their airspace, and at that time Sr. Com. Boone was in contact. "Report Major? "Sr. Commodore this aircraft truly soars like a dragon. You will never guess where I am right now? "Where? "Ready for this, I'm in Zantara over the country of Zairet.

"That's wonderful, it looks like our Supersonic Dragon project works to expectations. "It sure does! "It seems like you just left. "I did, the Star Drive Engine works to perfection. Would I be permitted to fire the SQ-Laser cannons and other weapons to get the feel of how they operate?"

"Negative not at this time, we don't want the energy signatures from your weapons to be detected by the Protrerian High Command on that part of the planet. Return to Cangla City and if you go to the old abandoned test range, there you may test the SQ-Lasers as well as the Plasma Pulse Cannons, the Protonic EMC-Missals and the Neutronic EMC-Torpedo's.

The test range is shielded and there you will not be detected, when you are ready to fire your weapons you must exit Stealth mode before the weapons array will operate. There is an energy buffer around the old abandoned test range we had installed especially for this reason. "Affirmative sir. "If that is all to report at this time, I'll leave you for now, Sr. Com. Boone out."

This time I rose to 27, 000 metrics then I slowly began accelerating all the way up to Mach ten. After viewing the radar, I deactivated Stealth mode as I reappeared. I engaged the Omagon 2115 Star Drive Engine, which in turn activated the Electronic Flux Inducer, and secs later the Ionic charge formed the swirling wormhole in my path. As I flew into it, the cockpit filled with breathable oxygen once again as the craft excelled to Star Drive one then Star Drive two.

Forty-five secs later of the same rough conditions I felt earlier, I deactivated the Star Drive engines and exited the swirling wormhole and decelerated to Mach three as I immediately reactivated Stealth mode and disappeared nearing Cangla City.

I lowered altitude to 500 metrics as I flew around the city bypassing the military facility. I eased the speed back further as I continued to drop altitude until I was down to 50 metrics then slowly my craft entered the abandoned test range. "'PAT', activate weapons," I said and when I was in range, 'PAT' detected a target. "Maj. Teldat, there is a target 50 metrics to the port side. "I see it 'PAT', many thanks," I said as I exited Stealth mode and fired the double barreled lasers as targets exploded all around.

Next I opened the bay entry-ways and fired a Protonic EMC-Missal. 'I wonder how the generator conjured up my weapons ammunition?' I asked myself as the EMC-missal exploded right on target. I pressed the white finger touch pad that lowered the Plasma Pulse cannons then as a target appeared, I fired. I looked out the port window and could barely see the outline of the cannons ammunition as it blew the targets to bits. "Wow, what power," was all I said upon impact.

"'PAT' advise me again, what is my total compliment of Protonic EMC-Missals? "You have a total of fifteen prior to expelling any of them, after depleting your supply the Comodrone Electronics P-52 Hydrogenic Generator will require ten mites time to recharge and create the next compliment. The same goes for the Neutronic EMC-Torpedo's; except your total compliment is ten and it will require twenty mites to recharge. "Understood," I said as I flew over more targets and fired the SQ-Lasers, the Plasma Pulse cannons and expelled more EMC-Missals.

After I had expelled my compliment of EMC-Missals, I accessed the menu in my helmet and switched to my

EMC-Torpedo's and as the next target came into sight I fired. The torpedo hit its mark and disappeared, almost immediately the target powered off and the laser that was firing at my craft lost its power and deactivated. Giving me the opportunity to target it and destroy it with my lasers. I did this a few more times as I destroyed the remainder of the targets. At that time I accessed the menu again and deactivated the EMC-Torpedo's.

'Utterly amazing,' I thought as the bays sliding metal plate automatically closed as I pressed the white finger touch pad on the flight stick and the cannons raised back into the wings.

"'PAT', as everything is electronic, just how would I get the results of my score? "As we flew through the test range, I recorded your score which I tallied and you scored 100%," 'PAT' relayed. "Many thanks," I said as I reactivated Stealth mode, climbed altitude to 15, 000 metrics and left the test range heading away from the city.

While heading toward Vertgren Isle I recharged my weapons ammunition then started getting to know what each touch pad and monitor on the instrument panels were for, with 'PAT's' assistance. After a few mites Sr. Com. Boone voice came over the com-link.

"Maj. Teldat I have Dr.'s Armitage and Graham present. They would like to inquire how the craft handled after you engaged the Star Drive engine? If you activate the communications monitor you will be able to talk to them directly."

I raised the face shield of my helmet then located and activated the satellite link of the communications monitor. "Greetings Dr.'s Graham and Armitage," I said as they appeared on the monitor.

"The Star Drive engine works unbelievably grand, but flying within the wormhole was very rough, it was almost like the aircraft was barrel rolling out of control. I felt a bit uneasy as I entered but after I got used to traveling at that speed, the feeling of uneasiness subsided. All in all it works grand," I said as I beamed proudly.

"That is because of external oxygen, you will notice this whenever you fly within ZarCedra's circumference, but that feeling should be eliminated if you ever need to fly outside this planet's circumference. Does everything meet your expectations?" Dr. Graham asked. "It does and surpasses them and I'll welcome the opportunity to learn other things this aircraft can do.

"How does the weapons handle?" Dr. Armitage inquired. "Wonderful, the SQ-Laser artillery, Protonic EMC-Missals, Neutronic EMC-Torpedo's and XTR-9000 Plasma Pulse cannons are very sensitive but work unimaginably grand. "They must, I heard you as you flew through the test range. My internal com-link receiver works to expectation," Sr. Com. Boone replied.

"That is wonderful Major but remember to say "out" when you are through talking to anyone; I wish you grand success on your mission" Dr. Graham said. "Affirmative, many thanks" I answered then the monitor went dark. "That is all for now, grand luck Major, Sr. Com. Boone out. "Many thanks sir, Maj. Teldat, out."

I lowered my face shield as I continued my flight north. 'PAT' and I talked of, "rules and regulations," to pass the time. When we were through, I thought of the lady I was leaving behind. 'My precious Gods, I love her so, if it is in my best interest let me return safely so I can again be in her company,' I thought as I looked at the landscape below go whizzing by.

"Major Teldat, there is a Jr. Com. Lancton to talk to you via satellite from the Eclipse Military Facility, Division Gaznor Ometga-North Western Quadrant," 'PAT' informed me. "Affirmative, many thanks 'PAT'," I replied as I raised my face shield, turned on the satellite link of my communications monitor and seen Sr. Com. Boone and Jr. Com. Lancton on a split screen. As I seen the two Commodores, I saluted.

"Maj. Teldat, I heard you tried and like the Supersonic Dragon 228-D Spy Jet Stealth Aircraft," he said as they both returned my salute. "Affirmative sir, it flies quiet, smooth and flies as fast as a dragon. "I also heard you were over the Zantaran Continent; explain the experience? "Affirmative sir, I was ordered to take this craft up and test the Star Drive Engine; in my observation, it works A OK." I said as I grinned from ear to ear.

"So you give our secret project two thumbs up? "Affirmative sir I do; I'm sure if I had a third thumb it would be up as well," I said as the two senior officers chuckled. "I'm not sure how citizens were ever able to keep this magnificent craft a secret; I'm guessing a few trittons," I said after the laughter subsided. "Actually, it has taken five and a half trittons from start to finish; the aircraft has been finished for over a tritton but the Star Drive Engine was just completed this tritton. That is why this tritton has been included in its designation." Sr. Com. Boone said.

"I also received the opportunity to fire the weapons when I returned to Cangla City; I was permitted to fly through our old abandoned test range behind the Grinshaw Military Facility. "How did that go Major? "Better than expected sir, I fired the SQ-Lasers, spent off a total of ten Protonic EMC-Missals, a few Neutronic EMC-Torpedo and volleys of cannon fire and destroyed every target. "Grand, I'll look forward to meeting you soon, Jr. Com. Lancton out," and his side of the communications monitor extinguished and only Sr. Com. Boone remained.

"You will be on Vertgren Isle only to take Digital Cinematic and assist in any way possible. Remember the Antrerian Race are our consociates, they tried their best to assist us during the Grand War we had so many trittons ago against their sister planet, Protreria."

"One more thing if you engage your autopilot or instruct 'PAT' to fly the aircraft then go back to your storage locker at the aft of the cockpit you will discover a black leather pilot's jacket, it will assist in keeping you warm on Vertgren Isle.

I raised the face shield then looked at 'PAT'. "The craft is now under your control," I said as I transferred control to her flight stick. "Affirmative Major Teldat." I removed the 'HUD' helmet then disconnected my safety belts and got out of the seat.

I went to the rear of the cockpit, opened the narrow closet entry-way and retrieved the garment. I looked it over, front and back then put it on and it fit grand, I also noticed it was quite warm for the thickness; I reached into a pocket and pulled out a pair of avionics sunglasses.

I returned to the pilot's seat, connected my safety belts and replaced my helmet. "Many thanks 'PAT'," I said as I took over the controls as I looked at the communications monitor. "Many thanks very much for the jacket and the sunglasses, Sr. Commodore."

As we were discussing the mission in grander detail, I took a better look at the leather jacket. I noticed it has a crest with N.Z.C.M.Co/S.H.Z.C.A embroidered on the front port breast, Maj. J. Teldat on the starboard arm, the tritton 2115 on the port arm and I remembered reading Supersonic Dragon 228-D SJ Stealth embroidered on the back. "I hope you are ready for the frozen North? "Affirmative sir I am ready now, many thanks again."

"You are welcome again but remember on the p.a.r you return to Cangla City pack it away; so no one in the Protrerian High Command sees it. May the Gods smile on the success and safety of your mission Major, if for any reason you need to be in contact with me don't hesitate to contact me, Sr. Commodore Boone out. "Maj. Teldat out," I said as the communications monitor went black.

"All right 'PAT' let's get this mission started," I said as I advanced speed to Mach six. "'PAT', what would the ETA be at Star Drive one? "Eleven mites," she said. I deactivated Stealth mode and the craft reappeared, I increased speed from Mach six to Mach ten, I looked at the radar then lowered my face shield as I advanced the Star Drive Engine.

As soon as the swirling wormhole was in front of me, I flew into it then went to Star Drive one as the cockpit filled with breathable oxygen. I kept a close watch on the countdown timer as I went through the rough, windy wormhole. This time the uneasy feeling I felt earlier was much easier as I was getting used to the havoc traveling at star drive speeds wreaked on my body.

Eleven mites later I pulled out of Star Drive and flew out of the swirling wormhole as the golden modules and rod disappeared back into the frame of the craft as I decelerated to Mach four.

"We've arrived at last 'PAT'," I said as soon as I arrived at the coordinates of the Eclipse Military Facility, Alphan Omegator-NWQ. I pressed the finger touch pad that activated two-way communications. "Eclipse Military Facility, this is Maj. Teldat of N. Z. C. M. Co/S. H. Z. C. A. requesting permission to set down? "Affirmative Major, you are cleared." So I slowed to a stop, while hovering I pushed down on the flight stick as the craft's wings tilted upwards. The landing gear automatically lowered as my craft slowly hovered down.

When I was on the freshly fallen snow-covered tarmac, I contracted the port wing as it slid out of the way of the main hatch. I turned everything off, disconnected my safety belts and left the pilot's seat. I zipped my jacket, removed the electronic keycard then opened and lowered the main hatch platform. "'PAT' would you care to accompany me as I see the Junior Commodore? "Affirmative Major, I'm unsure if you are aware but since I was created this aircraft is the only place I've been. "Well come with me and this will be the second," I said with a smirk. "Do you have a jacket or something? "Negative, the uniform I have on should suffice. "Affirmative," I said as we stepped on then lowered two metrics to the snowy ground, as an airman came out to block the wheels of my craft while the cold wind & snow swirled around us.

I put on my pair of avionics sunglasses as we stepped off the main hatch platform as I looked at 'PAT'.

"'PAT', RAISE AND CLOSE THE MAIN HATCH PLATFORM," I shouted as the wind howled. As the cybernetic version of 'PAT' and I met up with the airman. "WHERE WOULD I FIND JR. COM. LANCTON?" I shouted "INSIDE MAIN HEADQUARTERS," the Lance Corporal replied as he pointed. "MANY THANKS," I yelled and we went inside the front foyer of the partially buried main headquarters structure.

Upon entering we went down a few steps to a female Sergeant. "Grand p.a.r ma'am, I am Maj. Jeroque Teldat and I am to report to Junior Commodore Lancton upon my arrival."

"Greetings and grand p.a.r, just a moment." The Sergeant said as she pressed a pager button on her comp. console, a moment later Jr. Com. Lancton was depicted on the monitor. "What can I do for you Sergeant? "Sir, there is a Maj. Teldat here to see you, do I permit him to enter? "By all means, Sergeant. "Affirmative sir, at once. You may enter Major, the Jr. Commodore is expecting you," she said with an incredible smile. "Many thanks Sergeant." I replied as I returned her smile then 'PAT' and I went towards the Commodore's entry-way as I pressed the door chime.

A moment later the metal entry-way slid open. "Enter Maj. Teldat." We entered and saluted the Jr. Commodore then stood at attention in front of his desk, as the entry-way quietly closed behind us.

"Welcome to my outfit, stand at ease," Jr. Com. Lancton said as he returned our salutes then stood to shake my hand. "Many thanks sir this is my cybernetic co-pilot 'PAT'. "Very grand to meet you," the Jr. Commodore said as he shook her hand.

"The Supersonic Dragon Spy Jet Stealth must fly magnificently well for you to be here so soon," the Jr. Commodore said as he sat back down. "Affirmative sir, it flies unbelievably grand, we would have been here sooner but I only flew at Star Drive one," I said with a grin. "That was quick enough."

"As you know we are being revisited by the Antrerian Race. Nothing drastic has taken place between them and the Protrerian High Command because as of yet the Protrerian's are unaware of their presence here. The reason they are here is that, scientific information revealed that the planet of Antreria's sun is about to go nova. So their main Mother Crafts are cloaked and that race is secretly settling on Vertgren Isle."

"ZarCedra Force is also unaware of their presence here for the time being but we won't be able to keep it from them for long. Hopefully the Antrerian's will have everything here on ZarCedra before they do. We members of the Secret Humanarian ZarCedra Alliance are allowing them to settle here because of their assistance during the Grand War against the Protrerian High Command in the times elapsed. It's unfortunate that we were defeated and the Protrerian High Command has ruling power over our Planet. Your orders are to go up and take Digital Cinematic & keep them under surveillance."

"Question sir? "Go-ahead Major. "If the Antrerian Mother Craft are cloaked, how is it I can take Digital Cinematic of them? "Acceptable question, it is true their Mother Crafts are cloaked but their transport crafts are unable to cloak at this time but the energy signatures of their transport craft are being masked for the time being," the Jr. Commodore explained. "Affirmative, in other words you want me to spy on them sir?"

"Negative, although your craft is technically called a, "Spy Jet," we don't want you to spy on them per say but keep them under surveillance while they are taking refuge here, so the Protrerian High Command don't interfere at least until they are completely settled. "Affirmative sir, when would you like us to go up?

"The p.a.r's are quite a bit shorter in this part of our Planet, so go up for a short time this mid-p.a.r and just look for anything out of the ordinary. "Affirmative sir; and just let me say that it is a pleasure serving with you. Although it is only for a short time, I hope it will be pleasant. "I too," the Jr. Commodore said then he pressed a button on his desk and a part of the wall opened exposing a huge flat paneled monitor and depicted was a map of ZarCedra.

Jr. Com. Lancton walked over then reached for the pointer from its place beneath the monitor. "The Antrerian's are based 200 kiloms north of the settlement of Fratare. Although they brought structures with them, with their digits of citizens we advised them to use an old abandoned military base to use and build upon to start their city. The Antrerian's contacted us requesting our assistance because our planet is the closest M-class planet to them and the Humanarian members of ZarCedra offered to assist them if they were ever in need of our assistance and if we were in a position to assist."

"We also thought this would be the perfect time for them to settle here and try to establish permanent peace between them and the Protrerian High Command. This mission gave us the perfect opportunity to test the prototype Supersonic Dragon," he said then put the pointer back where he got it. "Affirmative, I am ordered here to comply with all orders you convey. "Very grand Major, after you finish your initial flight, twilight sustenance will be served at 17 hundred epocks in the main mess hall. "Affirmative sir."

Jr. Com. Lancton walked back to his desk and switched the pager button on his computer console. "Sgt. Sullivan, your presence is requested," he said as he returned his attention back to 'PAT' and I.

"Major, Sgt. Sullivan will show you to the bunker you will be sharing while you stay with us; does 'PAT' also require quarters? "Negative sir, I have an alcove aboard the Supersonic Dragon," she said. Just then the entry-way chimed and in walked the lovely Sergeant Sullivan, as the entry-way slid closed behind her.

"Affirmative sir, you requested my presence!" She exclaimed with an exquisite smile. "I did air citizen, show Maj. Teldat to a bunker and issue him a few of our uniforms for him to wear while he is with us. "Affirmative sir," the Sergeant replied as she looked at me and smiled once again.

"Come with me, sir. "I'll be awaiting your report Major," Jr. Com. Lancton said, as the three of us were about to leave the chamber. "Affirmative sir," I replied then the Sergeant, 'PAT' and I vacated his office.

"Just a moment Major, I need to check the availability of quarters," she said as she went to her desk and checked her computer terminal. "If I am no longer needed I will return to the craft," 'PAT' said. "Affirmative you are dismissed," I answered as she walked away. "Right this way sir," Sgt. Sullivan said after closing the file and we walked through the underground military facility to the Officer's Quarters.

"This will be your quarters, rest your chin on the chin rest then activate the record button so your retina can be scanned then state your rank and name." I did and my retina was scanned and my voice recorded, after I did the entry-way-slid open.

"Very exquisite," I said as we entered the chamber. "You will be sharing quarters with another officer, a Captain Lorii

Casper. I will now go retrieve your uniforms, feel free to look around until I return," Sgt. Sullivan said as she left.

'Very exquisite accommodations indeed,' I thought then I investigated the large Intervision flat screen monitor that was placed in a wall in the front chamber. "This is grand," I said. A few mites later the Sergeant returned with the uniforms and handed them to me. I put them on the lounger then we vacated the quarters, as I made a mental note that my quarters were in chamber, 'yellow twenty-three.'

We discussed the weather and customs relevant to the area on the way back to her desk. "I have to return to my craft, you have a pleasant p.a.r," I informed Sergeant Sullivan as I turned and walked away. "You as well!" Sgt. Sullivan exclaimed as I went up the steps and out the entry-way.

I fastened my leather jacket then pressed the left wing of my winged com-link. "'PAT', open and lower the main hatch platform," I said as I left the warm confines of the secretive military facility and continued through the blowing wind & snow to my craft.

As I got to the main hatch I stepped on and rose to the cockpit. "Greetings 'PAT'," I said as I entered and inserted the electronic keycard. "Greetings Major," 'PAT' acknowledged as I raised, closed and sealed the main hatch platform. I went and sat in the pilot's seat and fastened my safety belts then activated the engines.

As they roared to life, I put on the specially designed 'HUD' helmet as I lowered the face shield. "Map of the area," I requested and instantaneously a map illuminated on the lower portion of my visor. I mapped the coordinates to Fratare, Vertgren Isle then 200 km north. 'PAT and I "discussed our flight plan" as I had the port wing slide forward then extend.

I pressed the finger touch pad that activated two-way communications. "Tower, this is Maj. Teldat; I'm ready for liftoff, can I commence? "Affirmative, you are blue to go." I pulled slightly on the flight stick, the wings lowered and the craft started to rise as the landing gear raised automatically while I hovered up to 1500 metrics then halted my ascent. I leveled the wings and activated Stealth mode as the aircraft vanished; I raised the face shield visor, checked the radar as I started advancing forward then lowered my face shield.

Flying at Mach ten, I flew by Fratare and over to the coordinates I was given to the Antrerian settlement. After a few mites, I eased the speed back as I lowered altitude as we got to one hundred and fifty metrics from the settlement.

I stopped, hovered there unseen observing the Antrerian's transporting supplies. "'PAT' activate the telescopic view screen so we can get a better view," I said as I raised my face shield. We discovered they were transporting supplies and personnel via shuttlecraft to their base settlement in an old abandoned military base, from their cloaked mother craft above the planet.

I activated the XT-165 DigiCam and recorded all that was going on; I tapped the right wing of my winged com-link and called Sr. Com. Boone. "Sr. Com. Boone, come in. "Go ahead Major," the Sr. Commodore thought.

"Sir I am currently near the Antrerian base settlement, observing and recording the events happening in the area. "Does it look like the Antrerian's are doing anything out of the ordinary? "Negative sir, right at this moment they are transporting supplies and personnel to their settlement. I'm recording everything so you'll have the opportunity to retrieve and view the micro disk when I return to the Grinshaw Military Facility. "All right Major keep me informed on all events until your return, Sr. Com. Boone out. "Affirmative sir, Maj. Teldat out."

"We should advance closer to attain a better view," I suggested to 'PAT' as I looked around. "Affirmative Major." I maneuvered the aircraft forward sixty metrics and hovered there to get better recordings. After a few mites I flew around the huge Antrerian base settlement a while longer recording all that I saw.

Thirty mites later I turned the XT-165 DigiCam off and flew back to the Eclipse Military Facility, it took a while as we flew at 200 knots/e. I raised my face shield as 'PAT' and I observed and enjoyed the snowy scenery on the return flight, still learning how the craft maneuvered.

When I arrived, I deactivated stealth mode and my craft reappeared as I activated two-way communications. "Tower, this is Maj. Teldat, am I cleared to set down? "Affirmative Major you are," so I pushed the flight stick straight down until I heard the click as the wings raised and the landing gear lowered as I hovered down to a landing area. As I touched down, the tower contacted me.

"Maj. Teldat you are to follow Cpl. Tompkins and he will direct you to the turbo-lift pad that will lower your aircraft into our underground hangar. "Understood," I responded as I taxied the craft following the Corporal to the almost invisible turbo-lift pad. "'PAT", contract both wings. "Affirmative Major," she acknowledged as the wings folded inwards as I pulled onto the huge turbo lift. A mite later the pad started to lower out of the frigid cold and into the warm confines of the gigantic underground hangar 250 metrics below the surface.

When the turbo-lift pad ceased its descent, I taxied my craft off the pad and in as far as I safely could then I turned the main ignition off and removed the 'HUD' helmet and disconnected my safety belts. "'PAT', I was informed that you have an alcove at the aft of the cockpit where you go when not in use. "That is correct sir. "Grand I'll see you in the morrow, slide the port wing," I commanded as I got out of the pilot's seat. "Affirmative Major." I ejected the electronic keycard then stepped out of my flight suit, set it aside, removed my beret from my shoulder loop and put it on as I grabbed my duffel bag.

"Have a grand twilight Major," 'PAT' said. "You as well," I said with a smile as I opened and lowered the main hatch platform then exited the craft. After arriving at the floor I tapped the left wing of my com-link. "Many thanks 'PAT', raise and seal the main hatch platform. "Affirmative Major."

After receiving directions, I went off in the direction of Jr. Com. Lancton's office. Mites later I was standing in main headquarters, and in front of Sgt. Sullivan. "Greetings again ma'am, I am to see the Jr. Commodore upon my return," I said with a smile. "Greetings Major, of course you are, the Jr. Commodore said you are to enter when you returned. "Many thanks," I replied as I turned and went to Jr. Com. Lancton's office, removed my beret, activated the chime then entered as the entry-way-slid open then closed behind me.

Upon seeing the Jr. Commodore, I stood at attention and saluted. "Sir, I recorded the Antrerian transport craft as they transported personnel and supplies from their cloaked mother craft down to the abandoned Military Base. Nothing out of the ordinary seemed to be going on, besides they do have S. H. Z. C. A's permission to establish a settlement here in the North."

"They do, but the Humanarian members of ZarCedra's Administration should have inquired about the type of operations they would be involved in after they settled here on ZarCedra before secretly agreeing to let them reside here. "Relax Jr. Commodore, Sir; we don't know if they are here to cause any problems with the Protrerian High Command. Maybe it's the Humanarian Race's role to bring the two races together here on our planet and reintroduce peace into their lives."

"You're absolutely correct Major, for now we should keep the two races under surveillance and offer the Antrerian's any and all assistance they may require. In the morrow when you fly over there, inquire if they require any type of assistance and inquire of any materials that they may require at this time. "Affirmative sir!"

"Do you have everything to make your stay here more comfortable? "Affirmative sir, many thanks! "If there is anything else you require, don't hesitate to request it. "Affirmative sir, many thanks again, if there is anything else you will be the first to know. "One more thing Major be here in the morrow morn at 07 hundred 30 epocks for a briefing. "Affirmative sir. "You are dismissed Major," the Jr. Commodore said as we saluted each other. I turned and as I neared the entry-way, it slid open and I departed, as the entry-way silently closed behind me.

"Grand p.a.r ma'am," I said to Sgt. Sullivan as I returned her smile then made my way to my new quarters. When I got to chamber yellow twenty-three, I respectfully removed my beret then chimed the entry-way. The lovely Capt. L. Casper answered it wearing a plush robe.

"Greetings. "Greetings ma'am, I'm Maj. Jeroque Teldat and I'll be your quarter's mate for an octapar or so. "Captain Casper, Lorii," she added as she extended her hand to shake with mine. "My quarters are your quarters, you may enter," she added with a very cute smile. "Your slumbering quarters will be at the end of the corridor on the port side. "Many thanks, ma'am. "If you'll excuse me, I'll go put on proper attire. "Affirmative," I said as she left and I opened my duffel bag and removed the latrine supplies. I brought them to the latrine then brought my uniforms and duffel bag to my slumbering quarters.

When I was through putting my things away, I removed my jacket and beret then went back into the front chamber area to relax. Capt. Casper walked into the chamber dressed in a khaki shirt and pants; she went into the sustenance replenishing area and went to the personal sustenance and liquid replenisher. "A cup of Brigolia tea, 90° centigrade," she requested. A second later it appeared; she picked the cup up and blew as she took a sip.

"Would you care for anything to quench your thirst?" She asked as she retrieved the Intervision flat screen monitor's universal remote from the counter and tossed it to me. I caught the electronic device and turned the view screen on. "Negative but many thanks."

"Is there anything you would like to view? "Negative, I've got to record this p.a.r's report but many thanks," she said as she went to her computer console then took another sip of her tea. "Won't I bother you with the Intervision monitor activated? "Negative, as long as you keep the decibel level low," she said as she sat.

While getting started Capt. Casper heard a loud rumbling sound come from my stomach. "In need of sustenance are we?" She asked with a smile on her pretty lips. "In desperate need," I said as I rugged my gut. "Capt. Casper how is the consistency and flavor of the sustenance served here at this military facility? "They are both wonderful," she answered as she looked over at me. "We recently received new-updated versions of the sustenance replenishers in the mess hall so we can order anything that it has programmed into its memory bank. "Grand," I said as I lowered the decibel level even lower on the Intervision monitor.

"We could dispense with the usage of rank titles when we are alone," I said as I looked at Capt. Casper. "Grand, they were getting to be a bit of a nuisance anyway. "Call me Jeroque or Teldat and I'll address you as Lorii or Casper. "Affirmative," she responded. "Now I need silence from you," she said as she started working on her report.

Meanwhile I started flipping through the channels and stopped at a game show titled, 'For All the Marbles'. I viewed this program until 16 hundred 50 epochs. "I will finish my report after our twilight banquet, we should take our leave now," Lorii said as she saved her work on the comp-console.

When she was ready, we turned everything off and went towards the entry-way as I put on my beret. "Illumination off," Lorii said as the entry-way slid open and we both vacated the quarters. The entry-way quietly closed and locked behind us as we continued to the mess hall for our banquet.

When we arrived, we went to the sustenance replenishers and looked at the sustenance order board then ordered our banquets. After receiving our platters we put them on trays then we went to retrieve a swill and silverware. We went to a vacant table; sat, removed our berets and started talking as we both consumed our banquets.

"Why do you think the Antrerian's picked our Planet to occupy rather than any other M-class planet in this sector? "Our two planets are the closest M-class planets in proximity than any other and they did try to assist us during the Grand War. Besides their sun is about to go nova. How could the Humanarian race refuse?"

"I bet the Protrerian High Command will be up in arms when they discover they are here," she said, and then took a swill of her beverage. "Hopefully they will give peace a chance, our planet is a fair size and I believe our three races can try to work together to live in a peaceful manner. If not there is always a neighboring solar system with M-class planets. If any resistance occurs, we should know right after the Protrerian High Command discovers they are here on ZarCedra," I said as we continued to consume our banquets.

A little later we both finished our banquets and beverages, we put our trays away then walked from the mess hall. "Would you care to go to the aspergym for a game of raquerball?" Casper asked as we were on our way back to our barracks "That's a grand idea, it beats sitting in our barracks all twilight. "Grand, turn down this corridor and the aspergym is at the far end."

When we arrived, I went into the male locker chamber and went to the equipment resonator. "I require a towel, a large T-shirt, medium gym shorts, size 12 court shoes and a racket for raquerball," I requested. Secs later the supplies materialized, I retrieved them and went to change. A few mites later I picked up the racket, walked into the gym and waited for Casper.

She walked out with her hair tied back, wearing a tight black and white T-shirt and shorts ensemble that hugged every curve of her immaculate body; exquisiteness right down to her white court shoes. "Teldat are you ready?" Casper asked as she twirled her racket in her hand. "Ready, ready for what, to beat your gorgeous backside? Affirmative, I am," I said with a laugh as I walked over to where she was standing. "Never in your delightful twilight fantasizing, will you ever beat me," she said with a giggle as she programmed the computer console for games of raquerball.

We walked half way across the gym and waited a few secs for the far wall to reconfigure for our game, secs later a ball fired from a spigot on the wall that suddenly appeared in front of us. When it did, Casper hit the ball and after sinking it into one of the four target holes on the far wall, a buzzer sounded as lights illuminated around the hole as the scoreboard gave her a point next to her name. "Ha, match that smoogaroo," Casper said. "You are in doubt if you think I will not try" I said as the ball fired from the spigot towards me and I hit it, it missed the target I was aiming for and it bounced back towards Casper. Ah very unfortunate," Casper said as she hit the ball.

We played for the next two epocks as sweat poured from our bodies and we had managed to work off the calories of our twilight banquet. When we concluded, Casper won with the final score of eight to five. "Many thanks for the exercise Jeroque and being a grand challenger, it's now time for a hyper shower," she said with a smile. "I will see you shortly unless you want a shower companion," I said as I raised an eyebrow. "Too bad so sad but you have to be female if you want to follow me," Casper said with a smile. "Very unfortunate," I said as I entered the male change chamber.

About twenty mites later we both met in the hall and made small talk as we walked to our barracks. "I want to say many thanks as well for the exercise this twilight," I said as Casper stooped to get her retina scanned. "Capt. L. Casper," she stated then the entry-way slid open. "Anytime as long as you don't mind me being victorious," Casper said with a smirk as we entered our quarters. "Ha, you better enjoy this triumph this time because it will be your final victory! "Only in your fantasizing," Casper said as we entered.

"Illumination on," she said then went to the sustenance replenishing area for a mineralized water. "Teldat, would you like a container of mineralized water? Casper inquired. "Affirmative, that would be most refreshing. "Many thanks," I said; a few secs later she tossed it to me as she went to her computer console. I took a big swill then went to my slumbering chamber and to my duffel bag and retrieved my electronic think pad. I went back to the front chamber area where I entered in the happenings of this p.a.r and results of my initial flight of the Supersonic Dragon 228-D Spy Jet Stealth.

An epock went by and Casper e-mailed her report to Jr. Com. Lancton's office. She stretched then went over to the sustenance and liquid replenisher. "Two glasses of calcium supplements, 20° centigrade," after it materialized she handed me a glass and we drank. "Time to slumber, 05 hundred epocks comes a might quick," she said after she finished her swill.

"When you are ready to retire, just say illumination off. "I will, many thanks. "Pleasant twilight," we both said as Casper went to her quarters and got ready to retire. I finished entering my report into my think pad then I thought it was also time to retire as well. "Illumination off!" I said as I got up, put my glass away then took my electronic think pad to my slumbering chamber and got ready to retire.

Later that twilight after I retired, I found myself in the middle of another twilightmare. I dreamt that I was enjoying a peaceful flight flying over the serene landscape, my surroundings was quite a bit brighter and that is when I realized I was flying a prototype aircraft.

All of a sudden big dark clouds started billowing around my craft. Thunder crashing all around me as strikes of lightening flashed all over. I still heard a voice warning me of the closeness of each lightning strike as I carefully flew through the storm trying to dodge each bolt as I flew toward a tunnel of churning air; all of a sudden I seen a bolt of lightning strike my craft. That's when everything went dark and that's when I woke shouting "NO" and soaked in sweat.

I knew by the sight and feel of the craft also by the voice of the female citizen warning me of the lightning strikes that it was the prototype Supersonic Dragon 228-D Spy Jet Stealth I was flying and the voice I heard was in fact 'PAT', my cybernetic co-pilot. I tossed and turned for the next few mites trying to figure out any meanings to my twilightmare, at long last I couldn't think of any so I again closed my eyes and drifted off in slumber.

P.A.R 3

As I entered the sustenance replenishing area, Lorii brought me a hot caffinated brew. "Grand morn Lorii, many thanks. "Grand morn Teldat, enjoy. As we were talking I turned the Intervision flat screen monitor on. We sipped our morn brew, talked more and listened to the early morn news.

"Weather Warning: The Eastern part of the region was getting ready for a severe electrical storm," we heard the weather person say. "Oh my Gods," I said as my face turned white. "What's wrong?" Lorii asked with grand concern.

"My twilightmares, they are coming true," I said as I downed my hot caffinated brew. "What is your meaning? "In my twilight escapades, I am flying a prototype craft when all of a sudden big dark storm clouds billow around me with lightning striking all around. I try feverishly to fly through it but alas my new craft gets struck by lightning and that's when I wake up."

"Hmm, I heard around that the Secret Humanarian ZarCedra Alliance is testing shield technology, by chance is your prototype craft equipped with a shield? "Affirmative, it is. "If you think you are in any danger of the storm, use it," Lorii said as she drank what was left in her cup. "Agreed," I answered as we turned everything off then exited our quarters and went to the Officer's Mess for our morn banquet.

Capt. Casper and I were talking & consuming our banquet when Jr. Com. Lancton entered the mess hall and stopped at our table, we both halted and saluted.

After returning our salute the Jr. Commodore looked at me. "Major instead of meeting me later this morn, I will brief you now. Maj. Teldat, since we won't be sending you up until 11 hundred epocks for your next mission; you are to report to Flight Sergeant Melbourne's Flight Course and explain the grander aspects of Aero Dynamics to her recruits. She will be in her chamber at 08 hundred epocks, you are to report to chamber TFS 14 and tell her you are ordered to express your technical skills pertaining to Aero Dynamics! "Affirmative sir!"

Jr. Com. Lancton's demeanor softened as he smiled at me. "I was conversing with Sr. Com. Boone earlier this morn and he brought to my attention that this p.a.r is your Birthp.a.r. "Affirmative sir, it is! "Can I ask, what is your age? "I turned thirty-three trittons, sir. "I wish you a wonderful Birthp.a.r and I hope it's grand," he said as he patted my shoulder, turned then left.

"I also wish you a Happy Birthp.a.r and I hope all your desires come true," Capt. Casper seductively said as she looked over at me with a gleam in her eye, an immaculate smile then she squeezed my hand. "Why many thanks little lady; there is sufficient time before I am expected to be at Fl. Sgt. Melbourne's class to check on my 'SS Dragon'," I told Capt. Casper as I looked at my timepiece and flashed her a smile of my own. "Grand p.a.r Captain," I said still with a mischievous smile as I rose. "You as well," Capt. Casper said as I went to dispose of my tray then walked from the mess hall putting on my beret.

'I could always contact 'PAT' via com-link and ask her if she is operational but I want to see everything first hand,' I thought as I continued through the underground halls of the military facility to the hanger my spy jet was in. I felt the warmth of the huge underground hangar as I entered, and was glad I parked in here rather than out in the frigid cold.

I pressed the left wing of my com-link as I walked to my craft. "Grand morn 'PAT', lower the main hatch. "Grand morn Major; affirmative. Grand Birthp.a.r sir, how are you feeling this p.a.r? "Many thanks 'PAT', A little unnerved. "Whatever are you unnerved about, Major? 'PAT' asked as I waited patiently for the main hatch to open then lower to the floor. "I will tell you in a mite," I said as the main hatch lowered.

I stood on the lowered main hatch platform and went up to the cockpit where I inserted and activated the electronic keycard. "I am unnerved about something I heard this morn on the early morn news," I told 'PAT' as the instrument panels illuminated; I went and sat in the pilot's seat. "Hopefully it's nothing," I said as I put the 'HUD' helmet on.

"'PAT', how much Liquid Napricyte[2] SDC remains in the Star Drive Engine?" I asked as she sat next to me as I tried not to let the news of the storm bother me. "¾, of a vile," she said as it also flashed on the lower portion of the face shield. "With all the flying in Star Drive we've done I figured I would have used more," I said as I checked the level of fuel and oil in the two main engines and tanks, I seen I had sufficient amounts of each. "PAT, how much water remains in the Comodrone Electronics P-52 Hydrogenic Generator? "The level is at the $9/_{10}$ Marker. "Grand many thanks 'PAT'."

When I was through, I removed the 'HUD' helmet, got out of the pilots' seat then went to remove my electronic keycard. "'PAT', I am a guest speaker in a flight class in a few mites, I was ordered by Jr. Com. Lancton to express my knowledge of Aero Dynamics to a class of recruits," I said as I went and got on the main hatch platform. I lowered to the floor as I pressed the left wing of my com-link. "'PAT", you can now close the main hatch platform. "Affirmative Major."

After the main hatch sealed, I looked at my timepiece and seen it was 07 hundred 54 epocks as I walked out of the hangar.

'What would be the most interesting thing I could speak about to the class?' I thought as I walked back through the halls. I turned a corner and met up with few younger officers. "Where would I find chamber TFS 14? I asked. "Turn right at the next corner and walk to the end of the hall. "Many thanks," I said as I continued on my way.

I followed the directions and stopped in front of chamber TFS 14 then buzzed the entry-way chime. A sec later the entry-way slid open and standing in front of me was a grand looking redhead with the prettiest sparkling turquoise eyes I ever saw in my 33 trittons. "Affirmative sir, can I assist you?"

"Affirmative ma'am, I am Maj. Jeroque Teldat and I am an instructor in the field of Aero Dynamics, at the Grinshaw Military Facility in Cangla City, in the Honorary Regime of Placaden, Tanglar. Since I won't be needed until 11 hundred epocks, Jr.

Com. Lancton has ordered me to talk to your recruits of my extensive knowledge of Aero Dynamics."

"Welcome and enter, she said with a delightful smile as she turned to her recruits. "We have a visitor from the Grinshaw Military Facility in Cangla City, in the honorary regime of Placaden, Tanglar. The floor is yours Major," she said as she looked at me.

"Greetings ladies and gentle folk, I am Maj. Teldat and I am here to explain about the new prototype Supersonic Dragon 228-D Spy Jet Stealth Aircraft that had just been constructed and introduced by N.Z.C.M.Co/S.H.Z.C.A."

"The first thing I must inform you of is the wing span of my craft is quite large and last twilight I was told to park my craft in the underground hangar. I was able to because the wings on my craft splits and folds then contracts to the fuselage of the aircraft. In order for my main hatch to open when the wings are contracted; the wing on the port side slides back a metric or so out of the way of the hatch way. This craft is approximately five times larger in size than the Stealth aircraft of this p.a.r or in the times elapsed and to power it, it uses two huge F405-F1D3 afterburning engines."

"For defense, my craft is equipped with a Sareden Quantum Laser Cannons that fires from atop the cockpit. Also there is a sliding metal plate under the nose of the craft, which slides out of the way when I am about to fire the Protonic Electromagnetic Cluster Missals or the Neutronic Electromagnetic Cluster Torpedo's."

"In addition, my craft is equipped with two XTR-9000 Plasma Pulse Cannons, one in each wing. I have access to the Quantum Lasers and the Plasma Pulse Cannons at all times but I only have a total of fifteen EMC Missals and ten EMC torpedo's at one time. After I deplete that supply, I must recharge my weapon's array before I can expel more, which takes a total of 30 mites time."

"On my craft I have a Comodrone Electronics P-52 Hydrogenic Generator, which supplies the necessary energy to create the ammunition for my craft's entire arsenal of weapons;

therefore I never need to reload. But in order to give it that explosive punch the weapons need, I must keep my generator supplied with a special radioactive compound called Liquid Napricyte[2] at all times."

"On another note, one of the main reasons the craft I am testing is classified as a spy jet aircraft is this craft's invisibility factor. When I engage my craft's Stealth mode capabilities, the entire craft vanishes from sight as well as radar hence the name spy jet. Another reason is its ingenious type of propulsion engines, the recently invented Omagon 2115 Star Drive Engine which operates in conjunction with another smaller engine called the Electronic Flux Inducer."

"With the two main propulsion engines I can access speeds up to Mach ten, then when the Star Drive engine and EFI are engaged it will increase my craft's speed to Star Drive one then Star Drive two. I'll explain all about these engines in more detail in a moment."

"Let me first tell you about 'PAT'; 'PAT' plays a double role in the operation of my aircraft. First, she is my cybernetic consociate and co-pilot and sec, she is my craft's onboard talking super computer. The letters P. A. T. is an anagram for Prototype Advancements in Technology, so in short we call her PAT."

"Her main purpose is to keep the craft in control and in flight; she was also created to assist me with any question, problem or dilemma I may encounter; therefore, cutting the need for additional co-pilots for a craft of its size and dimension. I then explained all about the speeds my craft could attain with the engines and electronic Flux Inducer equipped to my aircraft...."

*****

A little later, I looked at the timepiece on the wall and seen it was nearing 11 hundred epochs so I started to wrap things up by stating. "If I give positive feedback of this craft's performance they will mass-produce the craft; this craft will undoubtedly revelutionalize military air travel as we know it and it will be one step closer to ridding our planet of alien dictatorship. Are there any questions?"

"Affirmative sir, will we get the opportunity to view this craft in operation? "At 11 hundred epocks I will be leaving to continue my mission, if you go to the front foyer area and peer out the narrow window you will be able to see me liftoff. "Grand," they all replied "Since it is almost 11 hundred epocks, you may all leave at this time," Fl. Sgt. Melbourne told her recruits.

"I have to leave to report to the CO before I depart, have a grand p.a.r and it was a pleasure meeting you," I said as I smiled at her and returned her salute. "It has been a real learning experience having you as a guest in my class, many thanks and have a grand p.a.r, adioso for now. "Grand-adioso," I answered as I turned then left the chamber.

On my way to Jr. Com. Lancton's office, I saw Capt. Casper walking towards me. "Greetings," we both said in passing. A few mites later, I stopped in front of Sgt. Sullivan desk.

"Greetings Sgt. Sullivan, I'm here to see Jr. Com. Lancton," I said with a smile. "Greetings Major, affirmative I will let him know you are here." The Sergeant said with a smile as she pressed the call button on her computer's cinematic cam and contacted the Junior Commodore. A sec later he was depicted on the monitor.

"Can I assist you Sergeant? "Affirmative sir, Maj. Teldat is here to see you. "Send him in Sergeant. "Affirmative sir. You may go right in Major," she told me. "Many thanks Sergeant," I replied then removed my beret and entered the office.

As I entered, I saluted my senior officer. "Welcome and a pleasant morn to you. "Grand morn again sir, are there any last mite orders before I lift off? "Negative, just go to the Antrerian Base and be in contact with Administer Ambassador Kruni and see if there is anything we in the Secret Humanarian ZarCedra Alliance can do for him and his citizens? "Affirmative sir, is that all? "Affirmative it is for the moment, dismissed," the Jr. Commodore said as he saluted.

"I will depart immediately," I said as I returned the salute. "Take care," the Commodore said as I turned to leave. "Many thanks sir," I replied as I went out the entry-way. I smiled at Sgt. Sullivan as I put my beret back on, winked at her then left the area.

I went straight to my quarters, put on a fresh flight suit then put my leather jacket on and went toward the underground hangar. I tapped the left wing of my com-link. "'PAT' I'm on my way, lower the main hatch platform," I said as I continued to the hangar.

When I arrived at my craft, I stepped on the platform and rose to the cockpit. "Grand p.a.r again," I said to 'PAT' in a chipper voice as I raised and secured the main hatch platform.

"A pleasant morn once more Major," 'PAT' answered as I inserted the electronic keycard then sat in the pilot's seat, strapped myself in and activated the ignition system. I put my 'HUD' helmet on as 'PAT' and I activated a few touch pads and the engines roared to life. I waited a few mites then I taxied the craft to the elevation pad and rose to the surface.

I pressed the finger touch pad that activated two-way communications as I extended the wings. "Tower, this is Maj. Teldat am I cleared for lift off? "Affirmative Major, you are blue to go. "Many thanks," I acknowledged as I pulled slightly on the flight stick. The wings tilted downwards and the craft started to rise as the landing gear rose.

I flew closer to the front foyer of main headquarters, and as I did I sounded the air hooter then I activated stealth mode and my craft vanished as I continued to hover skyward. As I reached 10,000 metrics I leveled the wings as I eased the flight stick forward and advanced speed to Mach eight.

"'PAT', do you have any suggestions as to what I should first discuss with the Administer Ambassador in charge of the Antrerian settlement? "That matter should be taken up with Sr. Commodore Boone. "Agreed, Many thanks 'PAT'," I said as I tapped the right wing of my com-link. "Sr. Com. Boone, come in."

Almost immediately my CO came over the speaker in my helmet and he was depicted on my communications monitor.

"Grand to hear from you Maj. Teldat," he thought as he returned my salute. "Grand to hear from you as well sir, how is everything in Cangla City?" I asked as I raised my face shield. "As grand or as unfortunate as when you departed depending on how you want to view at it, how are things going on the mission? "I am currently on my way to make contact with the Antrerian Administer Ambassador to see if they require any type of assistance?" I reported as I neared the Antrerian settlement. "Do that Major, and then relay the results to me."

"I was curious to know sir, is there anything else you can think of that you want discussed with the Administer Ambassador? "Negative Major, not at this time. "Affirmative sir," I said just as I entered the airspace over the alien base as I started to descend. "Got to go Sr. Commodore, Maj. Teldat out. "Sr. Com. Boone out," he thought as the communications monitor went black.

I touched the pad to exit stealth mode and the craft again became visible. I activated two-way communications once again and asked for permission to set down.

"This is Chanta Gabries, asking who you are and why you request to set down?"

"Chanta Gabries, I am Maj. Teldat representing a division of the North ZarCedra Military Coalition called the Secret Humanarian ZarCedra Alliance. I come to speak to Administer Ambassador Kruni, wanting to personally welcome your race to planet ZarCedra and to provide whatever assistance the Humanarian members of this planet could offer."

"Sact, er, many thanks for the hospitality, I give permission to set down next to and enter our golden temple," Chanta Gabries said.

"Many thanks," I answered as I lowered the landing gear and set my aircraft down where directed. As the engines wound down, the port wing contracted and it slid out of the way of the main hatch. I disconnected myself from the pilot's seat, removed my helmet as I got up then went over and removed the keycard. "'PAT' you are with me," I said as I opened the main hatch, lowering it until it formed the platform. We both stepped on and lowered to the snowy ground.

I looked over at 'PAT'. "'PAT', raise and close the main hatch platform. "Affirmative," she acknowledged then instantly did what I asked as we continued into the golden temple.

Once inside Chanta Gabries met us. **"Greetings, I am Chanta Gabries, wait in this area for Administer Ambassador Kruni's arrival."**

"Many thanks," I replied as 'PAT' and I looked around. "The skin of the Antrerian citizens also had bluish-green pigmentation but it's considerably lighter than the Protrerian's. They have lengthy dark hair and almost the same rigid forehead except the bones of their foreheads protruded in the opposite directions than the Protrerian's but they had almost the same strong odor. Also, Antrerian males were similar in height as Protrerian males," I quietly said to 'PAT' as he walked away.

A few mites later, Administer Ambassador Kruni entered the chamber. **"Welcome to the Antrerian Base Humanarian delegates,"** he said as he bowed. "Greetings from the Humanarian citizens of ZarCedra," I told him as we returned the bow.

"Let us walk as we talk," Administer Ambassador Kruni said. "As I relayed earlier to Chanta Gabries, the Secret Humanarian ZarCedra Alliance welcomes you and your citizens to this planet and if there is anything we can do to assist in making this planet your permanent abode, don't hesitate to ask. We know what is about to happen to your sun in the Currecuse Sector and we hope to remain with peaceful relations with your citizens. Especially after your citizens tried to assist us in the times elapsed against the Protrerian Invasion during the Grand War of 2015," I said as I walked beside the Ambassador.

"Our deepest thanks, and we would also like to say many thanks to the Humanarian residents of ZarCedra for extending their hospitality in our time of need. But at the present time we have no need for assistance; if we do we will be in contact. "Very well."

"Can I offer refreshments to seal peaceful relations between our two races? "Agreed," I said as we entered a gathering chamber and sat at a table. "What is your pleasure?" A female Antrerian asked as she came to us and bowed.

"The females of the species are not as attractive as the Protrerian females. They too had ridges on their foreheads but they didn't add color, the ridges were clean and plain.

Their voices were higher and much softer than the males of the species. They are similar in height as Protrerian females, they too have four succulent breasts but wore loose clothing unlike Protrerian females who wore tight clothing," I quietly told 'PAT".

"We will have three Krisa Ales. "Immediately," she muttered as she turned and walked away. I started talking to Administrator Ambassador Kruni about the customs relevant to the area.

As I was talking, the female attendant returned with the ales and set them down. **"Sactumi,"** Administer Ambassador Kruni said as he pulled a glass towards him. **"Sactumi is the Antrerian equivalent to the ZarCedra words, many thanks."** Administrator Ambassador Kruni explained.

When we were alone, we took our tall slender glasses and toasted to peace and to seal Vertgren Isle a sanctuary. After our toast, we set our glasses down.

"Wonderful tasting ale; what is it made from? **"From Krisa berries that once grew in abundance on our planet and filtered zima or water, the remaining ingredients are sacred. I hope this land is far enough out of the way and we can settle and expand in the northern region without upsetting the Protrerian High Command? We like a much warmer climate but under these circumstances I know that is out of the question."**

"My apologies but affirmative it is, for your other inquiry the Tanglarian Administration's Humanarian representatives will try to keep your presence here a secret for as long as we can. **"Sactumi,"** he replied as he bowed.

"We Humanarian's of ZarCedra have no objections to having you here but you probably already know the Protrerian High Command will for the assistance your citizens had given our citizens in the times elapsed. As for the Brilain's, the authorized proprietors of this Isle, they haven't objected as of yet to your arrival so I think it safe to say you and your citizens can stay," I said as I returned the bow.

"I would like to extend our gratefulness to the Humanarian leaders of ZarCedra for the chance they are giving us, in our time of need. "Affirmative," I said as we took another swill and finished our ales. "I have duties yet to complete, I will now walk you back to the entrance of our temple," Administrator Ambassador Kruni said as he started to rise.

"First can you give me a reason as to why your skin color is lighter than the Protrerian High Command citizens, if you don't mind me inquiring? "I don't mind; it is because our abode planet of Antreria is closer to our sun and it is much warmer than the planet Protreria, that is why we Antrerian prefer a much warmer climate," Administrator Ambassador Kruni said as we all rose then he walked 'PAT' and I back to the front entry-ways where we entered.

"It was very pleasant to meet with you, until next time my consociate, take care," I said as we once again bowed to one another. Then he turned and walked away as I turned towards 'PAT'. "'PAT', lower the main hatch platform," I said as I refastened my jacket and we walked out to the Supersonic Dragon.

We went up to the cockpit and entered, 'PAT' raised then sealed the main hatch as I inserted and activated the electronic keycard. I sat in the pilot's seat touching the touch pad that extended the port wing then fastened my safety belts, put the 'HUD' helmet on and activated the aircraft.

I pressed the right wing of my com-link and called Sr. Com. Boone. "Sr. Com. Boone, come in. "Just a moment," Sr. Commodore Boone thought.

"All right, go ahead Major," Sr. Com. Boone thought a few mites later. I raised the face shield as I activated the communications monitor and saluted as Sr. Com. Boone returned my salute.

"Sir, 'PAT' and I had met with the leader of the Antrerian's. I told him we knew of the devastation that was about to happen to their sun. Administer Ambassador Kruni said he hoped it was all right for his citizens to settle on this Isle here in the Northern region?"

"If it was up to me I'd allow them to stay as long as they wanted but it isn't and when the Protrerian High Command discovers their presence here on this planet we all will pay

Hellatiously, for that I'm sure. But tell me, what was your response?" He thought.

"I told the Administer Ambassador that the Secret Humanarian ZarCedra Alliance had no objections to their presence here on this planet. "Grand, we just received word from the Humanarian members of Brilain's Administration. They relayed a message and said that the Antrerian race will be allowed to settle on Vertgren Isle and area as long as they remain in the North," the Senior Commodore thought as he shifted his seating position. "Affirmative, I will relay that message to the Antrerian Ambassador the next time we converse. "Is that all to report Major?

"Negative one more thing, I was told to say many thanks to the Humanarian citizens of ZarCedra for their hospitality. But the Antrerian citizens do not require anything at this time; if they do they will be in contact. Now that's all to report at this time. "All right Major, many thanks, Sr. Com. Boone, out. "Maj. Teldat, out," then the communications monitor went black.

I lowered the face shield of my helmet as I hovered up to 10,000 metrics and slowly increased speed to Mach six. I pressed the finger touch pad that activated two-way communications. "Jr. Com. Lancton, come in?"

A moment later Jr. Com. Lancton was depicted on the communications monitor, as soon as we seen each other I saluted. I started to tell the Junior Commodore what had conspired at the Antrerian Base and everything pertaining to my assignment when all of a sudden big dark storm clouds started billowing in around my craft; I also heard the horrendous crash of lightning around me.

"Jr. Com. Lancton an abrupt storm suddenly appeared," I said as I suddenly remembered the twilightmares I had.

"Return to base A.S.A.P before the static electricity in the lightning reacts with the new form of technology of your aircraft!" Jr. Com. Lancton ordered. "Affirmative, you'll have my report soon," we signed off as I maneuvered cautiously through the storm. I loosened the neck of my jacket and flight suit as I advanced speed to Mach ten.

"Maybe if I use the Star Drive Engine, we will get to the secret military facility before the storm arrives," I said to 'PAT'. Just as I activated the Omagon 2115 Star Drive engine and after the golden modules and rod were visible, the ionic energy began encircling my craft. As my craft was just entering the electromagnetically swirling wormhole, and as I was about to engage the craft's shield but before I got the chance a giant bolt of lightning struck the craft and everything went black....

*****

What seemed like a few secs later I exited the swirling wormhole. I didn't know precisely how long I was unconscious but I figured it wasn't long considering my craft was still in the air and in one piece.

"'PAT' what is our current location? "We are way off course; we are currently nearing the Northern pole. "Say what," I said as I grabbed the flight stick, leveled the fighter, slowly stopped advancing forward, rotated my craft 180° and returned to Vertgren Isle.

"Why are we so far off course?" I asked 'PAT'. "Unknown Major." I repressed the finger touch pad that activated two-way communications. "Jr. Com. Lancton, come in?" I called his name a few times but received no reply. So I pressed the right wing of my com-link and called Sr. Com. Boone. "Sr. Com. Boone come in Sir!" But all I received was static. I activated two-way communications once again. "Calling anyone in the immediate vicinity?" I feverishly asked but was unable to reach anyone.

I lowered altitude to 1700 metrics then accelerated to Mach ten then engaged the Star Drive Engine, as soon as the swirling wormhole appeared I flew into it and went to Star Drive one.

After flying a few mites I exited the wormhole then decelerated to Mach five, and flew to the coordinates of the secret military facility as I decelerated to 50 kps I was bothered by this sudden turn of events; considering all the rain clouds, thunder and lightning had all but vanished. As I arrived, all I seen was snowdrifts as far as the eye could see, not a sign of life anywhere.

"'PAT', what in Hellatious is going on, where is the secret military facility? "Unknown, like yourself I too was off line when we were struck by lightning." I stopped and hovered over the coordinates where the military facility was supposed to be and wondered what happened to everything? "'PAT', what is the exact time?" I asked. "14 hundred 45 epocks," she said. I decided to fly down to the Grinshaw Military Facility in Cangla City.

"'PAT' if you are unable to tell me precisely what happened during the storm, can you give me a possible scenario?" I asked as I accelerated to Mach ten.

She went silent for a moment then beeped. "Unknown sir, my circuits are unable to account for the time interval I was off-line; if I had to venture an hypothesis I would have to say by the absence of alien COM chatter and the difference in planetary star charts we are not in the right time period. "Say what? I hope you are mistaken! "I am never mistaken Major, but in this instance I hope I am."

I increased speed and flew awhile at Mach ten then I activated the Omagon 2115 Star Drive Engine and flew within the swirling wormhole, Star Drive one then Star Drive two, and flew the windy roller coaster flight for a few secs.

After that time, I disengaged the Star Drive Engine and exited the wormhole and as the golden rod and modules disappeared into craft, I slowed to Mach five then activated stealth mode and the aircraft disappeared. "'PAT' what is my current position?" I asked looking around for some sort of milestone. "We are currently over the Honorary Regime of Placaden. "Understood," I said as I increased speed and flew at Mach seven until I was at the outskirts of Cangla City then decelerated to a halt.

"First I'll try the com-link one more time," I said as I tapped the right wing of my com-link. "Sr. Com. Boone, come in." Still no answer, so now all I could do was use two-way communications. I activated the touch pad on my 'HUD' helmet. "Calling the Grinshaw Military Facility, come in."

"Who is this and why are you using this frequency?" I was asked quite abruptly. "This is Maj. Jeroque Teldat of the

Grinshaw Military Facility, let me talk to Sr. Com. Boone! "My apologies Major but we have no Sr. Commodore by that name currently stationed at this military Facility. "What do you mean, I just finished talking to him a few mites ago? "Land and you'll be permitted to discuss your situation with Sr. Com. Bancais; you are cleared to land on runway three.

"Negative tower, I have no need for a runway. "What do you mean, what are you flying? "I am flying a prototype hover controlled Stealth craft. "My apologies Sir, I didn't hear of the Air Brigade inventing a newer version of the Stealth Aircraft besides the Nightingale 228-A Stealth but it's not hover inclined."

"I thought they discontinued manufacturing the Nightingale 228-A Stealth when they started manufacturing the Nighthawk 228-B Stealth? "What do you mean the Nighthawk 228-B Stealth, I've been stationed here since 2009 and I've only heard of the Nightingale 228-A Stealth.

"2009, what do you mean you have been stationed here since 2009? "Affirmative sir, I have been stationed here six and a half trittons. 'How many trittons?' I asked myself reeling from the realization that "PAT's" hypothesis was indeed correct and we in fact went back in time. "What tritton is it, wait don't tell me now I'll be down momentarily." I said as I pressed the touch pad that made my craft reappear.

As it did I raised the wings and lowered the landing gear then I hovered to the ground next to an H-14 aircraft. "You were correct 'PAT' when you told me we traveled through time. If that air transportation controller spoke the truth, it is in the locality of a centritton." I said as the engines wound down. "Affirmative Major, I told you I am never wrong!" 'PAT' stated. "I know you did 'PAT', don't get all full of yourself," I said as I contracted the port wing then removed my 'HUD' helmet. I unbelted myself and got up, withdrew the electronic keycard as I released the main hatch platform then stepped on.

"Remain on-board and I'll return shortly," I said as I started lowering. As I neared the tarmac below, I looked around and seen a circle of Military personnel gazing at me in disbelief.

They continued watching as I stepped off the main hatch platform and pressed the left wing of the eagle on my chest. A microsec later a voice emitted. "Affirmative Major, go ahead. "Raise and close the main hatch platform," I ordered as I glanced around me. "At once Major," the voice replied as I put my beret on.

Right away I noticed the difference in the look of the military facility. Main headquarters', it had a quarter as many levels and everywhere I looked, I couldn't see a Protrerian official anywhere. 'You know what this means Jeroque, don't you?' I thought.

I walked to the tower section of main headquarters and entered the structure. 'I should dismiss my curiosity and go directly to the CO but I just have to know,' I thought as I took the turbo-lift up to the 12th level to see the air transportation controller and find out just what's going on? A few mites later I entered the air transportation control chamber. "I'm Maj. Teldat," I said as I entered and the Sergeant jumped to his feet.

"To answer your question sir, this p.a.r's date is 06.28.2015," the Sergeant said as he sat back in his chair. 'Wow, what a Birthp.a.r I'm having,' I thought. "I have to talk your Commanding Officer immediately, it is of the up most urgency! "That would be Sr. Com. Bancais; you will find him in his office. Go back to the turbo-lift, go down to the main floor, turn right and his office is at the end of the hall. You will see an office area, ask his secretarial assistant to see Sr. Com. Bancais then go to the blue entry-way marked CO," he said with a puzzled expression on his face. "Many thanks," I said as I turned to leave.

"A sec sir?" I stopped then turned towards the puzzled Sergeant. "What is it Sergeant? "What is the reason you asked the tritton and what do the digits 2115 on your flight jacket mean? 'That's kind of obvious,' I thought but I also wanted to keep things quiet until I spoke with the Sr. Commodore. "You'll find out in time, now if that's all I'll take my leave," I said as I turned and walked out.

I followed the Sergeants direction and returned to the main floor and a few mites later I arrived in an office area, it was bustling with activity but there was no one at the reception desk so I went to the Senior Commodore's entry-way. I rung the entry-ways chime and waited a sec. "Enter," I was told. The entry-way didn't slide open as expected, so I turned the knob. After I entered, I saluted then closed the entry-way.

"Sir, my name is Maj. Jeroque Teldat, and what I have to report will be hard to believe but it's the absolute truth! "All right Major go ahead," the Sr. Commodore replied as he got comfortable as he chewed on the butt of an unlit cigar.

"Sir, like I said my name is Maj. Jeroque Teldat; I am a test pilot and an instructor specializing in the field of Aero Dynamics. Because I am a specialist in that field and a test pilot, the Military wanted me to test their advanced version of the Stealth Aircraft then use it on a secretive mission. I was ordered to test and use the prototype Supersonic Dragon 228-D Spy Jet Stealth."

"The Military hasn't constructed such an aircraft by that name." The Commodore said as he took the butt of the cigar out of his mouth. "Not yet but they will in the tritton 2115. "What do you mean they will? "Let me go on and I'll elaborate. "Then go on already!"

"Affirmative, I was on a top-secret mission up over Vertgren Isle and on my return to my military facility this p.a.r I flew through an electrical storm. Everything was going fine until my craft was struck by lightning. If I were flying a normal aircraft that would have badly damaged or even destroyed my craft but look I seem to be fine; a little shook up but fine nonetheless. But I have somehow gone back in time, by the looks of it a centritton."

"How is that possible airman? "My craft, the Supersonic Dragon 228-D Spy Jet Stealth, has Star Drive speed capability and uses a special radioactive chemical solution called Liquid Napricyte[2] Star Drive Compound. Which enables my craft the maximum air speed of Star Drive two, or Mach ten * twenty, which is equivalent to Mach 200."

"In order to attain Star Drive speed, I have a third engine called the Omagon 2115 Star Drive Engine and an Electronic

Flux Inducer. The combination of this engine and this device and the chemical solution of the Star Drive Engine creates an Ionic swirling Humanarian-made wormhole, as I fly into this wormhole I can travel Star Drive speed within ZarCedra's oxygenated resistant atmosphere and gravitational pull."

"What I believe happened, was that the electricity in the lightning reacted with this chemical solution, just as I was entering the wormhole creating a rip in the time gamut, thus, causing my craft and I to travel back in time. I know this sounds fantastic but it is the only reason I can surmise for being here at this time interval."

"Plus being here prior to 07.01.2015 there is something that is of up most urgency I must inform you of then you must inform the entire planet. "And what may that be?" Sr. Com.

Bancais asked as he sat forward in his chair. "First I want you to know I am for real and everything I am informing you of is the absolute truth."

Sr. Com. Bancais removed the cigar butt from his mouth again. "Let me get this straight, you're telling me you are from the tritton 2115 and you are in possession of an advanced military aircraft and there is something you must tell me?" "Affirmative sir, that is correct and I can prove I am from the time yet to come. "How, what?

"Well, the jacket I'm wearing and the difference in the uniform you and I have on and by this," I said as I rolled up my sleeve and produced my digital Timor 6500 visual and talking timepiece on my left arm. "On my right arm up by my shoulder is a tattoo of a patriotic eagle with the tritton 2109. That was the tritton I entered the Military." I also produced my military tags. "My military tags have my rank, name, serial digits and birthp.a.r; it also has the tritton of my admittance in the Military."

"When will I be able to see this mysterious aircraft and you tell me what is so imperative? "Soon sir, but first let me inform you that my craft is equipped with advanced weapons for defense. Also, its stealth capabilities are astounding; it has a cybernetic onboard talking super computer named 'PAT', which stands for Prototype Advancements in Technology. My craft is hover capable; therefore, I do not need the use of a runway of any type for liftoffs or landing."

"Hmm," Sr. Com. Bancais said and by the look on his face, not really believing a word I was saying. "If you expect me to fully believe your story airman, produce this technically advanced miracle aircraft. "Affirmative sir, let's go!" I said as Sr. Com. Bancais put his cigar butt back in the ashtray, stood and put on his beret. The two of us walked from the office, out a rear entry-way, down a hall then out of the structure.

While walking I saw Sr. Com. Bancais read my flight jacket as we continued to the aircraft. When we neared the huge craft we saw a circle of recruits around it. "Break and disperse," Sr. Com. Bancais said as I pressed the left wing of my com-link.

"'PAT', open and lower the main hatch platform." When the hatch opened it lowered to form the platform then it lowered to the tarmac. "Very impressive," Sr. Com. Bancais said as he looked at the massive, sleek craft. On the side of the aircraft, Sr. Com. Bancais saw the depiction of the ferocious dragon. "That dragon sure looks impressive, doesn't it?" I asked as I looked at him and seen his smile. "It sure does," the Sr. Commodore said.

"Look above the cockpit, you will see a turret with double barrels, that is where my aircraft's laser emits from. Down here is a sliding metal plate and from there I can launch either Electromagnetic Cluster Missals or Electromagnetic Cluster Torpedo's. The differences between the two armaments are, EMC-Missals are an explosive charge and explodes on contact. EMC-Torpedo's is a charge that when it strikes a target with a working operating system, it is automatically absorbed and cuts power leaving it vulnerable to attack. I have additional weapons but for now I will keep quiet about them."

"Right this way sir," I said as I ushered him towards the main hatch platform. "Now stand completely still," I told the Sr. Commodore and a few secs later the platform started to rise.

When the platform stopped its assent, we entered the cockpit as I fished the electronic keycard from my pocket then inserted it in the designated port. "Sr. Com. Bancais I would like to introduce you to 'PAT', my cybernetic onboard talking computer. "How do you do Commodore? "Pleasant to meet you, who are you?" The Commodore asked. "My name is 'PAT' which is an anagram for Prototype Advancements in Technology. My main function is to control this aircraft and offer Maj. Teldat any and all assistance I am able.

"That will be all for now 'PAT'. "Affirmative Major," she acknowledged then went silent as I directed Sr. Com. Bancais attention to the helm of the cockpit.

"This is a recently constructed prototype craft; I was testing it when I was transported through time. I am unsure how everything operates as of yet, but I will as soon as I locate the operations e-manual," I said then started explaining all the touch pads and mini-monitors on the instrument panels then I produced the 'HUD' or Heads up Display helmet. Sr. Com. Bancais put the helmet on as I activated it then the face shield lowered and he seen one by one everything it had to show.

I "explained everything" the Sr. Commodore saw when he activatedthemenu,fromfuellevelstoarmamentcomplementation and from shield strength to targeting scanners and everything in between. I raised the face shield of the helmet. "Let me raise the face shield then look around the instrument panels, you will not notice a two-way communication device anywhere. "You are correct Major. "I have two-way communications built into the 'HUD' helmet. Lower the face shield then activate this finger touch pad by the starboard ear position and contact the tower."

He did what I asked and secs later he contacted the tower. "Tower, this is Sr. Com. Bancais, what is the status of the radar? "Sr. Commodore, the radar is clear nothing to report. "Affirmative airman, many thanks, out. Very impressive Major," Sr. Com. Bancais said. Awhile later after he was thoroughly impressed with the headgear, I pressed the touch pad above the visor of the helmet, the face shield rose and he removed it.

"Very impressive indeed," the Commodore said again as he left the pilot's seat. "Does 'PAT' also have an impressive

HUD helmet? "Negative, as she has a direct link with the crafts computer, my inkling is the creators of this craft didn't inkle she required one."

"Back here," I said as I went to a back overhead compartment with Warning Radioactive and a depiction of the radioactive symbol on it. "In here is a metal radioactive safe case containing a supply of 200 milliliter vials containing my supply of Liquid Napricyte^2 Star Drive Compound. Which my Star Drive engine combines with electrical energy then sent to the Electric Flux Inducer where it is converted to ionic energy for my craft to travel its grand speeds."

"In the compartment above it there is a radioactive safe suit and breathing apparatus I must wear when handling the Liquid Napricyte^2 Star Drive Compound. Now if you have seen everything in the cockpit I'll show you the engines. "Carry on," he said with a smile.

The Sr. Commodore and I stepped on the main hatch platform and we lowered to the ground. "Sir, do you have something we can stand on that will bring us up to the tail section of the aircraft?" I asked as we stepped off the main hatch platform and I looked around. "Unfortunately, I neglected to put a hover-board on board my craft prior to being transported through time."

"A hover-board you say, that would be something to see! Affirmative I have something; airmen go get an Automatic Mechanized Lift," Sr. Com. Bancais told two airmen that stopped to look at the huge aircraft. "At once sir," the young airmen said as they jogged off.

I pressed the left wing of my com-link. "'PAT', open the tail portion of the craft." As she was doing that, the airmen returned in an armored utility vehicle towing the AML. After a few mites, it was locked in place. Sr. Com. Bancais dismissed the airmen then he and I stepped on and we rose up to the mighty engines.

We stepped onto the metal walkway surrounding the engine galley. We walked over to the metal ladder and climbed down into the engine galley. "Here we have the two huge F405-F1D3 after burning engines; I am using these engines most of the time. Until I engage the Star Drive engine, which is over here," I smiled and said as I moved over to it and patted it a couple times.

"This engine is called the Omagon 2115 Star Drive engine. 2115 is the tritton they invented this Star Drive engine that is why it is included in its designation. Right next to it is the Electronic Flux Inducer or EFI for short. I have a golden rod and modules attached to my craft, which protrudes from the craft when needed. It is impossible to travel star drive speed within ZarCedra's oxygenated resistant atmosphere and gravitational pull without them. You see this insulated wire that leads from the EFI to the back of the aircraft to the first two golden modules? "I do. "Those two modules are fixed, but there are other golden modules strategically positioned around my craft that only appear when I activate the Star Drive engine.

"My Comodrone Electronics P-52 Hydrogenic generator powers the Omagon 2115 Star Drive engine as well as the EFI. This Star Drive engine creates a powerful electric charge, which is combined with the Liquid Napricyte^2 SDC then it travels to the EFI. In turn, the EFI converts that special electrical charge to an Ionic charge. This Ionic charge encompasses my craft going from golden module to golden module electromagnetically, until it reaches the longer golden rod attached to the nose of my craft."

"From there, it expels the stream of Ions out in front of my craft creating a swirling Humanarian-made wormhole. Flying through this wormhole allows my craft to reach Star Drive speeds as I fly within ZarCedra's oxygenated resistant atmosphere and gravitational pull. Since within this wormhole there is no oxygen, I have tanks of compressed oxygen that is circulated throughout the cockpit allowing me to breathe normally while I fly within the wormhole."

"The Liquid Napricyte^2 Star Drive Compound enters at this point," I said as I pointed to a black radioactive safe metallic cover. "The vial of this pale blue gel chemical solution is attached to and enters the electronic injection unit on the side of the engine. There is a gauge and beeper inside the cockpit on the instrument panel and on the view screen inside my helmet's face shield; which shows me the levels of all fuels, I have remaining. "I see," the Commodore said in the same very impressed tone.

When I was through showing the engines, I started explaining the Comodrone Electronics P-52 Hydrogenic Generator in more detail. "This generator supplies the energy needed to activate everything pertaining to Stealth mode. Also, all my weapons ammunition are created using this generator, which is also combined with the Liquid Napricyte^2 compound so I don't ever have to worry about having to re-supply."

"In addition, this generator supplies the energy needed to allow my craft to operate its full-bodied shield and power everything else that requires energy to operate." When I was through explaining everything about the engines, we made our way back up the ladder and along the walkway then stepped back onto the AML and lowered to the tarmac.

I tapped the left wing of my com-link. "'PAT' you can now close the tail section of the aircraft. "Affirmative Major."

"Sir, excuse me for a mite," I said as I walked away. I went back to the main hatch platform then went up to the cockpit to retrieve my electronic keycard then left the cockpit. I stood on the main hatch platform and descended, I tapped my com-link a second time. "'PAT', raise and close the main hatch platform; I will return later adioso for now," I said as I stepped off. "Affirmative Major," 'PAT' acknowledged as the main hatch platform started to rise.

"Did you enjoy the sightsee?" I asked Sr. Com. Bancais as I turned towards him. "Very impressed, follow me back to my office." A couple mites later we arrived back inside the office.

"Have a seat Major. I am very interested in the Supersonic Dragon Stealth Aircraft you have in your possession and I know it belongs to the Military and only issued to you but I still want your permission for a closer evaluation? "You may as long as you don't have it disassembled in any way; like I mentioned earlier there is something of the up most urgency I must inform you of. Because I am from the times yet to come, I know of a few very important facts that will unfold in the next few p.a.r's. "By all means what is it that you must tell me."

"In the next few p.a.r's we will be engaged in an intergalactic war here on ZarCedra. "With whom?" Sr. Com. Bancais asked as he sat up in his chair. "With an alien race known as the Protrerian High Command. "Who are they?" The Commodore asked as he once again chewed on the butt of his unlit cigar.

"The Protrerian High Command is a race of alien beings, who reside on a planet in the Currecuse Sector of the Dalnary Galaxy called Protreria They are Humanarianoid with facial structure and skin color differences; males of the species grow to the height of three metrics. The female of the species differs as well although they are shorter, only growing to a maximum of two metrics tall; they have four breasts because instead of having one or two offspring, they have a litter of as many as four at a time."

"If what you say will happen, I won't let your aircraft be permanently disassembled, you have my word." The Commodore said as he removed his cigar, placed it in his ashtray, half stood, reached across his desk and shook my hand. "Then I see no reason not to let you take a close evaluation."

"All right, while we inspect your craft, you will be a guest at this Military facility. Do you have anything else to wear besides what you have on? "Negative sir, under this flight suit I have on a uniform but that is all I have with me. "Affirmative," the Commodore said as he pressed the intercom button on his desk. "Lance Corporal, your presence is requested," the Sr. Commodore ordered. "I didn't see a coreman at the front desk when I entered your office. "That was because he was on an errand when you entered and when we left then returned to my office we used the rear entrance. "Affirmative Sir," I said.

"Affirmative sir," the airman said as he entered the office. "Maj. Teldat this is LC Gervais. LC Gervais this is Maj. Teldat," the Sr. Commodore said as he stood and made introductions. "Maj. Teldat will be staying at this military facility for a while, so will you find an empty officer's quarters for him and issue him a few uniforms?

But first, direct Maj. Teldat as he taxies his craft into hangar three. "Affirmative sir. "Pleasant to make your acquaintance," the Lance Corporal said as he turned towards me.

"Twilight banquet will be available at 17 hundred epocks and it will be available in the mess hall," Sr. Com. Boone said as he sat back in his chair. "Many thanks sir," I replied as I saluted then LC Gervais and I turned and was about to vacate the Senior Commodore's office. "Major, I want to see you in the morrow morn at 08 hundred 30 epocks. "Affirmative sir," I said then LC Gervais closed the entry-way. We stopped at his desk where he checked the availability of quarters. After, we both proceeded down the hall then out the main exit.

"Wow, is that your craft? "Affirmative, it is. "It looks mighty impressive," LC Gervais said wide-eyed. "Before I show you to your quarters will you first taxi your craft into hangar three, right over there in the largest of our hangars," LC Gervais said as he pointed to the hangar. "By all means," I said as I turned and immediately walked away as I pressed the left wing of my com-link.

"'PAT', lower the main hatch platform," I ordered as I continued to my craft. A few mites later I had both wing contracted then I taxied my huge craft into the hangar. "'PAT' remain onboard and I'll talk to you later. "Affirmative sir, 'PAT' said as I withdrew the electronic keycard then left the craft. After I had the craft secure I went and rejoined the Lance Corporal. "Right this way Major," LC Gervais said as we walked from the hangar to his armored utility vehicle.

LC Gervais unlocked the entry-ways with a remote handheld device and when we arrived we got in. We went down a couple blocks and stopped in front of a bluish-gray structure. We exited the vehicle and went towards the structure.

"Where are you stationed sir? "Not far from here Lance Corporal," I said not really wanting to tell him that it wasn't where I was from but when. "Right through here," LC Gervais said as we climbed a step. "Your chamber will be in OQ-1; right next to the entry-way we have the newly installed retina scanner. If you'll rest your chin on the padded chin rest and..."

"I know how to operate it airman! "How, it has just recently been invented? The Grinshaw Military Facility is the first military facility to have them installed. "Perhaps I will tell you later," I told him. After my retina was scanned and voice recorded, the entry-way slid open and we entered.

"Illumination on," I said as I looked around the front chamber of the Officer Quarters. "How on the Planet did you know the lights were voice activated? "I have my ways of knowing Lance Corporal. "Affirmative Major, but you're starting to freak me out!"

"Major will you follow me into the slumbering quarters? "Pleasant chamber," I said as we entered. "Illumination on; I'm glad you like it. Come over to the footlocker and place your thumb on..."

"I also know how to unlock the footlocker," I said as I placed my thumb on the scanner pad as it scanned it. "Maj. Jeroque Teldat," I said and the clasp beeped then unhooked and the lid slid open and I looked through it. "Close," I said as we turned and walked back into the living chamber.

"These quarters are empty because it is reserved for visiting officers; since you are the only visiting officer currently at our military facility you are free to use it alone. "Many thanks airman," I said as I continued to look around. The Lance Corporal started to tell me where the mess hall was located.

"I also know where it is, many thanks," I said stopping him in mid-sentence. "Affirmative," he said, as he looked at me a bit confused. "I will now go get some extra uniforms and would return shortly; may I ask what size you wear? "I take a grand shirt and pants with a 91.4 centric waist. "Affirmative, in the meantime look around and get comfortable with your surrounding; I will return shortly."

As I was left alone to look throughout the quarters, I checked out the quaint little Intervision flat screen monitor; I was going through its thirty-six channels when LC Gervais returned with the uniforms. "I didn't know the length of your stay so I only grabbed a few uniforms," he told me as he handed them to me.

"I am unsure as well, hopefully this will be enough, if not I will request more. "All right, if you need to use a public conversing device for any reason there is a gribbit PCD at the far end of the hall and remember that chow is at 17 hundred epocks," he said as he left my quarters. A sec later I went out into the hall. "LC Gervais, hold up a mite. "Affirmative sir what would you like?" He asked as he turned around just as he was about to go out the entry-way.

"Would you know a location where I could acquire shaving and other latrine supplies? "Sure, there is Mac Guire's Handiness Supplies down the boulevard; there you can acquire all the necessities you require. "That is grand but I have no form of currency," I told the young Lance Corporal. "Remain here and I'll see if I can get Sr. Com. Bancais's signature on an emergency monetary unit voucher for you. "Many thanks," I answered as I turned then went back into my new quarters.

'Monetary unit voucher? Oh of coarse credits were introduced after the Protrerian High Command took over ZarCedra,' I thought as I put the uniforms away then removed my flight suit. A few mites later I went into the front chamber and got comfortable as I anticipated the return of the Lance Corporal.

A while later, I finally heard the entry-way chime. "Enter," I said and the entry-way slid open to let LC Gervais in. "Here you go," he said as he handed me a signed voucher. "The reason it took longer than expected was because Sr. Com. Bancais was away from his office and I had to wait until he returned. "That's understandable airman," I said as I looked at the signed voucher.

"What is the significance of the digits on your flight jacket and can you tell me how you knew how to operate the retina scanner for the entry-way, operate illumination, unlock the footlocker and how you knew the location of our mess hall?" I sighed as I removed my flight jacket. "Affirmative, I'll tell you a few things; promise me that you will keep what you hear confidential? That is a direct order! "Affirmative, I promise!"

"First of all, the 2115 is the tritton I am from. In that time we have the same entry-ways, footlockers and illumination that operate in the same way, and the main mess hall is still at the same location, except in the tritton 2115, officers have our own mess lounge located in the main headquarters structure."

"Here on the front of my jacket it says N.Z.C.M.Co/S.H.Z C.A., I'm guessing you know what N.Z.C.M.Co is but since in my time we lost the war we will have in a few p.a.r's to an alien race. Almost a centritton later a secret division of N.Z.C.M.Co is created called the Secret Humanarian ZarCedra Alliance, which I am secretly a member of."

"Second, you have seen I have in my possession a prototype Spy Jet Stealth, which is stated on the back of my jacket, Supersonic Dragon 228-D SJ Stealth. I say prototype because my spy jet craft is one of a kind, in my original time I was supposed to test and use this craft on a secret mission. If I gave the craft a grand assessment, it was then going to be massed produced and used to lead Humanarian kinds fight against alien oppression. The Supersonic Dragon 228-D Spy Jet Stealth has a Sareden Quantum Laser Cannon and other futuristic weaponry, and as you saw, it is approximately five times the size of this p.a.r's Stealth aircraft."

"Third, is the special prototype Omagon 2115 Star Drive Engine. It was just invented and introduced by Humanarian scientists in the tritton 2115. My craft's Comodrone Electronics P-52 Hydrogenic Generator supplies the electricity to power my craft's Star Drive engine. Unfortunately I was hit by lightning as I flew through an electrical storm; theoretically the only reason for my craft and I to be in this time period I can surmise is that, the lightening had a remarkable effect on my Star Drive engine's chemical accelerant and the spiral wormhole I was entering, causing a tear in the time gamut transporting my craft and I back in time one hundred trittons."

"Wow, so you are from the times yet to come! "Affirmative but, remember keep what you have heard classified, remember that is a direct order" I said as I looked him straight in the eyes. "Affirmative sir, I will!" After everything was said, LC Gervais and I left my new quarters. The entry-way closed behind us and we continued out of the barracks. "Adioso," LC Gervais said as he went towards his armored utility vehicle.

"I have to return to main headquarters, would you like a ride to the gateabode? "Many thanks but I think I'll walk. "Affirmative," he said as he drove away and I headed for the gateabode.

I looked up and noticed the sun was still high in the sky as the heat beat down upon me. When I arrived at the gateabode I interrupted the MP thumbing through a periodical. "Uh hmm," I said clearing my throat! The MP set the publication aside and came to me. "What can I do for you sir? "I need directions to Mac Guire's Handiness Supplies."

"Affirmative, will you first sign out?" He said as he handed me a ballpoint and clipboard. "You mean manually? "Affirmative, what other way is there to sign out? "Unknown," I said as I took the primitive ballpoint and clipboard, looked at them a few secs then signed it. "Mac Guire's Handiness Supplies is about 150 metrics to your right," the MP told me as he pointed. "Many thanks," I said as I handed back the primitive clipboard and ballpoint, and walked away going in the direction I was directed.

While walking my mind started wandering and I was inkling of my bride to be and wondered, 'would I ever get the chance to be in her arms again?' Then I remembered the wish I made and what I promised if I could change the times elapsed.

Just then I came to Mac Guire's Handiness Supplies and entered. I looked around the fairly busy store and slowly found everything I needed, as a female citizen came up to me with a basket. "Can I assist you with anything sir? "Negative, many thanks ma'am," I said as I accepted the basket and deposited my supplies into it then went to get myself a frosty swill.

After I was through gathering the supplies I needed I went to the exquisite cashier and smiled. "Greetings grand looking. "Greetings," the cashier said with an exquisite smile in broken English. I smiled as I took the supplies out of the basket and set the articles down on the counter and thought she had a cute accent. The cashier started totaling everything I had gotten on the cash register.

"You sure live in a grand city," I said trying to start a conversation, as I reached for the voucher then handed it to the young citizen. "Oh, a voucher from the Military? "Affirmative ma'am, I just got in the city and the military gave me an advance until I receive my first pay," I said as I took her ballpoint and signed it then handed her the voucher. "Can I ask your name?"

"Topanga," she said as she flashed me another exquisite smile. "Greetings Topanga, my name is Maj. Jeroque Teldat, glad to make your acquaintance," I said as I kissed her hand. "Hee hee," she giggled and gave me the change remaining from the voucher. I looked at the parchment monetary units and metallic gribbits. 'This looks pretty strange,' I thought then put it into my pocket as I collected my bag of necessities.

I winked at Topanga as I grabbed my frosty swill and was about to leave. "Wait just a mite," she said as she reached for a piece of parchment and ballpoint then jotted her full name and abode personal conversing device digits. "I don't do this very often, in fact this is the first time but you look like you need to talk," Topanga said as she handed me the slip of parchment. "Give me a call sometime and we could converse? "Affirmative," I said as I read the piece of parchment.

"Topanga Shrenka," I said as I deposited the piece of parchment into my pocket. "Call me anytime I get off at five but don't get to my abode until about six," she said with a twinkle in her eye. "I most definitely will," I said as I picked up my soft swill and bag. "Have a grand p.a.r, adioso," Topanga said still smiling. "Grand-adioso and have a pleasant p.a.r as well," I said as I exited the shop.

I walked back to the military facility still mesmerized by Topanga's striking exquisiteness. When I arrived at the gateabode, I signed back in then went to my barracks. I set my bag and frosty swill down as I placed my chin on the chin rest as my retina was scanned. "Major Jeroque Teldat," I said then after it confirmed my identity and voice pattern the entry-way-slid open, I retrieved my bag and swill then entered.

"Illumination on," I said as I set my beverage aside then took everything from the bag and brought it to my personal latrine. At that time I checked the time on my timepiece and read 16:05 epocks. 'I have a while to wait before chow,' I thought as I finished my frosty swill. I went into the front chamber and turned on the Intervision monitor. I watched military programs until it was 17 hundred epocks, at that time I switched the Intervision monitor off then went to the mess hall for my twilight banquet.

In the mess hall, I received my tray of sustenance; grabbed eating utensils and a swill then went to sit by myself at a corner table. 'Wow, real homemade sustenance, all I ever seen was replicated banquets. This Military Facility sure looks grand without Protrerian High Command military personnel around,' I thought as I glanced around then removed my beret.

While I ate, a few military personnel came over and sat at my table. I introduced myself then they all did.

"That huge military aircraft we saw you in earlier, is it issued to you? "Affirmative it is, after it was constructed I was the only pilot trained to operate and fly that prototype Stealth Aircraft. "We saw as you all of a sudden appeared how'd you manage that? "My craft is top secret; my apology but there is nothing I can elaborate further."

"Would we be able to see your aircraft in mock action sometime soon? "Count on it," I said then took a swill of my beverage then finished my banquet. "What is your meaning?" I was asked. "I am not at liberty to leak that information at this time, you'll all find out soon enough. Now if that is all, I have to take my leave, it's been grand to meet you all and I hope we can have our banquets together again," I said as I put my beret back on, picked up my tray, placed it on a dirty tray cart then walked out.

As I walked down the boulevard I met up with LC Gervais. "Did you get all you needed from Mac Guire's? "Affirmative, many thanks Lance Corporal," I answered then informed him,

"I must be going. "Grand p.a.r," we both said then departed company. I looked at my timepiece and seen it was 17:55 epochs. "Alarm time 05 hundred 30 epochs. "Complete," it replied as my timepiece sounded two high-pitched beeps!

I was on my way to my barracks when I decided to go talk to 'PAT'. So I changed directions and went towards my craft. I tapped my com-link, "'PAT', I'm on my way to the craft, lower the main hatch platform." A few mites later I arrived and went up to the cockpit. I sat in the pilot's seat and turned to face 'PAT'.

"'PAT', you realize we have a chance to rewrite our times yet to come if we participate in the upcoming war? "Affirmative Major. "If we do assist in this time period will it in turn change the life I had in my own time for the better? "You know Major, changing the events of the times gone by can cause major problems to our time line. "I realize that 'PAT' but imagine if we can erase the Protrerian's from ever taking over ZarCedra, I think it would be worth taking that risk."

"Affirmative Major, it would make Humanarian life more bearable; if you have that much faith, I will assist you with everything I have," 'PAT' said. "I appreciate that 'PAT', many thanks," I said as I stood and patted her shoulder.

I went over to and inserted my electronic keycard and activated the ignition system then I returned to the pilot's seat and sat. I put on the HUD helmet and checked the levels of all fluids. "All Fluids are still at maximum capacity,' I told 'PAT' as I took off the HUD helmet.

"That is something I would have known, all you had to do was ask!" 'PAT' exclaimed as I went to remove the keycard. "I know 'PAT', many thanks but I like to do things myself when at all possible. I am off to my quarters, keep radar on and contact me if you detect anything out of the ordinary around the planet. "Affirmative Major, enjoy your twilight. "You as well, raise and seal the main hatch after I step off. "Affirmative Major," 'PAT' said as I got on the main hatch platform and lowered to the tarmac below and went to my barracks.

As I continued on my way I reached into my pocket and retrieved the parchment Topanga Shrenka gave me. 'I really do need a consociate to talk to, I wonder if she would like to have refreshments and talk awhile? There is an antique gribbit PCD at the end of the hall in my barracks I was told, I think I'll ring her,' I thought to myself.

When I entered the structure I went straight to the public conversing device. "I hope she got to her abode already," I whispered. I picked up the receiver and deposited a quint gribbit into the designated slot. I heard the "ding ding" as the hexigonical coin entered then I punched in her digits and waited as it chirped. A few chirps later I heard an unfamiliar ladies voice say, "Greetings".

"Greetings, would Topanga be at her abode yet? "Sure she just entered; may I inquire who's calling? "Affirmative, this is Maj. Jeroque Teldat. "Ok hold a sec? "Affirmative ma'am," I said and a few secs later I heard Topanga's angelic voice.

"Greetings Jeroque," she said with a sigh.

"Greetings Topanga, how are you?"

"Grand."

"I was wondering if you would like to go for refreshments or something because I really do need a consociate to talk to?"

"Sure, when?" she inquired with a squeal of delight.

"How about now, if at all possible?"

"Sure, I will meet you at the front gate of the military facility in about an epock. A moment of silence went by. "I was curious to find out how long it would take before you called me and I was hoping it wouldn't take you too long."

"Did I keep you waiting too long Topanga?"

"No you didn't and I am surprised it was this quick!"

"Affirmative my dear, I will be awaiting your arrival," I answered with a smile.

"All right, see you soon, adioso for now," she said then we both hung up.

*****

'Is it a grand idea to discuss the situation I have found myself in with someone who wasn't military personnel? I need to talk to someone and it might as well be a consociate. I know I don't know her very well but she is someone Humanarian I feel I could comfortably talk to,' I thought as I hung up the gribbit PCD and went to the retina scanner by my quarter's entrance.

My retina was scanned as I stated, "Maj. Jeroque Teldat." Only after it confirmed my identity and voice pattern did the entry-way slide open. I entered my barracks, removed my beret then went to the latrine to shave to look presentable for my consociate. I smeared shaving gel on my face and tried to shave the best I could, not being used to a razor that can actually cut me. 'Considering all I've used all my life was an electronic laser blade. Which wasn't an actual blade and I had the comfort of the lasers under a triple foil to rid my face of stubble,' I thought as I continued.

After I finished and a few nicks later, I splashed on a bit of after-shave lotion and winced in pain as it stung my cuts. "A bit of time to wait until Topanga's arrival." So I grabbed some latrine butt wipe to dab the blood on my face. "Illumination off," I said as I went into the front chamber, turned on the Intervision monitor and watched the news broadcast.

After the news program ended I thought it was time to get going so I switched the Intervision monitor off. "Illumination off," I said as I put on my beret then went out the entry-way as it slid closed and locked behind me.

I walked to the gateabode to sign out and while I patiently waited for exquisite Topanga's arrival; I talked to the MP. A few mites later we heard the sound of a hooter as I turned I saw the most awesome auto pull up to the front gate. "That is my ride, talk to you later. "Adioso Major and have a pleasant twilight," the MP said.

"Greetings Topanga, how are you?" I asked as I opened the gull wing entry-flap and got into her auto. "Pretty grand," she said with a lovely smile as my entry-flap automatically closed when I secured my safety belt. Topanga put her auto in reverse and backed onto the boulevard then drove off. "Where would like to go Jeroque?" Topanga asked with an incredible smile.

"I'm unsure, you decide. "All right," she said as she turned a corner then looked over at me and seen that I had a faraway look in my eyes. "A koob gribbit for your inklings," Topanga said as she smiled then squeezed my hand. "I have a lot on my mind but I was wondering if I should trouble you with my problems or not?" I asked as I smiled at her. "Go ahead; everyone else does besides you thought it important enough to chime me."

Just then Topanga pulled into the parking lot of a Mac Doan's Bistro. She drove around to the drive-thru order board; "I haven't had my twilight banquet yet so I shall order myself a burger and a box of sweet cakes. Would you like anything?" Topanga asked as she looked over at me. "Just an unsweetened iced caffinated brew. "Is that all? "Affirmative, I already had my twilight banquet but many thanks." Topanga turned and activated the talk button and "placed her order."

"All right ma'am pull around to the window." Topanga pulled around to the window and a few secs later she received her order. I was in the process of handing her some monetary units to pay. "Put your monetary units away, I'll treat, besides you only ordered an iced caffinated brew the rest of the order is mine."

She paid and after receiving her order and monetary units and metallic gribbits change, Topanga drove to a secluded parking stall and parked her 2010 Cavintro Toranado Fastback. "Ok tell me what you have on your mind," she said as she powered off her vehicle. "Affirmative," I said then slowly started to relay my story as Topanga started to consume her burger.

"First of all, this p.a.r 0628 is my Birthp.a.r. "Happy Birth p.a.r, how many trittons are you?" Topanga excitedly asked. "Thirty-three," I told her as I fidgeted with my brew cup then took a sip of my iced caffinated brew.

"What I have to say may sound unbelievable but everything I am about to confess to you is absolutely true. "Ok, go ahead. "I...am here from another time, the tritton I am from is 2115, and I was in the midst of testing a prototype aircraft. The Supersonic Dragon 228-D Spy Jet Stealth, I was flying through a thunder and lightning storm over Vertgren Isle when I was struck by lightning as I was flying into a wormhole. "Wait a mite, what's a wormhole?"

"Let me go on and I'll explain. If I were flying a normal craft, that in itself wouldn't have done more than destroy my craft or cause me to crash but as I said, I was flying a new prototype aircraft, which has Star Drive speed capability. What I suspect happened was the electricity in the lightning reacted with the special equipment and chemical solution it uses."

"The powerful radioactive chemical solution of that engine combined with the high voltage lightning and flying into the wormhole caused a remarkable effect, as though it caused a rip in the time gamut. It caused my craft and I to travel precisely one centritton in the times elapsed.

"Ok what's a wormhole; in order for my craft to fly at Star Drive speed within our planet's oxygenated resistant atmosphere and gravitational pull, I need to create a tunnel within ZarCedra's atmosphere to fly through. This tunnel has no resistant weighted oxygen and void of the pull of gravity that surrounds this planet. A wormhole is that tunnel. As there is no oxygen, I have tanks of oxygen equipped in my craft that fills my cockpit as I fly into it."

Topanga listened in amazement as she opened her box of sweet cakes and dunked them in her caffinated brew. "You are telling the whole truth, are you not"? "Affirmative, I am," I said as I grabbed hold of her hand and squeezed firmly. "Well," I said as I let go of her hand and let out a deep sigh. "I am stuck in this time with nothing but my co-pilot and craft." I looked over at Topanga and she had an unbelieving look on her exquisite face.

"There that is my story; I wouldn't blame you if you don't really take me serious. I'm not really sure I would if this happened to someone else but it happened to me and I know it's all-true! I can even provide physical evidence to back up my claim."

"Like what? "Like this," I said as I rolled up my sleeve and produced my Timor digital visual and talking timepiece on my left arm, on my right arm up by my shoulder I showed her part of my tattoo of a patriotic eagle with the tritton 2109. "That was the tritton I first enlisted in the Military." Topanga sat there with a surprised look on her face. I also produced my military tags that had my rank, name, birth tritton, and serial digits; it also had the tritton of my admittance in the Military.

"You are telling me the truth," she said with an astonished look on her pretty face. "Of coarse I am," I replied as I took another sip of my iced caffinated brew. "Your co-pilot, did you confer with him? "With her, I did a little but I have an inkling we should talk again. I do hope we can become grand consociates considering I did take a big chance in telling you my entire story," I said as I squeezed Topanga's hand again.

"Of coarse we can, and I will keep everything I have heard confidential," Topanga said then took a sip her caffinated brew and squeezed my hand in return. "Many thanks," I said as I kissed her knuckles. "Would I be able to view your aircraft sometime? "Affirmative of coarse, it is a lot larger than the conventional Stealth craft they have in this time period. So if I am allowed we could take a journey sometime then you can tell me what your true inklings are, agreed? "Agreed," she said as she leaned over to give me a peck on the cheek. "What was that for?" I asked with a smile.

"You must really feel lost, alone and out of place. "More than you could ever imagine. Topanga, tell me a little about your life?" I asked as we both finished our swills.

"Well my name is Topanga Shrenka, and I am 28 trittons old, I have never been joined in matrimony and I am currently unattached. I was born 02.10.1987 at the only Infirmary in Oskesar, Mankuer and that was my abode mate you immediately talked to on the PCD when you called my abode. Her name is Cheryl Kane and she is waitress/manager at the Grubby Gus Bistro and we became grand consociates in academe seminary as we took a business management course; we became instant consociates then abode mates a few trints ago and she is also 28 trittons old. Jeroque, I am more interested in your circumstance, tell me, what is it like when you come from?" Topanga asked as she sat on her leg to face me. "Affirmative," I said then winked as I met her gaze.

"They still play ice sports and stickball in my time but in the tritton 2029 a new game was invented. A game almost like the game of rugbitie but with major differences you have to see to believe. This new game is called 'Astroball'. It's more interesting and dangerous than rugbitie in this time period. "Well, that would be definitely something to view," Topanga said with a smile.

"But it is kind of eerie, you talking of things in the times elapsed that in this time period hasn't happened yet," Topanga said. "Hopefully with me being here some of the things I know of the times yet to come will turn out differently. "Like what? "Something you and everyone else on the planet will find out in a few p.a.r's."

"It is still fairly early would you care to do anything?" I asked changing the subject as I looked at my timepiece and seen the time. "What would you say to viewing one of this p.a.r's top flicks? "That sounds like a grand diversion," I replied as I kissed her hand again.

Topanga turned as she put her leg down in front of her and attempted to start her auto. At that instance I stopped her. "Before you start; could I look the auto over?" I asked a bit overjoyed. "Agreed," she replied as she stopped what she was doing and sat back. "I have never received the opportunity to observe a vehicle as antique as yours in perfect condition, no offence? "No offence taken," Topanga said as she smiled.

I excitedly exited the vehicle as Topanga followed, I slowly started walking around the auto, and I checked under the wheel wells then stood as I kicked the tires. "Driver's used to do this, I read in the times elapsed archive when I was in Scheduled Seminary. They did this to check to view if they had sufficient air in the tires."

I looked the vehicle over from front to rear; I especially liked the purple and black paint job also the gull wing entry-flaps gave it an exquisite look. Topanga smiled and as she did I could see much of the same qualities I seen in Tsarina. I started to feel a bond that was drawing us closer together.

"Topanga could you raise the hood so I can take a look at the engine?" I asked as I rubbed my hands together. "Agreed," she said as she reached into the opened drivers' entry-flap, pressed a button on the dash and the hood unlatched then automatically opened. As I peered under the hood, Topanga came up behind me and put her arms around my midsection and squeezed.

"As long as I am around you'll never be totally alone. Time to get going or we'll miss the start of the flick," Topanga said as she kissed my shoulder as I peered under the hood. A few secs later we got back in the auto and Topanga pressed the button that closed the hood. I sat in the passenger seat and fastened my safety belt as the entry-flaps closed.

"Can I inquire, what type of fuel your auto's engine operates on? "My auto is a tribrid, it operates using solar energy or original trigolfueline or water," she said with a smile.

Topanga started the engine and pulled from the parking lot and drove south along Coravel Boulevard. "You look quite dashing and debonair in your uniform," Topanga said as she looked over at me. "What would you like to view oh you probably don't know anything that is playing. "Not really," I replied with a partial smile.

"I'll agree to anything you would like to view. "All right, then we'll go to the flick abode down this boulevard," Topanga said as she turned a corner. After traveling a few blocks Topanga pulled off the boulevard and parked her auto then powered off the engine.

Topanga and I exited the auto as she pressed a button on a hand held device and locked the entry-flaps as well as armed the alarm then we walked up the walkway. Topanga smiled at me and noticed I still had a troubled look on my face.

"What is troubling you now, grand looking? "Nothing really, I was just wondering how, if ever, I was going to get back to my time where I belong. "Don't worry you and your co-pilot or the military will hopefully come to some conclusion," Topanga said as she rubbed my arm. "You are correct, I'll worry about that when the time comes in the interim we'll have a grand time," I said as I took her hand then kissed it as we neared the flick abode.

"Two for Splendor 3," Topanga said when we arrived at the ticket wicket. Topanga paid and received the tickets then we both walked into the structure. "Tickets?" The thin young usher asked as we entered the flick abode. Topanga handed him the tickets, he tore them in half, kept half then handed Topanga the other halves. "Enjoy the flick citizens," he said as we entered further.

The first place Topanga and I went was the concession stand. "Would like anything? "Indeed, can I have a fruit nectar and a small container of citrus corn? "Is that all? "That's it, remember I just ate," she said with a smile.

Topanga and I waited in line a couple mites then ordered what we wanted; I paid for it then deposited the remaining monetary units in my pocket. "Many thanks, that's very kind of you." Topanga said as she took her treats. "My pleasure Topanga, it was very kind of you to listen to my troubles."

We both headed for the flick auditorium to await the start of the flick. We found two seats together and sat, ate bites of citrus corn, took sips of our beverages and talked until the start of the flick. Then the lights dimmed and I reached over and squeezed Topanga's hand. "Many thanks again for lending an ear in my time of need and for suggesting the flick, it's a grand diversion. "You are very welcome; glad I can assist in your time of need, and Happy Birthp.a.r," she whispered as she looked deep into my eyes, squeezed my hand back then kissed my cheek.

As the flick started I sat closer to Topanga as she rested her head on my shoulder. "When will you know if you can give me a ride in your aircraft?" She whispered as she looked up at me. "I'm not sure, soon I hope. In the morrow Sr. Com. Bancais wants to examine my craft in more detail, hopefully sometime soon. "Me as well," she said as she gave me a kiss on the lips.

As soon as the kiss ended I quickly turned away. "What's wrong?" Topanga whispered. "I can't really say except that when we kissed I had a vision of my betrothed Tsarina. I know we most likely will never view each other again but I need time to let that sink in. "I will always be here for you, take all the time you need," Topanga said as she ran her fingers along my lips. "Many thanks," I said as I tickled her to ease the tension I was feeling.

We watched the rest of the flick enjoying our swills and citrus corn, laughed at the amusing parts and felt sorrow at the sad parts of the flick.

After the flick finished we got up and exited the flick auditorium along with all the other patrons. "How did you like the flick?" An usher asked Topanga and I as we reached the entry-way. "It was a grand depiction, I have seen this flick before; it is a classic," I replied. "What do you mean, this was the first showing of that flick and it was just released? "Oh, I must have been inkling of some other flick and it reminded me of this one," I said inkling fast then Topanga and I left the flick abode.

Outside the sun had gone down completely and the boulevard lights and commuter transportation lit the boulevard but with the illumination of the three moons we still could see clear.

"How many times have you viewed that flick Jeroque? "About five times but it gets better every time I view it. "C'mon Birthp.a.r gent and I'll drive you back to the military facility," she said with a very cute smile. "All right my exquisite one," I said as we walked back to Topanga's auto.

Topanga took out her mini remote, pressed a button and disarmed the alarm then it unlocked the gull wing entry-flaps. She pressed another button and the entry-flaps opened and we both got in as we started discussing what we would be doing the next p.a.r. As Topanga drove me back to the Grinshaw Military Facility.

A little while later Topanga pulled up to the gateabode and gave me a kiss, this time I went with it and kissed her back. "Call me in the morrow?" Topanga asked after the kiss had concluded. "Affirmative," I said as I got out of the vehicle. "Many thanks for making my Birth p.a.r memorable, grand twilight my exquisite one. "Anytime handsome, grand twilight and I really hope you had a pleasant latter part of your Birthp.a.r with me. "I did, you made it very grand, many thanks again, adioso," I said as the entry-flap closed. "Grand-adioso," Topanga said as she started backing on to the boulevard and honked as she drove away.

'Time to go sign myself back in,' I thought to myself as I walked to the gateabode. "Did you have an enjoyable twilight?" The MP asked as I signed back in. "Affirmative we both did," I said as I handed back the clipboard.

"My consociate Topanga and I went to talk for a while then for my Birthp.a.r we went to a flick," I said as I looked at my timepiece. "I have to get going, grand twilight," I told the MP then I retired to my barracks.

After I let myself in, I turned on the Intervision monitor and switched to the melodic compositional Entertainment channel and listened to the retro composition then went to find a jotter and ballpoint then jotted in the happenings of my trip through time. 'Quite a bit has happened this p.a.r but I made a grand consociate, her name is Topanga Shrenka. Topanga sure is a kind hearted young lady,' I thought as I jotted. I continued to document the happenings of this p.a.r for the next epoch. Then I got ready to retire for the twilight.

*****

Halfway to the early morn as I slumbered I started having another twilightmare. I was telling 'PAT' all the things I had told Topanga the twilight before and she got really upset.

"You shouldn't have explained our situation with someone who wasn't military personnel," she said a bit irate. "But I had to tell someone who would give me a Humanarian perspective, I decided to tell Topanga on account she is a bright citizen. "You told the Sr. Commodore, he is Humanarian, and don't you think he is a bright citizen? "Of coarse I do but…"

And that is when I awoke. "What was that about?" I asked myself out loud. I looked at my timepiece and asked the time. "04 hundred 23 epocks," it relayed. I laid there a few more mites trying to figure out the meaning of my twilightmare; I couldn't so I turned on my side and retired once again.

P.A.R 4

As I was standing in line at the mess hall waiting for my first banquet of this p.a.r, I adjusted my beret. 'Banquets were quicker and more accessible in the times yet to come using a sustenance replenisher but the way they cook and prepare the sustenance in this time period tastes a lot better,' I thought to myself as I inched closer to getting my banquet.

I then thought of everything I had told Topanga the twilight before. 'Was I right to tell her everything of my ordeal? I had to turn to someone, and I'm glad it was Topanga,' I thought smiling to myself.

A few secs later the line started moving and I received my morn banquet. I went to retrieve eating utensils and caffinated brew then went to a vacant table and sat. While I started on my banquet I thought more of everything that was about to unfold in the next few p.a.r's.

A bit later as I was taking a swill of my morn caffinated brew, when a Captain walked to the table I was sitting at. "Grand morn Major, may I join you? "Grand morn, be my guest. My name is Maj. Jeroque Teldat," I said as I shook his hand.

"Capt. Joque Jericho and it's grand to meet you; grand p.a.r this morn is turning into, isn't it? "It sure is. "I haven't seen you around before, were you stationed here long?" The Captain asked then took a swill of his caffinated brew. "Negative, I arrived the p.a.r before this one."

"What is your area of expertise? "I am a test pilot and instructor," I said then took another swill of my caffinated brew. "Instructor, you instruct in what field? "I instruct in the field of aero dynamics. What is your area of expertise, if you don't mind me asking? "Negative I don't mind; I'm just a regular pilot," The Captain said then began to consume his morn banquet. At that moment I finished my banquet. "It was grand meeting you but now I must take my leave," I said as I put my beret on then stood and gathered my tray. "Have a grand p.a.r," I said as I turned to leave. "Adioso," Capt. Jerico said as I walked away.

After I dropped my tray off, I went to hangar three to check things over on my craft. As I entered the hangar I pressed the talk button on my timepiece. "08 hundred epocks." I tapped the left wing of my com-link and contacted 'PAT'. "Grand morn 'PAT'; Sr. Com. Bancais, a couple of scientists and their E-Tech team will arrive shortly to take specifications of the aircraft."

"Grand morn Major; affirmative, I'll anticipate their arrival. "Open and lower the main hatch platform." As it started lowering, I started inkling of Tsarina, the love of my life that was possibly gone forever. 'Gods on high, I do love her, why did you make me leave her?' But I received no answer so I got myself together and went up to the cockpit. "So what did you do last twilight?" I asked as I inserted my electronic keycard then started inspecting the instrument Panels.

"I ran self-diagnostics, made sure all fluids were at acceptable levels then I went to my alcove, sat then powered down until you contacted me this morn. How was your twilight Major? My twilight was enjoyable and a bit jubellious, I had a get together with a consociate and then we went to a flick in celebration of my birthp.a.r," I said as I put the 'HUD' helmet on so I to could check the levels of water, fuel, oil and Liquid Napricyte^2 SDC I had remaining. The water, oil and fuel levels were low but the level of Liquid Napricyte^2 SDC was at the $^7/_{16}$ marker.

"But last twilight I had a twilightmare that has left me a little baffled. "What was your twilightmare about? "You were upset that I discussed our situation with my consociate Topanga. The reason you were upset with me was because you didn't agree that I should discuss our situation with someone who wasn't military personnel. But I had to tell someone who would give me a Humanarian perspective. "Upset, why was I upset? "I'm not sure because at that time I awoke. Maybe it was nothing but a twilightmare, we'll leave it at that," I said as I changed subject.

"The differences between the time we had come from and the time we have found ourselves in are quite astounding," I told 'PAT' as I checked other things in the helmets' main menu. "Affirmative Major, it is," 'PAT' said.

When I was through, I took the helmet off, got out of the pilot's seat then went and dislodged the electronic keycard. "Adioso for now 'PAT', raise and close the main hatch after I have lowered to the floor," I said as I left the cockpit. "Affirmative Major," 'PAT' acknowledged as I lowered to the floor. I looked at my timepiece and seen it was 08 hundred 20 epocks, so I proceeded to main headquarters and Sr. Com. Bancais office.

As I arrived in front of the Senior Commodore's secretarial assistant, my timepiece informed me it was precisely 08 hundred 30 epocks. 'Right on time,' I thought as I removed my beret.

"Grand morn LC Gervais, the Sr. Commodore is expecting me," I said with a smile. "Grand morn Major, let me inform the Commodore you are here," he said as he pressed a button on his primitive intercom system. Sr. Com. Bancais your 08 hundred 30 epock appointment is here. "Send the Major in. "You may enter," LC Gervais informed me. "Many thanks Lance Corporal," I replied as I entered the Sr. Commodore's office.

"Grand morn Sr. Commodore, sir," I said as I stood at attention and saluted the commanding officer. "Grand morn Major, stand at ease," the Sr. Commodore replied as he returned my salute. "Where would you like to speak?

"Excuse me sir, if it is all right with you I'd like to accompany you and your scientists as you inspect my craft? Like I conveyed the p.a.r before this one, I know a few very important facts that will take place in the next few p.a.r's. I want to make sure nothing happens to my craft or super computer because I know I will be expected to offer my assistance! I love this world and I'd do everything I could to save it. The times yet to come I am from isn't up to this p.a.r's standards and I believe it is my civic duty to prevent it from ever becoming reality again; no matter how much I stand to lose."

"What is your meaning? "That doesn't matter at this moment, just remember to alert the planet's leaders and advise them that we are going to be involved in a war with an alien race known as the Protrerian High Command. This war will commence

07.01.2015 at precisely 11 hundred epocks, and that they will attack by air and land. "Agreed. If you want to accompany me to your aircraft then let's get going.

"Affirmative Sr. Commodore, I'm right behind you." Sr. Com. Bancais stood up and placed his chewed cigar butt in his ashtray. "Excuse me sir, may I ask you what those cigars taste like? "You've never tasted them?" Sr. Com. Bancais asked with an inquisitive look. "Negative sir."

"All tobac products were outlawed in the tritton 2016, way before my time so I have never received the opportunity to try them. "Here son take a couple, they are the best-imported cigars from Mateo we have received yet," he said as he opened the box of cigars on his desk. "Many thanks sir," I said as I took a couple. I deposited them in the breast pocket of my uniform then put my beret back on as we both left the office.

"If I'm needed for any reason I'll be in hangar three checking out Major Teldat's aircraft," Sr. Com. Bancais informed Lance Corporal Gervais. "Affirmative sir."

Sr. Com. Bancais and I disappeared around the corner and eventually out of main headquarters. A few mites later we both reached the hangar before the scientists and their E-Tech team, so I decided that we would wait for them in the cockpit of my craft.

I tapped my com-link. "'PAT', open and lower the main hatch platform. "Affirmative," she acknowledged as the main hatch platform opened and lowered to the floor.

When it was down, Sr. Com. Bancais and I stepped on the platform. "Stand still for a few secs until the platform starts to rise." When we arrived at the cockpit we entered and I went over and inserted then activated the electronic keycard as everything illuminated.

"You remember 'PAT'," I said just as 'PAT' removed herself from her alcove at the rear of the craft. "Of course I do, how are you this p.a.r?" Sr. Com. Bancais asked as he returned her salute. "Very well," she said as she smiled and walked towards us.

"This craft has the same type of radar repellant coating as the Nightingale 228-A Stealth they have in this time period but as you are probably aware, it's not 100% effective. Finally, my craft is coated a combination of black, brown and gray then depicted is the orange dragon," I said as we turned and went to the instrument panels.

"Remind me again of the weapons and ammunitions this impressive aircraft has for defense? "Affirmative sir," I said as I took a deep breath. "I have a total of five types of weapons; they are the Sareden Quantum Lasers, Protonic EMC-Missals, and Neutronic EMC-Torpedo's. Finally, my craft is equipped with two XTR-9000 Plasma Pulse Cannons, one under each wing. These cannons fire a deadly stream of plasma shells."

"Protonic EMC-Missals are electromagnetically created missiles, like all missals they explode on contact. Neutronic Electromagnetic Cluster Torpedo's however, are made up of energy like my craft's missals except they do not have an explosive charge; rather they cut electronic power to whatever it comes in contact with leaving it vulnerable to attack. All my weapons ammunition are self-loading."

"I also have a Comodrone Electronics P-52 Hydrogenic Generator: After I deploy fifteen EMC-Missals, this Hydrogenic generator requires ten mites time for the generator to generate enough electricity to refill my compliment of EMC Missals back to fifteen and twenty mites to bring my compliment of EMC-Torpedo's to ten. The generator keeps the SQ-Lasers and the XTR-9000 cannons charged at all times so it has an unlimited supply of ammunition at all times. Also, it supplies my Omagon 2115 Star Drive engine and Electronic Flux Inducer, my craft's full-bodied shield and everything else electronic on my craft electrically charged. Although before my weapons will operate, I have to tell 'PAT' to activate them before they will fire."

"My craft has all the Stealth capabilities of the Stealth craft of this p.a.r, except for one very important feature. "And what may that be?"

"When my craft goes into stealth mode it vanishes from sight as well as radar. In stealth mode my craft is 100% undetectable from any radar because the craft itself is equipped with EM absorbent Panels for its cloaking privileges. I activate a touch pad and the craft vanishes from sight and it will remain invisible and undetectable for as long as I remain in Stealth mode."

At that moment Sr. Com. Bancais and I heard the scientists and their electronic technician team.

"Sr. Com. Bancais is that you in the cockpit?" A female voice asked. "Affirmative it is, I am accompanied by Maj. Teldat and his cybernetic co-pilot," Sr. Com. Bancais stated as I lowered the platform so they could also inspect the cockpit. "Come see this citizens, you've got to inspect this aircraft's cockpit."

When everyone was up in the cockpit they looked around in disbelief. "I would like to introduce you to 'PAT'; her name is an anagram, standing for Prototype Advancements in Technology. Her main function is to control this craft and offer Maj. Teldat any and all assistance she is able," Sr. Com. Bancais said. "Grand to meet you," they all said as they shook hands. I picked up the 'HUD' helmet and handed it to the female scientist. "Here ma'am, try this on."

She put it on her head as I activated the finger touch pad that lowered the visor. "'PAT', activate the HUD helmet and produce a map of Cangla City?" I asked and the aerial map of Cangla City appeared on the lower portion of the face shield view screen. "Ask any address in the city and 'PAT' will locate and produce an image of it as soon as she locates it," I told her.

"'PAT', produce an image of 6696 Lockhart Drive?" 'PAT' started producing images of Cangla City until she located the boulevard then the red brick two-story abode. "Amazing that is my address but how can she do this at this speed?

"Technology of the times yet to come and this p.a.r's satellite network," was all I said. "'PAT', in turn access water, fuel and Liquid Napricyte[2] levels, weapons, ammunition, and armament display.

"This is so cool," Dr. Clements said as everything one by one flashed on the lower portion of the view screen.

After Dr. Clements had seen everything it had to show, I raised the face visor then she removed it and handed to the other tech scientist.

The doctor then their E-Tech team had their turn as they one by one also viewed maps, weapon display, ammunition levels, fuel and Liquid Napricyte[2] levels, etc. After they had seen everything that the 'HUD' helmet had to show, the helmet was removed.

"If you will notice not anywhere on the control Panels is there a two-way radio. "You are correct Major," the two tech scientists said as they and their E-Tech team looked around. "There is a finger touch pad located here by the starboard ear position that I press to activate two-way communications. If I want to speak to anyone I have to activate two-way communications, however, if anyone contacts me it is automatically activated. In addition, if I press it a second time in quick succession, two-way communications will remain open until I press the touch pad a third time."

I activated my craft's communications monitor. "Citizens say greetings to 'PAT'. "Greetings PAT. "Isn't your cybernetic co-pilot also named 'PAT'? Sr. Com. Bancais asked? "Affirmative, but considering they are one in the same they work in conjunction with each other so all I have to say is 'PAT' and whatever I ask will be done. "Greetings Commodore and party," 'PAT' said. "The letters P.A.T., stands for Prototype Advancements in Technology. She is programmed to assist in controlling the craft in flight and to assist with whatever question, problem or dilemma that is asked of her, and the cybernetic version of 'PAT" is my copilot, she was created to assist me as I fly this craft," I told them all.

"'PAT', what is this p.a.r's date?" Dr. Clements asked. 06.29.2015," she immediately replied. "What was the date you and Maj. Teldat came from?" The other scientist asked. "06.28.2115," she answered and the female scientist gasped.

"You are correct sir," she said in amazement as she looked over at Sr. Com. Bancais. "My apologies sir, but when you first told me about the Major and his craft from the times yet to come, I thought you were finally losing your thinker."

"This is just the beginning, around the instrument panels you'll see digits of mini monitors, gauges and touch pads. They inform me of things such as, my altitude, cockpit pressure, if the electromagnetic missile/torpedo bay hatch is open, if the landing gear is up or down; also, if the wings and wing gears are raised or lowered, extended or contracted, and altitude level, etc.? I have a communications monitor, a monitor that gives me a direct link to my XT-165 DigiCam and over here on this instrument Panel is the monitor that informs me of my air speed at the time I am flying; to name a few."

"You can see on this monitor or on the inside of the 'HUD' helmet's visor if you say current air speed and it will flash in the far right hand corner of the visor. The lowest air speed is 0 knots per epock, because I can stop my craft and hover motionless in mid-air, and at regular air speed my craft can travel as fast as Mach ten."

"Then, if this touch pad here is pressed," I said as I pointed toward a purple touch pad. "It'll engage my craft's Omagon 2115 Star Drive Engine and I fly through a Humanarian-made swirling wormhole, which allows me to travel at Star Drive speeds. "

"How is that possible? "I have technically advanced golden modules strategically placed around my craft, which are hidden until needed. When my Star Drive Engine is engaged, electrical power is combined with a Liquid Napricyte[2] compound, this special electrical charge travels to the Electronic Flux Inducer which converts the special electrical power to Ionic power and this current of ionic power travels through an electrical wire then the ionic power encompasses my craft electromagnetically along those golden modules and the charge finely reaches a golden rod on the nose of my craft. The Ionic charge is then shot out in front of my craft, which creates a swirling Humanarian-made wormhole, I fly into it and I access Star Drive speed. Press it once for Star Drive one; press it a second time for Star Drive two."

"What kind of fuel do you use to reach Star Drive speeds?" Dr. Alexander asked. "My Star Drive Engine doesn't operate using a fuel, instead it is powered by my craft's Comodrone Electronics P-52 Hydrogenic Generator and that chemical substance I use, which is called Liquid Napricyte[2] SDC. "Liquid Napricyte[2] SDC, what is that?" Dr. Clements asked as she raised her eyebrows.

"That is the special type of chemical solution designed to give my Omagon 2115 Star Drive Engine the additional power it needs to advance to Star Drive speeds. "What does the SDC stand for?" Dr. Alexander inquired. "That anagram stands for Star Drive Compound. "But, this chemical substance plays a double role. "What is your meaning? I was asked. "What I mean is, this chemical solution allows my craft to excel its Star Drive speed; also it supplies my weapons the explosive power to cause major destruction."

"Do you have samples of this compound we can observe?" Dr. Clements asked. "Affirmative, at the rear of the cockpit, in that compartment which has the radioactive symbol and the words Caution Radioactive," I said as I went to the rear of the cockpit and opened a security compartment and retrieved a medium sized metal case. The metal case also had a radioactive symbol and beneath it the words, "Liquid Napricyte[2] SDC, Caution Radioactive."

"How much of that chemical solution do you have remaining?" Dr. Alexander asked. "I have eight, 200 ml vials remaining. "Would I be able to acquire one of the vials to break down the composition and attempt to duplicate and produce more of this chemical solution?" Dr. Alexander inquired. "Why? "I am planning to take schematics of the Omagon 2115 Star Drive Engine and Electronic Flux Inducer to try to reproduce them and I will need to duplicate the chemical solution in order to power it. I put the case back on the closet shelf and closed it.

"For what is about to happen in the near times yet to come, I absolutely give my permission. "That imperative information you informed me of earlier?" Sr. Com. Bancais inquired. "Affirmative sir, but there is a bright side I didn't mention. When everything looks hopeless, we will receive assistance from another alien race," I said with a smile.

"Another alien race?" Sr. Com. Bancais asked surprised as he raised an eyebrow.

"Affirmative, they are an alien race known as the Antrerian's, the Protrerian's and Antrerian's are aliens who live on sister planets in the Currecuse Sector of the Dalnary Galaxy. These two races have been at war with each other for a very long time, but they stopped fighting when they discovered their sun would eventually go nova and extinguish."

"That is when the Protrerian's somehow discovered our Planet and they will attack us and take it for themselves. The Antrerian's find out that they are taking our Planet by force and try to stop them.

"Then you know how the war concludes?" Sr. Com. Bancais asked.

"Aliens! And what's this about a war?" Dr. Clements asked. "Just a moment ma'am. Not precisely sir, I know how it concluded in my time line but as I am now in this time line, I'm not really sure. Let's hope with the firepower I have, I can make a difference to that outcome."

"To answer your question Doctor, on 07.01 at 11 hundred epocks our Planet will be attacked by an alien race, but not to worry most of the citizens in power are being notified and steps are being taken to prepare for what is to come. Now I'll show you scientific citizens the engines."

"How many engines does this aircraft operate on?" Dr. Clements asked a bit more calm. "This craft operates on two huge F405-F1D3 afterburning engines, for normal flying exorcises and a third engine I just explained, the Star Drive engine for times I need to be somewhere very fast. 'PAT', you may accompany us if you so desire."

The nine of us left the cockpit and lowered to the hangar floor. "If you'll notice on the top of the cockpit, if you stand a ways away from the craft you can see the Sareden Quantum Laser Cannons. Here below the nose of my craft is a sliding plate; from here I fire my craft's Protonic EMC-Missals and/or Neutronic EMC-Torpedo's."

"A moment citizens," I said as I looked at 'PAT'. "'PAT', raise the main hatch platform and slide the port wing forward then extend the wings. When that is complete lower the XTR-9000 Plasma Pulse Cannons. "Affirmative Major," she said and secs later the huge cannons lowered on a turret, one from under each wing. "These cannons fire a deadly stream of electromagnetic plasma shells. So my craft is a deadly predator at all times! "PAT', now raise the cannons and lower then raise the wings." As the wings tilted downwards I explained the significance.

"When the wings are in the downward position I can ascend up to a desired altitude. I have a touch pad inside my craft that levels the wings and I can fly in any direction I choose. The same rule applies to setting down except, as you can see the wings rise and I can descend straight down, which cuts out the need of a runway."

"You mean this aircraft is somewhat like a Helijet when it comes to takeoff and landings?" Dr. Alexander asked. "Sort of the same principle," I said. "'PAT', open the tail section engine cover." Immediately the rear of the craft opened and slid forward.

"Go retrieve an automatic mechanical lift," Sr. Com. Bancais told two of the E-Tech's. "'PAT' accompany them and give them a hand," I said as I walked over to and I quietly whispered to Dr. Alexander.

"Dr. Alexander, are you mated in matrimony and if you are, would her name happen to be Shannon? "I am mated in matrimony and affirmative, her name is Shannon. "Do you happen to have a male off-spring by the name of Joshua? "Negative, but my mate is expecting our first off-spring soon and we were planning to call the little tyke Juliana if it is a female or Joshua if it is a male, why?"

"Believe me, it will be male and many trittons over the horizon I will be engaged to your great granddaughter, her name will be Tsarina. Maybe, depending on what conspires in the near times yet to come. "What is your meaning? "Can you give me your abode address so we could talk face to face? "Affirmative," he said as he jotted it down on a blank piece of parchment at the back of his clipboard. When he finished jotting, he took the parchment out and handed it to me.

"You can stop by this eve after our twilight banquet. "Grand, many thanks; is it ok if I bring a consociate?" I asked as I looked at the address and noticed his address was the same address Tsarina and I resided for the last five trittons. I then remembered she had mentioned that the abode was in her kinfolk's possession for many generations. I then folded the piece of parchment and put it in my pocket. "Affirmative, bring whomever you like as long as you believe they can be trusted with the information that needs to be discussed," Dr. Anderson said.

At that moment, 'PAT' and the E-Tech's returned in an armored utility vehicle towing the AML, when it was disconnected and locked into place, everyone stood on it and we all rose to the metal walkway that surrounded the engine galley. We stepped onto the walkway, went over to and climbed down a metal ladder then turned towards the mighty engines.

"These are my two main F405-F1D3 afterburning engines, I use most of the time my craft is in flight. Over here is the infamous Omagon 2115 Star Drive Engine," I said as I turned to face it. "I administer a vile of Liquid Napricyte[2] SDC in a side port under this protective cover. I turn the vile of this chemical solution until I hear a beep, letting me know it is locked securely."

"What is the maximum Star Drive speed again?" Dr. Clements inquired. "My maximum Star Drive speed is Star Drive two. "Which is how fast?" Dr. Alexander inquired.

"When I am in Star Drive one, I can reach the speed of 10* faster than Mach ten and Star Drive two is 20* faster.

"You mean to tell us this massive aircraft can fly that fast? "Affirmative it can," I answered with a grin.

"Over here is the Comodrone Electronics P-52 Hydrogenic generator, which supplies power to the Electronic Flux Inducer, supplies the weapons array with the power to create all my craft's weapons ammunition. Power my full-bodied shield & allowing my craft to power its awesome stealth capabilities, also it powers everything else that requires electronic power on this craft."

"Over here next to the infamous Star Drive Engine is the Electronic Flux Inducer, which converts the mixture of Liquid Napricyte[2] enriched electrical power to ionic power then runs the precise amount of Ionic energy through this electrical cable that runs from it to the back of the craft. It then electromagnetically encompasses my craft going from each golden module to the longer golden metallic rod on the nose of my craft. Which shoots the Ionic charge out in front of my craft creating a swirling Humanarian-made wormhole, which allows me to fly Star Drive speed within ZarCedra's oxygenated resistant atmosphere and gravitational pull."

"This wormhole is oxygenated resistant meaning there is no oxygen, in order for me to breathe; for this reason, I have three oxygen tanks filled with compressed oxygen allowing a maximum of 96 epocks," I said as I opened a hatch and pointed to the tanks. "As I fly into the wormhole or break ZarCedra's atmosphere, the oxygen is automatically pumped into the cockpit allowing me to breathe normally. So when you take schematics of the Omagon 2115 Star Drive engine and EFI you must take the tanks of oxygen into consideration. The ride through this wormhole is quite erratic, almost like flying this craft along an unimaginable twisty roller coaster."

"Another contribution made to the defensive system is the installation of Inertial Dampeners- which are a replacement for motion compensators that uses graviton emitters to dampen the effect of quick acceleration, make sure you include them in the schematics you take"

"This is all I have to show you at this time," I said as I turned towards my party. "Maj. Teldat would be needing his craft in the next while so if you dismantle anything you must make sure you immediately reassemble it after the schematics are taken," Sr. Com. Bancais told his scientific staff and their E-Tech team. "Affirmative sir," they all replied.

"All right you citizens can start taking the specs you need so we can duplicate the Star Drive Engine, Electronic Flux Inducer and everything else that makes this craft fly at Star Drive speed," Sr. Com. Bancais told them as he and I climbed back up to the metal walkway, went to the AML then descended to the floor.

"It's 10 hundred 45 epocks," Sr. Com. Bancais said as he looked at his timepiece. "Come to my office after your mid-p.a.r banquet; for now you are free to leave" Sr. Com. Bancais told me as we got to the floor. "Affirmative sir! 'PAT' remain here and oversee the progress of these fine doctors and their E-tech team; assist in anything you can to make their progression as smooth as possible. "Affirmative Sir."

"Oh one more thing, these scientists and their tech team should be finished late this eve, so don't worry, your aircraft is in grand hands," Sr. Com. Bancais said. "Affirmative sir; the keycard is still engaged in its port, if the scientists need to access anything electronic in the craft, they will require that keycard. But if they want to dismantle anything electronic the keycard must be ejected from its port, if not it could result in electrocution. So I'll leave it with you, just make sure you let the scientists and their E-tech team know that and you can return the keycard to me later. "Count on it," he said as we saluted then I turned and began to leave.

I stopped then turned around as I seen Dr. Alexander at the rear of the craft waiting for the AML. "Dr. Alexander I will be in contact with you later this p.a.r, adioso everyone. "Affirmative," he acknowledged. I left the hangar and marched out towards my barracks.

When I arrived, I had my retina scanned and voice pattern identified then the entry-way slid open and I entered my quarters, I turned the Intervision monitor on and turned to the melodic compositional channel as I removed my beret then I retrieved the jotter and ballpoint. I opened it to the next blank parchment and jotted in the happenings of the morn up to this time.

When I finished I went into the latrine to freshen up a bit, I looked at my timepiece and discovered it was almost time for my mid-p.a.r banquet. I left the latrine and replaced my beret upon my head, turned the Intervision monitor off then left my barracks going towards the mess hall as I started inkling of the things that were happening, the citizens I have met and the things that were about to happen according to my times elapsed archive. 'I really hope the citizens of this time take my warnings to heart, that existence was hellatious on ZarCedra with the Protrerian's in control. I hope I can make a difference in the upcoming war without disrupting the times yet to come too much and hopefully this time maybe the citizens of ZarCedra could become the victors and stay in control of our planet,' I thought as I kept walking.

A few mites later I arrived at my destination and walked into the mess hall for my mid-p.a.r chow, just as my timepiece "beeped" and informed me it was "12 hundred epocks."

I walked in and in a few mites of standing in line I received my banquet. While I was getting a cold swill and silverware, I looked down and noticed the cigars in my breast pocket. 'Oh yeah the cigars, these should taste grand,' I thought then went to a table, set my tray down, removed my beret, sat and started consuming my banquet.

A few mites later, some of my new consociates entered the mess hall for their mid-p.a.r banquet then came to join me at my table. "Greetings, everyone said as they sat, then made small talk, as we all consumed our banquet.

After I finished, I put my beret back on then started gathering my tray. "Time to take my leave but first does anyone have anything to spark my cigar with? "Affirmative, here you go Major," A Sergeant said as he handed me a few mini sparking sticks. "Many thanks," I said as I put them in my pocket. "Grand p.a.r everyone," I said as I grabbed my tray, went to drop it off then went out to the designated puffing area.

As I got there I took out one of the cigars, lit it, and took a big drag. Well I coughed, sputtered and gagged. "Grand taste but hard on the lungs." At that time a few other military personnel arrived at the designated puffing area to puff their tobac sticks and we exchanged pleasantries.

"Does anyone know Sr. Com. Bancais first name?" I asked. "Affirmative, his first name is Gregor; why? "Just curious," I answered as I took another drag of the cigar, again I coughed. "Are you all right? I was asked. "I think so, I'm just not used to puffing," I said as I turned three shades of blue.

I puffed half the cigar talking to the military personnel then I butted what was left, "Adioso," I said then went to my barracks.

When I arrived, I had my retina scanned and voice pattern identified then the entry-way slid open and I entered my quarters, I sat on the lounger a few mites while the chamber spun, after the dizziness subsided I decided to go to Mac Guire's Handiness Supplies to talk to Topanga.

'I wonder if she had a more exciting p.a.r than I?' I thought as I went to the latrine. A few mites later I left my barracks and walked to the gateabode. 'It sure feels grand to have an exquisite citizen close enough to care so much about me,' I thought as I walked.

I stopped at the front gateabode. "Greetings Sergeant, how are you this p.a.r? "I'm doing pretty well. "Grand, can I sign the roster?" I want to go to Mac Guire's Handiness Supplies. "Affirmative Major," he said as he handed me the clipboard and ballpoint. I signed it then passed it back to the Sergeant. "Take care," I replied as I turned and went down the boulevard.

A few mites later I was in front of the shop and I gazed through the window. The sun was glaring so bright I couldn't see the faces of the female citizens that were working so I put my hand next to my face, blocking the sun as I seen Topanga's gorgeous face.

Seeing she was there I entered, and said "greetings" to my pretty consociate. "Greetings Jeroque, how has your p.a.r been?" she asked as I walked up to her. "Pretty bland, I presented and explained my craft to Sr. Com. Bancais, a couple scientists and their Electronic Technician team then I went for my mid-p.a.r banquet."

"Would you be interested in going to my abodement later this mid-p.a.r? "I would except, later this mid-p.a.r my CO wants to talk to me then I am to go see Dr. Alexander after my twilight banquet. "Oh is there something physically wrong? She asked with grand concern. "Negative he isn't that type of doc, he is one of the scientists stationed at the military facility."

"Oh." Just as I started explaining why, a couple citizens entered the shop. "It's my turn to assist these patrons, I will return shortly," Topanga said as she rubbed my arm and walked away. After they found everything they had come in for; they paid for their purchase then left the handiness shop.

"Continue," Topanga said as she came around the counter. "Dr. Alexander will eventually be the great grandfather of the young female citizen I was betrothed to in the tritton 2115. "Oh really? "Affirmative, but you are more than welcomed to accompany me if you so desire?" I asked with a smile. "If you or Dr. Alexander don't mind me tagging along? I would be happy to!"

"Grand, could you pick me up at 18 hundred epocks? "What time, I'm not too familiar with military time after 12 hundred epocks," she confessed.

"Oh 6:00 this twilight," I said with a grin. "Why are you grinning? "Because, all the consociately things I've gotten from you, it finally feels grand to give you some assistance even if it was assisting you with the time; also, it is pleasant of you to want to accompany me. "I want to assist you any way I can. "Many thanks my dear," I said as I quickly embraced her just as a few more citizens entered the shop.

"You and your coworkers are busy; I will take my leave now and see you at six this early twilight. I will meet you at the front gate abode when you arrive, adioso for now," I said as I walked toward the exit. "All right, adioso," she said with a smile as I exited the establishment.

I started up the boulevard toward the military facility, when I got to the gateabode I signed back in. I looked at my timepiece and seen that it was 13 hundred 54 epocks. 'I better go check in with Sr. Com. Bancais,' I thought as I walked toward main headquarters.

As I entered I started inkling; 'should I leak information to the Commodore that he and a few other key military personnel form a secret division of N.Z.C.M.Co. Then after the Protrerian

High Command take over ZarCedra, he and his cohorts are stopped but the Sr. Commodore's work was continued after the Protrerian High Command's dectrittons of domination. At that time that division of N.Z.C.M.Co, in my time, adopts the name Secret Humanarian ZarCedra Alliance, anagrammed S.H.Z.C.A. I wonder if Sr. Com. Bancais is in his office or still with the E-Tech team in the hangar,' I thought as I continued on my way.

"Greetings LC Gervais, I come to talk to the Sr. Commodore, is he in?" I asked as I walked up to his secretarial assistant. "Affirmative he is, but now you can address me as Corporal; I've just been promoted," he said as he produced a second stripe on the arm of his uniform. "Congrats," I said as I shook his hand.

"Many thanks, just a moment and I'll tell Sr. Com. Bancais you're here and request to see him," Corp. Gervais said as he pressed the call button on his intercom. "What is it Corporal? "Sir, Maj. Teldat is here to see you. "Send him right in. "Affirmative Sir," he said then pressed the off button. "You may enter; the Sr. Commodore is expecting you. "Many thanks," I replied as I removed my beret then entered the Commodore's office and closed the entry-way.

"Grand mid-p.a.r sir," I said as I saluted. "Grand mid-p.a.r Major, your aircraft won't be finished with for quite a few more epocks, it will probably take until the wee epocks of the early morn but after that time you can use it at any time," Sr. Com. Bancais said as he returned my salute.

"Many thanks sir. "Negative many thanks to you; Dr. Alexander asked me to remind you to leave him a sample of your Liquid Napricyte[2] compound. "Affirmative sir, did you like everything you saw? "I did Major," he said with a grin that reminded me of a child in a sweets shop.

"The reason why I need my craft in the next few p.a.r's is because; some of this I already told you, the planet will be attacked but on this continent, the Cardola Territories will be attacked first, then Tanglar and Garlotia in quick succession."

"What is their reason? "The leading objective, they plan to take our secrets from our Energy Facilities; then almost immediately they change their mind and decide to take ZarCedra. The war will commence 07.01 at 11 hundred epocks, just have fighters on standby alert, ready to scramble when needed, because they will be needed to assist. "Affirmative Major."

"Call the Lanston Military Installation in Translete, in the Cardola Territories and have them start evacuating that city and set up ground forces, immediately. "Affirmative Major. "Other major cities in the Cardola Territories that will be attacked, if I can remember them all," I said as I scratched my head. "Are Dek-kred, Negra Parday, Dalarme, Satery, Mar Pader, Kelsar, Tal Aden and I believe Myfore. Other major cities on the Kor Bissal Continent that will be attacked in Tanglar are Ortice and Trigor. In Garlotia, Garlotian Palisades and Vroxen, you must warn those locations also so they can start evacuating those cities, ground forces will be needed as well. "Of coarse Major," the Commodore said as he jotted down the locations.

"A few p.a.r's after the war begins we will meet our new allies, and you Sr. Com. Bancais with three other military citizens will form a major military defense facility, a branch of N.Z.C.M.Co that will affect the entire planet. "What is it we do? "You should figure that out yourself but I will say, it is imperative and beneficial to the entire planet."

"Hmm, you can't give me an indication? "Well, you and a few other key military personnel will work in conjunction with ZarCedra Solar Department to set up what you need. "So I won't be alone in this venture? "Negative sir, our nation is not equipped with the technology at the present time."

"Eventually Tanglar will be more technologically advanced than the Cardola Territories but by that time the Northern ZarCedra Military Coalition will be joined with the rest of the planet if, the Gods forbid, the Protrerian High Command are victorious in the war, they will rename it to ZarCedra Force. Also, you and the citizens in your group were stopped in my original timeline, when the Protrerian High Command won the war and took over ZarCedra but your work was continued after the Humanarian's of ZarCedra were allowed in Protrerian society. In this time line, with my craft and I present, we must not allow the Protrerian High Command to become victorious in this war so the work you do can be implemented immediately."

"So it was written that we were defeated in this war," Sr. Com. Bancais said as he sat back in his chair. "Affirmative, but hopefully with my craft and I here now, hopefully we could change that outcome. Just make the necessary calls to have the major cities of the Kor Bissal Continent evacuated and protected immediately. So, so many civilian citizens won't be killed by falling debris. "Agreed," he said as he picked up his personal conversing device."

"Corporal get me the Lanston Military Installation in Translete CT, immediately," Sr. Com. Bancais said then hung up. Secs later Sr. Com. Bancais' PCD chirped; he picked up the receiver then activated the speaker as he hung up.

"Lanston Military Installation, Pvt. Johnston here can I be of assistance? "Private Johnston, this is Sr. Com. Bancais of the Grinshaw Military Facility in Cangla City, in the honorary regime of Placaden, Tanglar. Let me speak to your Commanding Officer immediately. "That will be Col. Stenwen, just a moment I will put you through. Immediately he was patched through and was speaking to the Colonel. "Col. Stenwen here. "Colonel, this is Sr. Com. Bancais from the Grinshaw Military Facility in Cangla City, in the honorary regime of Placaden, Tanglar; it has come to my attention that there will be a major air battle, commencing 07.01 at 11 hundred epocks. Start evacuating the city of Translete and set up ground forces, ASAP.

"Where did you get your information? Col. Stenwen asked quite abruptly. "From a reliable source, I will be in contact with your President and advise him of the situation that is about to happen in the skies above his Territory. "My hands are tied until I hear from President Torren. "I'll be calling him directly grand p.a.r," Sr. Com. Bancais said as he deactivated the speaker then activated his intercom.

"Corporal, get President Torren at the Beige Abode in Dek-kred, in the Cardola Territories on the PCD immediately."

Secs later the President was on the line as Sr. Com. Bancais activated the speaker once again. "This is President Torren, what can I do for you Sr. Com. Bancais? "Pres. Torren, it has come to my attention, from a reliable source that the entire planet will soon be involved in an intergalactic war and the site of the first air battle will be in the skies over Translete of the Cardola Territories. Shortly thereafter the cities of Dek-kred, Negra Parday, Dalarme, Satery, Mar Pader, Kelsar, Tal Aden and Myfore will be attacked in the Cardola Territories."

"When is this battle supposed to commence? "07.01 at 11 hundred epocks, I called the Lanston Military Installation in Translete and talked to a Col. Stenwen and apprised him of the situation but he said his hands were tied until he talked to you. "How reliable is your source and how did he get this information?" Sr. Com. Bancais looked at me.

"From a very reliable source, I believe everything he says to be very true, I will put together a summit meeting here at the Grinshaw Military Facility in the very near times yet to come and you can meet him personally. "All right I will call the Lanston Military Installation in Translete, as well as the other military installations you specified and have them start evacuating and setting up the necessary ground forces in those cities immediately. "Grand, you will be hearing from me soon President Torren, many thanks and grand p.a.r." With that said Sr. Com. Bancais pressed a button that deactivated the external speaker.

"Well Major the ball is rolling, now we wait. Do you have plans for this twilight? "Affirmative sir I do, a consociate and I will be going to see Dr. Alexander and his mate this twilight. I will be away from this military facility approximately three epocks."

"Was that what you and Dr. Alexander were discussing in private this morn? "Affirmative sir, he doesn't know this yet but in my original timeline he was a prominent figure in my personal life. "I see, and at what time will you be going over there? "After our twilight banquets are concluded about 18 hundred epocks, may I ask why you need to know? "Oh no reason, I am just curious?"

"Who is your consociate and when did you have time to meet anyone? "Affirmative, the p.a.r before this one I met the exquisite Topanga Shrenka at Mac Guire's Handiness Supplies. We met when I went for supplies and we became instant consociates. Then last twilight we went out to talk and then went to see a flick to celebrate my Birthp.a.r. "You do work fast," the Commodore said with a chuckle.

"We are just grand consociates, nothing more. "At least for now, I can hear it in your voice. "Negative, nothing more than grand consociates unless I'm unable to make it back to 2115. Or by chance we are victorious in this upcoming war this time and in that case my betrothed along with all Protrerian life will no longer exist in the time I come from. "I see." The Sr. Commodore said still snickering to himself.

"I should be heading back to my barracks and await twilight banquets, unless there is more you require me to do? "Negative you are free to leave," Sr. Com. Bancais said as he too stood. "I am planning on taking my craft up in the morrow morn so I'll need my keycard when your E-Tech team is finished. "Of coarse, I will deliver it personally when I get it from my scientists.

"Many thanks sir," I answered then we saluted as I turned to leave. "We have to get together to talk again," Sr. Com. Bancais said as I was heading out the entry-way. "Affirmative sir we will," I said as I walked by Corp. Gervais desk and replaced my beret.

I walked out of main headquarters and went to hangar three to check on my craft. After entering the hangar, I tapped my com-link. "Greetings 'PAT', is everything progressing adequately?" I asked as I arrived at my craft and seen her. "Affirmative Major it is," she said with a smile.

"Greetings Dr. Alexander, about what time should you and your E-Tech team be finished with my craft? "I should be finished by 17 hundred epocks, my E-Tech team on the other hand will work until finished, they said they should be finished between 23 & 03 hundred epocks," Dr. Alexander told me.

"Where should I deliver the vile of Liquid Napricyte[2] Star Drive Compound? "Don't worry about it; I will take a vile before I leave this p.a.r. "Remember it is radioactive, you must wear a radioactive safe suit when handling it, and place it in a radioactive safe container when transporting and be careful not to jostle it about, it is very volatile and sensitive to movement. "Many thanks for that bit of information Major; I will be careful. "Grand, see you at your abode at about 18 hundred 30 epocks," I said as I left the hangar.

Walking the few blocks to my barracks, I returned the salutes of a few junior officers. I entered my barracks then continued to the retina scanner by my quarter's entry-way, after my retina was scanned and my voice identified my entry-way slid open and I entered.

"Illumination on," I said, as I turned on my Intervision Monitor to listened to the nostalgic tunes that were playing on the melodic composition channel then I removed my beret and tossed it on the lounger. I looked at my timepiece and seen I had time for a quick shower before my twilight banquet and before meeting Topanga.

I gathered the things I needed then went to the latrine, I undressed then got in the soothing shower and wished Tsarina was with me so we could wash each other. 'Oh Tsarina how I miss you terribly,' I thought as the cool water showered over me. A few mites later after I was squeaky clean; I turned the water off, got out, dried off then got dressed.

'I hope the warning Sr. Com. Bancais gave Translete was in sufficient time. Because existing with the Protrerian High Command was hellatious, except existing with Tsarina; besides she was only half Protrerian,' I thought as I applied deodorant. A little later, after I had my short-cropped hair combed, I looked at my timepiece and seen that it was 16 hundred 05 epocks. 'Just under an epock to wait before I can go to the mess hall,' I thought as I vacated the latrine.

I gathered my jotter pad and ballpoint then went to the lounger as I continued listening to the melodic composition channel on the Intervision monitor. I started jotting the events of this p.a.r up to this time then I started inkling of Topanga. 'What a grand-hearted young female citizen she is,' I thought as I continued to jot all that happened up to that time.

When I was through, I turned the Intervision monitor off, grabbed my beret and put it on as I left my barracks and headed for the mess hall for my twilight banquet.

By the time I arrived, it was quite busy and I stood in a line of citizens waiting to receive our twilight banquets. I started talking to the citizen in front of me as we slowly moved down the line until we received our banquets. Our banquet didn't look all that appealing but it was fresh and didn't come from a sustenance replenisher so I was glad to get it. I took my banquet, received an iced caffinated brew, got eating utensils then went to find a seat; I finally found one in a corner occupied with younger officers.

"Is this seat taken? "Negative, you are more than welcomed to it," a Lieutenant told me. "Many thanks," I said as I sat. "My name is Lt. Stervol Borret," the young citizen said as he extended his hand in consociateship. "Maj. Jeroque Teldat," I said as I shook his hand then removed my beret.

"To my left is Lt. Pennty Sheroch and across from her is Capt. Keen Mason," Lt. Borret said as he made introductions. "Very grand to know you," I replied as I began to eat.

We all ate and talked for the next while until we all finished. I gathered my tray together, replaced my beret upon my head as I stood. "It was a pleasure meeting you fine citizens but now I must take my leave, have a grand p.a.r," I said as I turned and went to put my tray away.

I continued out of the mess hall then went to the designated puffing area to finish the other half of my half puffed cigar. Arriving at my destination, I lit up and was enjoying the flavor when others came to have a puff.

"What are your plans for the twilight? I was asked. "A consociate and I are going to visit Dr. Alexander," I said as I blew out a cloud of puff. "Who's your consociate? "Topanga Shrenka. "You mean that gorgeous blond citizen that works at Mac Guire's down the boulevard? "The one and the same," I answered as I took another puff.

"I'm impressed, for as long as she managed that convenience shop and it's been a couple trittons, she has never courted or associated with anyone from the military. Why are you so special? "Unknown, probably because I told her I was new in the city, and she could see I was in desperate need of a true consociate," I replied as I took the last puff of my stogie then butted it in the metal ashcan.

"It's been grand talking to you all but now I must take my leave, adioso," I said as I turned then left the designated puffing area heading towards my barracks.

After I let myself in, I sat on the lounger as the chamber started to spin again. "Whew," I said after the spinning subsided. 'Puffing is doing unscrupulous things to my system. Better stop puffing, you remember how addictive tobac is and the cancers it causes, the only thing that doesn't matter at this mite is that tobac puff was deadly to the Protrerian's, that is the reason they outlawed puffing,' I thought as I continued to sit.

I looked at my timepiece and seen that it was 17 hundred 50 epocks. 'Better get going, Topanga will be here soon,' I told myself as I grabbed my flight jacket and beret then exited my quarters. I put my beret on at once but waited until I got to the front gateabode to put my jacket on. I signed out then waited patiently for Topanga's arrival.

As I waited I reached into the breast pocket of my uniform and retrieved the piece of parchment with Jason Alexander's abode address. 'I hope Dr. Alexander arrived at his abode already and he and his mate are ready for guests,' I thought as Topanga pulled up in front of the gate.

"Grand p.a.r," Topanga said with a smile as I got in her auto. "Grand p.a.r my dearest," I said as I kissed her then fastened my safety belt. "Greetings handsome; what is the address to Dr. and Mrs. Alexander's abode?" she cheerfully asked. I looked into Topanga's exquisite blue eyes. "It's at 17455 Carrington Heights."

As Topanga backed onto the boulevard; the questions I wanted to ask Dr. Alexander swirled around my mind; I half heard what Topanga was asking? "How are you going to present me?" she asked again. "As my grand consociate, that is what you are, are you not? "Of coarse," she said smiling as she reached over and squeezed my hand. "Very grand consociates, I hope? "Of coarse," I said as I smiled and squeezed her hand back.

Topanga drove in the direction of Carrington Heights until she pulled into the driveway of the two-level yellow and white trimmed abode at 17455. "Grand abode," Topanga said as she parked her auto. "Affirmative it is," I agreed as I disconnected my safety belt. Topanga released hers as she pressed the engine off button then we both departed the vehicle as Topanga pressed the button on her remote and locked the entry-flaps and armed the vehicle's alarm.

Topanga and I walked up the walk towards the side entrance; I could see the black hair of a female peering out the window. 'If I didn't know Tsarina was back in the tritton 2115, I would swear it was she minus the rugged forehead and bluish-green and pink colored skin pigmentation,' I thought. When we got to the entry-way, I rung the chime and Topanga and I waited patiently until it was answered.

When the entry-way opened, Mrs. Alexander was standing there. "Enter we've been expecting you," she said with a lovely smile. "Over joyed to see you," Dr. Alexander said as he walked by the entry-way and continued to the front chamber and lit his tobac pip.

Topanga and I entered the abode and removed our footwear and jackets as I tucked my beret under the shoulder loop of my uniform then entered the front chamber to join Dr. Alexander.

"Grand twilight sir," I said as I shook his hand. "Delight me son and call me Jason, and this plump exquisiteness is my matrimonial mate Shannon. "Oh Jason halt!" She exclaimed with a smile.

"My name is Jeroque and this gorgeous young citizen at my side is a grand consociate of mine, her name is Topanga Shrenka. "A pleasure to make your acquaintance," everyone said as we all shook hands. "Delight us and have a seat," Jason said as he gestured towards the lounger.

"Would you like a caffinated brew or something cold to swill? Shannon asked. "Caffinated brew will be fine if it is no bother," we both said. "And I'll take a soft swill," Jason said. "No bother," she answered then went in her sustenance replenishing area.

"It is pleasant that you could make it over this twilight; so you are engaged to my times yet to come, great granddaughter? "Affirmative sir I am and hopefully by the grace of the kind Gods above, I will be able to somehow make it back when my job here is complete and hopefully she will still be around? "Why shouldn't she be?" Topanga asked. "For the reason that, changing the coarse of times elapsed can make drastic changes to the times yet to come in which I came."

"What job?" Jason asked. "I am unsure, whatever it is that I am here in this time for," I said as Shannon reentered the chamber with a tray of caffinated brew, cream, sweetener and Jason's soft swill. "Many thanks dear," Jason said as he received his soft swill and was puffing his pip as Topanga got up and assisted her.

"Does the 2115 on your jacket mean the tritton you are from? Jason told me you were from the times yet to come but couldn't share any additional information with me which included the tritton," Shannon asked. "It does, I don't know how much information he was permitted to tell you but I am currently, just recently betrothed to your great granddaughter, her name is/will be Tsarina; she is half Humanarian and half alien descent; Protrerian. "At least I know that our kin will go on," she said as she rubbed her tummy. "It does," I told her.

"So Topanga, when and where did you meet Jeroque?" Jason asked as he put his pip down to sip his soft swill. "Jeroque came into the Mac Guire's Handiness Supplies that I manage for supplies, the same p.a.r he arrived in this time. He bought his stuffs then we started having a conversation, it was busy but I could see that Jeroque wanted to talk longer so we went out for a caffinated brew then a flick that twilight," Topanga told him.

"Would you all like warmed pastry to consume as we swill our beverages?" Shannon asked. "Agreed," we all replied. "Would you like assistance?" Topanga asked. "Most definitely," Shannon said and both females left the front chamber to let us talk.

"Can you tell me the real reason you think you were brought back to this time?" Jason asked puffing on his pip once again. "Well, I shouldn't say because I'm not positive but what I suspect is that on 07.01 at 11 hundred epocks Central Time, this planet will be attacked by the alien race known as the Protrerian High Command but the Cardola Territories will be attacked first."

"I figured the Protrerian's were a grand race for the reason that you said my great granddaughter was half Protrerian. "Negative sir they are not, like I tried to convey earlier this p.a.r. This race of beings took over ZarCedra by force and had controlling power over all ZarCedra's inhabitants, and after dectrittons of Protrerian domination; Protrerian's and Humanarian citizens started mating and joining in matrimony, that's how your great granddaughter happened to be a fusion of both species. Don't get me wrong, if we do happen to be victorious in this war your kin will still go on, only they will be all Humanarian."

"To continue, in this time, a few p.a.r's from now we will receive assistance from the Protrerian High Command's archenemies known as the Antrerian's. Now the Antrerian's and Protrerian's were neighboring races from a nearby solar system in the Currecuse Sector of the Dalnary galaxy, very advanced compared to our standards. But even with the assistance of the Antrerian Armada we still lose to the Protrerian High Command and for the next 100 trittons we are under their reign, although relaxed for the last thirty trittons. I didn't fully answer your mate's question because with the advanced firepower equipped to my craft, I believe it will give our planet an advantage the Humanarian race didn't have in the original war in my timeline."

"Therefore in the event we do triumph in the war, your great granddaughter's Protrerian half will cease to exist. But like I conveyed, she'll still be born but be all Humanarian, so I don't want you to worry? "Affirmative!" Jason answered.

"In the original war its duration lasted about half a tritton but with me here now it will hopefully be over in less time. "Hmm, and what does the casualty rate look like? "In my timeline it didn't look grand, we took heavy casualties especially in major cities around Northern ZarCedra. In the first few Trints of the Grand War but as I am now here in this time line; I did tell Sr. Com. Bancais to warn and evacuate and send ground troopers to major cities around ZarCedra so many civilian citizens lives could be saved."

At that time Shannon and Topanga entered the front chamber with Topanga carrying a tray of assorted warmed pastry and Topanga set them down on the brew table. "Many thanks ladies," Jason and I said as we aided ourselves to the treats. "What were you two gentlefolk talking about?" Shannon asked as she smiled at Jason and I. "Important facts about the near times yet to come," Jason said not wanting to upset her in her impregnated state.

"With the prototype craft in my possession, I know it would make a big difference in the designing of the times yet to come Stealth aircraft," I perked up and said. "What type of aircraft do you have?" Shannon inquired. "I have what is known as the Supersonic Dragon 228-D Spy Jet Stealth. Something like the Nightingale 228-A Stealth the military has now but bigger and with a lot of added features. "Oh," she said.

"That is what my E-Tech team and I were doing this p.a.r, taking schematics of the engines and other equipment inside Jeroque's aircraft," Jason said.

We talked for a couple epocks longer getting to know one another, and in that time, the conversation turned and I started talking about the baby Shannon was going to have. "If you don't mind me telling you about him?" I asked. "We don't mind," Jason and Shannon both said.

"The baby Shannon will have will be male and she will name him Joshua, and then I told them about his adult life in the military prison camps set forth by the Protrerian High Command. That is until his release and forced to serve in the Protrerian military. Where he meets the exquisite female citizen he would join in matrimony. She will have a male off-spring and he grows up to be a grand citizen who joins in matrimony with a Protrerian lady. A little later in life they have three male and one female offspring, this female grows to be the stunning Tsarina, the female citizen I fell in love with."

After saying that, I looked down at my timepiece and seen the time. "It's getting late I should get back to the Grinshaw Military Facility," I said as Topanga and I smiled, stood and thanked the Alexander's for the nibbles. "We should get together again," Jason said. "Hopefully, that would be grand," I replied. Jason also stood, refilled his pip and lit it as he and Shannon walked us to the entrance. Topanga and I put our footwear and jackets on then I replaced my beret. "Have a grand twilight," we said as we shook their hands then left their abode.

A few mites later Topanga and I were pulling out of the drive and onto the boulevard. "What pleasant folks. "Affirmative, I agreed. "I enjoyed meeting the Alexander's, I'm glad you asked me along, many thanks," Topanga said as she squeezed my hand. "You are very welcomed huni buni," I replied as I kissed her hand.

"Topanga how would you like to go somewhere in my craft in the morrow? I have an extra helmet and there's plenty of space for passengers. "Affirmative Jeroque, I would love the opportunity to see and be a passenger in your craft, if I am allowed? "I say it's all right but the final answer has to come from Sr. Com. Bancais. "Of coarse it does, if he says it's ok when & where will we go?" Topanga excitedly asked. "Where, I haven't decided yet but I would like to lift off by 11 hundred epocks."

"Topanga would you happen to have a eat al fresco hamper? "Affirmative I have one, why? "I was inkling we could stop somewhere for our mid-p.a.r banquet, so can you fill it with a banquet for us? "Sure, I can't wait for the opportunity to finally see your craft," she said as she turned a corner. "My craft is very large and pretty amazing," I said as I looked at my timepiece and seen that it was 22 hundred 25 epocks. "Would you like to stop anywhere, Jeroque? "It's getting late; I really should get back to the military facility soon. "Agreed," she said as she drove in that direction.

A bit later, Topanga pulled up in front of the gateabode and parked her vehicle. "I really did have a grand time this twilight," Topanga said as she rubbed my arm. "I did too, being with you made the twilight with the Alexander's all-that more enjoyable," I said with a smile as I rubbed Topanga's shoulder. Topanga grabbed me by my tie and pulled me closer to her and kissed me hard and long.

When we were finished with the kiss, Topanga looked into my eyes and said, "I would go anywhere with you all you have to do is ask. "Many thanks and many thanks for your company this twilight," I said as I disconnected my seat belt and winked. "Pleasant twilight my dear, I bid you farewell. "All right until the morrow, have a grand twilight. "Have a safe drive to your abode and again have a grand twilight," I replied as I exited the vehicle.

The entry-flap automatically closed then Topanga honked as she backed onto the boulevard and drove off; I waved then went to sign back in. "Did you have an enjoyable twilight, sir?" The MP asked as he gave me the clipboard and I signed myself back in. "With an exquisite citizen such as Topanga how can I not have a grand twilight," I said as I handed back the clipboard and went in the direction of my barracks. "Take care," I said before I was out of ear shot. "You as well," the MP replied chuckling to himself.

When I arrived at my barracks, there was a note taped to the entry-way, it was from Sr. Com. Bancais. "I came by to inform you that your aircraft is still being worked on but as mentioned it will be finished with later, drop by my office in the morn to collect your keycard," Signed Sr. Com. Bancais.

I removed the note and had my retina scanned. "Maj. Jeroque Teldat," I stated then the entry-way slid open and I entered my quarters, "Illumination on!" I commanded as I took off my jacket and beret then got me a glass of water. Grabbed my jotter and jotted the happenings of my visit with the Alexander's then got ready and went to retire.

*****

In the wee epocks of the early morn I had a different twilightmare. I was back in the tritton 2115 and when I went to my abode to see Tsarina, Topanga was with me. I was telling Tsarina about my whole time traveling experience. "When I went back in time I had met and fell in love with Topanga; Topanga is the citizen I want to be joined in matrimony and spend the rest of my existence with. Although you are exquisite and half-Humanarian, I want a mate that was all Humanarian and we could have offspring that were pure Humanarian."

As soon as I mentioned that to her, I immediately awoke covered in sweat. I knew that vision wasn't possible because if I did manage to change times elapsed, Tsarina wouldn't be there because she was half Protrerian and all signs of Protrerian life would be erased from ZarCedra's times yet to come. And how was it was I able to get back to the tritton 2115?

'What was the meaning, if any, for this twilightmare?' I wondered as I lay in my retiring unit. 'Topanga is a sweet and very exquisite young female citizen but if I was ever to somehow make it back to my time, she probably wouldn't want to leave this time with me. But what was it she said this twilight, oh yeah, she'd go anywhere with me all I had to do was ask. I wonder, I'd never leave Tsarina unless I had no choice but I'll cross that bridge if ever the situation arose,' I thought further as I looked at my timepiece.

"Timepiece illumination on," I said and seen that it was 01:44 epocks. "Ohh, I got to get more slumber," I mumbled then said, "timepiece illumination off" and closed my eyes.

P.A.R 5

Considering this p.a.r wasn't a labor p.a.r there wasn't much of a line when I arrived at the mess hall. I grabbed a tray and received my banquet; I walked to the end of the line, got a caffinated brew and grabbed utensils. I walked to an empty table, put my tray down, removed my beret, sat and started consuming my banquet.

After I finished eating, I slowly drank my morn brew. 'I suppose it's about time to go see the Sr. Com. Bancais to get my electronic keycard.' I finished my brew, got up and put my jacket and beret on then disposed of my tray and walked out of the mess hall.

As I walked to main headquarters, I gave and returned salutes from passing officers, when I arrived at the main headquarters structure I entered. A few mites later I arrived at Sr. Com. Bancais office; there was a different person at Corp. Gervais desk.

"Grand morn, I am Maj. Teldat and I'm to see Sr. Com. Bancais," I told the Lance Corporal. "Grand morn, I'm Lance Corporal Acernan grand to meet you," he said with a salute. "Just a moment and I'll inform the Sr. Commodore you request to see him." He pressed a button on his intercom and buzzed the Sr. Commodore.

"What is it Lance Corporal. "Sir, there is a Maj. Teldat here requesting to see you. "By all means LC Acernan allow him to enter. "You may enter, Major."

"Many thanks," I replied as I walked to the CO's entry-way, removed my beret and knocked. "Enter." I entered, saluted and closed the entry-way then stood at attention. "Grand morn, sir."

"Grand morn, at ease Major; I see you got my parchment," the Sr. Commodore said as he returned my salute. "Affirmative sir!" Sr. Com. Bancais reached into his breast pocket and tossed me my electronic keycard. "I stopped by your barracks last twilight but you weren't back yet."

"Also, I wanted to inform you that there is an officer from military intelligence by the name of Capt. Johnlen Pane who somehow found out you are from the times yet to come and wants to interview you. What time would you like to talk to him? "At my earliest convenience when I have nothing on my agenda. As soon as I return this p.a.r, I'll be more than willing to meet him then. "Affirmative Major!"

"Do you have a destination set? "Negative, probably Skittar or Dimoor, I haven't decided yet but somewhere in Kifrae. I want to show my lady consociate my craft if that is alright with you Senior Commodore."

"Affirmative, I shouldn't permit you to go, that doesn't sound like a grand idea but you have been through a lot, so go but don't be too long and use the Liquid Napricyte[2] SDC sparingly. If your prediction for the coming p.a.r's comes true, you'll need it. At least until we are successful in duplicating the formula and stay away from any and all electrical storms! That's a direct order! "Affirmative sir, don't fear I will."

"Also don't be concerned about me allowing Topanga to see too much of my craft, all I plan to show her is the speed of my craft, nothing more. "That was going to be my next statement but you answered it before I was able to say it. "If that is all sir, I'll take my leave now? "As you wish. "If I'm needed for any reason, I'll be up in my craft. "Considering this p.a.r isn't a labor p.a.r, you won't be needed for any specific reason until later when you see Capt. Pane." Sr. Com. Bancais said with a smile. "Affirmative sir," I replied as I deposited my electronic keycard in my pocket and saluted Sr. Com. Bancais, I turned and vacated his office.

A few mites later I walked out of main headquarters and went down the boulevard going toward hangar three. When I arrived I entered then went to my craft.

"Grand p.a.r gentlefolk," I said greeting the two junior officers that were in the vicinity of my craft. "Grand p.a.r sir. "Would you citizens open the hangar entry-ways when I am ready to depart?" I asked as I walked by them. "Affirmative sir," they responded with a salute. I returned the salute then continued to my Supersonic Dragon.

I pressed the left wing of my com-link. "'PAT', open and lower the main hatch platform. "Affirmative," she responded, as it opened and started to lower.

When it was on the floor I stepped on and rose to the cockpit. "A warm welcome and grand p.a.r Major. "Grand p.a.r 'PAT'," I answered as I put on my flight suit, went and inserted my electronic keycard in the designated port. As it activated I went to sit in the pilot's seat.

"'PAT, how are you and is the craft in working order?" I asked as I removed my beret then put the 'HUD' helmet on. "I am grand, many thanks for inquiring. Affirmative, the E-Tech team was very gentle with the inner working of the craft and everything they dismantled, they immediately reassembled; the craft is in working order.

"Grand," I said as I buckled my safety belts then pressed the ignition touch pad. As I did my hand brushed up against a leaver and a side panel compartment opened to reveal the craft's electronic instruction manual? I picked it up and activated it then accessed the table of contents and read the correct terminology of the components of the aircraft.

I accessed page after page learning new things about my craft, I read further and found out that the golden modules protruding from the craft had a mixture of three different metals, 30% goldane, 30% silvertrivane and 40% iron-cylium.

"So that is why the charge electromagnetically circled the craft. I better inform Dr. Alexander about that." I then read that if the white colored finger touch pad on the helmet was activated, the face shield would rise and an eyepiece-targeting scanner would protrude from the helmet. "Neat." I read further and discovered if I had to I could manually press the aquamarine colored touch pad on my starboard instrument panel, the golden modules and rod would extend or retract from the frame of my craft. Otherwise, the Omagon 2115 Star Drive Engine would do it automatically when I activated or deactivated that piece of technology. I read further to discover my craft has Multi-Wave Sensors which is an advanced computational sensing system that transmits carrier signals through star drive fields allowing high signal resolution at greater distances.

I turned the electronic manual off then put it back in the compartment and planned to read the rest of the manual at a later time.

I taxied the craft out the hangar entry-way and as I did I blew the air hooter a couple times to show my appreciation to the two young recruits. I pressed the finger touch pad at the side of my helmet, which activated two-way communications as I taxied further into the open and extended the wings. "Tower this is Maj. Teldat, am I cleared for lift off? "Affirmative Major. "Many thanks," I said as I accelerated the engines a bit as the wings lowered further and the craft started to rise.

I hovered up to 1375 metrics; I leveled the wings and raised the landing gear. I turned 45° west then increased air speed a few secs until I entered the test range then lowered altitude. 'In the tritton 2115 this test range is no longer used regularly and there was another target area built in another location to take its place,' I thought to myself.

I maneuvered my huge craft through the target area; I pressed the white finger touch pad on my 'HUD' helmet. The face shield rose and an electronic eyepiece-targeting scanner protruded from the side of the helmet. "'PAT' activate weapons. "Weapons activated you may commence," 'PAT' said.

I lowered altitude even more and fired my lasers as well as the Protonic EMC-Missals and Neutronic EMC-Torpedo's at hidden targets for the next few mites destroying each target as soon as it appeared. "PAT', lower the XTR-9000 Plasma Pulse Cannons," as she did I looked at the port and starboard monitors. As soon as targets presented themselves I pressed the cannons firing finger touch pads and blew them away. I did this for the next few mites destroying all targets that came into view as I maneuvered my massive craft through the target range.

"There are no more targets remaining Major, you have destroyed each target expertly," 'PAT' reported. I repressed the white button on my 'HUD' helmet and the eyepiece disappeared and the face shield lowered as I had the cannons rise back into the wings.

"'PAT' what is the current time," I asked and it appeared on the lower portion of my face shield, 09:45 epocks it flashed. I lowered the wings, maneuvering the aircraft up to 3,000 metrics, as I raised my face shield and looked at my radar then lowered it again as I straightened the wings and accelerated to Mach ten.

"'PAT', how long it would take until I reach the West Coast of Tanglar at Star Drive one? "Six mites," she immediately replied. I engaged the Star Drive Engine and the golden modules and rod extended from the frame as the ionic energy encompassed my craft. As soon as the swirling wormhole appeared in front of my craft, I flew into it advancing speed and flew at Star Drive one for six mites as breathable oxygen flooded the cockpit.

I kept an eye on the countdown timer on the inside of my visor, and after that time I exited Star Drive speed and the swirling wormhole, finding out I was indeed at the West Coast of the regime of Brilains Sonba. I engaged Stealth mode once again and the craft vanished as I decelerated to Mach one. A few secs later I decreased speed even further and cruised at 100 kps.

I traveled a couple hundred kiloms up the coast. "The scenery is just spectacular in this part of the country, isn't it 'PAT'? "Affirmative Major it is. "The snowcapped mountains are breathtaking," I said as I circled around and slowly flew back to my point of origin.

I raised my visor and checked my radar as I accelerated to Mach ten; I disengaged Stealth mode, my craft reappeared then once again I activated my Omagon 2115 Star Drive Engine as I lowered my visor. Secs later the stream of ions formed the swirling wormhole and I guided my craft into it. I went to Star Drive one and flew east, in the direction of Tanglar's Head Military Facility in Cangla City.

Six mites later, I exited the swirling wormhole then decreased airspeed as I had the golden modules and rod retracted into the frame of my craft. As soon as I reached the outskirts of Cangla City, I flew the rest of the way at 50 kps then I lowered my craft's landing gear. As I arrived at the Grinshaw Military Facility I stopped forward motion and hovered in the air as I contacted the tower.

"Tower, this is Maj. Teldat, am I cleared to set down? "Affirmative Major you are. "Many thanks," I said as I looked around before I raised the wings, the landing gear lowered as my craft descended to the tarmac below.

"Affirmative, it looks like the scientists and their E-tech team assembled everything they dismantled correctly," I told 'PAT'. "Affirmative Major, did I not say that they had? "You did but I had to find out for myself."

I switched everything off and while my craft wound down, I removed the helmet and disconnected my safety belts. "The mountains, valleys and sea were spectacular, truly something to witness, wasn't it 'PAT'?" I asked as I contracted the port wing, slid it back then put my beret on. "You are correct but since you did not land Major, I could only see the landscape and sea from the air and from that view I have to agree with you, it was indeed spectacular," 'PAT' said as I ejected the keycard and popped the main hatch open. I waited as the main hatch lowered to form the platform.

"'PAT', I will return shortly with a guest. Raise and secure the main hatch platform as soon as I am on the tarmac. "Affirmative Major." I stepped onto the main hatch platform and lowered.

I returned to my barracks, went to the retina scanner and let myself into my quarters. I turned on my Intervision monitor to listen to the melodic composition channel, I removed my jacket and beret then went to freshen up. A few mites later I heard the entry-way chime. "Enter," I said as I left the latrine.

As soon as the computerized entry-way verified my voice, the entry-way slid open. "Greetings sir," I said as Sr. Com. Bancais entered. "I have the results of your pass through the target range, very impressive. "Many thanks sir, but you didn't have to bring the results to me personally; 'PAT' recorded my score as I flew through."

"She did? Oh well, here is a hardcopy of your results. Anyhow that isn't the only reason I came here; Capt. Pane from military intelligence contacted me and said he would be here at 15 hundred epocks. "Affirmative, I will be back by then but why didn't ," I said as I fastened the buttons on my shirt.

"When are you going to meet your lady consociate?" I looked at my timepiece and seen it was 10 hundred 45 epocks. "In about fifteen mites, Topanga will meet me at the front gate," I told the Sr. Commodore as I put my tie back on. When I finished I zipped my flight suit; put on my jacket and finally put on my beret.

"I will let the Captain know he would get his interview at that time. "Affirmative many thanks," I answered as I went to turn the Intervision monitor off. When I returned to the Commodore, he and I went towards the front entry-way as it slid open then slid closed and locked behind us and we departed.

Outside, Sr. Com. Bancais and I went to his armored utility vehicle and he got in. "Would you care for a ride to the gateabode Major? He asked as he started his armored utility vehicle. "Affirmative, many thanks sir," I said as I got in. "If anyone asks, you left the military grounds without my knowledge, and I have no knowledge of where you went, just make sure you are back before 15 hundred epocks," Sr. Com. Bancais said as he drove towards the gateabode. "Affirmative, many thanks sir."

When we arrived, the Sr. Commodore dropped me off and I went to talk to the MP. A few mites later I saw Topanga's auto pull up along the walkway. "I will be back momentarily," I told the MP as I walked over to her auto.

When Topanga exited I immediately embraced her and kissed her luscious lips. "How are you this p.a.r huni buni?" She asked with an incredible smile. "Better now that I am in your company," I stated as I returned her smile. "Oh how sweet, I feel better when I am in your company as well," Topanga said as I took the eat al fresco hamper from the back seat of her automobile. Topanga used her remote to lock the entry-flaps and armed her alarm. We walked to the gateabode and Topanga signed in.

We started walking towards my craft and as we neared it, Topanga was surprised at its size and appearance. "What a magnificent piece of technology. "You like, just wait until you feel the rush as we take flight.

"Can't wait," she replied as she reached over and squeezed my hand. At the craft I tapped the left wing of my com-link. "'PAT' open and lower the main hatch platform. Watch this my dear. "Watch what? "This," I said as the main hatch opened and lowered to form a platform then lowered to the tarmac.

I took Topanga's hand as we stepped on the main hatch platform. "Stand very still a few secs and the main hatch platform will start to rise." When we got to the cockpit Topanga took a quick look around in astonishment. "The interior looks absolutely amazing!"

"I'd like to introduce you to 'PAT', my craft's cybernetic super computer. 'PAT' this is Topanga; Topanga say greetings to 'PAT'," I said as I went and inserted the electronic keycard and the touch pads and monitors on and around the instrument panels illuminated.

"Greetings PAT. "Greetings Topanga. "The name 'PAT' is an anagram meaning Prototype Advancements in Technology," I said as I raised and closed the main hatch then I secured the eat al fresco hamper.

"Take a seat Topanga and make sure you buckle yourself in." I went to the back closet and took out my spare helmet and handed it to Topanga. "Here, put this on, the flight will get pretty rough. "Many thanks," she said as she accepted it and put it on as I removed my beret. 'PAT', don't you need a helmet?" Topanga asked. "Negative, a helmet is not necessary," she said as she went to her seat.

I went to the pilot's seat, sat then connected my safety belts, put on my 'HUD' helmet and activated the ignition. "Are you ready my dear? "Ready," she said as she finished connecting her helmet and smiled.

I pressed the finger touch pad that activated two-way communications. "Tower, this is Maj. Teldat am I cleared for liftoff. "Just a moment sir while a helijet lands near your position. "Affirmative," I answered as I pressed the ignition sequence, extracted the wing and my craft sprung to life.

"Where are we going? "Our destination is clandestine; I will inform you after we arrive." While I waited for permission to lift off, I lowered my face shield and quietly discussed the flight plan with 'PAT'. When we were through talking, I received permission for liftoff.

"Here we go Topanga," I said as I looked in her direction. I checked my radar then began to ascend straight up. "Absolutely amazing!" Topanga gasped as she looked out the window.

I halted our ascent at one thousand metrics; I leveled the wings and raised the landing gear. "If you enjoyed that, watch this," I said as I started advancing forward. I started out slow as we flew over the city and when we were a few kiloms past the suburbs I increased speed; Mach one all the way to Mach ten.

"Hang on my dear," I told Topanga as we rose higher, I raised my helmet's face shield and checked my radar for any obstruction. Seeing my predetermined flight path clear, I lowered the face shield then activated the Star Drive Engine. The golden modules and rod automatically protruded from the frame of the craft. The pale blue color of the Ionic energy electromagnetically encompassed the craft going to each golden module.

Almost immediately the Ionic energy shot out in front of the craft and formed a swirling wormhole. I directed the craft into it as the craft started shaking and turning this way and that, flying upside down then right side up as it went to Star Drive one then Star Drive two. "What's happening?" Topanga asked suddenly. "Don't worry my dear, it's just that we're traveling at a grand rate of speed and going into this wormhole is the only way to attain the speed I want," I explained calming Topanga in the process.

We flew through the wormhole for thirty-five secs. After that time I exited the wormhole and deactivated the Star Drive

Engine and slowed to Mach one. Just then I remembered reading the E-manual, I didn't have to press the aquamarine colored button to make the golden modules lower into the shell of the craft. If I just deactivate the Star Drive Engine they will lower automatically after a few secs. As I activated Stealth mode and the craft vanished from sight as the oxygen level returned to normal. "How did you like that my dear? "Wow, what a rush, the journey was grand!" she said grinning from ear to ear.

"You enjoyed that did you?" I asked as I flew over the lush green fields as Topanga looked out the window. "Absolutely I did, very much but where are we?" Topanga asked quite excitedly. I raised my face shield then looked at her. "Ready for this?" I asked Topanga with a grin across my face. "Indeed," she anxiously said.

"We are currently over Skittar. "You've got to be jesting right?" She asked in disbelief. "Negative, I'm telling you the honest truth; 'PAT', what is our current position? "We are on the coast of Skittar nearing the city of Corkel.

"I can't believe it, it felt like we were in the air for only a couple mites," Topanga said in disbelief. "We were, thanks to modern technology of when I come from. "Oh!" Topanga said. I decelerated then stopped and hovered over a small plantation.

I scanned the area then flew three hundred metrics beyond the plantation and halted forward motion; I raised the wings, the landing gear lowered as I slowly descended to the grassy field below.

"Going through that wormhole is the only way to fly at Star Drive speed within the ZarCedra's oxygenated resistant atmosphere and gravitational pull. Oxygenated resistant atmosphere means without weighted oxygen to slow my craft; therefore, I have tanks of compressed breathable oxygen that is slowly pumped automatically into the cockpit as I fly through the wormhole. "Understood," she said as the craft rested on the ground near a stand of saplings.

I switched everything off and while the craft wound down I contracted the port wing and it slid back out of the way of the main hatch platform. I removed the 'HUD' helmet; Topanga removed her own helmet then disconnected her safety belts and walked to me. I squeezed then kissed her as I released the safety belts I had on then got out of my seat. I opened the main hatch and lowered it to form the platform.

"'PAT', we will remain at this location awhile, feel free to join us or remain on the craft," I said as Topanga removed the eat al fresco hamper. "If there are negative objections I will join you and Topanga a few mites on the emerald isle then return to the aircraft and to my alcove." The three of us stepped on the main hatch platform as we lowered to the grass below. We looked around; Topanga held the basket with one hand and held my arm with the other.

"Welcome to Skittar huni buni," I said as I looked at her, winked and flashed a smile. Topanga squeezed my arm and kissed my lips and as we arrived at the ground, we stepped off. Topanga put the basket down and embraced me tightly.

"Out of the all the male citizens I have known in the times elapsed, you are the only citizen who has ever taken me anywhere foreign. Except my father when we vacated Oskesar, Mankuer," Topanga said as she picked up the basket again and we walked away.

"That's a shame," I said as Topanga, 'PAT' and I strolled further. "'PAT', raise then close the cockpits main hatch and keep the craft in Stealth mode for the duration of our stay on this Isle. "Affirmative Major."

"If you remain in Stealth mode, how will you know where you set down? Topanga asked as she looked back and couldn't locate the craft. "Well you see the tall grass where my craft rests; it's crushed where the wheels are, also, where the main hatch lowered to the ground. So even though my craft isn't visible, I know where it is. "Oh ok," Topanga said setting the basket down.

"I suggest a walk before our mid-p.a.r banquet," I said as I took her hand. "'PAT', you may remain here or go for a stroll yourself but I want time alone with Topanga. "Affirmative Major," she said then walked away.

I'm really glad we met, it's a shame you traveled back in times elapsed but just think, if you hadn't we would have never met and fall in love." Topanga told me as we walked through the meadow.

"You're correct but when I have done whatever I was brought back to do and my job here is complete, I will attempt anything I can to get back to my own time. "That is understood but in the meantime share yourself and be with me," Topanga said as she smiled and squeezed my hand then turned towards me and gave me a loving embrace. We both embraced each other firmer and kissed passionately. As we did I could feel the quiver in her body which told me it took a lot to say what she did and that made me give her a tighter squeeze.

"I do have strong quixotic feelings for you my dear Topanga, I would truly like for you to be that special lady in my life," I said as we continued to walk. "I do as well; definitely I do as well!" Topanga exclaimed and kissed my cheek as we strolled further along holding each other tightly.

"We should return for our banquet," Topanga said as we both turned around and walked hand in hand back to our al fresco mid-p.a.r banquet. When we got there, Topanga disconnected the comforter that was attached to the hamper. "Would you spread this out?" Topanga asked as she handed it to me. "Of coarse my sweet," I said as I smiled then winked at her.

After I did, Topanga came over to me and kissed me again then sat opening the hamper. She took out fried chicken, potato salad, creamed spinach and a small bottle of white wine. She also took out two wineglasses, a corkscrew, silverware and napkins. At that time 'PAT' returned. "You are welcomed to join us 'PAT', if you would like," Topanga said with a smile. "Many thanks but this is your time alone with Maj. Teldat, I will return to my alcove on the aircraft to regenerate. "Many thanks 'PAT', I said as she walked towards the craft. Topanga prepared two plates as I popped the cork of the tiny bottle then poured its two glasses.

"When did you have time to make this delicious mid-p.a.r banquet? "I got up early this morn and made it. "Many thanks," we both said as we handed each other our food and swill. As we did Topanga looked deep into my eyes and noticed the sparkle.

As we consumed our banquet and drank our wine we quietly conversed. We heard the animals of a nearby farmstead frolic in the background enjoying the mid-p.a.r sun. Topanga reached into the hamper and withdrew two cream puffs for dessert. "You are going to get me fat," I said with a smile as I accepted the treat. "Don't worry, I will still be yours if you do, besides I like a man with a little meat on his skeleton," Topanga said with a giggle.

For the next few mites we both enjoyed the treats, when we finished eating we wiped our faces clean. I assisted Topanga put the serving dishes back into the hamper then I lay down, put my arm behind my head as I pulled Topanga down on top of me and kissed her exquisite face.

As our lips locked I started rubbing Topanga's back, I wanted to rub farther down and rub her exquisite backside but I knew this wasn't the right time for that. So I rubbed back up her back then I started massaging her neck.

"Many thanks for the scrumptious banquet," I said when we finished kissing. "You're quite welcome kind sir," Topanga said as she fluttered her eyelashes. I couldn't resist I had to give her another kiss. When we were through, I squeezed Topanga one last time then she rolled off me and settled close by my side as we both closed our eyes....

*****

The next thing we knew 'PAT' awoke us via com-link. "Maj. Teldat come in? You have remained motionless for 62 mites; you must wake, it's starting to precipitate," 'PAT' said as we discovered the sun had disappeared behind big gray clouds and it started to drizzle. Topanga and I arose and gathered the hamper and comforter; hand in hand we darted for the craft.

"'PAT' had opened and lowered the main hatch platform so when we got to the platform, Topanga and I stepped on and as we neared the cockpit it started precipitating harder. By the time we reached the top, we were completely drenched as we entered. I closed the cockpit's main hatch as I shook the water from my body.

Meanwhile Topanga put the hamper away as she retrieved the comforter. "Come here Jeroque," and she used the comforter to dry us off. After I was fairly dry, I kissed Topanga then she dried herself completely then clasped the comforter to the hamper and went to sit and fasten her safety belt.

"Many thanks for waking us when you did 'PAT'. Did you enjoy yourself?" I asked Topanga as I looked at her and connected my own safety belts. "Yes, oh yes, more than you'll ever know! I enjoyed the landscape of the emerald isle, but I really enjoyed being with you. Your company was warm, delightful and charming. But the precipitation sort of dampened my spirit; although, being with you made it all worthwhile," Topanga said as she put on her helmet.

"Being with you my sweet Topanga enlightened my spirit as well," I said as I looked at her and winked. Topanga winked back and flashed me a big smile. I smiled back as I put on my 'HUD' helmet. "Are you ready for the flight back to Tanglar? "Ready," she said as she looked at me and smiled.

I started the engines then pulled slightly on the flight stick. My craft's wings leveled then lowered as we hovered up to 10,000 metrics. I leveled the wings as the landing gear rose as I lowered my face shield then thrust the flight stick forward; suddenly there came buzzing sound.

"Warning, the level of jet fuel in the starboard tank is at minimum capacity. "'PAT', what is the level of Liquid Napricyte[2] SDC remaining in the Star Drive Engine?" I asked as I switched to the alternate fuel tank. The level flashed on the lower portion of my face shield, I seen I had $5/_{16}$ of a vile. 'More than sufficient amount to return to Tanglar,' I thought as I advanced speed to Mach one then slowly advanced speed to Mach ten.

I activated the finger touch pad that raised my face shield and checked my radar and seen my route clear. "Hang on ladies," I said as I lowered my face shield. I exited Stealth mode as my craft again became visible. I engaged the Star Drive engine and the golden modules and rod protruded on the exterior of the craft. As soon as the swirling wormhole appeared, I flew into it and went to Star Drive one then Star Drive two and flew for thirty secs.

"'PAT', what is our current location?" I asked as I disengaged the Star Drive engine and exited the swirling wormhole. "We are over the Cushnor Regime."

I flew the rest of the way to Cangla City, in the honorary regime of Placaden at Mach four, so we all could enjoy the scenery. Shortly thereafter I flew over Cangla City and reduced airspeed to twenty knots per mite, and then halted forward motion as we hovered over the Grinshaw Military Facility.

I lowered the landing gear then raised the wings as I activated two-way communications. "Tower, this is Maj. Teldat requesting permission to set down? "Affirmative Major, you are cleared to land on Helijet landing pads 4, 5 and 6. "Affirmative," I said as I slowly descended to the landing areas below.

As the engines were turned off and winding down, I contracted the port wing then it slid out of the way of the main hatch. I removed my 'HUD' helmet as Topanga removed her own helmet, then we disconnected our safety belts. I went and retrieved my keycard then released the cockpit's main hatch. I assisted Topanga gather the hamper and comforter then we both exited the craft. We stood on the platform and descended to the tarmac below.

"I had a wonderful time and we should go up again," Topanga said as she set the hamper down and gave me a tight squeeze. "I'm sure we will my dearest," I said as I put on my beret and pair of avionics sunglasses as we started walking.

As we were nearing the front gate abode, Sr. Com. Bancais drove up to us and stopped, and I saluted. "Maj. Teldat, Capt. Pane is now here and requests his interview with you ASAP. "Affirmative, inform the Captain I will see him directly. "I'll inform him," the Sr. Commodore said then looked in Topanga's direction.

"I take it this is the exquisite young citizen you were waiting for earlier. "Affirmative sir, she is," I said with a smile. "Sr. Com. Bancais this is Topanga; Topanga greet my Commanding Officer, Sr. Com. Bancais. "Very pleasant to greet you," they both said as they shook hands.

"Did you enjoy the time you and Maj. Teldat spent together? "Yes I did, very much and you'll never guess where he took me? "Where, he told me he wasn't sure where he was going? "We went to a field behind a farmstead and plantation outside Corkel, Skittar," Topanga said with an exquisite smile. "Did he, that's grand; unfortunately I have business to take care of so I must take my leave, it was grand to greet you my dear and I hope you have a grand p.a.r. Don't be too long Major, I'll expect you directly," Sr. Com. Bancais said as he smiled, turned then drove off.

"What were you and Sr. Com. Bancais talking about?" Topanga asked as I walked her to the gate abode. "There is an officer from military intelligence who discovered I am here from a time yet to come and he wants to interview me," I said as Topanga signed out. "Many thanks," Topanga said to the MP then turned her attention back to me.

"What are you going to tell him? "I'm not sure, in all probability whatever he asks but as little as I can, at least for the present time," I said as I embraced her. "When are we going to get together again?" Topanga asked as she kissed my cheek. "I'm hoping later this eve or in the morrow morn, I will call you later after my twilight banquet, to inform you when and also to let you know how my interview went," I said as I walked her to her auto then kissed her lips. "Ok," she said when we were through then she used her remote to disarm the alarm and unlocked her auto as I put the hamper and comforter on the rear seat.

"Again I'd like to tell you that I had a grand and wonderful mid-p.a.r banquet date and I really enjoyed being a passenger in your aircraft;" she said as she turned towards me. "I'm glad you enjoyed our time together," I responded as I squeezed

Topanga, kissed her hand then she went and got into her auto.

She fastened her safety belt as her entry-flap lowered then she activated the ignition of the vehicle as she lowered her window and blew me a kiss. "Grand adioso, my huni buni," Topanga said as she pulled onto the boulevard. "Adioso huni buni," I said waving as she drove away then I turned and walked back on the base.

'Time to get this interview over with,' I thought as I walked towards main headquarters and Sr. Com. Bancais office.

A few mites later I entered main headquarters, took off my sunglasses then proceeded down the hall to Sr. Com. Bancais' secretarial assistant as I removed my beret.

"Grand mid-p.a.r," I greeted LC Acernan as I arrived. "Grand mid-p.a.r Major, you may enter, the Commodore is expecting you," the Lance Corporal said with a smile. "Many thanks Lance Corporal," I replied as I went to the partially opened entry-way, knocked then entered.

As I seen Sr. Com. Bancais, I saluted the senior officer then returned the salute from the Captain. "Welcome Maj. Teldat this is Capt. J. Pane," Sr. Com. Bancais said as I shook the Captain's hand. "I explained everything I knew to Capt. Pane but I didn't go into much detail I was awaiting your arrival so you can extrapolate everything pertaining to your ordeal," Sr. Com. Bancais told me. "Affirmative, would we be allowed to have the interview in your office or would you prefer if we went elsewhere?"

"My office will be fine, I have duties to perform out of the office, so I will take my leave and you two gentlefolk can get down to business," the Commodore said as he left. Capt. Pane took a voice recording device out of his briefcase. "Major, are you ready to commence? "As ready as I will ever be," I said as Capt. Pane pushed the record button on his primitive recording device.

"This is Capt. J. Pane and I am here this p.a.r with an Officer who claims to be from a time yet to come, follow me as I try to get to the bottom of his tale.

"For my first question Major, what is your full name?"

"Jeroque Teldat."

"What is your rank and serial digits?"

"Rank, Major First Class; Serial Digits, 697A39G."

"What tritton do you allegedly come from?"

"I come from the tritton 2115."

"Very interesting," the Captain said as he was also jotting in his jotter.

"What do you think the reason is, if any, why you were transported precisely one hundred trittons in the times elapsed?"

"Unknown," I told the investigator.

"Ok allow me to rephrase the question; was your trip through time meant to be or was it accidental that you found yourself in this time?" Capt. Pane asked as he shifted his seating position.

"It was purely by accident, in the time I am from ZarCedra had been taken over by an alien race known as the Protrerian High Command; they have controlling power over all ZarCedra, especially the military. But Humanarian scientists in the Secret Humanarian ZarCedra Alliance secretly constructed the craft I now have in my possession, which is the prototype Supersonic Dragon 228-D Spy Jet Stealth.

"Hold on a mite, the Planet is taken over by an alien race?" Capt. Pane asked with grand concern.

"That is correct but let me go on and I'll explain."

"To continue, I was on a top-secret mission up north, over Vertgren Isle when I found myself flying through an electrical storm. I was in the process of activating my Star Drive engine when a bolt of lightning struck my craft just as I was entering the swirling Humanarian-made wormhole. What I suspect happened, was the bolt of lightning's enormous amount of electricity reacted with the chemical solution my Omagon 2115 Star Drive engine uses for fuel. This chemical solution is called Liquid Napricyte[2] Star Drive Compound and that combination somehow caused a tear in the time gamut. That is the reason I believe I found my craft and myself in this time period."

"About the aliens, on 07.01.2015 at 11 hundred epocks precisely, our Planet will be attacked by a brutal alien race known as the Protrerian High Command. Even with the assistance of their archenemy the Antrerian Race and their Armada, we lose this war and for the next centritton we are under their reign. The reason I honestly think, why, I was brought back to this precise time, and that is to change times elapsed in our favor with my prototype Spy Jet craft."

"Let me get this straight, an alien race known as the Protrerian High Command attacks ZarCedra but in our favor we receive assistance from their enemies; another alien race known as the Antrerian Race's Armada. But even with their assistance we lose, so are they enslaved also?"

"Negative, they are able to escape captivity."

"So the Humanarian race is the only citizens who are enslaved?"

"Correct, and for the next seventy trittons the Humanarian race were looked down upon and treated like Humanarian waste. Shortly after that time the Humanarian's and Protrerian races started joining in matrimony and mating. After then and for the next thirty trittons we became almost acceptable in their society."

"Do all political heads of ZarCedra know of the impending war?" The Captain asked suddenly.

"Affirmative, they were all contacted and apprised of the situation; we'll find out more when we hear from of every country of ZarCedra, there is still a digit of countries we are waiting on."

"If we are able to survive and somehow become the victors in this war, how do you plan to return to your own time?"

"That too is unknown, then again if I can at all. If I am unable to, there must be a grand reason that at this time I just can't see."

"Uh hmm, why do you think your aircraft is referred to as a prototype?"

"Because, my craft has superior weaponry such as Sareden Quantum Laser Cannon, Neutronic EMC-Torpedo's, Protonic

EMC-Missals and double XTR-9000 Plasma Pulse Cannons. Also, my craft's Comodrone Electronics P-52 Hydrogenic Generator inverts illumination in such a way that causes my entire craft to become invisible to the naked eye as well as undetectable by radar, which is the reason it is also referred to as a spy jet.

It is also able to fly at great speeds to a maximum airspeed of Star Drive Two or equivalent to Mach 200. Furthermore it is hover capable, cutting out the need of a runway for lift offs or setting down."

"Principally that speed is incredible, how may I ask, does your aircraft accelerate to that speed?"

"I have an additional engine equipped on my craft called the Omagon 2115 Star Drive Engine, this engine with the assistance of another device; called the Electronic Flux Inducer creates the power to accelerate my craft up to its maximum speed."

"My next question is how precisely does your weapons ammunition self-reproduce?"

"All my craft's weapons ammunition is essentially made up of electronic energy, therefore my craft is also equipped with a Comodrone Electronics P-52 Hydrogenic Generator, which supplies my craft with all needed energy for its awesome defenses and everything else on my craft that requires electrical energy.

Also, it is connected to the Electronic Flux Inducer and shares the Liquid Napricyte[2]; which gives my weapons the explosive power to cause mighty destruction. "

"Affirmative. My final question at this time is can I see this so called Supersonic Dragon 228-D Spy Jet Stealth?

"You can under one condition that you must adhere to.

"What may that be?" The Captain inquired.

"You can see my craft but I won't allow any photographs."

Capt. Pane took a few secs to ponder this request. "I agree," he said at long last.

"Then let's get going."

Capt. Pane turned off his recording device then we both went towards the office entry-way. As we neared it, the entry-way opened and in walked Sr. Com. Bancais.

"Is the interview over with already", he asked as he chewed on the butt of an unlit cigar? "Negative sir, we are going outside to view my craft. Would you like to accompany us? "Affirmative, if you both have no objections? "Negative objections," we both said then the three of us went out to my craft.

"Sr. Com. Bancais is it safe to show Capt. Pane everything in my craft at this time?" I quietly asked the Sr. Commodore as we got outside "I believe it is safe as long as you don't allow any photographs be taken. Besides after 07.01 everyone will know of your presence here; affirmative I think it is all right, as long as you are agreeing to let this citizen take a gander," he whispered back. "Affirmative sir."

As we neared the huge craft, Capt. Pane's eyes opened wide. "Your aircraft is a lot bigger than the Stealth 228 fighters we have now and the sleekness is grand," he said in an awe struck voice. "Am I allowed to at least jot notes?" I looked at him and seen the anticipation in his eyes and it wasn't in my nature to disappoint when I didn't need to. "Affirmative you can. "All right!" Capt. Pane excitedly exclaimed as he took out his jotter.

"This magnificent craft is the craft in the time yet to come designing of avionics, I present to you the Supersonic Dragon 228-D Spy Jet Stealth," I said proudly as we walked closer to it. Capt. Pane immediately started jotting notes as I pressed the left wing of my com-link. "'PAT', lower the main hatch platform."

As it was lowering, I called Capt. Pane's attention to the Sareden Quantum Laser Cannon atop my craft.

"That turret is where I fire the lasers. It circles 360° and the Comodrone Electronics P-52 Hydrogenic Generator powers it, and it is ready to fire at all times.

Down here behind this metallic sliding plate is where I fire my Protonic Electromagnetic Cluster Missals and my Neutronic Electromagnetic Cluster Torpedo's. My weapons array can hold a maximum of fifteen Protonic EMC-Missals and ten EMC-Torpedo's at one time after they are expelled the generator requires time to create the energy to make its next compliment of missiles and torpedo's."

"What precisely are Protonic Electromagnetic Cluster Missals and Neutronic Electromagnetic Cluster Torpedo's," Capt. Pane asked as he jotted. "I will explain them in detail a little later." After saying that the three of us stepped onto the main hatch platform and went up to the cockpit.

"Greetings Maj. Teldat and guests. "Greetings 'PAT', you know Sr. Com. Bancais and this other officer is from military intelligence, his name is Capt. Pane," I said making the introduction as I inserted the electronic keycard. "Greetings Capt. Pane," she said. "Greetings; who are you?" Capt. Pane asked looking at her.

"I am called 'PAT', I am the cybernetic version of this craft's super computer; the letters 'P.A.T' in my designation is an anagram, which stands for Prototype Advancements in Technology. "Greetings, 'PAT'," Capt. Pane said again. "Greetings Captain. Then the Captain proceeded to ask her a series of questions.

"That will be all for now 'PAT'," I said after they concluded. "Affirmative Major," she said then went to her alcove and sat. At that time, I showed him the series of monitors, switches and touch pads that were on the forward, port and starboard instrument panels as I slowly explained the significance of each.

"Here Capt. Pane, put this on," I said as I handed him the 'HUD' helmet. "Affirmative," he said as he removed his beret then put it on. "This is my Heads Up Display helmet and it is an integral asset to flying my craft. "What does this do," he asked as he pressed one of the many finger touch pads on the helmet and the visor lowered. "'PAT', in turn produce maps of the area, the fuel levels, oil, water and the artillery levels."

"Absolutely amazing," Capt. Pane said as everything one by one illuminated inside the visor of the 'HUD' helmet. I then repressed the finger touch pad that raised the visor. "One of the many things I like about this craft is, look around the instrument panels you will not see a two-way radio," I said as Capt. Pane looked around.

"You are correct sir. But how... "I press the finger touch pad here, which activates two-way communications and I can talk to anyone I request. When someone is in contact with me my two-way communication activates automatically."

After everything was shown in the cockpit, I explained Spy Jet Stealth mode in greater detail. "My craft has the usual Stealth capabilities with the addition of an invisibility factor. Where my generator inverts illumination in such a way that my entire aircraft becomes invisible. "That is so cool, Capt. Pane said as he continued to jot in his jotter. "Time to go out and view the engines."

"Adioso 'PAT'," I said as I withdrew my electronic keycard. "Adioso Major and guests. Capt. Pane took a few more notes then the three of us left the cockpit and lowered to the tarmac. At that time, two airmen were walking by. "Airmen, go retrieve an automatic mechanical lift?" Sr. Com. Bancais ordered. "Affirmative sir," they both said and quickly went to retrieve the lift.

As we waited, I tapped my com-link. "'PAT', raise the tail portion of the craft. "Affirmative Major," she answered and the cover of the tail section started to rise then slid back.

A few mites later the two junior officers returned in an armored utility vehicle towing the AML. "Where would you like it sir?" The Corporal on the passenger side asked. "Take it to the rear of the craft and lock it in place, so I can show the engines to the Sr. Commodore and the Captain," I said then they immediately drove to the rear of the aircraft to do what was asked.

"Many thanks, you are both dismissed," Sr. Com. Bancais said after the AML was locked into place. The three of us stepped on then rose to the rear of the craft, and as we stepped onto the metal mesh walkway that surrounded the engine galley, we went over to then climbed down the polished metal ladder that led to the engines. When Capt. Pane was down I started explaining all he saw.

"Here we have the two huge main Comodrone Electronics F405-F1D3 afterburning engines. They propel my craft from 0 knots per sec all the way up to the top airspeed of Mach ten; I am using these engines most of the time."

"Over here we have the infamous Omagon 2115 Star Drive engine, as you can see it is separate from the main engines but when engaged they do work in conjunction with each other. "What is your meaning?" The Captain asked as he looked up from his jotter.

"When I reach my top airspeed of Mach ten, I have a touch pad on my port instrument panel I can press which allows me to advance from Mach ten to Star Drive one then if I press it a second time I go to Star Drive two. "What speed would that be? The Captain asked. "Star Drive one would be ten * faster than Mach ten and Star Drive two would be twenty * faster. "Wow that is some speed for a craft of this size, Capt. Pane said as he lifted his beret and scratched his head.

"What type of fuel does it use or is it the same fuel as the two main engines? "Negative, although all three engines work in conjunction with each other, this engine operates on power supplied by my Comodrone Electronics P-52 Hydrogenic Generator and the aforementioned chemical solution Liquid Napricyte[2] SDC is needed to reach those speeds."

"Do you have a supply of this chemical solution or how can you get additional supplies because I haven't heard of that type of compound. "I have my own supply but I did allow Sr. Com. Bancais' two top scientists to take a sample. If I am unable to return to the tritton 2115, they have the specifications of my Star Drive Engine and a sample of the chemical solution it operates on so they will be able to mass-produce them," I stated.

"But first, the Comodrone Electronics P-52 Hydrogenic Generator sends an electrical charge to the Star Drive Engine which mixes with the Liquid Napricyte[2] SDC then that mixed current travels to the Electronic Flux Inducer which in turn converts that mixed electrical charge to an Ionic charge and sends this charge through this insulated electrical wire to the rear of the craft," I said as I pointed to the insulated cable.

When my Star Drive engine is activated, my craft's golden modules and rod are automatically activated and rise from the frame of the craft. "Then this ionic charge electromagnetically encompasses my craft going to each golden module to the golden rod on the nose of my craft. From there that charge is shot out in front of my craft creating a swirling Humanarian-made wormhole; I fly into this wormhole which allows my craft to travel Star Drive speed within ZarCedra's oxygenated resistant atmosphere and gravitational pull."

"Being oxygenated resistant means without oxygen, in order for me to breathe while I am in the wormhole I have tanks of compressed breathable oxygen, which is automatically pumped into the cockpit. Oh sir! I did find my craft's instruction e-manual and I discovered my craft's golden modules and rod are comprised of three separate metals melted together. These metals are 30% goldane, 30% silvertrivane and 40% iron-cylium, inform your scientists about this. "I will," he said as he took out a small jotter & ballpoint then jotted down the information.

"To carry on, back here we have the Comodrone Electronics P-52 Hydrogenic Generator, which supplies energy to Stealth mode, the EFI, the craft's shield, supplies the energy needed to create my ammunition and power everything else on my craft that requires electronical energy to function. Another thing, I assume the Planet's continents various Military Coalitions now exists? "You assume correct Major they do exist," Sr. Com. Bancais said. "Well in the time I come from, after the Protrerian High Command took over ZarCedra they combined all ZarCedra's military coalitions to form 'ZarCedra Forces.' But as my craft was built secretly and not known to the Protrerian High Command, we decided to keep the name N. Z. C. M. Co. But we added S. H. Z. C. A., which stands for Secret Humanarian ZarCedra Alliance."

"That's about enough questions for now, Maj. Teldat wrap things up," Sr. Com. Bancais said. Capt. Pane jotted a few more notes then we went back up the ladder, then to the AML and lowered to the tarmac.

"Will the time ever come when I would be able to take depictions of your aircraft? "I'm sure there will be a time but not at the moment, jot what you must but I do not want to see my craft in any news parchments at least for the present time. "Affirmative," the Captain responded.

I pressed the left wing of my com-link. "'PAT' you can now lower the tail portion of the craft. "Affirmative Major. "May I ask a few more questions?" Capt. Pane asked Sr. Com. Bancais. "You may, if you make them quick", Sr. Com. Bancais said.

"Major, can you tell me what you think of this time? "What I will say is, it is a lot different from my own time. "In what ways? "Well in my time, apart from alien domination, most of the vehicles are hover controlled and those that are not have metal wheels and shock absorbing alloys for suspension; another thing, there is a ban on all tobac products and also a ban on the clearing of any forests."

"Do you have any kin in the tritton 2115? "Negative, and I am not joined in matrimony, that is the main reason why I was specifically picked to test the Supersonic Dragon in the first place, that and my extensive knowledge of aero dynamics," I said with a smile. "I see," he said as he kept jotting in his jotter. "Before I end this line of questioning, I have something else to show you," I said to the Captain. " What may that be? "This," I said as I pressed my com-link and asked 'PAT' to extend the port wing, and lower the XTR-9000 Plasma Pulse Cannons.

Secs later the wing slid forward and extended as the Cannons lowered and locked into place, one from each wing. "These Cannons swivel 180° and my generator also creates its ammunition.

"That is so cool, I have one final question; what do you miss the most about your own time? "That is an easy question, the Grinshaw Military Facility with my fellow peers. "I see," Capt. Pane said as he jotted more then closed his jotter. "Many thanks, that is the extent of the questions I have for this p.a.r but as I earlier stated, I reserve the right to ask more questions in the times yet to come. "Affirmative anytime," I answered as we vacated the area.

"What if any, are your plans for the remainder of this twilight?" Sr. Com. Bancais asked me as we were leaving the area. I looked down at my timepiece and seen that it was 16 hundred 34 epocks. "At 17 hundred epocks I plan to have chow," I said with a smirk. "After my twilight banquet, Topanga asked me if I would like to visit her abode. I said I would either this twilight or in the morrow, if I go in the morrow, this twilight I might take a jog around this military facility, maybe do a little weightlifting to work off those calories, take a quick shower then retire for the twilight. "Sounds like you got your twilight all planned out," Sr. Com. Bancais said as he patted my back. "Sounds like I do, sir."

Just then Lance Corporal Acernan and another airman pulled up in an armored utility vehicle then exited. Sr. Com. Bancais returned their salutes. "Sir, I would like to introduce LC Chadnere Luxton."

"Lance Corporal Luxton reporting for duty sir!" The young man exclaimed as he stood at attention and saluted. "Welcome," Sr. Com. Bancais said as he looked at the young citizen and returned his salute. "I have just been transferred from the Corruther's Military Facility, North West of here in Togor, in the regime of Talgoria," LC Luxton reported.

"This is Maj. Teldat on my left and Capt. Pane on my right," Sr. Com. Bancais said as he gestured towards the Captain and I. "Greetings," we said as we returned the young citizen's salute. 'Wow, the famous Lance Corporal Chad Luxton, I can't believe I'm actually meeting him,' I thought as I shook his hand.

"Since you are new to this military facility; you are to pair up and share quarters with Maj. Teldat and he'll brief you on what we are currently working on. Major, it looks as if your plans for the rest of the mid-p.a.r and early twilight have changed." The Sr. Commodore said as he turned to face me. "It sure has sir! "All right Major; take him to your barracks and settle him in. "As you say sir," I said as we all started walking.

"I have to leave to start jotting my report about the Major and his impressive aircraft," Capt. Pane said. At that time we all saluted, turned and went our separate ways.

"How long have you been in the Royal Tanglar Military?" I asked the Lance Corporal as we were walking towards my barracks. "I have in almost two trittons and I expect to serve at least thirteen more before I even contemplated leaving the military. How long have you served in the military? "Six trittons," I said as we entered the Officer's Barracks.

"May I ask, how long are you in for? "I'm in for the duration; I will retire when I have at least twenty trittons in, not before," I said as we continued down the hall. "That means you joined the Military in 2009? "Something like that," I said as we got to my entrance. "Place your chin on the chin pad and activate the record button. "After you do that, state your rank and name and have your retina scanned then enter this code," I said as I whispered it into his ear. "Then you can enter our chamber whenever you like."

"This retina scanner is something new, we didn't have in the regime of Talgoria. "I know, I was informed it had just been installed and if it works to expectations here they will install them at all military facilities throughout Tanglar."

LC Luxton followed my instructions and as soon as he finished the entry-way slid open and we entered OC-1. "Illumination on," I said as the overhead illumination illuminated. "Grand quarters. "It's adequate; your slumbering quarters will be in that chamber," I said as I pointed to a partially opened entry-way at the end of the hall. "Come with me and I will instruct how to open your footlocker. "Affirmative, LC Luxton said as we entered his chamber.

"Illumination on. This type of footlocker was also just introduced. To operate the lid, place your thumb on the scanning pad and at the same time press the record button; state your rank and name." He did what I asked and the lid slid open. "Now only you will be able to open this footlocker, so whatever you store in it will be secure."

"It's almost chow time, unpack your duffel bag and I'll be out in the hall using the public conversing device, when you are through come get me and we'll go for our twilight banquet. "Affirmative."

"By the way my first name is Jeroque, when we are alone you may address me by that designation. "Affirmative, although my first name is Chadnere, you and all citizens could call me Chad."

I left his slumbering quarters then our quarters and walked to the end of the hall where I picked up the receiver of the PCD. I deposited a metallic quint gribbit and entered Topanga's digits. Three chirps later the PCD was answered by Topanga's sweet angelic voice.

"Greetings."

"Greetings huni buni, what are you up to?"

"Greetings Jeroque, oh nothing really, I just got out of the shower a few mites before you called."

"How did you enjoy our flight?" I asked with a smile.

"It was most enjoyable! How did your interview go?

"It went fairly grand; I answered an arsenal of questions then I gave Capt. Pane a tour of my craft."

"Did you give much information of the times yet to come?"

"I gave as much information as I was asked then we went to view my craft but I was very adamant about not allowing any depictions be taken at this time."

"Grand, not too many citizens will take his tale seriously without depictions, not at first anyhow."

Just then LC Luxton exited our quarters and sauntered down the hall.

"Almost ready for chow? "Just about." I said.

"Topanga my dear, I have to get going there is someone waiting for me but I hope to see you in the morrow?"

"Who is she and what does she mean to you?" Topanga asked quite suddenly.

"Her name is Chadnika, she is about 170 cm tall and weighs, I am guessing about 55 kgs, and is she pretty!" I said trying to hold back a laugh.

"Oh really, is she prettier than I?" She playfully pouted.

"It's too close to tell, but she has pretty golden hair like you but she has the cutest brown eyes," I said as I pinched Chad's cheek.

"He's not telling you the truth, I'm a male citizen," Chad said as he tried to get away from me.

"Oh you prankster!" Topanga said with a giggle.

"Affirmative huni buni, I'm jesting; Chad is a he and he is my new partner, I have to brief him about the things that are about to happen so I'll see you in the morrow."

"Oh not this twilight?"

"Unfortunately not huni buni, I'll call you in the morrow morn when I can get away."

"All right until then I hope you and your consociate have a grand twilight."

"You too huni and I'll tell Chad."

We both said, "have a grand twilight" then we hung up.

*****

"Who was that? "That was my special consociate Topanga," I said as we walked away from the PCD. "Listening to you, you two sound like extra special consociates," Chad said with a grin. "She is very close and she hopes we both have a grand twilight. "All right," Chad said with a chuckle as he playfully punched my arm. "I hope you told her to have a grand twilight as well? "Affirmative I did and now I'm starved, let's go for our susten, er, twilight banquet before it's all gone and I waste away," I told him with a wryly smile.

"Looking at the size of you, that won't happen anytime soon," Chad said with a grin. "On another note, I noticed your leather flight jacket," Chad told me as we were on our way out of the structure. "What is the meaning of the digits 2115?" Chad asked as we walked up the boulevard. "I will explain that to you during our twilight banquet. "Affirmative," LC Luxton replied as we continued on our way.

A few mites later we came to the line of citizens filtering into the mess hall. LC Luxton and I stood behind LC Acernan and his consociate. "Greetings citizens." I said as we walked up behind them. The two gentlefolk turned to see LC Luxton and I. "Greetings sir," LC Acernan said.

"LC Luxton, did you settle into Maj. Teldat's quarters all right?" LC Acernan asked. "Affirmative I have, Maj. Teldat and I make a grand team. "Who is your companion?" I asked as I looked at the young Sergeant. "This here is Sgt. Jasontri Pane; he has just been transferred here from the Fartree Military Facility in the regime of Sangree a few octopars ago," LC Acernan answered.

"That is correct and I also have a brother stationed at this military facility, in military intelligence. His name is Capt. Johnlen Pane, we might see him around during our banquet; he usually has his banquets with me when he has the time," Sgt. Pane said as the line of citizens moved a metric or so. "I know who he is, we met earlier this p.a.r; grand to meet you, I am Maj. Jeroque Teldat," I said as I stuck out my hand to shake with the Sergeants.

"And this young military citizen beside me is LC Luxton. "Grand to meet you," both citizens said. At that time the line started moving again and we all made our way into the mess hall. The four of us eventually received our grub, swills and eating utensils then made our way to a vacant table. We all sat and removed our berets then started consuming our twilight banquet.

"So are you going to tell me what the meaning is for those digits on your flight jacket?" LC Luxton asked as he looked over at me. I looked at him then at all the other faces of the air citizens sitting nearby.

"Might as well get this out in the open, everyone will learn about it on 07.01anyhow." I looked around and all eyes of the citizens in the vicinity were on me. I cleared my throat then started. "As some of you know who I am and for those of you that don't, my name is Major Jeroque Teldat and I am from Cangla City." Just then a female air citizen came and sat near me and I continued.

"To recap, my name is Maj. Jeroque Teldat and I am from Cangla City, but I am not from this time period; I am from the tritton 2115. I looked in the direction of LC Luxton. "That is what the digits on my jacket meant." Everyone looked at me in amazement as Capt. J. Pane sat next to his brother.

"You are not telling falsities are you?" Maj. Manet asked then took a swig of her swill. "Negative, I am not! "How is that possible?" She asked a bit puzzled. "I have in my possession a highly sophisticated aircraft, known as the prototype Supersonic Dragon 228-D Spy Jet Stealth."

"228-D, we just acquired the Nightingale 228-A Stealth aircraft a few trittons ago," Sgt. Pane argued. "That may be but scientific citizens in the times yet to come have made significant advancements in technology," I said in my defense.

"I have seen this aircraft, and as far as I have been able to surmise everything Maj. Teldat is telling you about the aircraft is indeed factual," Capt. Pane said as he stood and looked over the crowd of air citizens.

"Would we also be able to view your aircraft?" LC Acernan asked. "Not at this time, everyone will be able to see it in operation on 07.01," I said as I sat and took a bite of my bread roll. "But I do have something to show you. "What is that?" Sgt. Pane asked.

"This," I said as I took my military tags out from under my shirt. "The tags give my rank, name, serial digits, birth p.a.r and the tritton I had entered the military, 2109. I also have a tattoo of a patriotic eagle on my upper arm, and on my wrist is a visual and talking timepiece," I said as I produced it for all to view.

"We should all meet somewhere in the morrow for a briefing on upcoming crucial events that is about to commence in the near times yet to come. "How about here on the grounds or we can go to Casablanca's Bistro, they do have a fairly grand gathering chamber," LC Acernan stated. "That sounds like a grand plan, I will leave it up to you to make the necessary arrangements Lance Corporal. "Affirmative sir," LC Acernan answered.

"Since the morrow's date is 06.31 we'll try to meet at Casablanca Bistro in the mid-p.a.r about 14 hundred epocks for our briefing, and hopefully I can get Sr. Com. Bancais to join us. "Agreed," everyone said.

At that time, everyone at the table finished their banquet then replaced their berets, then put their trays away and vacated the mess hall. "Capt. Pane, what are your plans for the twilight?" I asked as I put my own beret on. "I have a report to finish, grand twilight," he said as he too got up and vacated the mess hall.

"Got any plans for the rest of the twilight? "Nothing in particular," I said as I looked at my timepiece and seen the time. "I didn't have any set plans and it is too late in the early twilight to be making new plans. Maybe I'll just stay on base and do some jogging or something. "Or we can go back to our quarters and you can explain how you got to this time," Chad said as we were walking. "You of all citizens have that right," I said as I returned salutes from lower ranking officers walking by.

A few mites later we entered our barracks, at our entrance I placed my chin on the chin rest and let the scanner scan my retina. "Maj. Jeroque Teldat," I stated then the entry-way to our quarters opened.

"Illumination on," I said as I sat on the lounger as Chad sat on the lounger. I took a deep breath and started. "Well from the beginning," I said as I exhaled.

"A few planetary axis revolutions ago, I was handed orders for a top-secret mission and at that time I was issued the newly constructed prototype Supersonic Dragon 228-D Spy Jet Stealth Craft. The contents of the orders I was given, was to check up on the alien race known as the Antrerian's Race who were settling on Vertgren Isle. We the Humanarian military citizens of N. Z. C. M. Co. /S. H. Z. C. A, secretly agreed to let the Antrerian Race settle here on this planet because of their assistance in the war between ZarCedra and the Protrerian High Command that is about to unfold. "Well where do the Antrerian's fit in?"

"I was just getting to that, but first let me explain who and where these two alien races come from. Antreria and Protreria are twin planets in the Currecuse Sector of the Dalnary galaxy neighboring our own solar system, for centrittons the military forces of these two planets have been mortal enemies. Now it was common knowledge that Protreria almost distinguished their planet's natural resources and their sun was slowly going nova. Then one p.a.r their long range sensors discovered ZarCedra and our way of harnessing solar energy."

"What, do you mean to tell me they attack us to get our energy supply? "That is partly correct but let me explain further and elaborate in more detail."

"First, the Protrerian High Command attack ZarCedra and a few planet revolutions later the Antrerian's discover what they are up to and they dispatch their military armada to assist in protecting ZarCedra. At that time, the Protrerian High Command decide instead of just taking schematics of ZarCedra's Energy Reactor Facilities and to just take over ZarCedra and adopt it as their own; because their sun only had a centritton or so of life left in it. After Trints of heavy resistance and with the added strength of the Antrerian's, we still end up losing the war. "Wow, unbelievable, that is a big chunk of information that is hard to swallow," Chad said.

"But wait; let me give you my scenario as to why I believe I was brought back in time to this precise time period!"

"I believe, because I have the prototype Supersonic Dragon 228-D Spy Jet Stealth Craft in my possession, I feel that somehow we were supposed to be victorious in this altercation. Because we were defeated, this is the God's way of giving the Humanarian Race a second chance. "Now everything is starting to look a bit clearer," Chad said.

"Everything I have told you is part speculation and part factual according to my times elapsed archive and I believe it is up to my craft and I to participate in this war and to prevent it from becoming reality, again."

"Was there, I mean will there be heavy casualties?" Chad looked at me and asked with hesitation in his voice. I sat there and contemplated the idea of telling young Chad. After inkling a mite I decided to because he would know soon enough.

"According to the times elapsed archives I've read, affirmative there will be many citizens young and frail, military and civilians killed in action. To let you in on something I haven't revealed to anyone else but Sr. Com. Bancais.

Is that as the Protrerian's attack, he (Sr. Com. Bancais), A 2nd Lieutenant Haggis from the Fairchild Military Facility, Admiral Challid from the Tanglar Sea Patrol and Colonel Hagerty from ZCSA; invent and introduce an advanced military fighter called the Hugo C-15. All military personnel when first enlisted are taught all about it because of the important role in times elapsed it played during this war. From what I remember the specifications of this craft are as follows:"

Designers:	Bancais, Challid, Hagerty and Haggis Enhance N. Z.C. M. Co. (North ZarCedra Military Coalition)
Role	Four seated Sea/Air/Space Strike Shuttle
Weight:	15 metric tons
Engines:	Two Pratt and Whitney F200-350 Turbojets w/15875.7 kg. Thrust max.
Range:	1500 kiloms
Ceiling:	600, 000+ metrics.
Depth:	15, 000 metrics Below Sea Level
Maximum Speed:	Mach 7
Armament:	4-15mm Laser Cannons, 4-Torpedo/missal recesses and 6 weapons pylons
Radar Quality:	Long range, High quality Cedric radar.

"Those four men founded N. Z. C. M. Co but because we were defeated by the Protrerian High Command, they are who end up directing all military functions and they change the name N. Z. C. M. Co and all the other land masses of ZarCedra's military coalitions to ZarCedra Force. But after Humanarian citizens were allowed back into society, the Humanarian members of society started our military forces once again. Our secret military alliance decided to reintroduce the name N. Z. C. M. Co., and add the letters S. H. Z. C. A., which stands for Secret Humanarian ZarCedra Alliance."

"What are you inkling about?" I asked as I looked over at Chad's distraught look. "I know asking this isn't very ethical, but would you happen to know what happens to me? "Hmm I don't know if I should say, I said rubbing my chin. I'm afraid if I tell you that I would be disrupting the natural course of times elapsed too excessively. 'And you become the first champion in this intergalactic war,' I thought.

"Tell me," Chad begged. "All right I will reveal this much; according to the military data I studied, your fighter will be destroyed just after the Protrerian High Command's Energy Extractor Craft first enters ZarCedra's atmosphere."

After saying that, I could see that Chad got more fidgety in his seat. "Do you know of my mission? "Affirmative, all military personnel in the time I am from know of your valiant kamikaze flight to destroy the beams that were draining one of ZarCedra's power supply facilities."

"Do I stop them?" He asked a bit distraught. "That craft you do but there are three other energy extractor craft at the other energy facilities. They drain a bit and electronically take schematics then it is at that time the Protrerian High Command change their actions, and that is when they initialize a full-scaled attack for possession of ZarCedra."

"Eventually the Antrerian Armada arrives and joins forces with ZarCedra, but the advancements the Protrerian High Command had made to their armed forces even defeats them."

"So is that when we lose? "Well after half a tritton of heavy resistance, affirmative. The Antrerian Armada was able to escape but banished from this planet, and then the Protrerian High Command started their reign."

"But because I have come back to this particular time with a prototype craft in my possession, I believe I am here to prevent the Protrerian High Command from defeating ZarCedra."

"If you do make that happen then my demise will stand for something." I looked at him then seen the trickling tear drop roll from his eye. "Affirmative buddy I will do my best to try to prevent it from happening but if I am unable to, your demise will indeed be for something. "Many thanks."

"There are many features to my craft that I haven't mentioned to anyone and may just give me the edge I need," I said as I looked over at Chad. "May I enquire what those features are? "Unfortunately those features are classified for right now, but soon all will be known; now, that is about all I could reveal at this time."

"Well, things will hopefully work out," I said as I got up and patted Chad's shoulder. "I'm going for a shower then I'm going to retire for the twilight, when you are ready to retire just say illumination off and the illumination will extinguish," I told him as I messed his hair. "Affirmative, many thanks," Chad said as he tried to get away.

"Ok partner, I'll see you in the morrow morn," I said as I laughed then went toward my slumbering quarters, got my slumbering garments then went to the latrine for my shower.

P.A.R 6

Early the next morn, I went into the front chamber to await Chad while he got ready so we could go for our morn banquet. "Don't take too long, we want to get to the mess hall before all the grub disappears," I hollered. "Don't get your underthings in a twist, remember this p.a.r's date is the p.a.r of the God's and we are allowed an extra epock to slumber, so I don't think the mess hall will run out of banquets for a while; I'll be ready to go in a few mites, think you can wait that long?" Chad hollered out the latrine entry-way.

I rubbed my stomach as it made a grumbling sound. "I can but my stomach can't, so don't take all this planet's axis revolution, ok? "I'll be out when I'm grand and ready, so you'll just have to delay!

"You know I could report you for insubordination! "True, you are the higher-ranking officer but if you do that you'll lose a grand abode mate. 'He's correct, a smart ass but correct,' I thought as I switched on the Intervision monitor and watched the early morn news until Chad was through in the latrine.

When he was, I turned everything off, we grabbed our berets then we both went for our morn banquet. As we were walking we met up with LC Acernan and a grand-looking blonde female officer. As we met, LC Acernan and the Lieutenant saluted me. "Grand morn," I said as I smiled politely and returned their salute as I shook their hands.

"Grand morn ma'am I am Maj. Teldat and the fly boy beside me is LC Luxton. "Greetings, my name is Lt. Barb Brucetti," she said with a delightful smile. "Enjoyable to greet you and I hope to see you around this military facility; where are you off to? "To see Sr. Com. Bancais, Lt. Brucetti was just transferred here and she has to check in with the Sr. Commodore," LC Acernan answered. "Affirmative, we must meet in the mess hall later to discuss something of importance," I said as I looked at LC Acernan. "Affirmative sir but for now we must be going."

"What a pleasant young female citizen," I said as I turned around and watched her walk away. "She isn't bad but remember you have a no doubt exquisite lady consociate, if any one should be gawking, it's me," LC Luxton replied as we continued toward the mess hall. "Ok little buddy you're correct gawk all you want," I replied as he turned around just in time to see her and LC Acernan turn a corner. "Darn too late, she's gone," LC Luxton said as he turned back around. "Too bad so sad," I said with a smirk as we continued to the mess hall.

When we arrived, we entered and each grabbed a tray and waited in line until we received our morn banquet then went to a table. After LC Luxton and I sat, LC Luxton fixed his morn caffinated brew as we started discussing, our plans, for this p.a.r.

By the time we were half done our banquet the whole gang was together, LC Acernan also returned with Lt. Brucetti. "Would anyone have a problem if we sat? "Negative problems, sit and be my guest," I said as they sat. "Did you talk over what you needed to with Sr. Com. Bancais? "Affirmative, and I am to report to you Maj. Teldat, and you are to brief me on what I am to know for the morrow; is now a grand time?

"Well, I can give you and everyone nearby a short rundown of what's about to happen," I said as I took another sip of my black brew.

"To start, in the morrow at precisely 11 hundred epocks we are going to be attacked by an alien race known as the Protrerian High Command. They first attack us for our precious energy and secrets of how to harness the sun's energy. Which are being used at the four Energy Reactor Facilities around our planet, but in time they will change their mind and decide to just take over ZarCedra and adopt it as their own."

"The reason they attack is because their Planet is running out of natural energy and they aren't able to supply more, fast enough to sustain life and because their sun is slowly going nova and will extinguish in about a centritton. On the brighter side we do receive assistance from their archenemies that reside on their sister planet of Antreria."

"Other key military personnel and I are to meet at Casablanca Bistro just down the boulevard at 14 hundred epocks this mid-p.a.r, to discuss the war in grander detail; if LC Acernan was able to reserve their banquet hall? "Although this p.a.r is the p.a.r of the God's and they are not supposed to open until 10 hundred epocks, there was someone there when I called earlier this morn. I was able to reserve the chamber for an epock at 14 hundred epocks," LC Acernan said.

"Grand, LC Acernan drive Lt. Brucetti to Casablanca's Bistro for 14 hundred epocks and our situation will be further explained at that time. "Affirmative," they both responded then took a sip of their swills. "Now, if everyone will excuse me, I must be off, until then I bid you all farewell," I said as I replaced my beret, got out of my seat, picked up my tray then walked away. I put my tray on a dish cart then headed for the exit where I ran into Sr. Com. Bancais.

"Maj. Teldat, I need to brief you in anticipation of the morrow's attack," the Sr. Commodore stated as he returned my salute. "Sir, a few key military personnel and I are to meet at Casablanca Bistro at 14 hundred epocks, I was going to ask you to meet us there. "That time would be superior, I'll see you there; I might be tardy a few mites," he said. "Sir, try not to be tardy too long, we only have the banquet chamber for an epock. "Affirmative Major, he said as we saluted again then we parted company.

I continued out of the structure and returned to my barracks where I went straight to the PCD. I deposited a metallic quint gribbit then entered Topanga's digits and waited patiently as it chirped. When it was answered, Topanga and I arranged our morn plan. "I will meet you at the front gate in about fifty mites. "Grand, I can hardly wait to be in your company my dearest. "And I can hardly wait to be in yours," she said then we both said "grand adioso" and hung up.

I walked to my barracks then up to the retina scanner by my quarters, had my retina scanned and my voice identified then entered to await Topanga's arrival. "Illumination on," I said then turned the Intervision monitor on and listened to the melodic composition network as I glanced out the window and watched recruits as they jogged by and I reminisced the times I ran around this military facility in my time.

I looked farther across the military facility and could see aircraft take off and land from various runways. 'It would be a different story in the morrow when fighters would take off and few, if any, would return after the war begins,' I thought to myself. I watched military citizens walk by my barracks along the walk and thought, 'affirmative it will be a different story in the morrow.'

I looked at my timepiece and seen that it was 08 hundred 56 epocks. 'Almost time to sign out,' I thought as I went to the latrine to freshen up a bit. After a few mites I exited the latrine and decided it was time to go wait for Topanga at the gate abode. "Illumination off," I said then turned the Intervision monitor off as I exited my quarters and the entry-way silently slid closed behind me then I continued out of the barracks.

I made my way to the gateabode and when I got there I found the MP reading this p.a.r's news. "Uh hmm," I interrupted and the MP set the news aside, stood and approached. "Is there any new grand news to report?" I inquired with a smile. "Not much," the MP said coming toward me.

"I'm here to sign out to leave for the p.a.r. "Got a hot date, do you?" The MP asked with a smile. "I think I do." Just then we both heard a honk, we looked in its direction and seen my ride. "Time to go," I said as I signed the roster. "Carry on reading the p.a.r's news," I said then went to Topanga's auto.

"Grand morn huni buni," I said as I got into her automobile and fastened my safety belt as the entry-flap lowered. "Grand morn," Topanga said as she smiled quite lovely at me. "You look particularly radiant," I said as I kissed her luscious lips. "Many thanks for the compliment, I wanted to look grand for you," Topanga said as she smiled and backed out onto the boulevard. "You do huni buni, you really look spectacular."

"Many thanks Jeroque, where would you like to go to start our p.a.r together? Topanga asked as she drove off. "I was inkling about viewing your abode? "We can, Cheryl, my abode mate mentioned that she had a few errands to run and will be out most of this p.a.r," Topanga said with a smile.

"Grand, I would like to be alone with you, so we could talk. "About what, anything in particular you want to discuss? "More about where we are going with our affiliation and the things that are going to happen in the next few p.a.r's," I told her as she turned a corner. "All right," she replied. "We shall talk soon my exquisite one," I said as I picked up her hand and kissed it.

Forty-five mites later Topanga pulled up alongside her abode structure then switched her auto off. "We got here faster than usual," Topanga said as we removed our safety belts as the entry-flaps rose. "Probably because this p.a.r is the p.a.r of the God's and not the usual amount of commuter transportation on the boulevards as work p.a.r's," I said as we exited the vehicle and the entry-ways closed behind us.

"I finally get to view your living quarters," I said as Topanga pressed a button on her remote and locked her vehicle; the chirping sound after that told her the alarm was set. We walked hand in hand into her abode structure.

"Our accommodations aren't much but my abode mate and I like to call it our abode," Topanga said as she looked at me. As we ascended the stairs, Topanga's abode mate descended and stopped.

"Greetings, I'm Cheryl, Topanga's abode mate. You must be Jeroque? Topanga has mentioned a few things about you, but she neglected to tell me how grand you look," she said with a smile as she held out her hand to shake with mine. "Never you mind Cheryl, his love belongs to me, find your own male citizen," Topanga said with a devilish smile. "Ok Topanga, I was only being truthful," she replied as she smiled again in my direction.

"You better be off before I hurt you," Topanga said with the same devilish smile. "Pleasant to meet you Jeroque, I must be off now before Topanga hurt's me," Cheryl said with a laugh then continued down the stairs. "Adioso," Topanga and I said as Cheryl continued toward the front entry-way.

"Pleasant young lady, maybe next time we could talk longer and get better acquainted," I said as I gave Topanga a squeeze. "C'mon," Topanga said as she pulled away and we continued up the stairs. 'Grand body,' I thought to myself as I watched Topanga's back side as it wiggled back and forth while we continued up the stairs. We both stopped in front of the entry-way that had the digits 204; Topanga removed her keys from her shoulder bag and unlocked the entry-way.

"Would you like a cool refreshment?" Topanga asked as we entered her living quarters and we removed our footwear. "What do you suggest? "How about a tall cool glass of limonade," she suggested smacking her lips. "Sounds grand," I said as she went into her sustenance replenishing area.

While she was out of the chamber, I looked around her living chamber. "You and Cheryl have an impressive abode," I said as I inspected a landscape of watercolor hanging on her wall. "Many thanks," she said as she re-entered the living chamber with a tray of refreshments.

"For instance the artist, Chantel Lalonde, who painted this landscape; in a few trittons this landscape of watercolors and all of her artwork will be priceless. "Really? Now I know if I needed a substantial amount of monetary units, I could always peddle it," Topanga said with a laugh. "All jesting aside; if you haven't yet, you should get this depiction insured because soon it will be worth a small fortune," I said as I turned around and joined Topanga on the lounger for our glass of limonade. "It hasn't been insured, but knowing that it will soon be worth something; I definitely will insure it."

I turned slightly to face Topanga, as I did Topanga took my face in her delicate fingers and kissed my lips. She sat closer and started rubbing my chest. "Not just yet huni buni, we should first discuss our positions in grander detail," I said as we both sipped our swills.

"I thought we did when we went to Skittar?" Topanga asked as she set her glass down. "So did I but something is bugging me and I can't figure out just what?" I said then took another

Wings Of Time

sip of my delicious swill. After I set my glass on a coaster on the brew table, I took Topanga's hand in mine.

"Topanga I find you exquisitely attractive and I thank the Godly paradises that I was able to meet and fall in love with you. I know that by being here in this time, gives me the opportunity to change the times elapsed of the Planet in the time I am from. But if I do that, I know I'll give our Antrerian consociates a stronger advantage with the craft I have in my possession. With this added advantage we have a better chance of being victorious in this war, but if by chance we end up winning, I know I will lose the love of the female citizen I have been in love with for the last five trittons. By being victorious in this war will mean we will have defeated the Protrerian High Command and they will no longer live with us in the times yet to come. "Uh huh," Topanga said then took another sip of her swill as I continued.

"Well that will mean all Protrerian life on ZarCedra will be erased and Tsarina being half Protrerian and half Humanarian, she will no longer exist as the female citizen I fell in love with. I know by being victorious in this war will make living all that much better in my own time but is losing her really worth it? I already made up my mind to assist in the upcoming war with everything I can but I can't stop inkling about the love I still have for Tsarina. "

"What does your heart tell you?" Topanga asked, as she looked deep into my eyes. I didn't have to ponder the question for more than a microsec before I answered, then I softly took her face in my hands and made my decision once and for all.

"I do love Tsarina more than you will ever realize but if I had your love I would indeed give everything I've got to be victorious in this war. "If it's my love you want you have it; because, as you know I have been in love with you ever since that first p.a.r you walked into Mac Guire's Handiness Supplies," Topanga told me as she kissed me intensely.

"That's grand to know because I feel I have fallen in love with you too," I said as I tickled her to ease the tension we both were feeling at that moment.

"I am to meet a few military personnel at the Casablanca Bistro near the Military Facility at 2 o'clock this mid-p.a.r," I told Topanga as I squeezed her knee then we both took another sip of our limonade. "What is the meeting about?" Topanga asked as she set her glass down. "To discuss the upcoming war on the continents of ZarCedra, especially the attack that is going to happen above Tanglar, Cardola Territories and he rest of Kor Bissal."

"Would I be allowed to accompany you or is it confidential? "This isn't an official meeting so it would be all right if you accompanied me, besides I will need you to give me a ride," I said as I smiled at her. "Are you quite sure because I could always drop you off then return to my abode? "Negative, you are a part of my life now and I believe we will all benefit if we all knew where and when we will be attacked," I replied then kissed Topanga's nose.

Topanga stood then finished the rest of her limonade as I too took the last sip of my own beverage. "Would you like another?" Topanga asked as she took my glass. "Negative, but many thanks huni buni," I said as Topanga smiled then disappeared into her sustenance replenishing area.

A moment later she re-entered the front chamber and rejoined me on the lounger, she reached for the Intervision monitor's remote and started roaming the airwaves. "Would you like to see or hear anything in particular?" She asked as she fluttered her eyelashes. I thought a moment then not knowing what was being played on Intervision at this point in time. "Can you get the melodic composition channel? "Sure," she replied as she flipped to the appropriate channel. For the next few mites my eyes were glued to the Intervision monitor screen.

As my attention was on the screen, I barely felt the warmth of Topanga's hand start roaming up my leg to my thigh. She stopped there and tickled me and that's when I felt her. I looked deep into her exquisite blue eyes and a sec later we were in the midst of a quixotic kiss.

A few mites later I stopped Topanga in the nick of time as she was releasing the snaps of her chemise. "As exquisite as you are and as much as I would like for you to continue, we should talk and get to know each other better before we go any further; for the time being anyhow," I said as I looked at her and took her hand in mine.

"All right," she replied as she sat back and refastened the snaps. "Besides, there isn't sufficient time for intimacy at the moment; I would like to take my time taking in the exquisiteness of your being. Maybe there will be sufficient time later this mid-p.a.r? "Grand," Topanga said as she sat on my lap and we were once again in a quixotic kiss.

"Are you getting famished? Would you enjoy a toasty or something?" Topanga asked as she rubbed my stomach. "A toasty sounds grand; what kind of toasty are you planning to prepare? "It's a surprise," she said smacking her lips. "Sounds grand, my huni buni. Would you like assistance in preparing our mid-p.a.r banquet? "No you just stay in here and watch the melodic composition channel and I'll call you upon completion.

"Are you sure? "Quite," she said as she stood, bent over and gave me a quick peck on the cheek then walked towards the sustenance replenishing area. As she neared the entry-way, I couldn't stop myself from glancing at her perfect little backside as she entered.

Once she was out of sight, my eyes diverted towards the IV monitor screen and I watched and listened to the composition as I looked down at my timepiece and seen that it was 12 hundred epochs. I sat back, closed my eyes and started inkling of the things I wanted to discuss at the meeting this mid-p.a.r.

I thought about Tsarina, and for that matter all Protrerian High Command citizens. 'Is what I'm about to do really rational? Was it rational what the Protrerian High Command did when they took over ZarCedra?' I thought to myself as I reconfirmed my stand. "For all the pain and hardship they put Humanarian kind through, I will fight with everything I've got not to let them take this Planet from us again," I whispered to myself.

'What would the possible repercussion to the times yet to come be after the start of the war; my meddling with times elapsed events would cause? Well if it can ease some of the pain and suffering the Humanarian race has been put through, it would be worth it.'

As I sat there inkling and with the low murmur of the Intervision I barely heard Topanga's angelic voice. "Our mid-p.a.r banquet is ready for consumption." I shook back to reality and stood, stretched then started for the sustenance replenishing area.

As I entered, I saw Topanga bring our mid-p.a.r banquet to the table. "Many thanks huni buni," I said as I sat next to her and removed my beret. "You are very welcomed grand looking," she answered as she got up to pour us each a glass of milk. After she sat, we both ate our mid-p.a.r banquet engulfed in quiet conversation.

During our conversation I told Topanga, "all who were to meet at Casablanca Bistro and that we were going to have a fairly quick in-depth discussion concerning the morrow's attack." I finished my mid-p.a.r banquet, pushed the plate aside and swilled my milk.

Topanga smiled in my direction and I marveled in her exquisiteness. "What are you inkling about right now?" Topanga asked as she sat back. "I was just admiring your sheer exquisiteness and I was inkling that I am a lucky citizen to have you in my life. "Many thanks kind sir," she said as she kissed my hand then she smiled affectionately at me for the longest time.

"Time to clean the dishes before we leave," Topanga said as she started gathering them. I put my beret back on then assisted her, a few mites later we cleaned the sustenance replenishing area spotless then went into the front chamber to relax for a few mites. We both listened to the melodic composition as we, "discussed the things we were going to do after the meeting."

A little later we both decided it was time to get going. The Intervision monitor and illumination was extinguished then we put on our footwear and left the abode and Topanga locked the entry-way. We descended the stairs hand in hand and out to her auto. Topanga removed her auto's remote from her shoulder bag, disarmed the alarm and unlocked the entry-flaps. We raised them and got in. After we both fastened our seat belts, the entry-flaps automatically closed; Topanga started her auto then she pulled onto the boulevard.

A bit later Topanga was intertwining through the commuter transportation as we both jested and laughed. At long last, Topanga pulled up alongside Casablanca Bistro; she switched the ignition system off then we left the auto. Topanga locked the entry-flaps behind us then armed the security alarm. On the walkway, Topanga and I came together, holding hands as we walked to the Bistro.

When we entered a hostess came to greet us. "Are you here to meet with other members from the Grinshaw Military Facility?" She asked as soon as she seen my uniform. "Affirmative ma'am we are," I said as I returned her smile. "Follow me," the hostess replied.

Topanga and I followed the young lady to a back meeting chamber filled with citizens I had asked to meet me here. "Grand mid-p.a.r," I said as Topanga and I sat. "Would you both like a refreshment?" The hostess asked. "I would like an unsweetened soda?" Topanga asked. "Can I have a black iced caffinated brew? "I will have it delivered to you immediately," the hostess said as she turned and left.

"Do you know how long Sr. Com. Bancais will be?" I asked LC Acernan. "There are a few things he had to take care of first before he could meet us, he didn't say how long he would be but he did say he wouldn't be too long. "Many thanks Lance Corporal," I said just as a waitress came into bring Topanga and I our swills and to take the swill orders of everyone else who hadn't received one yet.

"What would everyone else like to swill?" She asked as she put our swills down. She jotted down what each wanted. "Grand mid-p.a.r Trinacia, how are you this p.a.r?" Maj. Manet asked as the waitress got to her. "I am doing fine but I have been functioning 14 p.a.r's straight without a p.a.r off," the waitress said as she rested her hand on her hip. "I hope you get a p.a.r time off soon. "So do I," Trinacia answered.

"I would like to introduce everyone to a grand consociate of mine," Maj. Manet said getting all our attention. "Everyone this is Trinacia Belzar; Trinacia this is some of the military citizens I am stationed with. "Greetings," everyone said as she continued taking swill orders then went to retrieve them.

"Now, as we wait for Sr. Com. Bancais arrival, I will update everyone on what's about to happen for the next while. Especially those citizens who haven't heard of the terrible time we are in for as we begin this Grand War. As most of you know the tritton I am from and for those of you who haven't I come from the tritton 2115, so everything I am about to tell you is factual according to the times elapsed archives I've studied," I said as I took a sip of my iced brew.

"Starting in the morrow 07.01.2015 at precisely 11 hundred epocks ZarCedra will be attacked by the alien race known as the Protrerian High Command. I read that this war is supposed to last half a tritton but in the first few Trints the fighting will be the fiercest, even after we receive assistance from their arch rivals, the Antrerian Armada."

"Who are they? "The Antrerian Armada belongs to a race of beings that reside on the sister planet to Protreria called Antreria. The Antrerian Armada and the Protrerian High Command have been at war with each other for many centrittons. They will come to our aid 07.06.2015 mid-p.a.r, so until then we must fight the Protrerian High Command alone."

"If the Protrerian's and Antrerian's are enemies, why do the Antrerian's take so long to intervene?" LC Acernan asked. "Because, they want to see how strong our military is, plus their planet is a grand distance away. Even at the grand speeds they are able travel it takes a few p.a.r's to arrive here," I told him as Sr. Com. Bancais and other high ranking officials entered the chamber.

"Greetings everyone, my apologies for our tardiness. I have with me a few members of the head of Tanglarian Defense," he said as he entered. Trinacia our waitress returned to the chamber with a tray of refreshments and started handing them out. Mites later she looked towards the distinguished looking older gentlefolk. "Would you gentlefolk like something cold to swill? "A soda for me, my acquaintances will have? "The same. "Six sodas my cutie. Any particular essence?" She inquired. "Surprise us my dear. "Sure, I'll be back directly," she said as she smiled and left.

"Now what were you young citizens talking about?" Sr. Com. Bancais asked as he lit a fresh cigar. "I was just saying when we get attacked in the morrow it will be fierce and is supposed to last half a tritton. I say supposed to because that is how long I read it would last in my times elapsed archive. But by me being here now with the prototype Supersonic Dragon 228-D Spy Jet Stealth in my possession, we will have an unfair advantage and the war just might be over sooner than expected."

"Hmm," Sr. Com. Bancais said as he and his cohorts had a discussion between themselves.

As they had their discussion, I smiled lovingly at Topanga then looked at the fine prints hanging on the wall. At long last Sr. Com. Bancais looked up. "I was in contact with most of the planets leaders and many of them agreed to a satellite conference later this mid-p.a.r. Before long this entire Planet will know of the threat facing ZarCedra in the morrow," the Commodore told everyone. "Grand," I said.

"Excuse me, I heard your aircraft has superior weapons, precisely what types of weapons are equipped?" A Commodore MacIntyre asked. "My craft is equipped with Sareden Quantum Laser Cannons, two XTR-9000 Plasma Pulse Cannons which fires an unlimited supply of artillery fire. The Sareden Quantum Lasers are located atop my cockpit and the XTR-9000 Plasma Pulse Cannons are located, one under each wing."

My craft is also equipped with a limited supply of Protonic Electromagnetic Cluster Missals and Neutronic Electromagnetic Cluster Torpedo's. "What precisely do you mean by limited supply of electromagnetic cluster missiles and electromagnetic cluster torpedo's and for that matter what precisely are they?" A Commodore Sparks asked. "Allow me to go on and that will be explained in a few moments," I said as I looked in his direction.

"Additionally, equipped to my craft is a Comodrone Electronics P-52 Hydrogenic Generator; this generator creates all my weapons ammunition and is combined with Liquid Napricyte[2] to give it the explosive power it needs to cause major damage. My weapons array holds a maximum of fifteen Protonic Electromagnetic Cluster highly explosive charges and ten Neutronic Electromagnetic Cluster Torpedo's, which are not explosive."

"What Neutronic EMC Torpedo's do is, when they are fired and strike a target they drain that target of all electronic power, leaving it defenseless. After I expel my supply of missals, I must recharge ten mites before I get my next compliment of fifteen missiles and after I expel my arsenal of Torpedo's, I must recharge my weapons array twenty mites.

"Let me get this straight," Commodore Mac Entire, said. "You actually have a generator on your aircraft that creates your highly explosive arsenal of weapons! How is that possible? "I'm not precisely sure but what I am sure of is that it will most likely be explained in my craft's instructional e-manual, I will know more about this as soon as I read it further. " Understood, many thanks," the Commodore said.

"This aircraft you have in your possession, the Supersonic 228-D Spy Jet Stealth has other major additions unlike the aircraft of this p.a.r; can you elaborate on a few of those features?" A Sr. Commodore Tobious inquired.

"Affirmative. One of the most important features is my Omagon 2115 Star Drive engine. It operates in conjunction with an Electronic Flux Inducer; the combination of these two engines allows my craft to travel Star Drive speed within ZarCedra's oxygenated resistant atmosphere and gravitational pull."

"Precisely how fast is Star Drive speed and how does it attain that speed? "I first have to inform you that my fastest normal airspeed of my craft is Mach 10; Star Drive one is 10 * faster than Mach 10 and Star Drive two is 20 * faster; it is equivalent to Mach 200."

"Two, my craft attains those speeds by my Comodrone Electronics P-52 Hydrogenic Generator supplying power to my Omagon 2115 Star Drive engine, which is mixed with a radioactive chemical solution called Liquid Napricyte[2] SDC. This mixed electrical power is transferred to my Electronic Flux Inducer, which converts the special electrical power to Ionic power. This Ionic power travels through a cable to the rear of my craft then electromagnetically encompasses my craft going from golden module to golden module until it reaches the longer golden rod on the nose of my craft. From there the Ionic power shoots out in front of my craft creating a swirling Humanarian-made wormhole. This wormhole is free from the effects of oxygen and the pull of gravity."

"Three, because this wormhole is free from oxygen my craft is also equipped with tanks of compressed oxygen, which 'PAT', my cybernetic co-pilot and super computer expels automatically into the cockpit thus, allowing me to breathe. This Humanarian-made wormhole, when I fly into it is very rough, if you can imagine riding a very twisty roller coaster. "Many thanks Major, for your insight."

Topanga turned towards me and whispered. "I know some of the officers at the table but there is a lot of citizens I don't, so if it's convenient could you present me? "Affirmative," I replied as I squeezed her leg then cleared my throat. "Before we go any further I would like to present my lady consociate to those who haven't met her, her name is Topanga Shrenka."

"Glad to meet you," most of them said and the rest said, "Grand to see you again. "When and where did you two meet and how long have you two been coupled?" Lt. Brucetti asked Topanga. "Jeroque, I mean Maj. Teldat and I met the first p.a.r he arrived here and I felt an immediate attraction towards him. We met at Mac Guire's Handiness Supplies where I'm a supervisor, this handiness mercantile is located about 6 blocks down the boulevard," Topanga told Lt. Brucetti. "Oh" she said in a depressed tone.

"Understand I was betrothed to a female citizen who was of Humanarian-Protrerian descent. But for the reason we are here presently is that if, by the grace of our Gods, we happen to be victorious in this war, she and all Protrerian life will cease to exist in the time I am from; and I will be betrothed to no one. "Out of curiosity, what is the young citizens name?" LC Acernan asked. "Her name is Tsarina Alexander. "Any relation to Dr. Alexander?" Capt. J. Pane inquired. "She is," I answered then took a swill of my iced brew.

"If we happen to be defeated in this war, she will be his great granddaughter," I answered as Trinacia the waitress entered the meeting chamber with Sr. Com. Bancais and his group's soft swills and handed them out, smiled then left at once. "If we do happen to be victorious in this war, she and all Protrerian life will cease to exist in the time I am from."

"Well to change the subject, as you know the craft I have is a prototype craft and it has some additional important features but although in spite of that fact many of the aircraft that go up in the morrow will parish; I can only assist as much as Humanarianly possible. Above Translete, Cardola Territories will be the site of the first attack then many other major cities around the Planet."

"Sr. Com. Bancais I know has already contacted President Torren of the Cardola Territories. They have already started evacuating and military reinforcing the major cities of that country and hopefully all other countries that will be involved in air and ground wars. Sir, have you been able to contact the President of Garlotia to warn him of the attacks?" I asked as I looked at Sr. Com. Bancais "Affirmative, which is one of the reasons why I was tardy. The cities of Garlotian Palisades and Vroxen are being evacuated and military reinforced as we speak. Additionally, so are the cities of Ortice and Trigor, here in Tanglar. "Grand, many civilians would be saved by that action."

"The four Solar Energy Reactor Facilities situated around the Planet will be targeted at first but fear not, before they are seriously damaged the Protrerian High Command ceases their attack on them and decide to keep them intact and to just take over ZarCedra."

I looked at the time and seen our time was almost up. "Let's adjourn this meeting for now and if Sr. Com. Bancais is able to set up a summit meeting we can go into additional detail then," I suggested as I looked around the chamber then back to the Senior Officials. "My apologies to cut the meeting short Sr. Commodore, but like I said we only had an epock. "That's ok Major, it's me who should apologize for arriving tardy."

"Later this twilight or in the morrow morn I will give you a list of air citizens in your squadron," Sr. Com. Bancais said as he looked at me then flicked the ashes from his cigar. "Affirmative," I replied as everyone finished their swills, stood, saluted the commanding officers and started for the entry-way.

"Let's all be ready for the morrow, it sounds like it will be one hellatious p.a.r," Sr. Com. Bancais said then swilled what remained in his glass. "What are your plans for the rest of the mid-p.a.r?" The Sr. Commodore asked as he looked toward Topanga and I. "Unknown sir," I responded as I looked at Topanga with a mischievous smile as she swallowed the last sip of her swill. "We could always go back to my abode; my abode mate should be out for the rest of this p.a.r," she suggested with a smile and gleam in her eyes as she stood. "Affirmative; it looks as if I will be going back to Topanga's abode if you have no further need for me?" I responded as I finished my tall glass of iced brew.

"Sounds like it will be one hellatious p.a.r in the morrow; come to my office when you return to the military facility later this p.a.r so you can be briefed on any last mite objectives," Sr. Com. Bancais said.

"All finished?" The waitress asked as she entered the chamber. "All through," I said with a smile. "Who gets the damage?" She asked as she waived the bill in the air. "I'll take that, I will sign it and let the military pick up the tab, since this was a military briefing, unofficial but military all the same," Sr. Com. Bancais said as he accepted the bill. "Many thanks ma'am, have a grand p.a.r," I said then we headed out toward the hostess. "Adioso," Trinacia replied with a smile then proceeded to clear the tables.

Sr. Com. Bancais, his associates, Topanga and I went to the hostess station; when we got there Sr. Com. Bancais signed his designation to the bill. "Add a 20% gratuity to this bill for the waitress, put this bill with the rest of the bills for the Grinshaw Military Facility, and have a grand p.a.r," Sr. Com. Bancais said with a wink. "I will, many thanks sir and I hope you all have a grand p.a.r also," the hostess said.

The eight of us left the air-conditioned Bistro into the muggy heat of the mid-p.a.r, as we neared our vehicles we stopped walking and I turned towards Sr. Com. Bancais.

"I will return to the Grinshaw Military Facility about 17 hundred epocks; everyone have a grand p.a.r," I said as I saluted. "Affirmative and you two have a grand p.a.r as well," he said as he returned my salute then Topanga and I went towards her spectacular auto as Sr. Com. Bancais and his cohorts went towards their vehicles.

"Is there anything you have to do before we go back to my abode?" Topanga asked as she disarmed her auto's alarm and unlocked the entry-flaps, after they rose we both entered. "Negative my darling, I'm all yours for the rest of mid-p.a.r," I answered with a smile as I raised my eyebrows a couple times. "Grand, then off to my place we go."

We both fastened our seat belts as the entry-flaps closed; Topanga pressed the start button then she pulled onto the boulevard as we talked of the things we were going to do to each other. A little later Topanga pulled up alongside of her abode structure, red faced and a bit flustered then switched the engine off.

"Well here we are," she said with a smile as she leaned over for a kiss. When we finished, Topanga and I removed our safety belts then exited the auto, as Topanga used her remote to lock the entry-flaps and set the alarm. When we arrived at the main entry-way, I held it open for my exquisite Topanga. "Many thanks kind sir," she said with a smile and a wink as she entered. As we mounted the stairs I held Topanga's hand as we went up to her abode. We stopped in front of her entry-way and jested as Topanga unlocked it then we entered. We both removed our footwear; I went and sat on the lounger as Topanga went to the sustenance replenishing area to get us both something cold to swill.

While she was out of the chamber, I removed my beret then closed my eyes and started inkling to myself. 'About everything that was said at the meeting, my presence here in the 21st centritton and when I am through with everything here, will I be able to get back to the tritton 2115? Or will I be stuck in this time. Also, if we do happen to be victorious in this upcoming war, this time around will things remain the same? Everything except the taking over of ZarCedra by the Protrerian's, or will everything change? If I'm successful at rearranging times elapsed, what would the repercussion be to the times yet to come? Tsarina, she is a wonderful female citizen; what would I ever do without her?'

Just then Topanga re-entered the chamber with two glasses of limonade and I entertained a thought. 'What is the possibility of Topanga returning to the 22nd centritton with me? If I'm at all able to return to the time where I belong? "Here you go grand looking," she said as she handed one of the glasses to me. "Many thanks huni buni. "You're quite welcome," she said as she set her glass down on a coaster and grabbed the remote for the Intervision monitor.

She switched it on, and we continued to watch melodic composition cinematics then Topanga went to her slumbering quarters to grab a comforter. When she returned she came back and sat on the lounger next to me.

I took Topanga by the hand and pulled her down on top of me and I kissed her luscious lips. "I really feel unsure of what to do," I said as I looked deep into her exquisite blue eyes. "About what? "After my job in this centritton is complete, what if it isn't possible for me to return to my time? "I'm not in a position to tell you what to do because I don't know about the times yet to come and you are your own citizen. So all I can suggest is follow your heart and hope for the best, and remember I said I'd always be here for you, that means endlessly," Topanga said as she sat up then took a sip of her swill.

"Many thanks huni buni, you are correct I am the only citizen who can tell me what to do so I will just use my intellect. Thanks again," I said as I guided her face close to mine and softly, passionately kissed her soft lips again. One thing led to another and soon both of us had our garments off and we snuggled naked under the comforter. Our hands slowly caressed each other's flesh and the next thing I knew we were both on cloud ten.

I softly kissed Topanga's skin; I started at her toes then kissed up her legs, and showered little kisses over her thighs and stopped at her belly button. As I licked her flesh, my hand was busy kneading her soft but firm awesome breasts. I moved my hand under Topanga and while leaving wet trails of saliva around her belly button I messaged her round taut little bum.

Topanga moved slightly and she started rubbing the hair on my chest as she left little wet trails around my muscular stomach. I lifted her chin, kissed her on the lips then I lowered my head and sucked her nipples. At long last we slowly made passionate love for the rest of the mid-p.a.r.

"I love you very much," Topanga told me as I rolled off her. I wiped the sweat soaked wisps of hair from her face. "The feelings are very much mutual, I love you too so very much my love," I said as I kissed her again then we both forced ourselves up. "My you have an exquisite body," I said, as we got dressed. "Many thanks kind sir, as do you," Topanga replied with a smile.

After we dressed, I took off my air brigade ring and with a smile I gave it to Topanga. "Here huni buni, I should have given this to you the other twilight," I said as she accepted it and placed it on her ring finger. "Things will be hectic for the next while so unfortunately I probably won't be around much but I will be here the first chance I get. "All right," she said a bit sulky. "Do you have to get back to the military facility soon? "Affirmative, it's about time I had my twilight banquet then Sr. Com. Bancais wants to see me after that," I told her as I rubbed her back.

"You could always have your twilight banquet here," she said as she tidied up the front chamber. "I would but I already told my CO I would return to base by 5 o'clock," I said wiping the hair from in front of her exquisite eyes. "Aughh", she pouted. I lifted her chin and gave her another kiss then we put our glasses away, put on our footwear; I put on my beret then we headed out the entry-way.

After securing it, we went down the stairs and exited the structure. Topanga removed her auto's remote and turned the alarm off and unlocked the entry-flaps. We got in the auto and mites later we were intertwining through the city boulevards talking of our wonderful mid-p.a.r together as we drove back to the Military Facility.

Topanga pulled up to the front gate abode and I leaned over for a kiss. "I really enjoyed our time together this p.a.r and I will call you, have a grand twilight," I said as I smiled, winked then got out and closed the entry-flap. "I had a wonderful p.a.r as well, I hope you enjoy your twilight too," she said as she too winked, smiled and blew me a kiss then backed onto the boulevard, put her auto in gear and drove off.

I turned and walked to the gateabode to sign back in. "Did you have an enjoyable p.a.r?" The MP asked as I signed back in. "Affirmative unimaginably grand," I answered with a grin. Then I turned and disappeared in the direction of my barracks.

When I arrived in my quarters, LC Luxton was there jotting his report. "Greetings buddy, glad to see you back, Sr. Com. Bancais had requested your presence as soon as you returned, he wants to see you immediately. "Many thanks buddy," I responded as I changed direction and exited our quarters. I walked the few blocks to main headquarters, entered and went to Sr. Com. Bancais office. When I arrived, I saw LC Acernan getting ready to leave. "Greetings Maj. Teldat, the Sr. Commodore is expecting you. "Many thanks Lance Corporal," I answered as I removed my beret then went right into the Sr. Commodore's office.

As I seen Sr. Com. Bancais, I stood at attention and saluted. "Maj. Teldat reporting as directed sir! "At ease Major; sitting here is Commodore Moncton with his aide Capt. Lancing from the Manning Military Facility in Trios and sitting over here is Admiral Fenton and Lieutenant A.V Benallie of the Cardola Territories

Sealtese Military Installation located in Sreel, Tembar, CT. You'll also notice Commodore MacIntyre, Commodore Sparks and Sr. Commodore Tobious who you met this mid-p.a.r are also present. "Of course," I said as I saluted and shook hands with every one present.

"The reason I requested you now is that in a few secs, The Prime Minister of Tanglar-PM Trembley, The President of the Cardola Territories-Pres. Torren, The King of the Candor Isles-King Smith IV and His Majesty's Ariel Forces out of the Candor Isles would contact us, via satellite." Sr. Com. Bancais said as he pressed a button on his desk and a portion of the wall slid up producing digits of monitors.

With a flick of a switch on a hand held remote, and from their remote cinematic units, each of the high ranking citizens the Sr. Commodore had mentioned were present on the monitors.

"Maj. Teldat is now present, you can proceed with your preliminary investigation," Sr. Com. Bancais reported. "Greetings Major, for my first question; what is your full rank, serial digits and the date you joined the Royal Tanglar Military?" The Prime Minister of Tanglar, the Honorable Prime Minister Trembley asked.

"Rank, Major First Class, serial digits are #697A39G1, 03.15.2109, was the date I entered the Royal Tanglar Military. "How are we to know you are telling the whole truth?" President Torren of the Cardola Territories asked.

"The tritton I entered the RTM is printed on the military tags I wear & tattooed on my arm, more proof is the prototype craft I have in my possession. "Affirmative, if you could elaborate on your special aircraft? Admiral Fenton asked.

"Affirmative, my craft is a prototype Supersonic Dragon 228-D Spy Jet Stealth, powered by two oversized F405-F1D3 afterburning engines and it has the accelerating speed of Mach ten. Additionally, it has a third engine called the Omagon 2115 Star Drive engine it operates in conjunction with another device called the Electronic Flux Inducer, which enables my craft to attain Star Drive speeds within ZarCedra's oxygenated atmosphere and gravitational pull."

"What is your top Star Drive speed?" Acting Commander Spiel of His Majesty's Air Command asked. "My craft has the top air speed of Star Drive two, which is the equivalency of Mach ten * twenty or Mach 200. "Wow, that is some speed," Commodore Sparks said as he started jotting in a jotter. "Affirmative, it is."

"What type of fuel does your aircraft use?" King Smith the IV asked. "My two main F405-F1D3 afterburning engines uses regular jet fuel. But the Star Drive Engine uses a special chemical solution called Liquid Napricyte² SDC. "Do you have a supply of that chemical solution on hand?" Admiral Fenton asked. "I have enough for a while then I will require more," I responded.

"Maj. Teldat was gracious enough to provide us with a vile of the special chemical solution so we can duplicate when needed. Additionally my two top scientists and their E-tech team took specifications and schematics of the Star Drive engine, Electronic Flux Inducer in addition to his aircraft's armaments and also its generator. Because all its ammunition is created by the P-52 Hydrogenic generator and it also uses the Liquid Napricyte² SDC for its destructive weapons," Sr. Com. Bancais said.

"Wonderful, all my military aircraft will be on standby alert; when this Grand War commences I will dispatch them in force," President Torren said "I too," Commander Spiel said. "The same with us," everyone else chimed in.

"What does this alien race want so badly that they are willing to declare war on our planet?" Prime Minister Trembley asked. "It is noted in the times elapsed archive I had studied that their abode Planet, 'Protreria,' is running dangerously low on natural energy and because their sun is close to going nova. Scientists on their planet somehow discovered that the citizens of planet ZarCedra uses solar energy, and we have discovered a way of creating and storing this energy at the ZarCedra's various Solar Energy Reactor Facilities; at first, they plan to attack us for our secrets," I told the Prime Minister.

"But why don't they just ask, I'm sure we can work something out? "They do not believe they have to ask for anything, they just plan to attack and take it, and then almost immediately they change their mind and decide just to take over this planet, and claim it as their own because their planet is on a steady decline to being uninhabitable."

"When precisely is this attack expected to take place?" Prime Minister Trembley asked. "In the morrow morn, 07.01.2015 at precisely 11 hundred epocks, the initial attack will be above the City of Translete, CT. "That city as well all the other cities I was informed of are being evacuated and military protected as we speak; don't worry I will be in touch soon," President Torren said then his cinematic screen went dark.

"But let me say to the remaining planet leaders, there will also be attacks over every industrial country of ZarCedra. "Affirmative," they all acknowledged. "Sr. Com. Bancais has already warned us about that," Prime Minister Trembley said then his monitor went dark.

"Aircraft transporters were already dispatched from the north and south Sephren Sea to assist where needed," the King of the Candor Isles reported then his and Commander Spiel's monitors extinguished.

"I'll send detachments of Military Seals to assist in the evacuation of Translete, if President Torren hasn't already," Admiral Fenton said. "Not to worry Maj. Teldat, the planet will be secure by the time of the invasion in the morrow, count on it," Commodore MacIntyre said as he chewed the butt of an unlit cigar. Just then Prime Minister Trembley's screen illuminated once again and in the Prime Ministers place was his military advisor, Maj. Commander R. J. Lalonde.

"Sr. Com. Bancais and Maj. Teldat, there will be troopers from the Tanglar Army dispatched to the major cities of Tanglar ASAP. "Affirmative," we both acknowledged then the screen went dark.

"Ok Major, who would you like in your squadron?" Sr. Com. Bancais asked as he turned to face me. "As you probably already imagined, I would prefer to fly lead. For my two wingmen I would recommend LC Luxton and Sgt. Pane. Fill in the rest of my squadron with whomever you think would best compliment my squadron for the security of our continents. "As you wish, you will receive a list later this twilight."

"Now Commodore Sparks, Commodore MacIntyre, Sr. Commodore Tobious, Jr. Commodore Moncton and Admiral Fenton & their Aides would like for you to show them your famous aircraft. "Affirmative sir, it will be my pleasure. Right this way citizens; my craft is near hangar three," I said as I turned and ushered everyone out of Sr. Com. Bancais office. "Sr. Com. Bancais would you like to accompany us? "Negative, I have a lot to do in preparation for the morrow's attack but many thanks all the same, dismissed. "Affirmative sir," I said as I closed the entry-way and replaced my beret and walked with the military personnel out of main headquarters.

As we neared hangar three they couldn't miss the huge, sleek gleaming craft as Jr. Commodore Moncton let out a "whistle. "What exquisiteness, huge but exquisite all the same," he said wide-eyed "The sleek and aeronautic design isn't the only advantage my craft has, there's a lot I haven't even tested as of yet that should give us an edge," I said as we arrived at the craft.

"Gentlefolk I present the prototype version of the direction aircraft will take in times yet to come, the Supersonic Dragon 228-D Spy Jet Stealth. You'll notice printed on the side of my craft are the anagrams N. Z. C. M. Co/S. H. Z. C. A. You should know what N. Z. C. M. Co stands for but S. H. Z. C. A. stands for Secret Humanarian ZarCedra Alliance. Since my craft is a Supersonic Dragon someone thought it appropriate to have a depiction of a ferocious dragon," I said.

"Citizens if you'll look atop my craft you'll notice the two barrels of my crafts' Sareden Quantum Laser Cannons. Those barrels are 100% charged at all times and its turret swivels 360°, so there isn't much that can fly by me. I tapped my com-link. "'PAT', slide and extend the port wing then lower the port and starboard Plasma Pulse Cannons. Lady and gentlefolk I draw your attention to my crafts' XTR-9000 Plasma Pulse Cannons. On each wing these cannons swivel on a turret 180° from bow to stern, and fires a deadly stream of plasma charges; it is also 100% charged at all times."

"Below the nose of my craft you'll notice a circular plate. When I have a target in my sight, I have that plate slide and from there I fire my Protonic Electromagnetic Cluster Missals and/or Neutronic Electromagnetic Cluster Torpedo's. I have a total of 15 highly explosive Protonic EMC Missiles and they will explode on contact with any given target. To give them the explosive power to cause major damage, they share the aforementioned Liquid Napricyte[2] SDC solution."

"I have 10 Neutronic EMC Torpedo's at a time. They are not explosive in nature; however, when they strike a target, the torpedo will absorb all electronic power leaving that target utterly defenseless and open to attack. Now if you will follow me I'll take you up to view the cockpit, as I pressed the left wing of my winged com-link."

"'PAT', raise the Plasma Pulse Cannons, contract and slide the port wing then open and lower the main hatch platform. "Affirmative Major," she stated then secs later the cannons raised, the port wing slid forward and contracted as the main hatch opened and lowered to the tarmac. We all stood on the main hatch platform and it started to rise, as we entered the cockpit I could see by the expression on their faces that the military officials were impressed by the plush interior.

"In the times yet to come the military sure takes care of their officer's, don't they?" Jr. Commodore Moncton asked as he patted my shoulder. "Well, the Humanarian members do," I replied as I went and inserted my electronic keycard. "Greetings Maj. Teldat and grand twilight to you and your guests. "Greetings 'PAT', and many thanks," I said as I turned towards my guests.

"Lady and gentle folk I would like to introduce you to my cybernetic and on-board super computers named 'PAT'. "You neglected to inform us about her," Admiral Fenton said. "I did for a reason, 'PAT' is my left hand, my right hand, she is the eyes in the back of my head; she is all the co-pilots I will ever need all rolled into one super cybernetic onboard computer. The letters P A T is an anagram, which stands for Prototype Advancements in Technology."

"But why didn't you inform us about your cybernetic super computers in the Commodore's office? "I neglected to say anything about her because I wanted you all to witness her individually; Sr. Com. Bancais has already met her, now it is your turn. Say greetings to 'PAT'. "Greetings 'PAT'," they all said, as they looked dumb founded at the brightly lit instrument panels.

"Wow," I heard them say as everything illuminated. "Take a look through this," I said to Jr. Commodore Moncton as I picked up the 'HUD' helmet and handed it to him. Jr. Commodore Moncton sat in the pilot's seat and put the helmet on. I pressed the finger touch pad that lowered the face shield, immediately on the lower portion of the face shield he seen the menu, from there I am able to observe fuel levels, artillery ammunition levels, maps, etc. With a little assistance from 'PAT' and I, he had seen everything it had to show.

After a while everyone had their chance to view everything the 'HUD' helmet had to show, and then their attention was brought to the hand contoured flight stick.

"This craft is hover capable; therefore I don't have the need of a runway for liftoff or setting down. For liftoffs I pull up on the flight stick and rise, when ready to set my craft down, I decelerate until I am no longer in motion then I just have to push the flight stick down. If you'll noticed the array of colored finger touch pads jeweled on the sides of the flight stick they are there for me to fire my SQ Laser, the XTR-9000 Plasma Pulse Cannons, fire my Protonic EMC Missals and Neutronic EMC Torpedo's, to activate my full-bodied shield and to operate my XT-165 DigiCam."

"Also, when I enter stealth mode I'm not only able to jam radar but my craft is able to manipulate illumination in such a way that my craft itself becomes invisible from sight as well as radar, that is why my craft is known as a Spy Jet."

At that time I switched everything off and withdrew my electronic keycard. "Time for us to go view the engines before it gets too dark," I said as I ushered my guests to the main hatch platform.

"'PAT', raise the golden modules and extend the rod then open the engine cover of the craft. "At once Major," she said as she did what I asked then we all left the cockpit. As we got to the tarmac below the golden modules and rod protruded from the frame, I brought them to everyone's attention. "If you'll all notice the special golden modules and rod situated on the frame of my craft; remember them and I'll explain their significance in a few mites. 'PAT' assist me retrieve an automatic mechanical lift, so we all could view the engines and other equipment? "Affirmative sir," she said as we left the area.

A few mites later, we returned in an armored utility vehicle towing the AML, then we had it locked in place at the rear of the craft. My guests, 'PAT' and I stepped on and we rose. At the top, we stepped onto the steel mesh walkway, went over to and climbed down the silver polished metal ladder. "As you can see this craft has two huge F405-F1D3 afterburning engines, and with these engines my craft can excel as fast as Mach ten. I use these two engines the most when I am in the air; and they operate using regular jet fuel."

At that time, I brought everyone's attention to the now famous Omagon 2115 Star Drive engine. "How does this engine work?" Admiral Fenton asked. "To go to Star Drive speed this engine requires a powerful accelerant, that special accelerant is the aforementioned Liquid Napricyte^2 SDC plus this," I said as I presented the Electronic Flux Inducer.

"When the Omagon 2115 Star Drive Engine is activated it sends an electrical current, saturated by the Liquid Napricyte^2 Star Drive Compound to this Electronic Flux Inducer, and in turn the EFI converts that power to Ionic power and sends the Ionic current through this insulated cable to the rear of the craft. Where it splits and the charge circulates electromagnetically encompassing my craft from each golden module then travels to the longer golden rod on the nose of my craft, which are the golden modules and rod I had shown you a few mites ago."

"From the golden rod the Ionic charge is shot out in my path, which forms a swirling Humanarian-made wormhole. I fly into this wormhole and am able to fly at Star Drive speed within

ZarCedra's oxygenated resistant atmosphere and gravitational pull. The ride through this wormhole is very rough; it is like flying along a very twisty roller coaster. With the wormhole being oxygenated resistant, that means there is no oxygen. In order for me to breathe while I am in the wormhole, I have tanks of compressed breathable oxygen that is automatically pumped into the cockpit."

"My superiors decided to limit the airspeed to Star Drive two within the wormhole because that airspeed is considered the fastest I can safely fly within ZarCedra's boundaries."

"Can you tell me again precisely how fast Star Drive speed is?" Capt. Lancing asked as he looked around. "Star Drive one is Mach ten * ten and Star Drive two is Mach ten * twenty. "I still can't believe that speed is attainable," Sr. Com. Tobious said shaking his head.

I pointed to a covered compartment on the Star Drive engine. "I screw in a 200 ml vile of Liquid Napricyte[2] SDC here and the chemical solution is pumped through an injection port over here. "How much of this chemical solution do you have remaining?" Com. Sparks asked.

"I had eight 200 milliliter vials when I started my original mission, one was used then when Sr. Com. Bancais' military scientists came to take specs of my Star Drive engine they had requested a sample of the compound to duplicate the formula. So I now have six 200 ml vials of this very powerful radioactive chemical solution remaining. "I see, and this chemical solution is shared with your aircraft's weapons? "That is correct," I said.

"Is that going to be enough for the war that is about to occur?" Lt. Benallie asked. "It should be enough for a while, but then I will require more. "Is this the generator that supplies your aircraft with all the necessary electrical power?" Admiral Fenton inquired.

"That is correct sir; this is my Comodrone Electronics P-52 Hydrogenic Generator. My Sareden Quantum Laser Cannon's as well as the XTR-9000 Plasma Pulse Cannon's ammunition are self-reproducing with this generator, but this generator requires ten mites for it to fill my total compliment of Protonic EMC-Missals to fifteen and twenty mites for the EMC-Torpedo's. It also supplies all electronic power to my craft's electronic systems."

"What other functions does your aircraft possess? "My craft also has a full-bodied shield. I can sustain digits of hits before I must retreat and recharge or my craft is seriously damaged. Also, I am able to stop and hover in one position as I pivot my craft and fire my weapons."

"My craft is also equipped with an XT-165 DigiCam; my Comodrone Electronic P-52 Hydrogenic Generator also powers it so I can record up to 165 epocks of digital cinematics on a Dexter micro disk. And, I already mentioned about the invisibility factor my craft possesses; but if I must fire my weapons or activate the Star Drive engine I must reappear before my weapons or Star Drive engine will operate. My craft has other components that at this time I won't mention but should give ZarCedra's defenses a fighting edge in the upcoming war."

"Now that concludes the tour at this time," I said as we went to the ladder and climbed up to the walkway then we all went over to and got back on the AML and descended to the tarmac below.

"'PAT', you can now close the rear of the craft and lower the golden modules and rod." I said as I turned towards her. "Affirmative Major," she acknowledged then did what I asked.

"This version of the Stealth Craft is like all the previous Stealth Aircraft's in the times elapsed, in respect to its Stealth capabilities, except for its size, speed, weapons, the invisibility factor and hover capabilities."

"Tell us more of this Protrerian race? "Affirmative, they are air breathers, they require oxygen the same as we do; they are not as attractive as Humanarian's are in respect to their facial features, except the females," I said with a grin. "Protrerian's have bluish-green skin, a rigid forehead and a mellow odor about them."

"Males of the species grow to a maximum of three metrics tall and weigh up to 150 kgs. Females of the species only grow to the maximum of two metrics tall and weigh up to 65 kgs. They have four breasts and give birth to as many as four offspring at any one prenatal period."

"These alien citizens are advanced enough to require energy as we do, that is the reason they declare war. Unfortunately they give no advanced warning of their attack! I guess that is one of the reasons I was brought to this precise moment in time."

"What does the casualty outlook look like?" Capt. Lancing inquired with concern. "It doesn't look grand; casualties are heavy on both sides. Even with the assistance we receive from the Antrerian Armada, the war is supposed to last a grand half a tritton. But by me being here at this critical juncture in times elapsed and with the firepower I possess it just might be over a lot sooner than half a tritton."

"Many thanks for the insight of the war and letting us take a look at your aircraft; whatever you are here for I hope it improves our situation."

"One more thing," I interrupted, "the Protrerian High Command has four Energy Extractor Craft and they are the crafts that first attack the four main energy facilities around ZarCedra. But, their smaller, more maneuverable attack craft are the main craft that attacks ZarCedra. "Affirmative, many thanks for that bit of information Major; it's time for us to go, grand-twilight."

"Citizens get a grand twilights slumber, because all hellatious breaks loose in the morrow morn at 11 hundred epocks," Sr. Com. Tobious said then they all left heading in the direction of main headquarters.

"Grand luck in the morrow baby and may the Gods be with us," I said as I patted the tire of my craft. 'It's about time I had my twilight banquet,' I thought just as my stomach growled. "'PAT', you are welcome to join me for my banquet or remain with the craft. "Many thanks Major but I should prepare for the morrow's attack," 'PAT' said with a smile. "Affirmative 'PAT', grand twilight," I said as I made sure my craft was secure then I left the area and proceeded to the mess hall.

When I arrived and opened the entry-way, the place was almost deserted; only the cooking staff and a few air citizens remained. I grabbed a tray and assisted myself to what remained for my twilight banquet, went to get a cup of brew and eating utensil then I went to sit as I removed my beret.

As I sat, a siren sounded and a voice reported. "As of now this military facility is on full military alert and no one but the visiting dignitaries are permitted to leave the premises."

A few mites went by and as I finished my banquet, I pushed my tray aside then pulled my brew cup towards me. When I had swilled my brew, I gathered my tray, put my beret on, got up and went to discard it then I left the mess hall. I walked to the designated puffing area but it was deserted. 'No one around, I might as well give Topanga a call,' I thought as I changed direction.

I walked the few blocks across the military facility to my barracks; I climbed the step, entered then marched to the PCD at the far end of the hall.

At the PCD, I stopped to look at the time and seen that it was 22 hundred 34 epocks. "Hmm it's getting late," I said to myself as I deposited a quint gribbit and entered in Topanga's digits. Two chirps later, Cheryl, Topanga's abode mate answered.

"Greetings. "Greetings Cheryl this is Jeroque, how are you this twilight? "I'm doing ok. "Grand, would Topanga happen to be at your abode? "Yes she is, hold a mite and I'll retrieve her." In the interim, I read the names again that were scrawled upon the wall. A mite later Topanga's lovely voice emitted from the receiver.

"Greetings Jeroque, what's up?"

"Greetings huni buni, not much I just wanted to hear your voice. I would enjoy seeing your exquisite face as we talk but they haven't installed cinematic pcd's yet."

"Do you know when they will start installing them?"

"I know they are already invented but the first cinematic pcd's will be available to the general public and start to be installed in a few p.a.r's after the Protrerian High Command attack."

"That will be excellent," she said as she marveled at the idea of us both viewing each other as we conversed.

"Although cinematic pcd's were an invention created by Humanarian's, if the Protrerian High Command is victorious in this war, the Humanarian race won't be able to access them for many trittons."

"Many trittons, really?"

"Really, my sweet."

"Then that's one more reason I hope our planet prevails."

"So do I Topanga, so do I. Then maybe Sr. Com. Bancais scientists can hopefully figure out a way for me to get back to my own time where I belong."

"It would be wonderful if you could get back to your own time but then again it wouldn't."

"Why do you say that?"

"Because as you know, I've fallen hopelessly in love with you and it will hurt to lose you."

"Unless, you accompany me when I attempt to get back, if the situation ever arose?"

"What, you mean I would be able to travel through time with you?" Topanga excitedly asked with a shriek of delight.

"If it's at all possible and if we are able to be victorious in this war this time around. You know there is extra seating capacity in my craft."

"Oh Jeroque, knowing this makes me love you even more."

"I love you too huni buni but you have to inkle about this hard and long, because this attempt may not work at all. When I was struck by lightning the first time I traveled in times elapsed, what happens if I get struck again and I travel even further in times elapsed or Godly paradise forbid my craft detonates?"

"I would not care, I love you that much."

"You can always look at it this way; it's better to have love lost, rather than not to have loved at all."

"I know you are correct Jeroque but just inkle if we can get back to your time, it would be grand."

"Affirmative, it would."

"What did you do after I dropped you off?" Topanga asked changing the subject.

"All I am permitted to say is I had a very imperative meeting with military and other important officials, my apologies but the meeting itself is confidential."

"I understand Jeroque, my apologies for asking."

"What did you do?"

"After I dropped you off I went for a limonade with an consociate then returned to my abode and I've been here ever since."

"Did you enjoy yourself when you were out?"

"I did but I would have enjoyed myself more if you were with me."

"I just bet," I said jestingly. "What are your plans for the morrow?"

"I have to pay a few notices then at 1 o'clock I have to be at work."

"Well I hope you have a grand p.a.r and I will talk to you again as soon as I can, take care huni buni."

"You too and be careful."

"Don't worry huni buni, I will."

"Ok, remember I'm here waiting for you and I love you."

"I especially love you, grand twilight Topanga."

"Grand twilight, Jeroque."

"Adioso," we both said then we hung up.

*****

After I hung up the receiver, I turned and walked to the retina scanner by my quarters. I had my retina scanned, after my voice pattern was identified the entry-way opened and I entered. Chad was sitting in the armchair swilling a soft swill, listening to the melodic composition on the Intervision monitor while he jotted a letter. He looked up and smiled.

"What did Sr. Com. Bancais want? "I had a meeting with the Sr. Commodore and other military officials then after I let the officials view my craft. When I was in Sr. Com. Bancais office earlier I specifically asked for you and Sgt. Pane to fly wing citizens in my squadron in the morrow."

"You mean we'll be flying together, that's terrific. "Affirmative, it will be dangerous but at least I can keep an eye on you two; we will fly first sortie in the morrow morn. "Who else will be in our squadron?" Chad asked as he finished jotting his letter. "I only asked for you and Sgt. Pane, Sr. Com. Bancais will fill in the rest with whoever he feels will best compliment my squadron and give me the roster in the morn but I suspect there will be ten to fifteen aircraft in our squadron."

"Well, time to go hit the sack, big p.a.r in the morrow; grand twilight," I said as I went to the latrine. "Grand twilight, see you in the morn," Chad replied as he continued to watch and listen to the melodic composition channel. When I was in my twilight garments, I went to my slumbering quarters and grabbed my jotter and jotted in the events of this p.a.r.

When I finished, I put my jotter away then went to bed. "Illumination off," I said as I pulled the comforter over me then I closed my eyes and drifted off to a slumber.

P.A.R 7

At 10 hundred 20 epocks I was ordered to Sr. Com. Bancais office, A.S.A.P. I ran to main headquarters and entered, briskly walked down the main hallway until I came to Sr. Com. Bancais' secretarial assistant.

"Maj. Teldat reporting as ordered. "You may go right in Major; the Sr. Commodore is expecting you. "Many thanks," I replied as I removed my beret then went to the entry-way, rapped and waited a sec until I was instructed to enter. I entered, closed the entry-way then stood at attention in front of Sr. Com. Bancais' desk and saluted.

"Maj. Teldat reporting as ordered, sir! "At ease Major, as of 10 hundred 15 epocks, we lost visual and audio contact with every satellite in the upper ionosphere around the globe. I am certain our alien foe has destroyed them so they won't be identified before their attack. Here is the list of pilots that will be in your squadrons," Sr. Com. Bancais said as he handed me the list. I glanced at it and noticed LC Luxton and Sgt. Pane's names among the names of pilots in my squadron.

"You are the flight leader of the Potenza squadron, but I am also adding the Cretka and Molenka squadrons to your squadron to assist. You will have a total of twenty-nine other aircraft in your squadron and you are to immediately depart and enter the Cardola Territories air space and rendezvous at the Lanston Military Installation in Translete, CT."

"Inform them you are there under direct orders from President Torren to be in contact with Jr. Com. T. Stenwen. "Affirmative sir, is that all? "Negative airman, grand luck up there! "Many thanks sir," I said as I saluted and started to leave the office. "One more thing Major, I will inform the rest of the pilot's in your squadrons immediately and quickly brief them of the mission. So once your squadrons are ready, you can leave immediately. "Affirmative sir," I answered then left the office as I replaced my beret upon my head.

I tapped my com-link. "'PAT' lower the main hatch platform," I said as I ran out to my craft. When I arrived I went right up to the cockpit. I raised and closed the main hatch platform then went and inserted my electronic keycard.

"Grand morn 'PAT', ready to engage the enemy? "Grand morn Major, I'm always ready." She stated as the control panels touch pad lights and monitors illuminated. I quickly removed my beret and tucked it into my shoulder loop as I put my flight suit on then sat in the pilot's seat, as I strapped on my safety belts. "Affirmative 'PAT'," I said as I pressed the ignition button.

I put on my 'HUD' helmet then waited a few secs for my craft's engines to fully engage then I taxied past the helijets into the open. I tapped the finger touch pad on the side of my helmet that activated two-way communications. "Potenza, Cretka and Molenka squadrons are you ready to depart? "Affirmative," they answered as they one by one checked in.

"Maj. Teldat, I am Lt. "Cracker" Tibb's, leader of the Cretka squadron. "And I am Maj. "Swifty" Currant, leader of the Molenka squadron. "Grand p.a.r ladies and gentle folk, welcome to the Potenza squadron I want you all to immediately get airborne and I will meet you all at 1500 metrics. "Affirmative sir."

"Major, do you have a flying handle or would you like me to assign you one?" Sgt. Pane inquired as my squadrons one by one took off down the runways. "Negative Sergeant, I was never given one; whatever you come up with is fine with me. "Affirmative," he said as he went silent a few secs.

"How about Time Star? Considering your aircraft traveled back in time and travels at Star Drive speed. "Affirmative Time Star it is," I said as I reactivated two-way communications. "Tower this is Maj. "Time Star" Teldat requesting permission for liftoff? "Affirmative Major, you are cleared. "It's time to get airborne 'PAT', here we go," I said as I paid close attention to the ground crew as my craft immediately started to rise. We stopped rising at 1500 metrics, I leveled the wings, raised the landing gear and waited for my squadron to rise to the predetermined altitude.

When the squadrons were all together we flew in formation out of Cangla City. "Now let's get all your flying handles? LC Luxton, what is your flying handle? "'Gunner', sir. "Affirmative, Lance Corporal," I said with a smirk. Sgt. Pane what is yours? "Ace Flyer," he said with a chuckle. "Lt. Brucetti what is yours? "My flying handle is 'Baby Doll,' sir. "Sgt. Powiklet, what is yours? "Ginger Tart, sir."

After hearing the rest of the flying handles, I tapped the finger touch pad that activated two-way communications. "Maj. Teldat calling the Lanston Military Installation."

"This is the Lanston Military Installation; can we be of assistance Major? "I am the flight leader of the Potenza squadron, accompanied by the Cretka and Molenka squadrons from the Grinshaw Military Facility of Cangla City, in the honorary regime of Placaden, Tanglar. We are now entering the Cardola Territories airspace, under direct orders from President Torren to be in contact with the Lanston Military Installation and Jr. Com. T. Stenwen."

"I am Pvt. Konan, grand to make your acquaintance. "Private can you be in contact with your Commanding Officer and inform him that my squadrons will be landing in approximately 5 mites; this is flight leader Maj. "Time Star" Teldat, out. "Affirmative Major, he'll be awaiting your arrival, Lanston Military Installation out."

"'PAT' produce a map of Translete CT, so I can locate the exact location of the Lanston Military Installation. "Affirmative Major," she acknowledged as a map of Translete, Cardola Territories illuminated at the bottom of the face shield.

"Major "Time Star", are you excited about starting your first mission in this time?" Ginger Tart Powiklet asked. "Affirmative," I answered as a flashing red illuminator illuminated over the location of the military installation. I tapped the finger touch pad that activated two-way communications.

"Tower this is Maj. "Time Star" Teldat of the Potenza squadron accompanied by the Cretka and Molenka squadrons requesting permission to land? "You are all cleared to land on runways four, five and eight. "Affirmative," I responded then ordered my squadrons to, "land on the runways four, five and eight." I hesitated a sec then contacted the tower once again. "Tower, this is Maj. Teldat again, is there a place where I could set down? I am flying a prototype hover controlled craft that doesn't require a runway to land. "What type of aircraft are you flying?" Pvt. Konan asked as he looked at his radar and seen the huge blip.

"You haven't heard of this type of craft," I said as everyone in my squadrons started to lower their landing gear. "It's a Supersonic Dragon 228-D Spy Jet Stealth. It's like the Nightingale 228-A Stealth Aircraft but quite larger. "Larger you say, then you better lower to helijet landing pads 6 to 8. "Affirmative, inform Jr. Com. T. Stenwen to meet me as I land; it's of the up most urgency! "Affirmative Major," Pvt. Konan out. "Maj. Teldat, out."

I circled around until I seen the landing pads 6, 7 & 8, I stopped, raised the wings as the landing gear lowered and hovered down to the helijet landing areas below. After my craft was on the tarmac, I switched the engines off then contracted the port wing; after, it slid out of the way of the main hatch. I removed the 'HUD' helmet, unbuckled myself and hurried to the main hatch. "'PAT', I'll return momentarily," I said as I opened it then stepped on and lowered.

As I neared the tarmac, I looked over and seen a stern looking military citizen holding his beret as he walked over by a helijet next to the pads where I had set down. Upon seeing the officer in charge, I saluted.

"Who are you and what's so urgent that I had to drop everything and meet you?" The Jr. Commodore asked. "I am Maj. "Time Star" Teldat and there is approximately fifteen mites before all hellatious breaks loose over your city. "How do you know that? "Let's just say I have my ways of knowing and my knowledge is factual and precise. Now as you know we of the Royal Tanglar Military are under full military alert, I'm sure your President has contacted you and brought you up to speed with our situation?"

"Affirmative, he has and the city of Translete has been evacuated except for all military personnel but there has been no reports stating we are in any type of jeopardy. "Believe me sir there won't be, but we are going to be attacked from above at precisely 11 hundred epocks."

"Do you have squadrons ready for takeoff? "I have squadrons on standby alert; they can scramble and be in the air at a mite's notice. "Excellent, have them in the air immediately, it's almost 11 hundred epocks; I the command leader of the Potenza, Cretka and Molenka squadrons of the Cangla City detachment of the Royal Tanglar Military will be in the air awaiting their arrival," I replied as I saluted again, turned and started for my craft.

"After this attack I want you to report directly to my office and explain how you know the things you say will happen and I want you to explain the aircraft you fly!" The Jr. Commodore shouted after me. "Affirmative sir, promptly on my return," I said as I stepped on the main hatch platform.

I tapped my com-link. "'PAT' signal me at precisely 11 hundred epocks Central Time. "Affirmative Major," she responded as I pressed the relay button on my timepiece. "10 hundred 55 epocks," it informed me. When I arrived at the cockpit, I entered, raised then closed the main hatch and immediately went to the pilot's seat and buckled myself in ready for liftoff then replaced the 'HUD' helmet atop my head. "Time to kick some alien backside," I said as I activated my craft, slid then extended the port wing and both wings tilted downwards as my craft hovered skywards ass the landing gear rose inside my craft.

I tapped the finger touch pad on my helmet that activated two-way communications. "Maj. Swifty Current, Lt. Baby Doll Brucetti and Lt. Cracker Tibbs, get my squadrons airborne immediately," I said as I continued my ascent. "Affirmative Maj. Time Star," they acknowledged as they one by one started up the runways.

On other runways I saw the Translete detachment of the Cardola Territories aircraft takeoff and rise to my altitude. I hovered in the air then activated two-way communications. "Ascend to two thousand metrics," I informed, as helijets also started rising to the predetermined altitude. I also rose and as soon I reached the designated altitude I leveled the wings of my craft.

I accessed the menu inside my 'HUD' helmet then accessed my targeting scanner and activated it. The visor of my helmet rose and the scanner protruded.

Just then 'PAT' set off a "buzzer" and informed me, "it is now 11 hundred epocks precisely." At that moment I looked at my radar and seen about thirty waves of intergalactic spacecraft descending our way. "'PAT, activate weapons. "Activated," she said as they descended then branched out. Half of the Protrerian High Command attack craft flew toward our location as the rest flew east.

"Enemy craft heading in our direction and by the rate of descent of the other enemy craft, they are on a course to Zantara, 'PAT' reported. "Affirmative 'PAT', many thanks," I said as I tapped the touch pad for two-way communications.

"Lanston tower, we have fifteen waves of enemy attack craft also heading east, by the rate of their descent they are heading toward the Zantaran continent! "Affirmative, we will contact the proper established order of that continent. "Affirmative tower. 'PAT' raise shields," I said as I activated the XT-165 DigiCam.

"It's now time to roc citizens," I told everyone as I returned fire on the silver and blue metallic attack craft. As everyone else fell in and were engaged in airwars of their own. Destroying Protrerian High Command attack craft after attack craft, I spent off a Protonic EMC-Missal at the craft on Baby Doll's tail. Destroying it in the process.

"Many thanks Time Star," she said as I stopped turned 180° and fired off another Protonic EMC-Missal destroying the craft on my own tail. I glanced in all directions and seen both, the ZarCedra fighters and Protrerian High Command attack craft explode all around me as I kept firing the port and starboard XTR-9000 Plasma Pulse Cannons, the Sareden Quantum lasers and expelled additional Protonic EMC-Missals and Neutronic

EMC-Torpedo's and watched as spacecraft exploded or fell from the sky crashing to the planet below. From the corner of my eye I seen the black smoke of the anti-aircraft weapons on the surface as they fired at all enemy starships.

The initial attack lasted a grand forty-five mites then I saw what was left of the Protrerian High Command's Intergalactic attack craft gather together and head up towards the cosmos. I looked at my radar; the danger was gone so I had the cannons rise back into the wings as I disengaged the targeting scanner, as it disappeared back into my 'HUD' helmet. I lowered my face shield as I tapped the finger touch pad that activated two-way communications.

"Potenza, Cretka, Molenka and Translete squadrons the area is all clear for now, we'll fly back down to the Lanston Military Installation below and I will report to Jr. Com. Stenwen. "Affirmative," they responded as what remained of the squadrons flew back into the civilian deserted city of Translete. As we descended the jets that were badly damaged were the first to land. As soon as what remained of the aircraft and helijets started lowering to the ground, I tapped the finger touch pad that activated two-way communications and called the tower.

"Tower this is Maj. Teldat, have someone inform Jr. Com. Stenwen that what was left of the ZarCedra's squadrons that went up have now returned, severely damaged. "Affirmative sir."

I turned off the XT-165 DigiCam and dropped my shield, then recharged my Protonic EMC-Missals and Neutronic EMC-Torpedo's. I lowered my landing gear, and had the wings raised then after what was left of my own squadrons were safely on the tarmac, I hovered down to the helijet landing areas below. "'PAT' you are with me," I said as we both left the cockpit.

A few mites later we reported directly to Jr. Com. Stenwen. "Our forces took a real beating up in the skies over the city, I stated the shape the squadrons were in and I knew the Protrerian High Command will send more attack craft re-supplied. "How do you know all this and explain the aircraft you are flying!" Jr. Com. Stenwen demanded.

"Could I speak freely under extreme secrecy? "Of course Major, stand at ease and commence! "First and foremost, beside me is my cybernetic co-pilot, her name is 'PAT'; her designation is an anagram for Prototype Advancements in Technology. She is the cybernetic version of my onboard super computer. "Grand p.a.r Jr. Commodore," 'PAT' said with a salute. After Jr. Com. Stenwen returned her salute I slowly started to explain the predicament we have found ourselves in.

"Sir, the tritton we are from is 2115. That is why I know what is about to happen, I read about this war in my times elapsed archive. "You mean to tell me in your time this war with these aliens already took place? That is correct sir and we lost; that is why, I think we were brought to this precise moment in time. The reason is to try to assist in this war and prevent the Protrerian High Command from defeating our forces and taking control of our world. "'PAT' can verify everything I am about to tell you is the absolute truth."

"More about the prototype craft I have in my possession, which is the experimental Supersonic Dragon 228-D Spy Jet Stealth. This craft was built especially for the uprising of the Humanarian military after a centritton of alien domination."

"For its armament it has Sareden Quantum Laser Cannons and expels Protonic Electromagnetic Cluster Missals and Neutronic Electromagnetic Cluster Torpedo's and under each wing I have a weapons pylon that houses two XTR-9000 Plasma Pulse Cannons. My Comodrone Electronics P-52 Hydrogenic generator creates the entire load of various ammunition my weapons need, mixed with Liquid Napricyte[2] to give it the explosive power it needs to destroy, it also supplies power to the rest of the components on my craft that requires electronic energy to operate. Additionally, my craft is equipped with other highly sensitive prototype equipment."

"The original secret mission I was on was to settle the Antrerian citizens, another race of extraterrestrial beings on our planet before the Protrerian High Command knew they were here. Because the Antrerian Race attempted to assist us in this war barely escaped and were banished from ZarCedra, we should receive their assistance in a few p.a.r's. But in my time the Antrerian Race's abode planet of Antreria is about to be destroyed so they were secretly settling on ZarCedra and my mission was to see to their settling and try to bring the two races together peacefully when they were finally discovered on this planet."

"A few p.a.r's ago we were flying through a severe electrical storm and my craft was struck by lightning just as I was entering a wormhole. Part of the reason my craft is known as a prototype is because we finally broke the speed barrier that permitted us Star Drive speed. Otherwise being struck by lightning would have destroyed or badly damaged the craft in which I was testing."

"To travel Star Drive speeds my craft has a third engine, identified as the Omagon 2115 Star Drive engine; this engine is powered by my aircraft's Comodrone Electronic P-52 Hydrogenic Generator, additionally it also uses the Liquid Napricyte[2] compound as its accelerant."

"What I suspect happened was the high voltage of electricity in the lightening my craft was struck with, somehow reacted with that chemical solution in my Omagon 2115 Star Drive engine and generator as I flew into the oxygenated resistant wormhole and that caused a rip in the time gamut causing my craft to plummet back in time. Anyhow that is the only reason I can surmise at this time for explaining what precisely happened for my craft and I to be here at this precise juncture in time."

"Wormhole? Explain what that is! "Affirmative sir, this special Omagon 2115 Star Drive Engine works in conjunction with an Electronic Flux Inducer. My craft's Comodrone Electronics P-52 Hydrogenic Generator sends an electrical charge to the Omagon 2115 Star Drive Engine, which combines with the Liquid Napricyte[2] SDC then this special electrical charge, is sent to the Electronic Flux Inducer. The EFI in turn converts this specially mixed electronic charge to an Ionic charge, which is then sent along an insulated cable to the rear of my craft."

"When the Omagon 2115 Star Drive Engine is activated, many golden modules are activated and protrude on the outer shell of my craft and a golden rod is extended from the nose of my craft. This Ionic charge encompasses my craft electromagnetically going to each golden module until it reaches the golden rod. This charge is then shot out in front of my craft creating a swirling Humanarian-made wormhole, in other words a churning tunnel of air. I fly into this wormhole and I am able to fly Star Drive speed within ZarCedra's oxygenated resistant atmosphere and gravitational pull. I am able to travel to a maximum air speed of Star Drive two. Which is 20* faster than my top air speed of Mach ten."

"Oxygenated resistant atmosphere means there is no oxygen, in order for me to breathe my craft is equipped with tanks of compressed oxygen that slowly releases into the cockpit as I fly through this wormhole".

"Fascinating, that is some speed, Major. How do I know you are being completely truthful? "Believe him sir, everything he has told you is the absolute truth. "That's ok 'PAT', take a look at this for one thing," I said as I withdrew my military tags. Jr. Com. Stenwen stood to get a better look. The Jr. Commodore read my rank, name, serial digits and birth p.a.r then seen the tritton of my entrance into the military, '2109'."

"I have been in the military a little more than six trittons, if you want additional proof," I told the flabbergasted Jr. Commodore; "there is a tattoo emblazoned on my upper arm of a patriotic eagle also with the tritton of my admittance into the military." I rolled up my sleeve as high as I could to show Jr. Com. Stenwen. "If additional proof is required, we can now go examine my experimental prototype craft. "Affirmative," the Jr. Commodore answered.

We all left the office for the craft then one more time I explained my aircraft. "It sure is a grand size," Jr. Com. Stenwen said as soon as he seen my aircraft again. "Affirmative, it has to be," I answered. "How many co-pilot's are required to fly such a magnificent aircraft. "I am the only Humanarian pilot; cybernetic 'PAT", is my one and only co-pilot but her counterpart, the super computer is who keeps the craft in control and in flight." I said as I looked at 'PAT'.

"'PAT', lower the main hatch platform. "Affirmative Major," she answered and secs later it started lowering. Jr. Com. Stenwen looked at the aircraft and read N.Z.C.M.Co/S.H.Z.C.A-SS Dragon 228-D SJ Stealth, written on the side and seen the depiction of the ferocious dragon.

"After the Protrerian High Command took over ZarCedra, they changed ZarCedra's military coalitions and renamed it 'ZarCedra Force'. Our Secret Division of the North ZarCedra Military Coalition kept the initials N. Z. C. M. Co and added S.H.Z.C.A, which stand for Secret Humanarian ZarCedra Alliance. "Why is the port wing contracted and further back than the starboard wing? He asked. "That is because the wing needs to be out of the way of the main hatch for it to lower and raise."

"Now will you follow me?" I asked the impressed Jr. Commodore. "Affirmative," he said as we stepped on the main hatch platform and it started to rise bringing us up to the cockpit.

"What other surprises do you have on this aircraft? "A lot," I said as I inserted my electronic keycard turning the ignition system on, and as I did the touch pads and monitors of the instrument panels illuminated. "Outrageous," the surprised Jr. Commodore said.

"Here are the instrument panels, all these mini monitors and gauges allow me to see what my craft is doing also these touch pads are to manually activate various defense equipment like chaffer flares, ECM's, decoys and the like or I could access the main menu in my 'HUD' helmet or if I'm really pressed for time, I could ask 'PAT' to access a command immediately. Finally over here is my Heads up Display or 'HUD' helmet. Here place it upon your head and tell me what you think?" I said as I went over to the pilots seat and handed it to the Jr. Commodore. Jr. Com. Stenwen sat then took the helmet and placed it on his head.

"What's the big deal, it looks like the helmets we have now, and I thought you said there was a menu? "The difference is this; 'PAT' activate the helmet." Immediately the visor lowered as the helmet activated and the menu came into view. "Like I said, either access the menu or ask 'PAT' for things like fuel gauges. "'PAT', show me the fuel gauges." The menu disappeared and the fuel gauges appeared on the mini screen on the lower portion of the face shield. "It illustrates here that you have two main tanks for regular aircraft fuel, I guess this other gauge is for the Liquid Napricyte^2, Star Drive Compound. "That is correct, for the Weapon's ammunition and the Omagon 2115 Star Drive Engine I have told you about earlier."

"You mentioned earlier your maximum normal air speed is Mach ten, also you told me you have Star Drive two, do you have Star Drive one or does your Star Drive speed excel in powers of two?" Jr. Com. Stenwen asked as he accessed other components in the menu of the helmet. "My Star Drive engine excels from Mach ten to Star Drive one then Star Drive two. 'PAT' show the artillery levels as they are being recharged?"

"Recharged, you were serious? The stupefied Jr. Commodore replied. "Affirmative, like I said I have five types of weapons on this craft, as you can see on the lower portion of the helmet's visor."

"First are the SQ-Lasers Cannons although it is self-reproducing it still needs power to operate. It gets the power from the aforementioned Comodrone Electronics P-52 Hydrogenic Generator for its operation and artillery."

"Next, is the Protonic Electromagnetic Cluster Missals, which has a highly explosive Liquid Napricyte^2 charge; the Comodrone Electronics P-52 Hydrogenic Generator operates it too but my generator requires ten mites to recharge its ammunition to its maximum load of fifteen in my weapons array.

"Thrice, is the Neutronic Electromagnetic Cluster Torpedo's; which on the other hand are neutrally charged and drains electronic power from a target. My craft's Comodrone Electronics P-52 Hydrogenic Generator also operates it but the generator requires twenty mites to recharge its ammunition to its maximum load of ten. The reason it requires more time and has less in its compliment is because these torpedo's have a larger yield and requires more energy so not to drain my generator it can only supply my craft a maximum of ten at any one time.

"Fourth and fifth, are my craft's XTR-9000 Plasma Pulse cannons. These cannons are located within each wing, when I need them, I press a touch pad and they both lower from the wings. I don't have a limit to how many I have at any one time, so they are available at all times.

My craft also has a full-bodied shield. It also draws power from the Comodrone Electronics P-52 Hydrogenic Generator. Ask 'PAT', to show the shield strength. "'PAT', show me the shield strength?" And it flashed inside the 'HUD' helmets view screen. "The shield allows me to be under heavy attack and still be able to sustain numerous hits before my shield weakens, and I must retreat to recharge."

"Last and what I think is the most important feature, is my craft's invisibility factor. My generator reformats illumination such a way that it allows my craft to vanish from sight as well as radar, this vanishing technology is part of my craft's Stealth capabilities, allowing my craft to be somewhere unseen and undetectable. "Very interesting," the Jr. Commodore stated as he took off the 'HUD' helmet.

"Where do you keep your supply of Liquid Napricyte^2 SDC?" Jr. Com. Stenwen asked as he got out of the pilot's seat. "At the rear of the cockpit in an overhead compartment that reads warning, radioactive; it is stored in a radioactive safe case and inside are the vials of the Liquid Napricyte^2 SDC."

"Now if you'll follow me we will now go and observe my aircraft's different engines," I said as I went and switched off the power then disengaged the electronic keycard. Jr. Com. Stenwen adjusted his cap as we walked to the main hatch platform then lowered to the ground.

As we both stepped off, I pressed the left wing of my com-link. "'PAT' raise and close the main hatch platform then open the tail portion so we can view the engines. "Affirmative Major," she acknowledged as the main hatch platform raised and closed as the engine cover rose then slid forward. "Cool," Jr. Com. Stenwen said amazed!

"Do you have anything we can stand on that will raise us high enough to view the engines? "Affirmative," the Jr. Commodore answered as he got the attention of a couple curious core men. "Privates, go retrieve an automatic mechanical lift. "At once sir," the core men said as they hustled to get the object for the Jr. Commodore.

"My squadron and I would need to refuel before the Protrerian High Command sent out the next battalion of attack craft," I informed Jr. Com. Stenwen as we waited for the AML. "Do you know when the next battalion will be sent out? "I don't know precisely, unfortunately I'm not a psychosomatic foreteller, but one thing I do know is it will be soon and they will attack with a vengeance sir, by air and land."

Just then the core men returned in an armored utility vehicle pulling an AML. They got out, disconnected it then brought it to the Jr. Commodore, as we gave them a hand. "Many thanks, you may be on your way," the CO said after we set the AML in place at the rear of the aircraft. Jr. Com. Stenwen and I stood on the AML as it brought us up to the metal mesh walkway surrounding the engine galley.

We stepped on to the metal walkway, went over to the ladder that descended down to the engine galley as I started to explain the two huge F405-F1D3 afterburning engines. "These two engines I use most of the time I am in the air, they propel my craft to my maximum regular airspeed of Mach ten." Jr. Com. Stenwen was flabbergasted at the size and power of these engines.

I moved to the infamous Omagon 2115 Star Drive engine. "Since it had just been invented in the tritton 2115, the scientists that invented it included that tritton in its name. Right next to it is the Electronic Flux Inducer, this is the unit that converts the mixed electrical energy into an Ionic charge that electromagnetically encompasses my craft then shoots out in my path creating the swirling Humanarian-made wormhole that makes Star Drive travel possible within ZarCedra's oxygenated resistant atmosphere and gravitational pull."

"As I already explained, the Comodrone Electronics P-52 Hydrogenic Generator supplies power to form my artillery, power my weapons, full-bodied shield and activate the craft's Stealth capabilities as well as supply power to all other electronic systems on the Supersonic Dragon 228-D Spy Jet Stealth."

"You said your aircraft's main engines operate on regular jet fuel," Jr. Com. Stenwen said. "Affirmative, the same fuel as the rest of the aircraft use," I stated as I turned to look at him. "Affirmative, just leave your aircraft here and I'll make sure it and the rest of the jets in your squadron are refueled. Meanwhile you and your squadron should go clean up and have your banquets," he said as we climbed back up to the walkway then back to the AML then we started our descent to the tarmac below.

"Many thanks sir," I said as I saluted then pressed the wing of my com-link. "'PAT' wait until the craft is refueled, after it is, close the rear of the craft. "Affirmative Major," she acknowledged.

I then told Jr. Com. Stenwen where the fuel tanks were located. "Usually the fuel tanks are located in the wings of an aircraft but since the wings on my craft contain my XTR-9000 Plasma Pulse Cannons and the wings raise and lower, the scientists in my time thought it best to have the fuel tank located in the cover of the tail portion. Where the tail section separates from the fuselage you'll see two fuel caps, one on either side of the fuselage, I will need both tanks refueled," I said as I tapped my com-link once again.

"'PAT' activate the planet radar and contact me as soon as additional Protrerian attack craft enters ZarCedra's stratosphere. "Affirmative Major."

"Jr. Commodore, where precisely are the latrines located?" I asked as I seen the pilots of what remained of my squadrons come my way. "Straight through those entry-ways," he said as he pointed, "go down the hall fifteen metrics and you'll see the entry-ways, they are clearly marked. As for the mess hall, stay along the hallway go about twenty-one metrics further and you'll see the mess hall. "Many thanks again sir," I said as I turned and walked away.

"What a battle, where do we go to freshen up?" the remaining twelve pilots in my squadrons wanted to know as we got to the entry-way. "Follow me citizens," I said as we entered the structure.

They followed my direction and a few secs later we arrived at the latrines and went in. After we cleaned up, everyone met back in the hallway then we all went for our banquets.

When we entered the mess hall we each grabbed a tray then stood in line to receive our banquet. "Do you know when the next attack would take place?" Sgt. Pane asked. "I don't really know, but my craft is equipped with a planet radar and when any enemy attack craft enters ZarCedra's stratosphere, I will be notified. "Grand, that was my first taste of air to air combat and it felt grand," Sgt. Powiklet said. "Affirmative, it got my adrenaline going too, unfortunately we lost our comrades though," Lt. Tibbs added. "Affirmative and some of them were grand consociates," Sgt. Pane said as he looked away and said a silent prayer.

After we all received our banquets, we got eating utensils and a swill then went to a table and sat. As we ate we discussed the possible reason why I came back to this precise time, just prior to the beginning of this war. Just as we were about ¾ through our banquets there was a sharp "beep" from my com-link. "Fifteen, correction, twenty waves of intergalactic attack craft just entered ZarCedra's stratosphere by the rate of descent they are headed to this location," 'PAT' reported. "Understood, on our way," I acknowledged as we all rose.

"Here we go again!" LC Luxton said as everyone in my squadron got up and quickly ran out to our aircrafts.

Just as I arrived at my craft, the fuel tanker was just leaving and the tail portion of my craft lowered. "We have twenty waves of enemy attack craft incoming," I yelled out as I ran just as the base alarm sounded. "Your squadron's aircraft were also refueled, I'll dispatch multiple squadrons in the air immediately," Jr. Com. Stenwen told me as he ran off.

I tapped my com-link. "'PAT', lower the main hatch platform." When it was on the ground I went up to the cockpit, I closed and secured the main hatch, inserted my electronic keycard then went to the pilot's seat and buckled myself in as I put my 'HUD' helmet on.

After ignition, I extended and slid the port wing until it was in position. A sec later they tilted downward as my craft hovered up to thirteen hundred metrics, stopped, leveled the wings, and raised the landing gear. By this time my squadron was in the air and they all fell into formation behind me as we went to engage the enemy. I accessed the menu inside my 'HUD' helmet then accessed and activated my targeting scanner. The face shield rose and the scanner protruded. I looked at my radar and noticed the Protrerian's were almost on top of us.

"'PAT' activate weapons," I said as pressed the finger touch pad on my helmet that activated two-way communications. "Here we go citizens it's time to roc...once again," I said as I activated my craft's full-bodied shield then eased the stick forward even further as my squadron and I engaged the enemy with guns and lasers blazing. I slowed then stopped, hovered in midair rotating my craft as I lowered the Plasma Pulse Cannons. My fingers danced along the finger touch pads as I fired all weapons, destroying attack craft after attack craft.

I thought about using my craft's Neutronic EMC-Torpedo's once again but the enemy attack craft weren't that large and I thought using a Torpedo would just be a waste of critical artillery. So I destroyed a total of twelve attack craft using just my cannons, lasers and Protonic EMC-Missiles before the fighters and helijets from Translete arrived to assist. I tapped the finger touch pad on my 'HUD' helmet that activated two-way communications. "Welcome to this little battle air citizens," I said as they joined the air battle.

Everywhere I looked there were fighters and attack craft blasting at each other; even from the city I seen cannon fire from the ground troops firing at all alien attack craft that flew overhead.

The laser blasts of the Protrerian High Command attack craft almost looked animated until the realization that this was the real thing. Every time a fighter or helijet exploded into a grand ball of fire, that was one less pilot and aircraft fighting for ZarCedra's freedom.

We fought hard about two epocks when I destroyed the last remaining attack craft. "Many thanks 'PAT'," I said. "My radar is all clear," I told all that survived the attack, including the two remaining pilots in my own squadron as I raised the cannons then disengaged the targeting scanner and it disappeared back into my 'HUD' helmet. All that remained of the Potenza Squadron was Gunner Luxton and Ace Flier Pane and myself.

On our return flight to the Lanston Military Installation, I recharged my EMC-Missals and shield. "Forty ZarCedra aircraft squadrons are heading in our direction, arriving from off the East as well as the West coast of the Zran Continent. "'PAT' could you determine their identity? "Affirmative, they are parts of the Candory, Ghengist, Tormor, Skreel, Zand, Camael, Rasbur, Tesmir, Kronc, Urik, Quatae and Skittar Air Battalions arriving from aircraft transporters in the Oskretin and Sydoken Seas," 'PAT' reported.

"Brigadier Commodore Scalops of the Kronc Continents Military Coalitions reporting in, Maj. Teldat do you copy? "Affirmative, go ahead. "We heard you could use assistance, we were sent via aircraft transporters by our respective countries to offer all assistance necessary and that all military forces from around the planet, were lending any and all assistance in this intergalactic war. "Affirmative, where were you a couple epocks ago we could have used your assistance in the battle we just fought. "My apologies Major but our aircraft transporters just arrived and we were dispatched immediately," Brig. Commodore Scalops reported.

"Well, we welcome you and are thankful for all the assistance we can get; we are just heading back to the Lanston Military Installation in Translete, CT. The Commanding Officer in charge is Junior Commodore Stenwen; make sure you meet him upon your arrival, Maj. Teldat out."

I tapped the finger touch pad that activated two-way communications. "Tower of the Lanston Military Installation, this is Maj. Time Star Teldat; we have allied forces arriving from aircraft transporters off the east and west coasts of the Oskretin and Sydoken Seas, inform Jr. Com. Stenwen to also have a fuel tanker awaiting to refuel what's left of my squadron and my aircraft as soon as we land, Maj. Teldat, out. "Affirmative Major, Lanston Military Installation, out."

"'PAT', is there a way of keeping the weapon system activated at all times so I don't have to ask you to activate them every time we go into battle? "Affirmative Major, there is would you like to complete this task or would you like me to do it for you? "Inform me and I'll know how to do it in the times yet to come. "Affirmative, activate the menu in the 'HUD' helmet and go to your weapons list. At the bottom of the list you will see a check box for activate weapons at all times. Check mark this box and your weapons will remain activated at all times. "Many thanks 'PAT'," I said as I followed her instruction.

A sec later I set my craft down at the military installation and as I did there was a fuel tanker waiting for me. I powered down my craft as I contracted then slid the port wing out of the way of the main hatch. I released my safety belts then took off my 'HUD' helmet as I went and removed the electronic keycard. "'PAT', the craft will get refueled then we're off to the Pentiac Solar Energy Reactor," I said as I lowered to the tarmac and looked around the underbelly of my craft for any sign of damage.

I waited until the fuel tanker refueled my craft and was driving away when I re-contacted 'PAT'. "'PAT', I'll be right with you but first I must see the Jr. Commodore," I told her as I put my beret on then went in the direction of their main headquarters structure then to Jr. Com. Stenwen's office.

As I got to his office, I saluted and stood front and center in front of the Jr. Commodore's desk. "We had one horrific air battle in the sky above your city sir; we lost a lot of grand air citizens. But, with all the allied ZarCedra aircraft incoming from aircraft transporters off the east and west coasts, our continent should be well protected. "Affirmative Major."

"For now I must go to the Pentiac Solar Energy Reactor in the Southern region of the honorary regime of Placaden,

Tanglar and secure that location because it is one of the main targets of our extraterrestrial enemy. I trust you will take care of the two pilots remaining in my squadron in my absence? "Not to worry, they will be well cared for. "Many thanks sir," I said as I saluted, turned and left the CO's office then went to my craft.

I rose to the cockpit. "'PAT', keep radar on and inform me as soon as anything enters ZarCedra's stratosphere," I said as I entered. "Affirmative Major," 'PAT' acknowledged as I raised, closed then locked the main hatch then sat in the pilot's seat and safety belted myself in. I prepped my craft's engines as I removed my beret then put the 'HUD' helmet on as I extended the wing and it slid forward.

I rose to fifteen hundred metrics, lowered the wings and the landing gear raised as I slowly advanced forward increasing speed. As I flew I engaged stealth mode and my craft disappeared as I continued to the Solar Energy Facility.

After a few mites, I flew over the Grand Tarns of Placaden at Mach eight, as I was discussing "military tactics" with 'PAT'; I flew over Trigor. A moment later I was hovering over the Pentiac Solar Energy Facility, I lowered altitude to one hundred and fifty metrics, stopped and hovered as I disengaged stealth mode and my craft again became visible.

"'PAT', scan the area for any sign of disturbance or intruders. "Scanning Major.... The area is clear at this moment," 'PAT' reported secs later. "Many thanks 'PAT', I replied as I raised the craft's wings and lowered the landing gear then descended to the tarmac below.

I tapped the finger touch pad that activated two-way communications. "Maj. Teldat calling the Grinshaw Military Facility, come in?" I said as I set my craft down. "Sgt. Blair here, go ahead Major. "Sergeant, connect me with Sr. Com. Bancais, immediately. "At once Major."

Secs later as I was releasing my safety belts I heard. "Sr. Com. Bancais here go ahead Maj. Teldat. "Sr. Commodore, I request a battalion of armed soldiers, also six anti-aircraft cannons to protect the Pentiac Solar Energy Facility in Trigor.

"Affirmative Major, there will be a unit dispatched to that location immediately. Is that all? "Negative sir, I just set down at the Pentiac Solar Energy Reactor and I am going to secure this location and will remain here until your soldier's and munitions arrive; that is all for now. "Affirmative Major, Sr. Com. Bancais out. "Maj. Teldat out," I replied as I finished disconnecting my safety belts.

"'PAT' keep the radar on and inform me immediately upon the detection of any attack craft entering ZarCedra's stratosphere or any aircraft landing around the Facility grounds. "Affirmative, Major."

I removed my 'HUD' helmet as I contracted the port wing and as it slid back I went and opened the main hatch platform. "'PAT', you are welcomed to join me if you like? Affirmative Major, many thanks," she said as we walked on the lowered platform and lowered. As we arrived at the tarmac below, we viewed the front of the plant. There were citizen grounds crew doing various jobs on the property, they stopped what they were doing to watch us and look at my huge craft. "'PAT' raise and secure the main hatch platform. "Affirmative Major," 'PAT' acknowledged as we walked toward the main entrance of the plant.

We entered the huge structure and was fascinated with everything we saw as we walked up to a security citizen. "Greetings and Grand p.a.r. "Greetings, can I be of assistance?" He asked as he looked away from his security monitors. "Affirmative, I would like to see the person in charge of this facility, it is of the up most urgency. "Of coarse sir, his name is Dr. Shillingham and I'll call him directly," he said as he picked up the PCD. "Many thanks," I replied as the security citizen called the doctor as 'PAT' and I looked around.

"Dr. Shillingham is on his way and will be here momentarily," he said as hung up the personal communication device. "Many thanks," I replied as we walked away and continued looking at various depictions of the facility in the lobby.

We waited patiently until a gray haired scientific citizen in a white lab coat and black-rimmed spectacles walked up to us.

"Greetings and grand p.a.r, I am Dr. Shillingham," he said as we shook hands. "Greetings I am Maj. Teldat, and next to me is 'PAT'; of the Grinshaw Military Facility in Cangla City. If you haven't heard yet, war has just broken out between ZarCedra and an alien race, as of this morn at 11 hundred epocks. The Pentiac as well as the other three Solar Energy Reactor Facilities around our planet are the first targets of the enemy but do not be distressed excessively they won't be hit very hard. The abode planet of these aliens will eventually become uninhabitable so they will decide to take over ZarCedra as their new abode so they will eventually stop targeting and attacking these facilities," I explained.

"What am I to do?" Dr. Shillingham hesitantly asked. "Do not worry there will be troopers fully armed of the Tanglar Military dispatched to this location immediately to offer protection. While we are awaiting their arrival, will you show us around this fascinating facility? "Of coarse," Dr. Shillingham said as we walked from the lobby and down a corridor.

A while later Dr. Shillingham had shown and told 'PAT' and I of all the labor they were doing within the structure. "Accompany me to the exit and I will show you the other labor we do here? Dr. Shillingham said as we exited the rear of the structure. We were shown the three main gigantic stacks of the Pentiac Solar Energy Facility.

"These three stacks expel enough energy to create a continental section of protection to keep all of Tanglar and surrounding countries around the Northern Pole from the open space of the quickly deterioration of the ozone layer, which as you probably know is ZarCedra's protection from ultraviolet rays radiation and open space," Dr. Shillingham explained.

As we continued to receive the tour "PAT" interrupted. "Major, a transport plane is just setting down in an open field adjacent to the plant; it is accompanied by two F-16 Striker aircraft. "Affirmative many thanks 'PAT'," I acknowledged. "What is happening? "The plant's protection just arrived and they will remain here until after the enemy ceases their attack. "I see; do you know when that would be? "Negative, but hopefully it won't be long. "Ok," Dr. Shillingham said as we headed back inside the structure.

When we reached the main entrance, I saw a platoon of armed soldiers running in single file, and enter the structure through the front entrance. "We were sent to this location and to do everything you order," a Lt. Briggs reported as he saluted me. "Affirmative Lieutenant; take the anti-aircraft cannons and situate them around the structure and the energy reactors then protect this facility from all threats! "Affirmative sir," he acknowledged as he saluted, turned then left the structure.

At that moment 'PAT' interrupted again. "Enemy attack craft just entered ZarCedra's stratosphere, heading in this general direction. "Affirmative 'PAT'. Grand-adioso and many thanks Dr. Shillingham," I said then 'PAT' and I hurried toward the main entrance. "Wait, what should I do? "Just stay out of Lt. Briggs' way and he'll organize the soldiers and cannons. He'll have them situated where they would best protect this energy facility, in the meantime I'll try to draw the enemy attack craft away," I said as we went toward the entry-way.

At that moment, the pilots of the two F-16 Striker aircraft were entering the structure. "We have enemy attack craft heading this way, meet me in the air immediately," I said and we disappeared out the structure. "'PAT', initiate the activation of the craft and open and lower the main hatch platform."

When we arrived at the craft, we stood on the main hatch platform and went to the cockpit. After entering I closed and secured the cockpit's main hatch. 'PAT' extended the port wing then it slid forward. As the engines were already activated, I removed my beret and got in the pilot's seat. "Enemy at five thousand metrics," 'PAT' reported. "Affirmative," I acknowledged as we connected our safety belts then I put on my 'HUD' helmet. I pulled gently on the flight stick, the wings lowered as I ascended.

At one thousand metrics, I leveled the wings as the landing gear raised. I tapped the finger touch pad that activated two-way communications. "Sr. Com. Bancais come in? "Sr. Com. Bancais here, Maj. Teldat go ahead."

"Sir, I am about to engage the enemy over the Pentiac Solar Energy Facility, I request squadrons of fighters to assist in this attack. "Affirmative, they would be at your disposal in approximately ten mites."

At that moment I accessed the menu inside my 'HUD' helmet then accessed my targeting scanner and activated it. The face shield rose and the scanner protruded just as I activated my craft's shield. "Enemy attack craft at 12 o'clock," 'PAT' reported. "Maj. Teldat out," I said as I returned fire on the silver and blue metallic attack craft.

My craft shook as it was hit. "'PAT", damage report? "Damage minimal, shield strength is currently down to ninety three percent. "Affirmative," I responded as I fired at and destroyed the craft that was directly in my path as I tapped the touch pad that lowered my craft's Plasma Pulse Cannons, firing at the many attack craft on either side of my craft.

"There are two attack craft directly aft of us," 'PAT' reported. I stopped suddenly; let them fly by me then fired my laser cannons and destroyed them both. I looked around and noticed the two other pilots' of the Tanglar Military in their own battles. I turned my craft in the direction of the attack craft dogging them and spent off a Protonic EMC-Missal and the attack craft exploded in a magnificent array of pyrotechnic debris as my fingers danced on the finger touch pads along the shaft of my flight stick and fired all weapons.

There was no end to the alien attack craft; every time the other two pilots' or I destroyed an enemy attack craft there were five more to take its place.

By the time the squadrons of aircraft arrived from the Grinshaw Military Facility, there was only one of the two Striker aircraft remaining in the battle. "Assistance has arrived and it is time to kick some extraterrestrial butt," this is Capt. "Georgor" Piccini of the Areola Squadron of the Grinshaw Military Facility reporting. "Affirmative, we are terribly outnumbered," I reported as they joined the battle.

Just then my craft shook violently a few secs as I was struck on the starboard side. "Shield strength is down to fifty eight percent. "Affirmative, inform me when it gets down to twenty percent. "Affirmative, there is an attack craft at 2 o'clock. "Got him, many thanks 'PAT'," I said as I turned my craft's starboard cannon in the direction of the advancing craft and fired a Plasma shell and watched it explode. Just then I was attacked from aft; I quickly turned my craft to face my attacker and fired my laser cannons and blew that craft out of the sky.

As I flew to my next position, I checked the levels of fuel then the amount of Protonic EMC-Missals I had remaining. The fuel was sufficient but seen that I only had three Protonic EMC-Missals remaining so I continued fighting for the next ½ epock. "Shield strength is currently at twenty percent," 'PAT' reported "Acknowledged," I said as I destroyed yet another pesky attack craft.

At that time I looked at my radar and seen it was all clear of enemy craft so I disengaged the targeting scanner and it disappeared back into my 'HUD' helmet. I lowered my face shield just as a voice came over my helmet communication' array.

"Maj. Teldat you are to report to the Grinshaw Military Facility immediately for a conference. "Affirmative, I'm on my way. I tapped the finger touch pad at the side of the helmet and activated two-way communications. "Capt. Piccini, my radar is all clear of enemy attack craft at this moment and I was just ordered to report to the Grinshaw Military Facility. It's been grand fighting alongside of you and your squadron, hopefully we can fight together again, adioso!

"Affirmative Maj. Teldat and fighting alongside you and your impressive craft has been grand as well, I'll fight alongside you anytime, grand adioso," he responded as I broke formation.

"Many thanks," I said as I advanced speed to Mach six and charged my weapons and shield while I flew towards Cangla City. Meanwhile 'PAT' gave me a report of the intergalactic attack craft I had engaged and destroyed in the attack.

As I was entering the airspace over Cangla City, I slowed to fifty knots per sec then stopped and hovered over the military facility; I raised the wings as the landing gear lowered. I tapped the finger touch pad that activated two-way communications. "Tower, this is Maj. "Time Star" Teldat am I cleared to set down. "Affirmative, you are cleared. "Affirmative," I responded as I started descending to the tarmac below.

As soon as my craft was on the tarmac, I switched off the twin turbines and took off my 'HUD' helmet and disconnected my safety belts. I contracted the port wing and it slid back from the main hatch as I hopped out of the pilot's seat. I removed my flight suit then went to retrieve the electronic keycard and deposited it in the pocket of my uniform. "'PAT', you're with me. "Affirmative Major," she said as she got up and accompanied me as I opened then lowered the main hatch platform; we stepped on and lowered to the tarmac below.

I placed my beret atop my head; "'PAT', raise & close the main hatch platform." I looked at my timepiece and seen that it was 17 hundred 35 epocks, we then proceeded to main headquarters.

As we walked into main headquarters PAT and I discussed all the things that went on during this p.a.r and were going to report to Sr. Com. Bancais. We arrived at the main office area and went to LC Acernan. "Grand p.a.r Lance Corporal, I'm to report to Sr. Com. Bancais. "Of coarse Major, you may enter." 'PAT' and I went to the partially opened entry-way of Sr. Com. Bancais office; we removed our berets then knocked. "Enter and close the entry-way behind you." I did then 'PAT' and I stood at attention and saluted the commanding officer.

"You may stand at ease; I heard you had one hellatious p.a.r? "Affirmative sir! There were only two pilots left out of the squadrons that went with me to Translete, CT. And three aircraft remained of the squadrons you dispatched to the Pentiac Solar Energy Facility. All the other pilots regretfully met their destruction in combat," I said as we stood at ease. "I see; that's very unfortunate, that means we lost grand air citizens; fortunately you'll have a new squadron at your earliest convenience. "Many thanks sir"

"Now for the reason I asked for your presence. I received word this mid-p.a.r that the whole planet agreed to come together in our crisis with Protreria. "I knew they would, it was written in my times elapsed archive that they did.

"I had sent protection to the Pentiac Solar Energy Facility and requested protection to be sent to the other three Energy Reactor facilities as well. With your prototype aircraft I want you to personally go to each facility and make sure they are securely protected. "They are well protected that is one of the reasons why the Protrerian High Command decide to abandon them and take over ZarCedra."

"I see, and our extraterrestrial assistance won't arrive for some time, you say? "That's correct sir in four more p.a.r's, after our situation looks futile and a lot of our forces are defeated, that is when the Antrerians Armada arrive and attempt to protect us. When they do, we attempt to construct additional aircraft and artillery but there wasn't sufficient time and the Protrerian high Command start to be victorious in the war. "Understood," he said with a distraught look. "With you and your impressive aircraft here now, we might have a shot at being victorious this war?" The Sr. Commodore asked as looked at 'PAT' and I.

"Unknown sir, like I said before, that is the reason I'm hoping we traveled back in time for! "I see," Sr. Com. Bancais repeated as he walked to a chart of ZarCedra. Using his pointer he pointed to the position of every main command headquarters of each country's aerial defenses, around ZarCedra. "I would like for you, when you receive your additional Liquid Napricyte^2 compound, to fly around and be in contact with each key area and offer whatever assistance you fine citizens may be able to offer. "Affirmative sir!" 'PAT' and I exclaimed.

"There will be key officials and heads of numerous countries from around the globe present in an epock for a summit meeting. "Can I ask whom, sir? "Affirmative, there will be the Kings of Skittar, Candor Isles, Kaal, Corstal and Stannel. The Prime Ministers of Gergel, Tanglar, Tanzeer, Kirst, Garlotia, and Kalada will attend. Also, the Presidents of the most powerful countries such as Inuk, Iskut, Kashbul, Trasmir, Creyel, Belzak, the Cardola Territories and other key officials from each Military Coalition around the planet, will be present at our meeting."

"We finally have planet unity Major, I was told that would never happen in my lifespan but it has, too bad it was over our world being attacked by extraterrestrials but it is actually here."

"After our summit meeting I was inkling of offering swills at the base taverna this twilight, I hope you both can attend. "Affirmative, if nothing drastic occurs between now and then. "Let's hope not, but for now go get freshened up and have your twilight banquet, I will call you when our summit meeting commences. "Affirmative sir," I said as we saluted, turned and vacated the Sr. Commodore's office.

As we did, we replaced our berets then left the structure. "'PAT', return to the craft and I'll request you presence at the time of our summit meeting. "Affirmative Major," 'PAT' said with a smile, turned and left. I went to my barracks, when I got there I entered and walked up to the retina scanner, had my retina scanned, stated my rank and name then after the entry-way opened I entered. "Illumination on," I said then went and turned on the Intervision monitor; turned to the melodic composition channel then went to the latrine to freshen up.

After I spruced up a bit I decided to give Topanga a call. "Illumination off," I said as I went and turned the Intervision monitor off then left my quarters. 'I hope my lady is at her abode,' I thought as I went to the gribbit PCD. I deposited a quint gribbit then entered her digits. After a few chirps the PCD was answered by Topanga's lovely voice.

"Greetings."

"Greetings my huni buni, how is my darling this p.a.r?"

"Greetings Jeroque, I'm doing better now that I hear your voice. Where are you?"

"I am in the city at the Grinshaw Military Facility at least for this twilight. In the morrow I'll probably be in Translete, CT, or where ever the military sends me. Topanga how was your p.a.r?"

"It went business as usual until one o'clock after the mid-p.a.r break then there was a news flash on the IV monitor and radio saying that everyone was to go directly to their abodes and remain there until further notice. At this moment I am here with my abode mate and we are both fairly frightened."

"Everything will hopefully be ok huni buni and in a few short p.a.r's you and everyone else will be able to leave your/their abodes. 'Unless the Protrerian's are victorious in this war then all Humanarian citizens will be rounded up and incarcerated,' I thought to myself.

"When will that be?"

"After the Antrerian Armada arrives to assist in this war."

"Jeroque, I was inkling I might have a plan."

"And what would that be?"

"I was inkling maybe if I could, I would volunteer my services at the infirmary as an aide and try to be a small source of assistance in this war."

"That is a grand idea, then as you are doing something it will assist in taking your mind off what I'm doing out here. Well my sweets I just called to find out how you are doing and to hear your voice, I have to be going now but I will try to call and converse with you longer very soon, I love you & take grand care of yourself and I wish you success if you go ahead with your plans."

"Adioso Jero and take grand care of yourself too, and always remember I love you very much as well."

"Many thanks Topanga, I love you too; tell Cheryl I said greetings? Adioso for now," I said as I blew her a kiss.

"All right Jeroque," Topanga said then we both hung up.

****

'Now to get some grub, I sure am famished,' I thought to myself as I rubbed my gut. I walked out of my barracks and went to the mess hall returning the salutes of a few junior officers on the way. When I arrived, the place was hopping. I grabbed a tray then a toasty, a sweet roll and an iced caffeinated brew then went to a vacant table. I placed my banquet on the table; sat and rubbed my hands together. I removed my beret and took a swill of my iced caffinated brew, unwrapped then began to consume the toasty.

When I was through eating, I sat back and enjoyed my cup of iced caffinated brew. "Maj. Teldat report to Sr. Com. Bancais office Immediately," I heard over the P.A. I rose, put my beret back on, gathered my tray then put it on a dirty tray cart and left the structure as I headed where I was summoned. While on my way I tapped my com-link. "'PAT', we are summoned to Sr. Com. Bancais office for the summit meeting. "Affirmative Major, I'm on my way."

A few mites later I arrived at Sr. Com. Bancais secretarial assistant. "Maj. Teldat reporting as directed. "Affirmative Major you may enter," LC Acernan said. "Many thanks, I will momentarily. 'PAT' arrived and we went to and entered the Sr. Commodore's office where we met the Commodore and a couple delegates.

"We stood front and center and saluted the commanding officer. "At ease and follow us," Sr. Com. Bancais said as we went to an oversized adjoining meeting auditorium where seated at tables throughout the huge auditorium were the political representatives Sr. Com. Bancais had mentioned earlier and by the looks of it a lot more citizens were present than the Sr. Commodore had suspected.

Sr. Com. Bancais sat; as did everyone else, after he took a sip of water he pulled his microphone closer to him. "Now that everyone is present we can commence."

"Ladies and gentlefolk sitting to my right are Major Jeroque Teldat and his co-pilot 'PAT'; Maj. Teldat has been our main source of information of the major events happening around our planet."

"How do you all do?" I asked. "As everyone knows, all the citizens of ZarCedra's entire continental military coalitions have finally come together to join forces against this extraterrestrial threat. Let me just say that, that p.a.r has finally arrived. "It's about time; I just wish it were under better circumstances." President Torren of the Cardola Territories said.

Sr. Com. Bancais stood and walked to a huge electronic map of ZarCedra on the sidewall, he took a pointer and pointed to the chart. "As you all can see the blinking lights here, here, down here and down over here, are the locations of ZarCedra's Solar Energy Reactor Facilities and by this time they are all heavily guarded. But with the information Maj. Teldat has informed me of they will not be hit very hard."

"The Protrerian High Command will give up that idea and because their abode planet will eventually be exterminated anyway, they decide to just take over ZarCedra. But we, the Humanarian race will receive assistance from the Protrerian High Command's archenemies the Antrerian Armada; who occupy their sister planet of Antreria, in their solar system."

There was a murmur as the delegates talked amongst themselves. "When would the Antrerian Armada arrive and get involved?" Commodore Amy Shateer asked a few moments later. "Precisely five p.a.r's from this p.a.r but we cannot depend solely on their intervention; we the Humanarian race must fight and protect what is ours," Sr. Com. Bancais said as he looked at 'PAT' and I.

"Affirmative we must but why does it take so long for this Antrerian Armada to become involved?" President Kishtofen of Belzak asked. "Because the Antrerian Armada want to see just how strong we the Humanarian race are and even with the great speeds they can travel through space, it takes a few of our p.a.r's to travel from their planet to ours.

"Maj. Teldat, you mentioned the last time we spoke that even with their assistance we get are defeated," President Torren said. "Affirmative I did, and that is why I believe we were brought back to this exact time with my prototype craft; to assist and change that outcome."

"What type of aircraft do you fly?" Prime Minister Koster of Kaal asked. "As some of you know and for all of you who don't, the craft I fly is the prototype Supersonic Dragon 228-D Spy Jet Stealth. It is approximately five times the size of the current Stealth aircraft, and my craft has Star Drive speed capability. Which are two of the better aspects of the time I come from. My craft is hovering inclined, so I no longer have the need of a runway; I can ascend straight up and descend straight down."

"Tell them about the Omagon 2115 Star Drive Engine and the Electronic Flux Inducer," Sr. Com. Bancais whispered. "Affirmative sir," and in a deep voice, I started.

"First and foremost I would like to introduce 'PAT', my cybernetic co-pilot. The letters in her designation 'P A T', is an anagram standing for Prototype Advancements in Technology. She and her computerized counterpart controls and assist as I fly the Supersonic Dragon 228-D Spy Jet Stealth Craft.

This craft has the capability of flying to a maximum regular airspeed of Mach ten. Then when I activate and engage my Omagon 2115 Star Drive Engine it creates a powerful electrical charge. Golden modules and a golden rod are automatically raised from my craft. This electrical charge mixes with a special pale blue radioactive chemical solution called Liquid Napricyte[2] Star Drive Compound inside another smaller component called the Electronic Flux Inducer, which converts this electronical charge to a special Ionic charge.

This specially mixed charge encompasses my craft going through each golden module to the golden rod on the front of my craft. This charge then shoots out in front of my craft creating a Humanarian-made swirling wormhole. By flying into this wormhole, I can access Star Drive speeds within ZarCedra's oxygenated resistant atmosphere and gravitational pull."

"This wormhole being oxygenated resistant means that there is no oxygen to slow my craft and no oxygen for me to breathe. For this reason, I have tanks of compressed breathable oxygen that slowly releases into the airtight cockpit of my craft allowing me to breathe normally."

"Star Drive speed is equivalent to what speed?" The President of the Trall Republic asked. "Star Drive one is equal to ten times the speed of Mach ten and Star Drive two is equal to twenty times that speed. My maximum Star Drive speed is equivalent to Mach two hundred."

"It sounds like over the trittons the military has made significant advancements," the President of Kaal said. "Affirmative ma'am, the Humanarian members have but some of our greatest technological advancements were discovered by combining Humanarian and Protrerian technologies. To that end there is a lot more to my craft that I haven't had much of a chance to test as of yet, but… "But believe me it is more than sufficient to handle this intergalactic war," 'PAT'" cut in and said. "Could you go into a little more detail?" The Prime Minister of Tanglar asked.

"My craft is equipped with a Comodrone Electronics P-52 Hydrogenic Generator; this generator supplies my craft with the needed power to make its own armament of ammunition. I have Sareden Quantum Laser Cannons; my craft is also equipped with two XTR-9000 Plasma Pulse Cannons, one within each wing. When needed, one lowers from each wing and fire a deadly stream of plasma shells. The turrets swivel 180° to the port and starboard direction; which are always ready on command.

"Also I have Protonic Electromagnetic Cluster Missals as well as Neutronic Electromagnetic Cluster Torpedo's, my Protonic EMC-Missals need ten mites to recharge; at one time I have a maximum of fifteen. After I expel the entire load I must recharge to bring my compliment back to its maximum load. The same rule applies for my craft's EMC-Torpedo's accept; the charges are not explosive in nature. When fired, the torpedo strikes a target and eliminates all electrical energy leaving a target ultimately defenseless. For this reason, these torpedo's take more energy from my craft's generator and can only create ten energy charges every twenty mites."

"My craft also has a full-bodied shield and most importantly it has an invisibility factor. When I activate Stealth mode my generator is able to manipulate illumination in such a way that my craft is able to disappear from sight as well as radar. That is why my craft is classified as a Spy Jet."

"I also have a special Heads up Display or 'HUD' helmet where I can manually activate my weapons; it also supplies me with vital information when I access its menu. Like charts, graphs, maps, fuel, Liquid Napricyte[2] SDC & ammunition levels, etc. I get a visual electronic representation located on the lower portion of my face shield."

"But no matter how great 'PAT' or my craft is; I can only assist as much as Humanarianly possible. Although, I did tell Sr. Com. Bancais to take a few precautions, like evacuating major cities and reinforcing military security and the like, there will be significant loss of life military and civilian as there are in any war but let's hope with that warning I gave, a lot of citizen's lives will be spared.

"Will some of us receive the opportunity to view your aircraft?" The President of Inuk asked. "Affirmative, right after this meeting. "Great," I heard. "We finally have planetary unity, I am still unable to get over how every country of ZarCedra has come together to join forces in this war; I'll adjourn this meeting now so Maj. Teldat's craft can be inspected," Sr. Com. Bancais said as he looked around the auditorium.

"Before we do I must say something that was implemented just after the Protrerian High Command put into motion just after they took over our world and in my inkling was a good judgment call. And that was to appoint one President for the entire planet; each continent would have their own power for the most part but for anything requiring a final decision in something in particular that would be the President of the world's designation."

"Now, for those who have the time and wish to view my craft, follow 'PAT' and myself outside," I said as everyone stood. "Sr. Com. Bancais, would you care to view my craft once again? "Many thanks Major, but I have other things more pressing that requires my immediate attention and since I have already seen your impressive aircraft, I will meet you and our guests at Magwa's Taverna at 21 hundred epocks," Sr. Com. Bancais said.

"Affirmative sir," I answered as I turned towards the crowd of officials and officers. "This way ladies and gentlefolk," I said with a smile as we vacated the meeting auditorium.

We walked down the corridor then out of the structure, a few secs later we walked towards the Supersonic Dragon 228-D Spy Jet Stealth. "Remain here under illumination, I will taxi my craft into hangar three where it can be better seen then you all can meet me there," I told the group of officials. "Affirmative," they said as 'PAT and I walked off into the semi-darkness of the twilight.

As we walked towards my craft I looked over at 'PAT'. "'PAT' open and lower the main hatch platform. "Affirmative Major," she acknowledged. When we arrived we went straight up to the cockpit.

I went and inserted the electronic keycard then went to the pilot's seat as 'PAT' raised and closed the main hatch platform then sat. After belting myself in, I activated the ignition sequence and a few secs later my jet's engines roared to life. I put on the 'HUD' helmet then taxied the craft into hangar three.

When I took off the 'HUD' helmet, I peered out the window and sounded the air hooter to call the group of officials to enter the hangar. I saw the look of surprise and disbelief on their faces when they finally entered. I exited the craft and lowered to the floor.

"The main hatch platform could only hold about fifteen hundred kilos, I imagine. So I will have to make a couple trips but if you all have patients, in time everyone will view the cockpit.

A few mites later everyone was in the cockpit. "My apologies for the crampness but this craft wasn't constructed to accommodate this many citizens at one time," I told the party of citizens.

"By the grace of our Gods, how long did it take to construct this magnificent aircraft?" I was asked as everyone looked around. "It took a few trittons but they had just completed the Star Drive engine in the tritton 2115, which is why that tritton is included in the designation of that engine."

"I now call your attention to the multi-colored lights, touch pads and mini monitors of the instrument panels," I said as I sat in the pilot's seat and activated the ignition system. After explaining the significance of each, I individually let each person try on and view through the 'HUD' helmet. As they did I started explaining all they saw when they accessed the menu. A while later after my guests were thoroughly impressed with everything they saw in the cockpit, I ushered them to the main hatch platform, turned everything off, withdrew the electronic keycard then in time I brought everyone to the floor.

"Would we get the opportunity to see this aircraft in action?" King Smith of the Brilain Isles asked. "It is a grand possibility you will; I will be at various locations around the planet for the next while. "Will we also receive the opportunity to view the engines?" The Jroken Prime Minister asked. "Unfortunately there isn't time at the moment, as most dignitaries and officers will be leaving or going to the base taverna soon."

"But, if everyone will look above the cockpit of my craft you could see the Sareden Quantum Laser Cannons. 'PAT' extend the port wing and lower both XTR-9000 Plasma Pulse Cannons." As she done what I asked, I heard the gasp of the dignitaries. "I call your attention to my craft's Plasma Pulse Cannons; these are the cannons that swivel 180° and fires plasma shells. 'PAT' you may now raise them. Underneath the nose of my craft you will notice a sliding metal plate; this is where I fire my EMC-missiles and EMC-Torpedo's. Now this is all I could show at this time."

"Many thanks for the tour," they all said. "You are all welcome," I replied as my guests all departed the hangar. I looked at my timepiece; 'it is about time I went and got ready to go to the base taverna,' I thought.

After I had made sure my craft was secure, I tapped the left wing of my com-link. "'PAT', if I am needed for any reason don't hesitate to contact me immediately; if not I will see you in the morrow morn. "Affirmative Major, have a great twilight, 'PAT' out. "Many thanks 'PAT', Maj. Teldat out."

I headed towards my barracks; when I arrived I had my retina and voice scanned, after they were I entered my quarters. "Illumination on," I said as I removed my beret and went to the latrine to freshen up a bit. When I was through, I put my jacket and beret on. "Illumination off," I said as I headed out the entry-way.

I went toward the base taverna; on the way I met up with President Torren, Prime Minister Jean Luc Trembley and their aides. "Greetings again, why are you citizens walking; I figured you would get driven to the taverna?" I asked as I accompanied them. "It is an exquisite twilight, the weather is warm and clear besides by the light of ZarCedra's triple moons, we can see fairly clear... so we decided to take advantage of it and walk to the taverna," Prime Minister Trembley said as we continued on our way.

When we got there we entered the establishment, we saw Sr. Com. Bancais with a few other citizens sitting at a table. "Right over here ladies and gentle folk," Sr. Com. Bancais said as we came closer. "Affirmative sir," I said as we joined the Sr. Commodore and his companions.

"Glad to see you again," the Sr. Com. Bancais said to our party, as he returned my salute then he invited us to have a seat. The melodic composition was softly heard over the hum of conversation of the guests in the taverna. A barmaid came to us and took our swill orders then went to fill them. "Maj. Teldat I would like to introduce you to Flight Sergeant Crystal Colthamner and Major Matt Sumnerfelt," Sr. Com. Bancais said then took a sip of his swill.

"Maj. Sumnerfelt and Fl. Sgt. Colthamner will be among the pilot's in your new squadron." Sr. Com. Bancais said as we greeted one another.

"Sr. Com. Bancais already explained your ordeal to us, is there anything you would like to add Major?" Maj. Sumnerfelt asked. "Only one thing, the reason I suspect I traveled back in time is that we are somehow supposed to be victors in this war and because we weren't in my time period; I believe I was transported to this precise time with my prototype spy jet craft to lend my assistance and be victorious in this war!"

"That is some parable Major, how are we to believe what you say is true?" Fl. Sgt. Colthamner asked. "Believe him it's all true," Sr. Com. Bancais said. "That's quite all right sir, I've come to expect skepticism," I told him as I produced my military tags. The two military personnel stood to take a look, just as the barmaid returned with our swills.

"Many thanks little lady, just add them to my bill," Sr. Com. Bancais said as he winked. Sr. Com. Bancais returned his attention back to us as the barmaid walked away. "Maj. Teldat why don't you tell them about your aircraft? The Sr. Commodore said just before taking out a fresh cigar and lit it. "Affirmative Major, what type is it?" Maj. Sumnerfelt inquired.

"It is a tritton 2115 version of the Stealth Aircraft, called the Supersonic Dragon 228-D Spy Jet Stealth. "Really," Maj. Sumnerfelt said. "He's telling the truth," Prime Minister Trembley said. "Affirmative but considering there isn't sufficient time right now, you will see it in the morrow morn."

"It is about five times larger and has advanced features than the Stealth craft of this p.a.r," Sr. Com. Bancais said as he took a drag of his cigar and blew smoke rings. As the next ditty started playing, Fl. Sgt. Colthamner took Maj. Sumnerfelt by the hand. "Let's compositionally twirl Maj. Sumnerfelt," she said as she dragged him off towards the twirling floor.

"What do you think of Maj. Sumnerfelt and Fl. Sgt. Colthamner?" Sr. Com. Bancais asked once they were out of earshot. "Very gracious citizens but I hope they are grand in combat. They both are grand in action; both flew in Zand during peacekeeping missions. Also they were both indispensable during the war with North Zantara we had digits of trittons ago. So they both know their way around a fighter," Sr. Com. Bancais said matter of factly. "That's grand to know," I answered then took another swill.

"How long is this war supposed to last?" I was asked. "In the times elapsed archive I've studied it lasted half a tritton, but with me here and with the superior fire power I have in my possession; it could be over much sooner than predicted. "Explain? "Well I'm not positive I can but I hope I can reverse the outcome of this war where we are victorious with the assistance of the Antrerian Armada."

"That will mean a complete life style change, since it is a centritton in which you came. "Affirmative," I said as I took another swill of my beverage just as Maj. Sumnerfelt and Fl. Sgt. Colthamner returned, sat down and took a big swill of their beverages.

I turned to the grand-looking female Lieutenant sitting at the table behind me. "Would you care to compositionally twirl, my dear?" I asked with a smile. "It would be my pleasure," she said as she retuned my smile. I took her by the hand and we walked to the twirling floor.

****

"And what do you two think about Maj. Teldat? Sr. Com, Bancais asked Maj. Sumnerfelt and Fl. Sgt. Colthamner. "I'm not sure," Maj. Sumnerfelt said. "Take your time, I know what he says sounds outrageous but everything he has predicted so far has come true, so you should give him a chance. "Affirmative, we should see what else conspires before we pass judgment," Fl. Sgt. Colthamner said.

****

As the composition played, the young lady and I talked as we twirled and in no time I twirled my way into the young Lieutenant's heart. We swayed to the sound of the tune and I asked her name? "Lt. Cora Loo," she replied with a smile and hint of an accent. After her introduction I introduced myself. "I am Maj. Jeroque Teldat and it is my pleasure to meet you." She squeezed me tighter just as my winged communicator, "beeped." I backed away from the young Lieutenant as I tapped my winged com-link. "Go ahead 'PAT'."

"Major, fifteen waves of Protrerian High Command intergalactic attack craft just entered ZarCedra's stratosphere, by the rate of their descent they are on a course toward Negra Parday City in the Cardola Territories. "Acknowledged."

My attention returned to the lovely Lt. Cora Loo. "It was a pleasure compositionally twirling and getting to know you but right now I must go," I said as I squeezed her arm then ran toward Sr. Com. Bancais. "We have fifteen waves of enemy Protrerian High Command attack craft heading toward ZarCedra, Negra Parday City in the Cardola Territories to be exact. "Affirmative, I'll be in contact with the Military Coalition stationed there ASAP and notify them of the incoming," Sr. Com. Bancais said as he leapt to his feet.

"How can you be so sure of the incoming?" Maj. Sumnerfelt inquired. "I have a direct link with my craft's super computer and in my craft I have planet radar, 'PAT' my onboard super computer and cybernetic co-pilot just informed me of the incoming."

"Maj. Sumnerfelt and Fl. Sgt. Colthamner you're both with Maj. Teldat in the Potenza squadron, dismissed," Sr. Com. Bancais ordered. "Affirmative sir," they both replied as we ran for the exit. "The remainder of your squadrons will meet you in the air," Sr. Com. Bancais hollered as we were leaving the taverna. "Affirmative sir," I replied as I disappeared into the twilight racing towards hangar three and my craft. As I got there 'PAT' had already lowered the main hatch platform and I stepped on.

When I arrived at the cockpit, I raised and closed the main hatch as I fished the electronic keycard from my pocket and inserted it activating the electronic system. When I had my flight suit on, I jumped in the pilot's seat, connected my safety belts then activated the ignition system. I removed my beret, placed the 'HUD' helmet on as I taxied the craft out into the open.

When I did, I received clearance for liftoff. I extended the port wing and as it slid forward, the wings tilted downwards and my craft started to rise. I heard the wail of the emergency siren letting everyone know there were enemy attack craft heading toward ZarCedra.

After I ascended to fifteen hundred metrics, I stopped, raised the landing gear as the wings leveled. I waited patiently for the squadrons to leave the runways. As I waited, I raised my face shield and glanced at the radar and seen the Protrerian attack craft getting closer to ZarCedra over the Cardola Territories. "'PAT', it looks as if we are about to have a grand time engaging the enemy, I hope you are ready because here we go! "Affirmative Major, I'm always ready."

When my squadron was in the air, I lowered my face shield then all aircraft flew in formation towards Negra Parday City.

As we flew at the maximum Mach speed of my squadron, we all introduced ourselves and I got to know a little about each pilot.

Once we reached the Cardola Territories airspace, I tapped the finger touch pad that activated two-way communications. "Potenza squadron climb to two thousand metrics and intercept the enemy. "Two Protrerian Energy Extractor Craft just entered the atmosphere," 'PAT' informed me as we neared the city of Negra Parday. "Affirmative, many thanks."

I activated two-way communication again. "Maj. Teldat calling the Lanston Military Installation in Translete, CT; come in? "This is the Lanston Military Installation, go ahead Major. "Is Jr. Com. Stenwen nearby? I need to talk to him immediately; it is of the up most urgency. "Standby Major, I'll put you through." I checked my levels of artillery, power, fuel, oil, & water and seen everything was at maximum capacity as I awaited the Jr. Commodore.

"Maj. Teldat this is Jr. Com. Lanston, go ahead. "Jr. Commodore, there are fifteen waves of enemy attack craft heading towards Negra Parday City. "Affirmative Major, I will contact the proper authorities immediately to let them know they have enemy attack craft incoming; I will also dispatch reinforcements from this location ASAP. "I believe my CO already informed them of the incoming, on second thought do that and inform them of the larger Energy Extractor Craft incoming and that I am going to intercept! "Roger, Jr. Com. Stenwen out. "Maj. Teldat out."

I tapped the finger touch pad that activated two-way communications twice to keep the channel open. "Maj. Sumnerfelt come in. "Maj. Sumnerfelt here, go ahead. "This is Maj. "Time Star" Teldat, I am going ahead to engage the Protrerian Energy Extractor Craft that are descending towards ZarCedra. "Affirmative, want some company? "Definitely I do but considering my craft is much faster than the aircraft you are using, I'll go ahead and you can meet me there. "Affirmative Major," he replied as I advanced speed to Mach ten.

Since it was a clear twilight I was able to see the intermittent lights of the enemy Craft as we neared each other.

"Ten kiloms, five kiloms, there are now two Protrerian Energy Extractor Craft fifty metrics to the port side accompanied by a swarm of intergalactic attack craft," 'PAT' informed me as I decelerated. I accessed the menu inside my 'HUD" helmet then accessed my targeting scanner and activated it in twilight mode.

The face shield rose and the scanner protruded from my helmet with infrared twilight vision. "Affirmative, I see them," I said as I activated my shield and veered port then starboard dodging laser blasts. I fired laser fire of my own then let off a volley of Protonic EMC-Missals as I had the port and starboard Plasma Pulse cannons lower from the wings as I fired. Star craft after star craft fell from the sky but the more I shot down there were ten more to take their place.

"WHERE'S MY BACKUP, 'PAT'? "Five kiloms away, traveling at their current maximum air speed they will arrive in thirty-seven secs," 'PAT' answered. At that moment my craft shook a few secs as it was hit. "Damage report? "We lost secondary turbine power in the starboard engine, shields down to eighty percent. "We can't afford to take many more hits like that," I said as I spent off my remaining three Protonic EMC-Missals then spent off five EMC- Torpedo's. "Direct hit Major," 'PAT' reported as one Protrerian Energy Extractor Craft exploded in a gigantic fireball that lit the twilight sky.

Just as I started after the other craft, I heard Sgt. Pane's voice. "Time Star, Gunner and our squadron are mere secs from your position, we heard you might need a hand up here, grand buddy? "I can use all the assistance I can get. "I have arrived," Maj. Sumnerfelt said as he joined in the battle.

"Two more Protrerian Energy Extractor Craft just entered ZarCedra's stratosphere," 'PAT' reported. "That's four Protrerian Energy Extractor Craft, which should be the extent of them. Maj. Sumnerfelt, get a couple additional fighters to accompany you to take care of one of those Extractor Craft. "Negatory command leader, all fighters in my squadron are engaged in battles at the moment. Go get the two damned Protrerian Energy Extractor Craft yourself," Maj. Sumnerfelt ordered. "Affirmative, watch your six in my absence? "Affirmative, now get going!"

As I rotated my craft in the direction of the descending Protrerian Energy Extractor Craft I saw one of the aircraft in Sgt. Pane's squadron hit just after they arrived, luckily the pilot ejected because I saw the outline of a parachute open as their aircraft exploded in a great ball of fire and fall from the sky. For the next few secs I stayed assisting ZarCedra fighters in the air battle.

I fired laser blasts and electromagnetic shells from my craft's Plasma Pulse cannons as attack craft exploded all around my craft. I looked at my radar and saw that one of the two Protrerian Energy Extractor Craft changed direction and was heading in the direction of the Candor Isles as the other stayed on coarse and headed toward Sot Bissal. I quickly disengaged the Plasma Pulse cannons and they disappeared back into the wings. I had the targeting scanner retract back into my 'HUD' helmet as I lowered my face shield.

"Maj. Sumnerfelt, I have to go after the threat that now was on a direct course for the Candor Isles," I said as I high tailed it out of there. "Go Major; we can take care of things here." I flew off in the direction of the descending Protrerian Energy Extractor Craft as I watched the battle going on in my aft view monitor as I hoped, the ZarCedra fighter's would be all right in my absence.

"'PAT', the engine damage the craft had sustained, is it operational enough to make it to the Candor Isles? "Affirmative Major, but with recommendation that you do not over use the starboard nuesel until it is repaired. "Recommendation noted! Maj. Teldat calling LC Gunner Luxton, come in?"

"Gunner here, go ahead Major. "Gunner, go after the Protrerian Energy Extractor Craft heading toward Sot Bissal as I go after the one heading toward the Candor Isles. "Affirmative sir. "Get assistance before you depart, and when you get to Sot Bissal be in contact with the South Sot Bissal Military Coalition for additional assistance; remember the facts of my times elapsed archives I told you about. "Affirmative Major, how can I forget? It's the most important thing on my mind. "Take care of yourself little buddy and don't be a champion. "Many thanks sir, I won't."

I tapped my two-way communications finger touch pad again to extinguish two-way communications as I recharged my weapons ammunition and shield. I flew toward the Candor Isles advancing speed to Mach ten. 'I could easily take the Energy Extractor Craft now but it has too much security with it and my weapons ammunition needs recharging. "My craft could easily take out some but I most likely would need back up but everyone is currently busy," I told 'PAT' as I looked in my aft view monitor. "I better wait until we get to the Isle of Otra Gore in the Candor Isle chain where I'll acquire back up from the Brilain Military Coalition."

"'PAT' how long would it take that Protrerian Energy Extractor Craft to reach its target traveling at its current velocity? "Three mites. "Affirmative, how long would it take us at Star Drive two? "Thirty-five secs. "All right," I said as I climbed altitude, I checked the radar to make sure nothing was flying in my path.

Nothing was, so I engaged the touch pad that activated the Omagon 2115 Star Drive Engine. The golden modules and rod protruded as the Electronic Flux Inducer started the flow of Ions. It encompassed the craft, then shot out from the golden rod and formed the swirling wormhole. I guided the craft into it and went to Star Drive one then Star Drive two as compressed breathable oxygen flooded the cockpit.

I flew for thirty-five secs then pulled out of Star Drive speed, I exited the wormhole then decelerated the engines to Mach four as I went into stealth mode and my craft vanished from sight. I raised my face shield and looked at my planet radar and discovered I was over the coast of Otra Gore.

"Maj. Teldat calling the Brilain Military Coalition at His Majesties Air Defense come in? "Sgt. Fishneri here from Bri.M.Co, and His Majesties Air Defense in Craz, Maj. Teldat could I be of assistance? "Affirmative, is your Commanding

Officer nearby I have something of the up most urgency I need to make him aware of!" I exclaimed as I lowered the face shield of my 'HUD' helmet. "Affirmative sir, Acting Brigadier Commodore Becler is in his office, give me a moment and I'll patch him through."

"'PAT', produce a map of the Island of Otra Gore?" A microsecond later it flashed on the lower portion of my face shield and I knew precisely where to look as I scanned it for the Vista Solar Energy Reactor. I noted that it was N. E. of the small city of Brovut, Otra Gore.

"Brig. Commodore Becler here, Maj. Teldat go ahead. "Affirmative, many thanks sir; according to the planet radar I have equipped in my craft. We have a Protrerian Energy Extractor Craft on its way to the Vista Solar Energy Reactor. "Is that craft alone? "Negative sir, there are multiple alien attack craft accompanying it. "Affirmative, how long until they reach their destination.

"They will reach the Vista Solar Energy Reactor in approximately two mites, traveling at their current velocity. "Affirmative, I will immediately dispatch five squadrons of fighters to assist you, should that be sufficient? "Affirmative sir, I will be at the Vista Solar Energy Reactor in mere secs. "You will have reinforcements as soon as possible, Brig. Com. Becler out. "Maj. Teldat, out."

I flew closer to the Energy Reactor and as I did, I arrived just in time to see the sun peek its head over the horizon. The sky was an exquisite dim red-black color, as I reached the reactor I eased my speed to 20 kps then stopped completely. Hovering in midair, I scanned the area before all hellatious broke loose. I activated my XT-165 DigiCam and started recording the quiet surroundings of the reactor.

"It's too bad that in less than a mite this quiet peaceful facility will be in the middle of an air battle," I told 'PAT'. "Affirmative, I would say it is breathtaking if I had breath to take," 'PAT' said with a smirk just as she sounded a buzzer, just as the first attack craft approached. When the lead attack craft was close to my position, I accessed the menu inside my 'HUD' helmet then accessed my targeting scanner and activated it. The face shield rose and the scanner protruded from my helmet.

I exited stealth mode and my craft again became visible, I pressed the finger touch pad that lowered my Plasma Pulse Cannons then activated the full-bodied shield and started toward it with my laser cannon blasting. As I destroyed it, many attack craft swarmed around me. I targeted the craft before me and fired a Protonic EMC-Missal and destroyed it, the port and starboard Plasma Pulse Cannons fired at every alien craft that moved in the vicinity, just then His Majesties Air Defense, and the Craz Military arrived and joined the battle.

"Jr. Com. Melbek calling Maj. Teldat come in? "This is Maj. Teldat, go ahead Jr. Commodore. "Reinforcements have arrived. "You and your citizens are more than welcomed to join in," I said just as my craft shook as an attack craft got in with a lucky shot, which was a mistake on his part because I targeted the Protrerian High Command attack craft and fired a Protonic EMC-Missal and that craft exploded in a great ball of fire, taking two other attack craft with it.

For the next ¾ of an epock the battle was grueling. "Shield strength is down to fifty percent," 'PAT' informed me. I decided it was time to go after the Protrerian Energy Extractor Craft, which was now hovering over the Energy Reactor, in battle with many ZarCedra fighters. I flew towards the mammoth enemy craft as ZarCedra fighters and alien attack craft exploded all around me. I fired my laser cannons as I neared the immense craft in my path that dwarfed my craft significantly, as if it were a child's curio. I drew closer to the Energy Extractor Craft with its bigger laser cannons firing at me.

As my craft was hit, it shook uncontrollably as sparks flew from the side control panels; I fired a few more times. A sec later I heard an alarm go off. "Shield strength down to twenty percent," 'PAT' warned.

"Time to do some real damage," I said as I locked on and fired five Neutronic EMC- Torpedo's then fired five Protonic EMC-Missals in quick succession, making contact on five different sections of the Protrerian Energy Extractor Craft.

Secs later it exploded in a horrendous display of pyrotechnic debris. It quickly descended to ZarCedra below just missing the structure by literally centrics and it crashed in a bigger explosion. I turned my craft 90° and flew to assist my allies.

I blasted the Protrerian High Command Attack craft in my path then targeted the Attack craft that was firing at Jr. Com. Melbek's aircraft. The ship was able to somehow escape my every laser blast, so I targeted it with my eyepiece and when it was directly in the zone I fired an EMC-Missal and watched as it exploded. "Many thanks Major, if not for you I'm not sure I could have escaped that attack craft. "Many thanks are not necessary, glad I was here to assist."

That left one lone Protrerian Attack craft as it high tailed it out of the area up towards outer space. I disengaged the Plasma Pulse Cannons as they disappeared back into the wings; next I tapped the touch pad for the targeting scanner and it retracted back into my 'HUD' helmet as my face shield lowered. "The area is clear, everyone back to base including you Maj. Teldat," Jr. Com. Melbek said as he let out a cheer.

"Maj. Teldat what is the type of aircraft you are flying? The Jr. Commodore inquired as what was left of His Majesties Air Defense squadrons and I flew back to Craz. "Flight leader, this craft is a Supersonic Dragon 228-D Spy Jet Stealth. "I never heard of that type of aircraft. "I know it's quite new; I'll explain in greater detail when we set down. "Affirmative, meet me in Acting Brig. Commodore Becler's office and we will talk. "Affirmative sir," I answered as we flew toward Craz and the Brilains Military Coalition's main headquarters.

A mite later we flew over the city of Craz and above the Royal Buckinghart Military Command. The aircrafts started to land as I slowed then hovered in midair. "What is the problem Major? "My craft is a prototype, which has no need for a runway. Is there a landing area I could descend down to? "Of coarse," he said as he started to land his own fighter. "Set down in the deserted area near the helijet landing area. "Affirmative Jr. Commodore," I answered as I raised the wings as the landing gear automatically lowered then I slowly descended to the tarmac where directed.

As the craft was whining down I raised the port wing and had it slide out of the way of the main hatch. I deactivated two-way communications, removed my HUD helmet then disconnected the safety belts. "'PAT', you are welcomed to join me as I meet with the Brig. Commodore. "As you wish sir," 'PAT' said as we both got up and I removed my flight suit. I put on my beret then went to remove the electronic keycard; I popped the main hatch open and it lowered further to form the platform. We stepped on and slowly lowered to the tarmac below.

As we descended, I noticed the air citizens in the nearby vicinity stop what they were doing to watch us come from our craft. When we arrived at the tarmac secs later, we stepped off and I turned toward 'PAT'. "'PAT', raise and close the main hatch platform," I said as a female air citizen arrived to block the wheels.

"Where would I find Brig. Com. Becler's office?" I asked as we walked toward the Sergeant and returned her salute. "You will find him in main headquarters," she said as she pointed to a structure about one hundred metrics away. "Many thanks Sergeant," I said as we smiled at each other and 'PAT' and I walked off in its direction. I returned the salutes of a few air citizens as we neared main headquarters then entered the structure.

Sitting at the front desk was a pretty young female citizen by the name of Corp. Mekney. "Grand p.a.r Corporal, I'm Maj. Teldat, this is my co-pilot 'PAT' and I have been informed by Jr. Com. Melbek that he and Brig. Com. Becler wanted to see us as soon as we set down. "Just a moment Major," she said as she returned my smile then pressed a button of her primitive intercom.

"Brig. Com. Becler sir, there is a Maj. Teldat and his co-pilot here to see you, should I send them in? "Affirmative Corporal, on the double. "At once sir. "You may enter Major. "Many thanks," I said as I thought she had a very cute accent. "You are very welcomed," she said with a delightful smile and a twinkle in her eye.

We went to the Brigadier Commodore's entry-way and knocked. "You may enter." 'PAT' and I stood at attention, front and center and saluted the Brigadier Commodore. "Grand p.a.r; stand at ease. "Affirmative sir! "Jr. Com. Melbek informed me of a few things about you, Jr. Com. Melbek will be joining us in a few mites but in the interim tell me a little about yourselves and that big exquisite prototype metal bird you fly?" Brig. Com. Becler asked.

"Brig. Commodore sir, I will but it may sound a bit unbelievable but everything is factual and I can prove it," I said as Brig. Com. Becler motioned us to have a seat. "Affirmative airman, go ahead. "The first thing I should say is sitting beside me is my cybernetic co-pilot; her name is 'PAT'. The letters in her name is an anagram standing for Prototype Advancements in Technology. She and her counterpart are my craft's on-board super computers."

"Now, my full name is Major Jeroque Teldat. My rank is Major First Class, and the craft I fly is the Supersonic Dragon 228-D Spy Jet Stealth. "Curious, didn't the Tanglar Military just introduce the Nightingale 228-A Stealth a few trittons ago? "Affirmative they did but..."

Just then there came a buzzing sound from Brig. Com. Becler's intercom. "What is it Corporal?" Brig. Com. Becler asked as he pressed a button. "My apologies for disturbing you again sir but Jr. Com. Melbek is here. "Many thanks Corporal send him right in. "Affirmative sir, as you wish." A sec later the Jr. Commodore entered the office. As he entered, 'PAT' and I stood at attention once again and saluted the Jr. Commodore. He returned the salute and at the same time saluted the Brigadier Commodore. "As you were Jr. Commodore," Brig. Com. Becler said.

"Start again Major, from the beginning so Jr. Com. Melbek will know your entire tale. "Affirmative sir; beside me is my cybernetic co-pilot; her name is 'PAT'. The letters in her name is an anagram standing for Prototype Advancements in

Technology. She and her counterpart are my craft's on-board super computer."

"My name is Major Jeroque Teldat and I am from the Grinshaw Military Facility in Cangla City, in the honorary regime of Placaden, Tanglar. "Explain your aircraft!" Jr. Com. Melbek exclaimed. "Of coarse, I am currently flying the Supersonic Dragon 228-D Spy Jet Stealth. "How can you be?" The puzzled Jr. Commodore asked. "Didn't the Tanglar Military just come out with the Nightingale 228-A Stealth Aircraft? "I thought your Honorable King Smith IV would have notified you two about me by now?"

"He called earlier this morn, he did mention a few things about you but we thought we would make our own inquires. "Affirmative, to answer your question at this point in time they only have the Nightingale 228-A Stealth. In the tritton 2026 with direction of the Protrerian High Command, they introduce the Nighthawk B class; in 2079 they introduced the Ravenheart C class. The tritton I am from, by the way that tritton is 2115, and the Humanarian members of N. Z. C. M. Co/S. H. Z. C. A. secretly introduce the Supersonic Dragon 228-D Stealth Spy Jet."

"The Protrerian High Command is the invading alien military we are now at war with. In my timeline I was not here to assist in preventing them from taking over ZarCedra so they prevailed in this war. But in this timeline I am here with this craft, I hope with our assistance we will defeat them and stop the Protrerian High Command from taking over our planet."

"Unbelievable!" Brig. Commodore Becler gasped. "You say you are from the tritton 2115; what is your proof to back up this claim? "Well 'PAT' for one, the military tags I wear will tell a lot of vital information," I said as I withdrew them. Both men came closer to get a better view, as they read what was engraved on the small metallic plates. My rank, name, birthp.a.r and serial digits and the tritton I had entered the military. The tritton read 2109. "I have been in the service of the air brigade for six and half trittons."

"More proof is of course my flight jacket and the tattoo I have on my upper arm," I said as I took my jacket off and undid the buttons on the cuff of my shirt then rolled the sleeve as far as I could to show the two officers. Both men barely believed it. "If more proof is needed we could go look at my craft. "What you have shown us is proof enough but if you would allow us to view your aircraft that would be smashing. "By all means, we can go at your earliest convenience. "How does right now sound?" They both asked in unison. "Affirmative but after I really should be on my way."

"Will you stay at least for tea and crumpets?" Brig. Com. Becler inquired. "May I ask, what time do you have? "11 hundred 20 epocks," Brig. Commodore Becler said. "Calculating an eleven-epock time difference that would make it 24 hundred 20 epocks back at the Grinshaw Military Facility," I said as I looked at my timepiece.

"I think it's fair to say that we could stay longer but then I must depart. "By all means," Brig. Com. Becler said. "Follow me gentle folk," I said to the two senior Officers. The four of us walked out of their main headquarters structure and out into the drizzle, which had formed in the last few mites. We walked over to the Supersonic Dragon 228-D Stealth Spy Jet and Brig. Com. Becler let out a whistle.

"Your aircraft is a lot bigger than the Stealth Aircraft of this p.a.r and the futuristic look, looks right off a blooming si-fi flick disk," Brig. Com. Becler said. "Affirmative, it does have an advanced look compared to the current Stealth Aircraft and it has to be larger to accommodate the huge engines and firepower," I said as we got to my craft.

"You will notice under the nose of my craft a sliding plate, when I am prepared to fire my Protonic Electromagnetic Cluster Missals or Protonic Electromagnetic Cluster-Torpedo's that plate slides out of the way. Also on the top of the cockpit, if you stand back a few metrics you will notice my Sareden Quantum Laser Cannons."

"Electromagnetic Missals, lasers this is truly an unbelievable craft," Brig. Com. Becler said. "It sure is but that is not the extent of my craft's defensive weapons," I said as I looked at 'PAT'. "'PAT', extend the port wing then slide that wing forward then lower the port and starboard XTR-9000 Plasma Pulse Cannons."

As she was doing that I explained. "Sirs, my two plasma pulse cannons fire a deadly stream of highly explosive plasma shells. The turrets of these weapons rotate 180° from bow to stern and are operated by myself or if I am busy, by 'PAT'.

"'PAT' raise the plasma pulse cannons then slide back the port wing as you open and lower the main hatch platform. "Affirmative Major." The cannons started rising into the wings then in one motion the wing folded and slid back as the main hatch opened and lowered to form the platform. Then lowered to the ground, I ushered my guests on and all four of us went up to the cockpit.

A few secs later, I took out my electronic keycard from my pocket and went to insert in its designated port. By the look on their faces I could see that the two officers were impressed with the entire cockpit.

I went over and picked up the 'HUD' helmet. "Here try this on," I said as I handed it to Brig. Com. Becler, he was first to put it on as I activated it and the face shield lowered. "The lower portion of the visor gives a menu, where I can access vital information such as maps, fuel levels, ammunition levels, power levels, my shield strength, etc. "Simply amazing," he said as he looked at everything in the menu. "Here Jr. Commodore you must inspect this."

The two senior officers traded places and the Jr. Commodore put the 'HUD' helmet on. "I explained everything he saw as he went through the menu then I explained more about the SQ-Laser cannons, Protonic EMC-Missals, Neutronic EM-Torpedo's and the XTR-9000 plasma pulse cannons."

"Protonic EMC-Missals are Protonic infused and highly explosive electromagnetic cluster missals. Neutronic EMC-Torpedo's are the complete opposite. What I mean is, when I lock onto a target and fire a Torpedo; as it strikes its target it immediately drains all the energy from that target and leaves it powerless, leaving it vulnerable to attack. My Comodrone Electronic P-52 Hydrogenic Generator creates all my crafts weapons ammunition. "Fascinating, isn't it?" The Brigadier Commodore asked. "Quite," the impressed Jr. Commodore answered.

"The wonders of this craft doesn't stop there, this craft also has an invisibility factor connected to its Stealth mode capabilities, a full-bodied shield and it can travel grand speeds. "Tell me the fastest speed in which you can travel? "This craft can travel up to Mach ten, then if I activate this touch pad over here it will activate my craft's Omagon 2115 Star Drive Engine; at that time, golden modules and a golden rod will protrude on the outer shell of my craft then my Electronic Flux Inducer is activated."

"This EFI converts the electrical Liquid Napricyte[2] infused charge to an Ionic infused charge that electromagnetically encompasses my entire craft going to each golden module then finally to the golden rod. The Ionic charge is then shot out in front of my craft creating a swirling Humanarian-made wormhole; I fly into this wormhole, which propels my craft to Star Drive one. If I press the touch pad a second time I advance to Star Drive two within ZarCedra's oxygen resistant atmosphere and gravitational pull."

"Within this wormhole oxygen resistant means without oxygen, in order for me to breathe, I have tanks of compressed breathable oxygen that releases slowly into the cockpit," I told the two Officers.

"That's bloody amazing," Jr. Com. Melbek said as he took the helmet off. "Tell me, what speeds are Star Drive one and two? "Star Drive one is 10* the speed of Mach ten and Star Drive two is 20* that speed or equivalent to Mach 200. My Omagon 2115 Star Drive Engine may be small but it is very powerful, to operate it also draws power from my craft's Comodrone Electronic P-52 Hydrogenic Generator and uses a pale blue radioactive chemical solution, called Liquid Napricyte[2] Star Drive Compound."

"Humanarian military scientists in the time I am from invented this special engine and chemical solution and with me being a test pilot, I was the first pilot to test and use this aircraft. "Unbelievable!" They both exclaimed in an awe struck tone. "Very ingenious, but how did you manage to travel in times elapsed?" Brig. Com. Becler asked.

"I was on a secretive testing mission over Vertgren Isle when an electrical storm abruptly started around the area where I was flying. I had no choice but to cautiously fly through it. Before I was able to activate my shield, I was in the process of advancing the Omagon 2115 Star Drive Engine, and as I did and was just entering the swirling wormhole my craft was struck by lightning. Normally an ordinary craft would have crashed or exploded but as I was flying this prototype craft, something remarkable happened which transported me in times elapsed."

"This is only speculation but it's the only feasible reason I am able to surmise for what had happened. What I think happened, is the electricity in the lightning had reacted with the radioactive Liquid Napricyte[2] compound my Star Drive engine uses, causing a rip in the fabric of time. "Your onboard computer didn't record what had happened?" The Jr. Commodore inquired. "Negative, when we were struck by the lightning it shorted my system and I was off line during that time interval, 'PAT' said. "Fascinating," Brig. Com. Becler said.

"This concludes the tour," I said as I brought the two Officers to the main hatch platform. "'PAT' I am returning with these officers to Brig. Com. Becler's office; would you care to join us? "Negative but many thanks, I will return to my alcove until you are back on board. "As you wish 'PAT'," I said with a smile. "This was very interesting" Brig. Com. Becler added as we descended to the tarmac below then we stepped off the main hatch platform.

I pressed the left wing of my com-link. "'PAT' raise and close the main hatch platform," I said as the three of us walked back to the office area of main headquarters.

"There will be one more for tea and crumpets," the Brig. Commodore told Corp. Mekney. "Affirmative sir," she stated as she looked in my direction and smiled. "As you were," Brig.

Com. Becler said as the three of us disappeared into his office and he closed the entry-way.

"Take a seat and explain what ZarCedra is like in the times yet to come?" As I sat, I began. "To tell you the truth sir, I no longer know how things are but before I came to this time it was hellatious. Although we finally lived in peace with the Protrerian High Command there were a lot of Humanarian's who wanted to sever all relations with these aliens. One step closer to our freedom came the p.a.r when the Supersonic Dragon 228-D Stealth Spy Jet was constructed," I said as a smile formed across my face.

"Very interesting," the Brigadier Commodore said as the entry-way opened and the Corporal entered with a tray of tea, condiments, crumpets and jelly. She smiled and winked at me as she passed by where I was sitting. "Many thanks Corporal that is all, dismissed," Brig. Com. Becler said as she left. We all rose then went over to the tray of goodies and poured ourselves a cup of tea, added condiments then we each took a crumpet smeared with jelly.

"If the citizens in your time fought this war and were defeated, what makes you think we have a chance of defeating them in this time?" After I took a sip of my tea, I answered. "For one thing, in the original war I wasn't here with the craft I have in my possession; I think having that craft and traveling back in time to this precise time period, is the God's way of giving Humanarian kind a second chance. "I see."

"The reason I was ordered to Vertgren Isle, before everything happened, was to be in contact with the Antrerian Race as they secretly settled on Vertgren Isle and surrounding area. "Wait a minute, who are these Antrerians and how do they fit in the vast scheme of things?" Jr. Com. Melbek asked then took a sip of his tea.

"They are a race of aliens who reside on the planet of Antreria. Neighboring the Protrerian abode planet of Protreria in the Currecuse Sector of the Dalnary Galaxy. The Antrerian's originally assisted us in this war, but unfortunately even with their kind assistance we were defeated."

"Anyhow in the tritton 2115, their sun is about to go nova. Remembering the promise we made to them a long time ago, they secretly returned to our planet because our sun has a long life yet and we have a way of sustaining our planet with solar power. They came here and asked the Humanarian occupants of ZarCedra if there was a place on this planet they could reside. We secretly allowed them to settle on Vertgren Isle and surrounding area."

"You say they tried to assist us in this war but we were still defeated, if they did assist us in your time, where are they in our time?" The confused Brig. Commodore asked. "They haven't arrived yet, in my time it was a few p.a.r's after the war started before they arrived; so in this time they should arrive 07.05.2015. But as I am here now with my craft, we may no longer need their assistance, at least for the moment."

Brig. Com. Becler, Jr. Com. Melbek and I ate our crumpets and sipped our tea. "Many thanks for the refreshments and hospitality but now I should return to Tanglar since the peril here is over," I said when we were through then rose. "Many thanks Major, if not for you I would be a goner for sure," Jr. Com. Melbek said as he shook my hand feverishly. "Affirmative, with your assistance you made everything go a lot smoother; many thanks," Brig. Com. Becler said. "You both are very welcome and it was my pleasure to assist," I said as I went to put my cup on the tray.

"Would you mind if I took one more crumpet for the trail? "Or sky," Brig. Com. Becler said with a hint of humor in his voice. The two Brilain officers walked me to the entry-way and shook my hand. "Many thanks again," Jr. Com. Melbek said. I saluted the senior officers then left the office.

"Pleasant chap, I wonder if we'll ever get the pleasure of seeing him again?" Acting Brig. Com. Becler asked Jr. Com. Melbek as the entry-way closed. "Hopefully," the Jr. Commodore said, as they continued talking as I walked away.

"Let's chat a mite?" Corporal Mekney asked as I was passing her desk. "Certainly my exquisite one, what would you like to chat about?" I asked as I stopped in front of her. "How long will you be staying in Craz? "Unfortunately I'm not, I'm returning to Tanglar at once. "Do you think you'll return to Craz in the times yet to come? "Unknown," I said as I smiled at her.

"Well, if you ever do happen to come by here again, here are my PCD digits," Corp. Mekney said as she handed me a slip of parchment. I accepted it with a smile and a promise. "If I ever fly this way again I would by all means give you a call. "Many thanks and I hope you have a wonderful flight back to Tanglar. "It was a pleasure to make your acquaintance, but for now I must be on my way, adioso," I said as I picked up her hand and kissed it. "Adioso," she sighed with a smile.

I walked out into the damp Craz fog and made my way to my craft and pressed my com-link. "'PAT' lower the main hatch platform, I am on my way. "Affirmative Major," 'PAT' acknowledged as I began munching my crumpet. A few moments later I arrived at my craft, stood on the main hatch platform and rose to the cockpit.

'What's going to happen now? Now that three Protrerian Energy Extractor Craft have been destroyed and ZarCedra's Solar Energy Facilities were heavily guarded,' I thought to myself as I entered the cockpit and raised then closed the main hatch platform as I finished my crumpet.

"'PAT', check the planet radar to see if the fourth Protrerian Energy Extractor Craft had been destroyed or still in flight? "A moment Major," 'PAT' announced as she accessed the planet radar. "It stands to reason it has been destroyed, the planet radar is all clear from the upper ionosphere to ZarCedra's surface. "Affirmative, that is grand news," I said as I activated the engines and waited a few mites then I was ready for liftoff.

I tapped the finger touch pad that activated two-way communications. "Tower, this is Maj. Teldat requesting permission for liftoff. "You are cleared Major." I had the port wing extend and slide in place. The wings tilted downwards then rose straight up to two hundred metrics; I stopped, lowered the wings as the landing gear rose. I observed the levels of fuel in the two main engines. The craft's two huge engines were down to ½ of a tank and the gauge of the Omagon 2115 Star Drive Engine read ¼ of a vile.

'An adequate amount to get back to Tanglar,' I thought as I checked my timepiece and discovered that it was 02 hundred 30 epocks, Central Time. "'PAT' what are your predictions on how the war would turn out?" I asked as I turned the craft west then slowly started advancing forward.

"The four Protrerian Energy Extractor Craft were destroyed and ZarCedra's solar energy reactors were saved, apparently Lance Corporal Luxton was successful at completing his mission. If ZarCedra's forces are able to hold off the Protrerian High Command's attacks at least until the Antrerian Armada arrives on 07.05, in my calculations the war should abruptly end shortly thereafter. "Affirmative," I said as I checked my radar, seeing my route clear of obstruction I advanced speed all the way to Mach ten. Just as I was about to activate the Star Drive engine, there came a "warning buzzer."

"The damaged engine only has two mites of power remaining," 'PAT' reported. "It took thirty-five secs to arrive here, so it should take that long to return and there I will ease speed to Mach three as soon as we arrive back in Tanglar. Would that be sufficient? "Affirmative Major."

I advanced air speed to maximum Mach then activated the Omagon 2115 Star Drive Engine. As soon as the swirling wormhole appeared, I flew into it as my speed advanced to Star Drive one then Star Drive two. Thirty-five secs later I exited the swirling wormhole then decelerated to Mach three and discovered I was flying over the Honorary Regime of Placaden, Tanglar.

A few mites later I flew over Cangla City; I decelerated to fifty kps until I was over the Grinshaw Military Facility, where I halted position then hovered motionless. I tapped the finger touch pad that activated two-way communications. "Tower, Maj. Teldat here am I cleared to set down? "Affirmative Major, you are cleared to set down near hangar three next to the helijets. I raised the wings as the landing gear lowered and I descended to the tarmac below.

"Tower, have you heard from LC Luxton and the squadron that went to Sot Bissal?" I asked as my craft was turned off and whining down. "Negative sir we have been out of verbal communications since they departed. "Affirmative many thanks, Maj. Teldat out. 'PAT', could he and his squadron be located on the planet radar? "Negative Major, his nor any other Tanglar military fighter south of the Tanglar border could be located at the moment. "Affirmative," I replied as I removed the 'HUD' helmet and disconnected my safety belts. I tapped the touch pad that contracted and slid back the port wing, stood, stretched then went and removed my electronic keycard. I opened and lowered the main hatch platform as I removed my flight suit and put on my beret; I was about to step on when the tower contacted me once again.

"Sgt. Ryan Lalonde calling Maj. Teldat, come in?" I went back to the pilot's seat, sat down and replaced the 'HUD' helmet. "This is Maj. Teldat, go ahead. "Sir you ordered to Sr. Com. Bancais office immediately. "Affirmative I will report directly, Maj. Teldat out. "I wonder what Sr. Com. Bancais was doing up this late in the twilight and what he wanted to see me about?" I wondered out loud as I removed the 'HUD' helmet. "Unknown," 'PAT' replied. "Oh that was a rhetorical question 'PAT', I didn't expect an answer," I said as I got out of the pilot's seat. "Affirmative Major. Adioso 'PAT', I may be back directly, if not then I'll see you in the morrow but I'll have the engine looked at. "Affirmative sir, many thanks."

'I guess there is only one-way of knowing what the Sr. Commodore wants. "'PAT' raise and close the main hatch as soon as I'm down. "Affirmative Major." I went and stood on the main hatch platform and lowered to the tarmac. I marched my way to main headquarters then entered and went to Sr. Com. Bancais secretarial assistant. "Maj. Teldat to see Sr. Com. Bancais. "Affirmative Major you may enter. "Many thanks," I said as I removed my beret, went to his entry-way, rapped on it then entered. I closed the entry-way then stood at attention in front of the Sr. Commodore's desk.

"Maj. Teldat reporting as directed," I said as I saluted. "At ease Major, and have a seat." As I sat, Sr. Com. Bancais started. "First, Fl. Sgt. Colthamner just mites ago reported in to inform that the aerial assault with the Protrerian Energy Extractor Craft over Sot Bissal was a slaughter. She, LC Luxton, and three craft of the Sot Bissal Military Coalition, were the only pilots able to barely escape; the other twenty-five pilots and their aircraft were regretfully destroyed in battle. Fortunately Fl. Sgt. Colthamner got the opportunity to destroy the Protrerian Energy Extractor Craft; LC Luxton gave her the chance by flying toward the Protrerian Energy Extractor Craft and drawing its laser blasts. As Fl. Sgt. Colthamner fired her guns and released her missals, her weapons as well as the missiles on LC Luxton's aircraft were enough to destroy that Protrerian Energy Extractor Craft. "That's terrific! "It sure is, Fl. Sgt. Colthamner and LC Luxton had to stop at the Hemair Military Installation in Myfore, Grelacen to refuel; they both should return by morn."

"On another note, I had just received a PCD call from acting Brig. Com. Becler in Craz, in Brilain of the Candor Isles. He informed me of your heroism in the skies during that battle, very impressive. "Many thanks sir. "Negative Many thanks to you, and with the authority given to me by the military, you have shown exceptional heroic leadership skills and demonstrated commendable bravery in the heat of battle and for the saving the life of a Jr. Com. Melbek of Bri.M.Co; so I now advance you to the new rank of Junior Commodore."

"Also, for all you have done so far in this war, I give you this," he said as he opened a drawer and withdrew two little blue cases. He closed the drawer then opened the first box.

"This medal is for heroism and bravery in the line of duty." I accepted the medal with great appreciation. Sr. Com. Bancais opened the second little box and presented me with a set of Trioxen Leaves. "This Trioxen leaf worn on each lapel of your uniform collar portrays your new rank of Jr. Commodore. Congratulations; pin these to the collar of your uniform letting everyone know your new rank. Well Jr. Commodore, just a few more rankings then you'll be a Commodore. After a few trittons more then you'll be a full-fledged Sr. Commodore as I am "Affirmative sir," I said with a grin. "Do you know where we should go from this precise time?"

"Since we were able to accomplish in one p.a.r what couldn't be done in a half tritton of heavy battle. I'm not really sure, but we should remain on high military alert until the Antrerian Armada arrives here on 07.05. "Are you sure they will still come? "Negative sir, but it <u>was</u> written that they did come. "Affirmative, we will remain on high military alert until that time and if there is no further resistance from the Protrerian High Command, I will cancel high military alert. "Agreed Commodore, I concur."

"That is if I am still around," Sr. Com. Bancais said. "What do you mean sir? "I have had a PCD conference with Commander Hagerty at ZarCedra Solar Dept., Admiral Challid from the Tanglar Sea Patrol and 2nd Lieutenant Haggis from the Fairchild Military Facility, we discussed everything you told me and we will get to work on the Hugo C-15 aircraft ASAP. So the planet will have protection in the event of times yet to come attacks. "Very grand sir, I wish you grand luck in your times yet to come endeavors," I said as I stood to shake his hand. "Jr. Commodore you're dismissed," Sr. Com. Bancais said as we both saluted.

"Sir, before I take my leave, my craft took a few hits and my starboard nuesel of my craft's F405-F1D3 engines sustained damage, I was wondering if you could get an aircraft mechanic to take a look at it? I know it is very early in the morn, but it needs to be repaired at once in case I am needed. "Of coarse Jr. Commodore, go to your aircraft and I will call the on-duty aircraft mechanic directly. "Affirmative sir, many thanks, I set my craft down near hangar three next to the helijets. "Affirmative; one other thing Jr. Commodore, you have had one hellatious p.a.r, you have a right to slumber a couple extra epocks in the morn. Now you are dismissed. "Many thanks sir, pleasant twilight," I said as I saluted.

I turned, left the office and put my beret back on as I continued out of main headquarters; outside I went to my craft and waited a few mites until a mechanic drove up in an armored utility vehicle. "Grand morn Jr. Commodore, I'm Sgt. Fred Lalonde, what can I do for you? Sr. Com. Bancais called and told me that you needed my expertise." The Sergeant said as he saluted.

"Grand morn Sergeant, many thanks for coming; I lost main turbine power in the starboard nuesel, could you take a look at it and see if you can repair the damage? "Affirmative, taxi you aircraft into hangar three and I'll take a look at it for you."

We saluted again then the Sergeant drove around the corner of the hangar. I pressed the left wing of my com-link. "'PAT', lower the main hatch platform, I'm going to have your starboard nuesel repaired. "Affirmative, many thanks Major." I rose to the cockpit and a few secs later I taxied the huge craft into hangar three then powered off the craft.

"'PAT' I was advanced in rank to Junior Commodore, for everything that conspired in the skies above the Candor Isles. From this time forward you can address me as Jr. Commodore. "Congratulations Jr. Commodore, you are most deserving. "Many thanks 'PAT', so are you, more than you'll ever know," I said as I left the pilots seat and lowered the platform. "'PAT', when I get to the bottom raise the main hatch then raise and slide the engine cover," I said as I stepped on the main hatch platform and descended to the couple metrics to the floor. "Affirmative Jr. Commodore," 'PAT' said as I stepped off.

I went and assisted the Sergeant retrieve an AML. After we had it locked in place at the rear of the craft, we rose to the metal walkway then went over to and climbed down the ladder and to the damaged nuesel. "My craft was hit during the air battle before I left for the Candor Isle and damaged this engine's starboard nuesel. Can you repair it?"

The Sergeant looked at the damaged engine a few secs. "Not to worry Jr. Commodore, I'll have your aircraft repaired in no time." But the engine in my craft is much larger than the engines on all the other aircraft? "Don't worry, I'll repair it somehow even if I have to call in some favors from the Cangla City International Airdrome. "Many thanks Sergeant.

"My pleasure, come back later this p.a.r," he said as we climbed back up to the metal walkway, walked to and stepped on the AML then we lowered to the floor. "Affirmative, Many thanks Sergeant, grand twilight," I said as I walked away.

I tapped my com-link, "'PAT' I am retiring to my quarters for the twilight. Keep radar activated and contact me immediately if enemy attack craft are detected entering ZarCedra's circumference, Jr. Com. Teldat out. "Affirmative Jr. Commodore, 'PAT' out."

I went in the direction of my barracks and to the retina scanner when I got there I had my retina scanned. I accessed the core memory and pressed the record button. "New rank, same name; Junior Commodore Jeroque Teldat," I said then released the record button. After the scanner identified my retina and voice patterns, the entry-way opened and I entered my quarters. 'I hope both Fl. Sgt. Colthamner and LC Luxton are ok,' I thought.

"Illumination on," I said as I removed my jacket, footwear and beret then went to the latrine and got ready to slumber. After I finished, I extinguished illumination then walked back to the front chamber. "Illumination off," I said then went to my slumbering quarters. 'It's too late to call Topanga now, I'll contact her later this morn,' I thought as I checked the time and seen it was 02 hundred 45 epocks. I disrobed, changed into my slumbering garments and went to retire. I closed my eyes and almost immediately fell into a slumber.

****

I started having a wonderful reverie. Of Topanga and I, we were in the 22nd centritton because we were standing near my hover bike next to a waterfall. It was a warm twilight and the moons and stars shone brightly as I looked into Topanga's exquisite blue eyes. "You've made me very happy by deciding to accompany me back to this centritton where I belong," I said as I softly kissed her succulent lips.

After we had finished, Topanga looked deep into my eyes and smiled. "I am glad you asked me to join you in matrimony; you have made me the happiest female citizen in any time."

"You have made me very happy as well and I'll do everything in my power to make you as happy as I," I said as I looked at her and winked. I pulled her real close and hugged her tightly in my arms. I closed my eyes real tight and when I opened them again I was staring into the ridges of Tsarina's forehead. I jumped back as the wind started blowing and the pleasant twilight turned to a stormy one.

"Why Jero why, why have you destroyed our life? I would have given you anything you could ever want but you had to go back in time elapsed and erase Protrerian existence from ZarCedra, why did you do that? I will never forgive you for what you have done, never! I loved you once but by your actions I have to ask myself, did you ever love me?" All of a sudden she was naked.

"Take a grand look at my body for the last time; this is what you gave up the mite you turned your back on my race. I would have gladly bore you offspring, offspring you could have been proud of, with the ridges of my citizens on their foreheads. But you had to turn your back on me and my race, just think of everything you have given up!"

I awoke with beads of sweat soaking my pillow. "What have I done?" I said. "My apologies Tsarina but the fate of a free planet caused me to do what I have done thus far and the God's as my witness I won't stop until this planet is free of the threat of your race. I did and always will love you but I have to stop your race from taking over this planet so what happened once will not happen again."

I looked at my timepiece. "What is the time?" I asked. "05 hundred 23 epocks," my timepiece said as I lay back down and closed my eyes.

P.A.R 8

'09 hundred 35 epocks,' I said to myself as I looked at my timepiece. 'I should contact Topanga, before my morn banquet,' I thought as I put on my beret. I left my quarters and walked to the end of the corridor where I fished a quint gribbit from my pocket, deposited it then entered Topanga's digits. The PCD chirped three times then Cheryl, Topanga's abode mate answered.

"Greetings," she said with a happy giggle. "Greetings Cheryl and grand morn; how are you this p.a.r? "Fine, is this Jeroque? "Affirmative, would Topanga happen to be at your abode? "Greetings Jeroque, hold and I will get her. "Many thanks my sweet." I said as I heard her call Topanga and told her the PCD was for her.

A few secs later I heard Topanga's lovely voice happily say "greetings".

"Greetings and grand morn huni buni, how are you this p.a.r?" I asked as I played with the PCD cord in between my fingers.

"Grand now that I hear your voice, I always feel better when you call."

"I enjoy hearing your voice as well but I like it when we are together even more."

"I enjoy being with you as well huni buni. When am I going to see you again?"

"Unknown Topanga, soon I hope but there is another reason I'm calling."

"What is it?"

"You know we are on military alert?"

"Of course but what of it?"

"Four Protrerian Energy Extractor Craft attacked us last twilight, we fought two of them outside of Negra Parday then a second two Protrerian Energy Extractor Craft appeared then split up. One veered off in the direction of Sot Bissal while the other craft flew toward Brilain, Otra Gore to be exact. A squadron was detached to go to Sot Bissal, I was sent to Craz, Otra Gore with implicit instructions to be in contact with the Brilain Military Coalition and defend the Vista Solar Energy Reactor. After we engaged the enemy we fought a hard battle but our forces were able to overtake the enemy attack craft and Protrerian Energy Extractor Craft and be victorious in that battle."

"Grand."

"Wait! That isn't the best part."

"What is?" Topanga excitedly asked.

"After the air battle had concluded, I was asked back to Craz to meet with that city's Acting Commanding Officer of the Brilain Military Coalition, Brig. Com. Becler. We discussed things pertaining to this war then I gave Brig. Com. Becler and a Jr. Com. Melbek a tour of my craft's cockpit. When we returned to the acting Brig. Com. Becler's office I explained all about my time traveling experience as we had refreshments. Then when I was returning to Tanglar, the Brigadier Commodore contacted Sr. Com. Bancais to commend me for my bravery and heroics and for saving the life of Jr. Com. Melbek who was the commanding pilot of the unit I fought with during the attack. Then Brig. Com. Becler suggested that Sr. Com. Bancais advance my rank to Jr. Commodore, so from now on I will be addressed by all as Jr. Com. Jeroque Teldat."

"My compliments Jeroque, I'm so proud of you!"

"That's not all, for additional heroics I was also awarded the 'Silver Star' Medal of Honor."

"When will I be able to see you again? I know we haven't been apart very long but I do miss you terribly."

"We will remain on military alert until 07.05, but I'll see what I can do about getting together in the interim. All I can say is I will try my best to see you."

"I understand Jeroque."

"Well, I should go have my morn banquet now. I was allowed extended slumber this morn because I didn't return from Craz until the wee epocks of the morn. Ok huni buni, I will contact you again when convenient. Adioso for now my love, I love you."

"I love you as well Jeroque; oh Cheryl says adioso and we both hope you have a grand p.a.r."

"Tell her I said adioso, and many thanks & I hope you both have a grand p.a.r as well," I said then we both hung up.

****

I turned then marched down the hall and out of the structure. I stopped to check the time as I looked at my timepiece; '10 hundred 05 epocks,' I said to myself. 'It's about time I had my morn banquet before everything is gone,' I thought as I began walking again.

When I finally arrived at the mess hall, I smelled the aroma of the banquets as I entered; I grabbed a tray and received my banquet, then retrieved eating utensils and a hot caffinated brew. I brought my tray to a table then sat and removed my beret. I took a sip of my caffinated brew then began eating. As I ate there came a "beep" from my com-link.

"Jr. Commodore, twenty waves of enemy attack craft just entered ZarCedra's stratosphere," 'PAT' reported. "Affirmative," I responded as I gathered my partially eaten banquet, put on my beret then put my tray away as I started running out of the mess hall. "'PAT' from their rate of descent, what is and how long until they reach their destination? "Eight mites over the eastern seaboard of Kor Bissal."

My first destination was to inform Sr. Com. Bancais, to warn him of the incoming. After I arrived at the Commodore's secretarial assistant; I passed him saying, "I must see the Commodore immediately, it's of the up most urgency. "Of course Jr. Commodore, enter," LC Acernan said.

"Sr. Com. Bancais," I said as I opened his entry-way without knocking. "We have twenty waves of enemy attack craft descending down to the Eastern Shore of Kor Bissal. "Affirmative, as you take to the air I'll dispatch ten squadrons of fighters so you will have back up. Sgt. F. Lalonde called about fifteen mites ago to say your aircraft was fit to go and your keycard was engaged in its port & the engine cover was lowered and secure. "Many thanks sir; but how was he able to get the parts so quick? "I'm unsure, I think he had to call in a few favors; he truly is a miracle worker. "Affirmative he is, thank Sgt. Lalonde for me? "Affirmative, I will. "Talk to you in the air," I said as I saluted then darted away.

As I left the office I tapped my com-link. "'PAT', is the craft completely operational? "Affirmative Jr. Commodore the aircraft is, Sgt. Lalonde was very gentle and he had done a grand job. "Grand, lower the main hatch platform, I'll be there directly."

When I arrived at hangar three, I went straight to my craft and up to the cockpit and raised then closed the main hatch. "Grand morn 'PAT'," I said as I looked over at her. I removed my beret as I put my flight suit on then jumped in the pilot's seat. "Grand morn sir," she replied as she fastened her safety belts. I buckled mine; put on then activated the 'HUD' helmet as I had the port wing extended and it slid forward as I activated the ignition sequence. I tapped the finger touch pad that activated two-way communications, I tapped it a second time to keep the channel open.

"Tower this is Jr. Com. Teldat, clear me for lift off immediately," I said as I taxied my craft out in the open. "You are cleared Jr. Commodore. "Affirmative," I acknowledged as I pulled up on the flight stick and started to rise.

When I was up to five hundred metrics I stopped, hovered at that altitude as the landing gear rose then I lowered the wings and waited as ten squadrons of fighters left the runways.

"Jr. Commodore, this is Maj. Krewski of the Zattan squadron. "This is Fl. Sgt. Barnes of the Utanga squadron, where is the enemy heading?" I raised the face shield of my 'HUD' helmet and looked at my radar. "Maj. Krewski and various squadrons the enemy is descending upon Dalarme. Have your squadrons fall in behind me and we will fly to that location," I ordered.

I contacted the tower once again and reported. "Tower, the enemy is on a direct coarse for Dalarme, inform Sr. Com. Bancais we are flying there now, Jr. Com. "Time Star" Teldat out. "Affirmative Jr. Commodore, the Grinshaw Military Facility, out." The squadrons and I left the city heading toward Dalarme at Mach 5.5.

"Jr. Com. "Time Star" Teldat calling Maj. Krewski, come in? "Maj. Krewski here, go ahead. "I'm going ahead to Dalarme so there will be someone there when the enemy arrives. "Affirmative, we'll get there as soon as we can. "Affirmative," I said as I increased air speed to Mach 8 as I engaged stealth mode and my craft disappeared.

Approximately two mites later I arrived at the outskirts of Dalarme, as I disengaged Stealth mode and reappeared.

"'PAT' what is the name of Dalarme's Military Installation? "It is the Kinkade Military Installation," she responded a microsec later.

"Jr. Com. Teldat calling the Kinkade Military Installation come in? "This is the Kinkade Military Installation, go ahead Jr. Com. Teldat. "I'm calling to report we have twenty waves of Protrerian High Command attack craft descending toward Dalarme, they will arrive in approximately three mites dispatch additional squadrons immediately to intercept. There are ten additional squadrons that will arrive from The Grinshaw Military Facility out of Cangla City, in the honorary regime of Placaden, Tanglar. "Affirmative Jr. Commodore. "Jr. Com. Teldat out."

"Jr. Com. Teldat calling the Autobahn Military Facility in Negra Parday. "This is the Autobahn Military Installation, go ahead Jr. Com. Teldat. "I know a fighter in Sgt. Pane's squadron was destroyed but I was wondering is he all right? "Roger, it was in fact his aircraft that was destroyed and he was picked up unscaved on the outskirts of Negra Parday early this morn. "Grand to hear; we have enemy incoming over Dalarme, I request any and all backup assistance your Military Installation can send to assist. "Roger, I will inform my Commanding Officer and he will detach them ASAP."

"I was wondering if there is an unused fighter that Sgt. Pane could use to offer assistance in this air raid over Dalarme? "Unknown, I have to put your request in to the Commanding Officer as well; I will get back to you momentarily."

I waited a few secs for the multiple squadrons of fighters from the Kinkade Military Installation to rise to my altitude. "Maj. 'Vamp' Praline calling Jr. Com. Teldat, come in sir? "Jr. Com. Teldat here, go ahead. "We are under orders to follow your command, what are our orders? "Climb to fifteen hundred metrics and follow me, we are in for a major air battle in mere secs. "Affirmative sir."

"Sgt. Pane would meet you in the air above Dalarme," the Autobahn tower reported. "Affirmative, we are over Dalarme presently, have him and additional back up meet us here ASAP. "Affirmative, the Autobahn tower out. "Jr. Com. Teldat out," I said as I as took point and we climbed to a higher elevation. At that time, Maj. Krewski and Fl. Sgt. Barnes arrived in the skies above Dalarme and they fell in formation.

"Ok listen up everyone, get ready for a major air battle," I said as I accessed my targeting scanner and activated it. The face shield rose and the scanner protruded from my helmet. I activated my shield and a few secs later all ZarCedra fighters engaged the swarming alien attack craft. I halted position and rotated my craft to and fro using my Sareden Quantum Lasers to destroy all attack craft that came into view. Looking down at the city, I saw the artillery fire of the ground troopers fire at all alien attack craft that flew overhead.

Ten mites later I heard Sgt. Pane's voice. "It feels grand to be fighting alongside of you, many thanks for requesting me and getting me out of Negra Parday. I have a surprise for you. "Really, and what might that be," I asked as I blasted a few more attack craft. "Guess who my two wing citizens are? "Unfortunately I have no time for guessing competitions at the moment. "Affirmative, I have Fl. Sgt. Colthamner and LC Luxton as my two wing persons.

"How are you buddy?" LC Luxton asked. "Feeling a lot better now that I know you and Fl. Sgt. Colthamner are safe. "We are mere secs from your position," Fl. Sgt. Colthamner chimed in.

I fired off a few Protonic EMC-Missals and watched as attack craft after attack craft exploded in grand balls of fiery masses. At that time, I looked at my radar and seen more squadrons of Nautical fighters arrive as additional attack craft entered ZarCedra's stratosphere, heading toward Brilain.

"Jr. Com. Teldat calling the Kinkade Military Installation, come in?" I said as the attack craft dipped further. "Kinkade Military Installation here, Jr. Com. Teldat go ahead."

"We have multiple waves of Protrerian attack craft incoming heading toward Brilain, inform Brig. Commodore Becler of the Brilain military Coalition at The Royal Buckinghart Military Facility in Craz, Otra Gore immediately of the incoming so they can determine their exact destination. "Affirmative Jr. Commodore, at once."

"This is Com. Hemp calling Major Teldat, come in? "It's Jr. Com. Teldat now, go ahead. "We have been dispatched here from the K. B. N. S. Dragoon and the K. B. N. S. Dragozi aircraft transporters to lend assistance. "Any assistance is grandly appreciated; fall in at once."

"Sixteen additional waves of attack craft just entered ZarCedra's stratosphere," 'PAT' cut in and reported. "Acknowledged. Commander Hemp we have additional Protrerian attack craft incoming," I said. "I am mere secs from your position I will engage the enemy at once," he proclaimed.

"Five squadrons trail me including Sgt. Pane, Fl. Sgt. Colthamner and LC Luxton. "Affirmative," they responded. "Twenty additional squadrons of ZarCedra fighters from various aircraft transporters off the coast of the Oskretin Sea are joining the battle," 'PAT' reported.

As I led the squadrons I kept an eye on my radar and as soon as I met the enemy attack craft, I got a lock on my targeting scanner and fired my port XTR-Plasma Pulse Cannon. We fought hard for the next three epocks as enemy attack craft and consociately aircraft exploded all around.

"How long until the Antrerian Armada arrive to assist?" Fl. Sgt. Colthamner asked. "Who are they?" Com. Hemp asked a little bewildered. "Three more p.a.r's. "Com. Hemp weren't you advised of them? Fl. Sgt. Colthamner asked. "Negative," he answered. "The Antrerian Armada is the enemy counterparts of the Protrerian High Command we are currently fighting.

We should receive their assistance some time mid-p.a.r 07.05. "How do you know this information? "I have my ways," is all I said. "Affirmative, the Commander answered.

After all the enemy attack craft were destroyed and my radar was clear of attack craft at our altitude, I ordered. "All fighters remaining in my squadrons, to lower altitude and assist our forces below."

"When were you promoted to Jr. Commodore?" Sgt. Pane asked as we lowered altitude. "Early this morn as I fought the enemy in Otra Gore, Brilain. "You must have done a grand job to be promoted? Fl. Sgt. Colthamner asked. "How were you able to get back to Kor Bissal in time for this battle?" Com. Hemp inquired.

"Haven't you heard of his craft?" Fl. Sgt. Colthamner asked in a bewildered tone. "Negative, I was at sea and out of radio contact a few p.a.r's. What type of aircraft are you flying? "I fly a prototype Supersonic Dragon 228-D Stealth Spy Jet, which has Star Drive speed capabilities. "Wow, I noticed it was considerably larger but I didn't know it was supersonic. "It took less than a mite to get from Otra Gore to Tanglar. "Wow you've got to be jesting," Com. Hemp said just as we returned to the battle down below. We saw that the ZarCedra fighters were in unfortunate shape.

"Shield strength currently at thirty-five percent," 'PAT' informed. "Affirmative," I acknowledged as I fired off a Protonic EMC-Missal and destroyed the attack craft in my path.

Twenty-three mites later we destroyed all but two attack craft and they were flying in the direction of LC Luxton's fighter. So with my lasers firing, I started after them. "I have to do something to save him from certain destruction," I said aloud.

"Your shield strength is currently at two percent, going in is suicidal," 'PAT' said overhearing me. "Suicide or not I have to at least try to save him." I followed the craft that was firing at LC Luxton's fighter and fired my SQ-Lasers. "Got him," I said but I was warned too late of the attack craft that circled aft of my position.

That attack craft fired its laser, my craft's shield absorbed the first blasts but that drained the little shield strength my craft had remaining and the next blast blew away my craft's starboard wing tip. My craft shook uncontrollably as Fl. Sgt. Colthamner destroyed that alien craft.

"Time Star" Teldat are you unharmed?" Fl. Sgt. Colthamner inquired anxiously. "Affirmative, I am," I answered as I tried feverishly to control my wounded Dragon.

"'PAT', are you still operational?" I inquired in a frantic tone. "Affirmative sir; but we are losing altitude fast!" I worked with grand determination to control the craft as I descended faster and faster towards Dalarme's Kinkade Military Installation.

"'PAT', engage inertial dampeners," I said as I lowered the landing gear. "Engaged," she said as the craft stabilized. I contacted the Kinkade tower.

"Jr. Com. Teldat calling the Kinkade Military Installation, my craft is seriously damaged; have crisis vehicles standing by as I set down. "Affirmative Jr. Commodore, runway one is clear. "Tower, I am flying a hover controlled prototype craft that has no need for a runway," I said as I neared ZarCedra very quickly. "Affirmative, set down on the port side of the helijets. "Affirmative," I answered as I raised the wings. I was holding on to the flight stick with both hands as I started descending where instructed.

As I neared the tarmac, I saw two fire/rescue vehicles and an EMCV quickly approach with their colored lights flashing and alarm bells blaring. I lowered the landing gear and my wounded Supersonic Dragon landed with a thud. I quickly turned the ignition off, had the port wing contracted and it slid out of the way of the main hatch. "PAT, get me the fire extinguisher," I said as I removed the 'HUD' helmet. I disconnected my safety belts then got out of the pilot's seat and I lowered the main hatch platform.

I took the fire extinguisher from 'PAT' and stepped on to the main hatch platform then lowered to the tarmac. I ran to the smoldering metal mere centrics from the starboard XTR-9000 Plasma Pulse Cannon, I quickly sprayed the flames protruding from my craft. I did this until the fire/rescue vehicles arrived, and started spraying the damaged area of my craft.

"Are you all right? "Fl. Sgt. Colthamner, Sgt. Pane and LC Luxton asked as they came racing. "Affirmative, I am but my craft isn't," I said with a frown. Sgt. Pane looked and seen the smoking torn metal.

"Are you all right?" A Com. Magae asked as he came running. "Affirmative sir, everything but my aircraft and my pride but I'm physically unharmed. "Affirmative," he said as he returned my salute. "You are not needed this time, you are free to leave," Com. Magae told the emergency medical attendants. "Affirmative sir," they both said as they got back in the EMCV and vacated the area. Com. Magae turned back around to look at me.

"As you are ok, tell me what happened up there?" I relayed what had happened until I was hit and forced to land. "You're that pilot from the times yet to come, aren't you? "News sure travels fast. "It does when a savior arrives in the nick of time," the Commodore said as he shook my hand. "Jr. Com. Teldat, pleasure to meet you. "Com. Magae and the pleasure is all mine."

I looked at the damaged wing and was horrified when I realized the part of the wing that had been blown away was the part that housed the golden modules. Then in the back of my mind, I remembered the extra golden modules and rod in the cockpit and relief washed over me.

"Would your aircraft mechanics repair the damage to my craft?" I asked as I rubbed the wheel of my craft. "Roger, my military mechanics will have you ready to take to the skies in no time," Com. Magae said as he looked at the damaged area of the aircraft. "I have to tell you something very important, I have experimental equipment on my craft and in order for it to operate efficiently, golden modules must be attached to the new section of wing. "Golden modules, what are they for?" the Commodore bewilderedly asked. "Just a sec Commodore," I said as I tapped my com-link.

"'PAT', is there any internal damage? "Negative Jr. Commodore, the only damage is to the starboard wing itself, which has to be repaired. "That is understood and will be done as soon as possible, in the interim extend the port wing and then the golden modules and rod and then join me, there is someone I want you meet. "Affirmative, Jr. Commodore."

As the modules and rod were raised to the surface of my craft I pointed to them. "You see Commodore, if you stand away from my craft, those are the golden modules and rod I was referring to. "But Jr. Com. Teldat, I have no such modules! "That is understood, I have spare modules in my cockpit, just in case anything happened to the modules on my craft."

"Go get an aircraft mechanic out here ASAP!" Com. Magae ordered an airman standing nearby. "Affirmative sir at once," he said as he left. "I have heard a little about you and your famous aircraft," the Commodore said. "Have you? I hope it is all grand," I said with a hint of humor amidst the horror of my damaged craft.

"I have, but humor an old gent and tell me your entire tale," the Commodore said with a chuckle. Just as an armored utility vehicle pulled up and the airman returned with the aircraft mechanic.

"We will go to my office as soon as I introduce you my top aircraft mechanic. "Sgt. Noonsy glad to see you," the Commodore said as he shook his hand. "This is Jr. Com. Teldat of the Tanglar Military, and he has an inquiry to ask. "Glad to make your acquaintance," we both said as we shook hands.

"What can I do for you? "My craft here has sustained considerable damage in the last air battle and the starboard wing was hit. "I see," the Sergeant answered as he looked up and seen the smoldering metal of the partial wing. "If you look on the port side you will notice three golden spheres strategically placed on the wing in order for my prototype equipment to function properly. I have replacement spheres that need to be attached to a new partial wing precisely; can you repair it? "I believe so, taxi your aircraft into hangar #2," Sgt. Noonsy said with a smile.

"After you are finished, I'll be in my office in main headquarters," Com. Magae informed me. "Affirmative, I will see you then with my cybernetic co-pilot and she will elaborate in more detail about the craft. Grand, I will be in my office," the Commodore said as he walked away.

"'PAT', contract the port wing and lower the main hatch platform." After it was, I went and rose to the cockpit and a mite later I started my craft as Sgt. Noonsy got in his armored utility vehicle; I followed Sgt. Noonsy to the hangar. "'PAT', everything will be taken care of as they will repair the damaged wing. "Affirmative, and for not knowing what to do in such an occurrence, you handled the situation commendably. "Many thanks," I said as I brought the craft into the hangar. When the craft was all the way in; I switched everything off and contracted the wings. "You're with me 'PAT'," I said as we exited the craft and lowered to the floor.

"'PAT', I would like to introduce you to Sgt. Noonsy. Sgt. Noonsy, 'PAT' is my cybernetic co-pilot and onboard super computer. "Greetings Sergeant," she said. "Grand p.a.r," he hesitantly answered. "The letters P. A. T is an anagram, standing for Prototype Advancements in Technology. "Sgt. Noonsy, do you have an automatic mechanical lift? "Sure just outside, wait here while I have it brought inside."

He left and returned a few mites later with another airman in his armored utility vehicle towing the AML. After it was set up and locked into place, 'PAT', the Sergeant and I stepped on the lift and went up to examine the damaged area.

"Usually in aircraft predating my Dragon, the fuel tanks were located in each wing but as the wings of my craft contract, extract, rise, lower and contains my craft's XTR-9000 Plasma Pulse Cannons; the fuel tanks were put in at the top of my fuselage where the engine cover rises," I told the Sergeant, we examined the extent of the damage then we lowered to the floor. I looked at 'PAT' and said. "You can now extend the port wing but leave it in the back position so you can lower the main hatch." As she did, the Sergeant went to view the port wing then returned to me a couple mites later. "Affirmative this shouldn't be much of a problem to repair."

"Grand, accompany me to the cockpit," I said as we went to the main hatch platform. 'PAT' and I brought Sgt. Noonsy up to the cockpit, and he looked around in amazement. "Unbelievable," he said as he seen the instrument panels.   "If you have any question about the craft, just direct your questions to 'PAT'. "Affirmative, I will get to work on it immediately. You do have a grand aircraft," he said as he glanced around the entire cockpit. "Affirmative, I do," I said as a smile formed on my face.

"In order to use anything electronic on this craft you will have to use the electronic keycard. Over here, is the slot where the electronic keycard activates my craft," I said as I went over and pressed a button and it popped out. "I will give it to you but whatever you do don't misplace it, it's the only one I have." I said as I handed it to him. "Affirmative sir, understood, I will keep it on my person until needed."

I went to a back storage locker and withdrew a long black case. I set the case on the floor and opened it; I took out the modules and handed them to Sgt. Noonsy. "Here are the modules that need to be attached to the new partial wing. "These modules have to be mounted, in the exact same position as on the port wing. "Affirmative," Sgt. Noonsy said as I closed the case and put it back in the storage locker. When I was through, we headed for the main hatch platform. "If you need me for any reason, ask the internal computerized avatar of 'PAT' and she will notify me immediately. "Affirmative," he said as we lowered to the floor.

"Out of curiosity, about how long until my craft would be fit to fly? "Looking at the size and availability of materials, give me at least a p.a.r. "Grand, as long as it is repaired by mid-p.a.r 07.05. "Why is that? "Classified, let's leave it as because for now. "As you wish sir; now it is time to get to work. Don't worry your aircraft will have my undivided attention until repaired."

"Grand, now it's time I went to talk to the Commodore," I said. "'PAT' you're with me; also keep monitoring the circumference of the planet and contact me immediately when more Protrerian attack craft are detected entering ZarCedra's stratosphere. "Affirmative, Jr. Commodore," 'PAT" replied as we headed for the hangar entry-ways. Just before we stepped out I stopped and turned around.

"When you need to raise and close the main hatch platform and you're not in the cockpit where the computer could hear you; climb the right wheel, pull down then mount the partial ladder, open the little trap compartment and press the labeled touch pad. "Affirmative," the Sergeant answered.

"Where precisely would we find main headquarters? "Turn right when you get to the walk, go up the boulevard until you come to a red and white structure and it is right there you can't miss it, it has a Kor Bissal, Cardola Territories, and the Dalarme's Kinkade Military Installation flags flying in front and a big sign. "Affirmative, many thanks," I said as I removed my beret from my shoulder loop and put it on as we departed. We followed the Sergeant's direction and a few mites later we found main headquarters.

'PAT' and I walked up the stairs then entered the air-conditioned structure and went to the Corporal at the front desk. "Greetings sir, can I be of assistance? "Affirmative, I'm Jr. Com. Teldat and this is my co-pilot, we're here to see Com. Magae. "Affirmative Jr. Commodore, he is expecting you, you and your co-pilot may enter, right through that entry-way," the Corporal said as he pointed. "Many thanks," I answered as we turned and walked to the CO's entry-way, removed our berets, knocked then entered.

As we saw the Commodore behind an oak desk, we stood at attention, and saluted "Jr. Com. Teldat and 'PAT' reporting as directed sir! "Welcome to the Kinkade Military Installation. Stand at ease and elaborate about flying in time elapsed," the Commodore said as he returned our salutes. "Affirmative sir, but first I would like to introduce my cybernetic co-pilot; her name is 'PAT'. "I am present to verify everything Jr. Com. Teldat reveals about what is happening at the present time and will happen in the near times yet to come," 'PAT' said as she shook Commodore Magae's hand.

"The craft we fly is a prototype, the Supersonic Dragon 228-D Stealth Spy Jet and we come from the tritton 2115. To make a long story short, we were on assignment over Vertgren Isle when we flew through an electrical storm and I activated my Omagon 2115 Star Drive Engine. My craft's Electronic Flux Inducer supplied the correct amount of Ions to form a swirling Humanarian-made wormhole, and just as we were entering this wormhole the craft was struck by lightning."

"If we were flying a normal stealth craft that would have destroyed or at least badly damaged the craft, but as I previously mentioned we are flying this prototype craft. Its Omagon 2115 Star Drive Engine operates using a special pale blue radioactive chemical solution; this chemical solution is called Liquid Napricyte[2] SDC. I'm not precisely sure but what I suspect is the high voltage of electricity in the bolt of lightning that struck my craft somehow reacted with that special chemical solution."

"Flying into the wormhole as the lightning struck the craft somehow caused a rip in the time gamut, which plummeted the craft and us back in time elapsed to this time. The reason it had brought us back to this precise time, like I said isn't certain but it happened on my birthp.a.r and the wish I had made was to change the way we lived in the 22nd centritton. Because, in my time we had lost the war we are having at present with the Protrerian High Command and we have been living under their reign for one hundred trittons. I know this theory sounds fantastic but it is the only reason I can surmise at this time. "I see," the Commodore said as he shifted in his chair.

"Sir, the rest of my tale is like I already stated, that the Protrerian High Command we are now fighting are victorious in this war and they take over ZarCedra and we are under their reign. But, even with the assistance we receive from their archenemies, the Antrerian Armada, we still lose. "Oh, I haven't heard of them, fill me in."

"Well the Antrerian race occupies the neighboring Planet next to Protreria called Antreria, for eons these two races have been at war with each other. It has been known for many trittons that the Protrerian abode Planet was running very low of natural energy and their sun was slowly going nova. The Protrerian High Command somehow discovered the Humanarian race on

ZarCedra had found a way to create our own energy with the assistance of our Solar Energy Reactor Facilities and the sun in our solar system is young and full of life."

"Wait a mite, if their sun is dying the Antrerian Planet would also be uninhabitable, correct? "Affirmative sir that was my original secret assignment on Vertgren Isle, before my time traveling experience began. The Antrerian race was allowed to secretly settle in that part of the Planet and I was to make sure they settled before the Protrerian High Command discovered they were on this planet. We, the secret Humanarian members of ZarCedra's military and Administrations allowed the Antrerian race to settle on ZarCedra because of their assistance in this war."

"Why didn't the two races pick other planets to relocate to? I'm sure there are other planets better equipped to accommodate them. "Why, I'm not sure, but for some reason they wanted ours. I think the Humanarian race messed up in my time and this is the God's way of giving our race a second chance, and this time with us here we better not screw up. "That is a lot to swallow airman," the Commodore said as he leaned back in his chair. "I know sir but do you have another theory as to why I was brought back to this precise time period just p.a.r's prior to the start of this war? "Negative Jr. Commodore, I do not."

"When is the Antrerian's supposed to arrive? "Mid-p.a.r 07.05, which is why I asked your aircraft mechanic if my craft, would be repaired by then? "I see, what are your plans for the interim?"

"The first thing I plan to do is give my CO at the Grinshaw Military Facility in Cangla City, in the honorary regime of Placaden, Tanglar a call and explain my situation, and tell him that I will remain here until my craft is repaired. "Affirmative, what are you going to do after that?"

"Well I can't go back to stopping the Protrerian High Command from taking over ZarCedra at the moment so I just plan to stick around here. "Affirmative, you are welcomed to stay until your aircraft is repaired then go do what you have to, to kick the crap out of those extraterrestrial ternaries."

"You and your co-pilot are welcomed to grab a bunk here," he said as he picked up the PCD. "I will require accommodations but 'PAT' has an alcove aboard my craft. "Affirmative Jr. Commodore; Corporal, Jr. Com. Teldat will be staying on base for a while, while his aircraft is being repaired. Find suitable quarters for him," he said then hung up. "Many thanks sir; is there a personal communication device I could use to make an extended distance call? "Roger, you are welcomed to use my PCD," he said as he turned it towards me. "Many thanks very much sir, I won't be long," I said as I grabbed the receiver. "Just press the digit sign key for an outside line."

I followed his instruction then entered the digits for the Grinshaw Military Facility. A mite later I was transferred to Sr. Com. Bancais secretarial assistant.

"Grinshaw Military Facility, can I assist you? "Affirmative LC Acernan, This is Jr. Com. Teldat; connect me with Sr. Com. Bancais immediately. "At once sir, hold."

"Sr. Com. Bancais here, may I assist you? "Affirmative sir, this is Jr. Com. Teldat. This p.a.r in the air battle I was in my craft was hit. "Are you hurt, is there anything I can do," Sr. Com. Bancais asked with grand concern. "I'm fine sir but my craft lost a partial wing and the citizens here at Dalarme's Kinkade Military Installation said they would repair it immediately."

"It's very unfortunate to hear about your aircraft but I am glad you're ok, I'd hate to hear anything unfortunate has happened to you or 'PAT'. "Many thanks for your concern sir, I will be staying in Dalarme a p.a.r then I will return to Cangla City. "Affirmative Jr. Commodore, be in contact with my replacement on your return. I'll be at ZCSD to start on the Hugo C-15 project. "Affirmative sir, grand luck and have a grand p.a.r, adioso. "Take care," the Commodore said then we both hung up.

****

"On another note sir, we got those last enemy attack craft but one thing you can count on, they most likely won't be the last. "How do you know?" Com. Magae asked. "I don't know for sure but what I do know is the Protrerian High Command don't give up easily," I said.

"Many thanks Commodore, if that is all sir we'll now take our leave? "Affirmative, if there is anything else I will call for you; when you get famished you are welcomed to have your banquets in our mess hall," he said as he returned our salutes. "Many thanks for everything sir, it is a real comfort to know that we have grand associates here," I said as we all shook his hand, turned then left the Commodore's office.

"As I am no longer needed, I will now return to the craft," 'PAT said. "Affirmative 'PAT', dismissed. "Sir, if you would follow me I will show you to your quarters," the Corporal said with a smile. We left the air-conditioned confines of the structure. We got into an armored utility vehicle; the Corporal pressed the start button and the vehicle roared to life then he pulled onto the boulevard.

Going down K Boulevard, we passed a squadron of armed cybernetic recruit replacements crossing the compound. 'The Tanglar Military doesn't have cybernetic recruits besides 'PAT" but soon we will have them as well throughout all branches of the military,' I thought as we passed a few buildings.'

"Pleasant gent the Commodore is," I said as we pulled up alongside the blue barracks. "He is as long as you stay on his grand side," the Corporal said as he turned the ignition off and we both exited the vehicle. "What are the chamber digits?" I asked as we got to the front entry-way. "Chamber 7b. "I would also require latrine supplies and fatigues. "Affirmative sir let me show you your quarters first then I will fetch the supplies you require."

We both stopped in front of chamber 7b and the Corporal unlocked the entry-way. "Look around while I go get the supplies you requested. "Corporal, inform air commuter transportation control to keep a close eye on the radar because the Protrerian High Command will most likely strike again. "Affirmative," the Corporal replied as he left.

I started looking around and was content with the quarters. I pressed the wing of my com-link and contacted 'PAT'. "Go ahead sir. "Keep the long-range radar on and contact me as soon as anything enters ZarCedra's stratosphere. "Affirmative, is there anything else you require? "Not at this time. "Affirmative, 'PAT' out. "Jr. Com. Teldat out," I said just as there was a chime at the entry-way.

The Corporal entered the chamber with an armload of supplies. "Here we are sir." I took the stuff that belonged in the latrine so I could put them away. He had the fatigues I requested a clean sheet and comforter for my cot. "If you need anything else, don't hesitate to ask," the Corporal said with a smile. "Many thanks Corporal but that is all I require, except can you tell me where the mess hall is located? "Sure, it's just up the boulevard a couple blocks, is that all? "Affirmative it is, many thanks. "All right sir," he said as he turned and left my quarters.

I took the slumbering unit linen and went to make my cot. After I had finished I looked at my timepiece, seeing it was 17 hundred 34 epocks and decided it was high time for my twilight banquet. So I left the barracks and went up the boulevard to the mess hall.

I entered, grabbed a tray then stood in line and waited until I received my banquet, I went to retrieve silverware and a cold caffeinated brew then went to find a seat.

****

After I finished my twilight banquet and was on my way back to my barracks there came a beep from my com-link. "Go ahead 'PAT'. "Jr. Commodore sixteen waves of interstellar attack craft just entered ZarCedra's Stratosphere and by the rate of their descent they are returning to the Eastern seaboard of Kor Bissal. "Affirmative 'PAT', how long until they reach this vicinity? "Eight mites. "Affirmative, Jr. Com. Teldat out." I changed direction and started running for Com. Magae's office.

When I got there I entered main headquarters and stopped at the Corporal's desk. "I need to speak to Com. Magae immediately! "Affirmative sir, if it's that imperative, go right in." I turned and entered the Commodore's office.

"My apologies for barging in sir but we have enemy attack craft incoming. "That is important enough of a reason for barging in Jr. Commodore; do you know how many attack craft we can expect? "Sixteen waves, about one hundred and sixty attack craft are descending to the eastern seaboard of Kor Bissal. "How did you receive this information? "'PAT', my co-pilot just informed me, my craft is equipped with a Planet radar." Just then a siren wailed and the Commodore's PCD chirped.

"Com. Magae here, go ahead," he said as he answered and was informed of the incoming attack craft. "I can send up ten squadrons, have them in the air ASAP," he said then hung up. The Commodore picked up the PCD again and made a call to the Z.C.C Clandor and warned them of the incoming attack craft. "Also advise the Z.C.C Manedosar, the K.B.N.S Dragoon and the K.B.N.S Dragozi aircraft transporters to lend assistance as well," he said then put the receiver down.

"Sir, may I use your Personal Communication Device? "Affirmative." I picked up the receiver and called the Corporal "Corporal connect me with the Lanston Military Installation in Translete immediately."

A few secs later I heard; "Lanston Military Installation. "Can I be of assistance? "Affirmative airman, let me speak to Jr. Com. Stenwen immediately! "Jr. Com. Stenwen was replaced by Commodore Dodson," I was informed.

"Connect us immediately!" I said in a frantic tone. When we were, I told him. "I am Jr. Com. Teldat, we have multiple squadrons of incoming attack craft arriving in the eastern seaboard of Kor Bissal and I require assistance ASAP. "Affirmative, I'll dispatch ten squadrons to that position immediately. I am ordered by President Torren to lend all assistance I can to you, will you also be in the air as well? "Unfortunately I will be unable to partake at this time, earlier this p.a.r in battle my craft was damaged and it is currently being repaired. But If I can borrow a fighter, I will assist. "Affirmative," he said then we both hung up.

"I'll have to make a call to see if we have a spare aircraft that we can provide you with," the Commodore said as he picked up the PCD. A mite later he hung up. "My apologies Jr. Commodore but there isn't a spare fighter available at this time to lend you, you're going to have to sit this battle out for now. If I can get a fighter for you to use I'll contact you immediately. "Affirmative sir, many thanks," I answered as I saluted; turned and left the office.

"Many thanks Corporal," I said as I walked by him on my way out of main headquarters.

Walking down the boulevard I heard aircraft after aircraft leave the runways, and seen the helijets take off as I pressed the wing of my com-link. "Affirmative Jr. Commodore, go ahead. "'PAT', I understand you are unable to fly at the moment, do you know for how long? "Negative, it seems the Sergeant is having trouble acquiring the correct material he needs at the moment; it looks like it won't be anytime soon. "Understood 'PAT', in the interim can you keep me informed on how the air-to-air combat is going? "Affirmative sir, is that all? "It is for now, Jr. Com. Teldat out. "'PAT', out." I then continued to my temporary barracks.

I entered the blue barracks then unlocked chamber 7b and went to sit on the lounger. 'I wonder how Topanga is doing? She mentioned that she was inkling about joining a military infirmary; I wonder if she had yet? I guess I will keep wondering until I could call her,' I thought as I got up to use the latrine.

After, I located a ballpoint and jotter; I started jotting a report of the happenings of this p.a.r and since arriving in Dalarme. As 'PAT' kept me up to date with the battle going on overhead.

A couple epocks later, I finished my report as I set it aside; I looked at my timepiece to discover it was 21 hundred 12 epocks. Since the Commodore hadn't been in contact, I decided to hit the hay for some shuteye. Before I did I contacted 'PAT'. "'PAT' here Jr. Commodore, go ahead. "I will be out of contact for a few epocks, but if there was anything of extreme crisis to report, contact me immediately! "Affirmative Jr. Commodore, is that all? "Affirmative Jr. Com. Teldat, out. "'PAT', out."

I turned everything off, went to the latrine and brushed my teeth then walked to my slumbering quarters, undressed and crawled into my cot then drifted off.

*****

While I slumbered, I had another one of my upsetting twilightmares. I was up in my craft fighting Protrerian attack craft when I noticed Topanga with me. At that sec a storm brewed up around the craft.

"Why are you with me," I asked just as a bolt of lightning struck my aircraft. The craft exploded in millions of pieces. I awoke screaming, "NO!" I sat up then realized it was only a twilightmare. 'Why did my craft just explode,' I wondered for the next few mites. "Unless it failed because the voltage of electricity in the bolt of lightning has to be precisely the same as the bolt that struck my craft and brought us to this time. But how can I be sure if 'PAT' was off-line? 'I guess I will ask 'PAT' that question if the situation ever arises,' I thought as I rolled over, closed my eyes and went back to slumber.

P.A.R 9

When I finished getting ready for this p.a.r, I put on my beret and was about to go for my morn banquet when I heard a chime at the entry-way. I went and opened it and low and behold standing in the hall was Sgt. Pane and LC Luxton.

"Grand morn sir," they both said as they saluted. "Grand morn," I replied as I smiled and returned their salute. "Are you ready for our morn banquet?" Sgt. Pane asked. "I sure am," I said as we left my quarters and made our way to the mess hall.

After entering, we grabbed trays then received our grub and caffinated brew. We each retrieved eating utensils then went to a vacant table, sat and removed our berets. As we were eating Com. Magae walked up to us and we saluted.

"Jr. Com. Teldat, I want to see you in my office immediately following your morn banquet," Com. Magae said as he returned our salutes. "Affirmative sir," I answered then the Commodore turned and walked away.

"I wonder what the Commodore wants? "Probably wants to tell you we were almost defeated last twilight but we were able to come out on top at the very end of the battle."

"Were you two citizens among the pilots sent up last twilight? "Affirmative, but we were sent up at the very tail end of the battle and the squadron we were in took care of the last squadron of attack craft. Why weren't you up there last twilight? I figured you probably would have borrowed a fighter to be up in the thick of the action," LC Luxton queried. "I wanted to but unfortunately there wasn't a spare aircraft available. Hopefully my craft will be repaired soon and I can again assist, then those Protrerian butt-holes better watch out," I said with a grin as I consumed the rest of my morn banquet then finished my caffinated brew.

When I finished my morn banquet I gathered my refuse and placed it back on my tray. "It's now time to go see the Commodore," I told LC Luxton and Sgt. Pane as I rose. "See you around," they both said as I turned and walked away. "Affirmative," I muttered as I put my tray away then departed the mess hall putting my beret back on.

I gave and returned salutes from passing military personnel as I walked the few blocks to main headquarters.

When I got there I climbed the stairs then entered the structure. I walked up to the Corporal. "Jr. Com. Teldat to see Com. Magae as directed. "Affirmative sir," the Corporal said as he picked up the PCD. "Com. Magae, Jr. Com. Teldat is here, affirmative sir at once. You may go right in the Commodore is expecting you," the Corporal said. "Many thanks," I answered as I removed my beret then walked to the entry-way, knocked then entered.

As soon as I closed the entry-way, I stood at attention and saluted. "Stand at ease Jr. Commodore," Com. Magae said as he returned my salute.

"You asked to see me sir? "Affirmative Jr. Commodore, the reason is I had put a rush on the repair of your aircraft and it should be ready to fly later this morn or early mid-p.a.r. "Grand, do you know about what time precisely? "Not precisely, but I was told sometime early this p.a.r. "Affirmative sir, many thanks."

"The partial wing of my craft that needs to be repaired is about five times the size of this p.a.r's Stealth Aircraft, how were they able to complete so quickly? That is unknown but the Sergeant and his team worked all twilight. "Affirmative sir; is that all?

"Negative Jr. Commodore, I would like to know what you think of how this war is turning out? "Affirmative sir, with me being here we were able to succeed in what wasn't possible in my times elapsed archives, and that was destroying the four Protrerian Energy Extractor Craft. Now if we can add enough resistance to the attacking Protrerian High Command attack craft at least until the Antrerian Armada arrives to offer assistance, we should be all right."

"They should arrive mid-p.a.r on 07.05? "That is correct sir. "All right Jr. Commodore that will be all for now, stop by my office in a few epocks and your aircraft should be repaired. "Affirmative," I answered as I saluted, turned and left the office.

'I'll sure be glad when my craft is repaired because on p.a.r's like this I love to be airborne,' I thought as I exited the structure into the warm sunshine and walked up the boulevard. I looked at my timepiece and seen that it was 07 hundred 55 epocks. 'It sure has been a while since the last wave of Protrerian High Command attack craft flew this way, I better contact 'PAT' for a report,' I thought as I tapped the left wing of my com-link. "'PAT', report."

"There has been no alien attack craft activity in the area since last twilight, all quiet for now. "Affirmative 'PAT', contact me immediately upon detecting any attack craft entering ZarCedra's stratosphere. "Affirmative, is that all? "Affirmative," I answered. "PAT, out. "Jr. Com. Teldat, out"

As I was walking down the boulevard a set of dumbbells and other exercise equipment in the front window of a structure caught my eye. I walked into Sam's Abode of Exercise then up to the counter. "Would it be possible to lift some weights and workout awhile?" I asked the Sergeant. "Affirmative sir, what size gym clothing do you wear? "I take a large t-shirt and 91.4 centric gym shorts. "What dimensions of shoes do you require Jr. Commodore? "Dimension 12e. "Here you go sir," the Sergeant said as he handed me the gym clothing, footwear and a towel. "My name is Sgt. Meadows, go change and I'll spot for you. "See you in a few mites," I said as I went into the change chamber.

I found a locker, removed my beret and changed then put on the running shoes. I removed my winged com-link and pinned it to my T-shirt, picked up the key that was on the bottom shelf of the locker, put it in my pocket then closed the entry-way. I went into the gym where I warmed up by doing a few stretches. When Sgt. Meadows finally entered, we both went to the weight chamber.

I worked out for a total of 2 epocks on an array of different exercise equipment; I was on my way to another weight training device when 'PAT' interrupted.

"Jr. Commodore, fourteen waves of alien attack craft have entered ZarCedra's stratosphere, by the rate of their descent they are flying in this general direction. Wait five waves changed direction and are on a coarse for Sot Bissal," 'PAT' reported. "Affirmative," I acknowledged. "I must go change," I told Sgt. Meadows as I vacated the area. In a matter of a couple mites I had my uniform, beret and boots on. I ran out of the gym pinning my com-link communicator to my jacket as I ran in the direction of main headquarters.

I went straight to Com. Magae's office and burst inside. "Commodore we have enemy Protrerian attack craft incoming and waves of enemy attack craft on a course for Sot Bissal. "I'll call the Hemair Military Installation in Myfare and warn them that we have incoming alien attack craft and they can inform the Sot Bissal Military Coalition in Sri Montra," Com. Magae informed me.

"Six additional waves of Protrerian attack craft have entered ZarCedra's stratosphere and by the rate of their descent in my calculation they are on a direct route to the eastern seaboard of Sot Bissal. At their current speed they will arrive in five mites thirty secs. "Affirmative, 'PAT'," I quickly acknowledged.

"I'll have aircraft in the air immediately," Com. Magae said as he made a call to sound the alarm letting everyone know they have enemy attack craft incoming. 1 sec later we both heard the whine of the siren as it sounded throughout the base.

"Precisely how long until my craft is repaired and I can once again get airborne? "I'm not sure, I'll call the Sergeant and find out," he said as he picked up the PCD and called the aircraft mechanic. "Affirmative," he grunted after a mite of discussion then hung up.

"It is almost repaired, all that remains to do is mount the partial wing to the aircraft and tinted. "My craft getting tinted isn't imperative at the moment but me being in the air is; I'll take my craft as soon as the wing is attached. "Affirmative, go to your aircraft and I'll contact the mechanic once more and inform him to let you have it as soon as possible. "Affirmative, and get as many aircraft in the air as quickly as you can and when I could, I will fly at Star Drive speed to Sot Bissal and give all the assistance I can! "Affirmative." I saluted, turned then ran from the office.

I ran to the entrance and exited the structure, knocking a few cadets down the stairs as the entry-ways opened. "My apologies," I said, as I assisted them to their feet then I quickly continued to the only hangar large enough to house my craft. I arrived as the head mechanic was on the Personal Communication Device. "Affirmative," he said then hung up.

"That was Com. Magae, we have incoming alien attack craft and I was informed to let you have your aircraft as soon as my team had completed the installation of the repaired wing. As you can see that is almost complete," he said as he looked up. I followed his gaze and seen the new partial wing suspended from the ceiling by block and tackle, as the last row of bolts were riveted in place.

"We were going to seal & tint the wing to match the aircraft but Com. Magae instructed me to allow you to take your aircraft as is, as soon as possible" he said as he tossed me the electronic keycard. "Affirmative, many thanks very much for repairing my craft," I said as I caught the key card.

"There the wing is repaired; as there was a rush on the repair of your aircraft Jr. Commodore we weren't able to attach your golden modules as the rest of them, we affixed them to the outside of the wing," the Sergeant said as the wing was released and the aircraft lowered slightly. "Many thanks Sergeant, that should be grand as long as they align with the rest of them? "They are; your co-pilot advised us where to apply them. A few mites later, the team of mechanics lowered to the floor as I tapped my com-link.

"'PAT, to enter the swirling wormhole and travel at star drive speeds within the ZarCedra's' atmosphere, the craft has to be air tight, is the weld sufficient to hold in oxygen at those speeds? "Affirmative sir, the weld should hold but an undercoat of polyurethane would make the craft unmistakably airtight. I looked at Sgt. Noonsy and said, "I have to replace a vial of the Liquid Napricyte^2 SDC; if you and your team can apply the polyurethane undercoating on the wing in that time, do it. If not, I'll have it done at a later time, keep in mind we have enemy incoming and they will arrive in mere mites. "Affirmative Jr. Commodore, we'll have it done ASAP," he said as he and his team went to work.

"'PAT', open and lower the main hatch platform immediately." When it was, I got on the platform and went up to the cockpit. I quickly put on my radiation safe suit, grabbed the case of Liquid Napricyte^2 SDC and my breathing apparatus then went to the main hatch platform. "'PAT', raise and slide the engine cover so I can refuel the Star Drive engine," I said as I lowered to the floor.

"I require the use of an AML," I told the Sergeant as I stepped off the lift. "Affirmative; give me a hand," he told a couple members of his team. "Affirmative, they said as the Sergeant, the couple members of his team and I ran to position the spare AML from the side wall to the rear of the craft. Then they went to work retrieving the sprayer and polyurethane.

I picked up the case of Liquid Napricyte^2 SDC and my breathing apparatus as I stepped on the AML and rose up to and stepped on to the metal walkway. I jogged to the ladder; I put my breathing apparatus atop my head and climbed down to the Omagon 2115 Star Drive engine. I pulled my breathing apparatus down and over my nose and mouth as I removed the cover over the fuel injection unit as I changed vials of the radioactive chemical solution.

When that was complete I replaced the empty vial in the case and replaced the cover over the injection unit. When I was finished I removed the apparatus from my face as I quickly went back up to the AML then lowered to the floor. "Many thanks for everything Sergeant," I said as they were just finishing spraying the weld of the new partial wing and I removed the radiation suit.

When I had the suit off I tapped the left wing of my com-link. "'PAT', you can now close the tail section of the craft," I said as I went up to the cockpit; put the case of Liquid Napricyte[2] SDC and radiation safe suit away. I quickly removed my beret then put on my flight suit. I raised then closed the main hatch platform then inserted and engaged the electronic keycard. I went to the pilot's seat, sat then buckled myself in; I put on the 'HUD' helmet as I activated my craft.

I taxied my craft out in the open and at the same time I had the port wing extended as it slid and locked into place. I pressed the finger touch pad on my 'HUD' helmet that activated two-way communications. "Tower this is Jr. Com. Teldat, clear me for liftoff."

I accessed the menu inside the face shield of my 'HUD' helmet and checked the level of fuel I had in the fuel tanks. I saw that I had a sufficient amount so when my clearance for liftoff came; I lowered the wings and started to rise.

As I rose I made a mental note. 'That Sergeant and his technicians had done a better job of repairing the wing than they led on.' I stopped rising at one thousand metrics, leveled the wings then started advancing forward as I checked the radar for the location of enemy attack craft in the immediate vicinity. "I better assist here until reinforcements arrive before we head to Sot Bissal," I told 'PAT.

"Affirmative, Jr. Commodore enemy attack craft at one o'clock and the few Kor Bissal fighters that arrived first are in a bad predicament. "I have them in my sights, many thanks 'PAT'." As the enemy attack craft advanced I activated my craft's shield in the nick of time as the attack craft started firing their laser blasts. I lowered the two XTR-9000 Plasma Pulse Cannons and fired at all the enemy attack craft that moved. I veered to the port side firing the Sareden Quantum laser cannons destroying the two craft in my path.

Two mites' later reinforcements arrived. I pressed the finger touch pad and activated my two-way communications. "Flight leader of Dalarme's Kinkade Military Installation forces, if you have everything under control here I am going to lend assistance in Sot Bissal. "Affirmative go," he answered.

I checked the long-range radar as I deactivated the full-bodied shield. I raised the XTR-9000 Plasma Pulse Cannons back into the wings then I advanced speed to Mach ten. I activated the Omagon 2115 Star Drive engine and the remaining golden modules and rod appeared from the body of my craft, as soon as the Ionic swirling wormhole appeared I flew into it and disappeared. I went to Star Drive one then Star Drive two as oxygen filled the cockpit and the craft barrel rolled through the wormhole.

Thirty-seven secs later I pulled out of Star Drive and slowed to Mach six as I activated stealth mode and my craft vanished from sight. I flew forty-five kiloms off the coast of Sri Montra, Corstal where I saw the Corstalian aircraft of S.B.M.Co and alien attack craft in heavy battle. I deactivated stealth mode then activated my craft's shield as I joined in the battle.

"Who are you?" A surprised voice inquired at the sudden appearance of my aircraft. "I am Jr. Commodore Teldat, from the North Kor Bissal Military Coalition. "Welcome, any additional assistance is grandly appreciated, I am Jr. Com. Mendez."

I hovered in one position as I activated my XT-165 DigiCam then fired the SQ-Lasers and spent off a few Protonic EMC-Missals as I lowered the XTR-9000 Plasma Pulse Cannons and blasted at all enemy attack craft in my line of sight. At that moment ten squadrons of Kor Bissal and the Galatians fighters and helijets arrived.

"I am Com. Santon from the Hemair Military Installation from Myfare, Torxen in the Cardola Territories here to assist. "And I am Commodore Colandro, ordered here from the Caza Military Facility in Galatian Palisades also sent here to assist. "Welcome, join in," Jr. Com. Mendez said as he fired a missile at the craft before him.

As the air battle was commencing, everyone was amazed at the size, maneuverability and fire-power of my huge craft; they watched from the corner of their eye as my craft hovered in one position and pivoted from port to starboard then back to port, destroying all enemy attack craft in my path. Even though I destroyed attack craft after attack craft I still noticed consociately aircraft going down or exploding in flames.

After two epocks of heavy resistance, I overheard the discussion between Jr. Com. Mendez and a Commander Frolliana of the Tanzeer Nautical Air Command.

"I am the flight leader of a squad of thirty aircraft," the Commander reported. "Grand, you are more than welcomed to join in when you arrive," Jr. Com. Mendez said. At that time, I decided it was time to formerly introduce myself to Jr. Com. Mendez and Commander Frolliana. I tapped the finger touch pad that activated two-way communications.

"Time to formally introduce myself gentlefolk; I am Jr. Com. Teldat and I am from the Grinshaw Military Facility out of Cangla City, in the honorary regime of Placaden, Tanglar. "What type of aircraft are you flying? I have never seen such a magnificent aircraft! " Jr. Com. Mendez inquired. "What type of aircraft are you flying? Commander Frolliana also inquired. "This is a prototype craft called the Supersonic Dragon 228-D Spy Jet Stealth," I proudly stated. "Commander you should see this aircraft!" Jr. Com. Mendez exclaimed. "I will soon, I be almost to your position," Commander Frolliana said in broken English. "Jr. Com. Teldat, tell the Commander of your aircraft's firepower!" Jr. Com. Mendez said. "My craft's firepower consists of Sareden Quantum Laser Cannons, two XTR-9000 Plasma Pulse Cannons, Protonic Electromagnetic Cluster Missals and Neutronic Electromagnetic Cluster Torpedo's," I told the Corstalian Commander.

"I have a question for you Jr. Com. Teldat?" Jr. Com. Mendez said. "Ask away. "How can your aircraft sustain so many direct hits and still be unaffected? "One of the many important aspects of my prototype craft is its full-bodied shield; I can sustain many direct hits as long as my shield holds."

Just then Commander Frolliana arrived with his squadron and joined in the battle. "Amazing!" Commander Frolliana said as he seen my huge craft. Twenty more mites of grueling air battle followed and the sun was starting to dip over the horizon as the last enemy attack craft was destroyed.

I turned the XT-165 DigiCam off as I recharged my weapons and shield as the remaining military aircraft gathered together and flew toward Sri Montra's Scaltia Military Facility. "Many thanks for your assistance," Jr. Com. Mendez said to everyone. "My squadron and I must return to our aircraft transporters; grand to meet you Jr. Com. Teldat and I'm glad we could assist," Commander Frolliana said. He turned toward the open sea and the five aircraft remaining in his squadron flew in formation with him.

"My squadron and I need fuel desperately, before we head back to Myfare," Commander Santon reported. "As do the remaining aircraft in my squadron," Commodore Colandro stated. "Follow us to Scaltia Military Facility and your aircraft will be attended to as you and your squadrons have twilight banquets. Jr. Com. Teldat you can explain more of your prototype aircraft over your banquet as well," Jr. Com. Mendez said. "Affirmative, lead the way," I said smiling to myself as we flew.

"Is there a certain place I can descend to Jr. Com. Mendez? My craft doesn't require a runway to land," I said as we neared the Scaltia Military Facility in Sri Montra. "Amazing, you are permitted to land alongside the helijets. "Affirmative," I said as the remaining aircraft and I flew over the city.

When we arrived at the Scaltia Military Facility they landed as I stopped, raised my craft's wings, as the landing gear automatically lowered. As I descended to the tarmac below with the two remaining helijets.

I switched off the engines and as my craft was winding down, I contracted the port wing and had it slid back. "Raise the tail potion so the craft can receive fuel," I told 'PAT'. "Affirmative Jr. Commodore," she replied. I removed my 'HUD' helmet then disconnected my safety belts and left the pilot's seat. I retrieved the electronic keycard and deposited it in the pocket of my flight suit as I put on my beret.

"You are welcomed to join me 'PAT', if you so desire? "Affirmative I desire," 'PAT' said as I went over opened the main hatch platform; we both stepped on and lowered to the ground. We got to the ground just as Jr. Com. Mendez arrived by armored utility vehicle.

"A pleasure to finally meet you face to face," Jr. Com. Mendez said as his Commanding Officer also came out to meet me.

"Commodore Monteyez at your service, anything you desire or need will be at your disposal. "Gratchias Ameigon," I said in not very grand Sot Bissalian. "Are you getting famished?" Commodore Monteyez inquired. "Considering I haven't consumed anything in a few epocks, I am so famished!" I said as I rubbed my stomach. "I am Jr. Com. Teldat and beside me is 'PAT', my cybernetic co-pilot," I told Commodore Monteyez and Jr. Com. Mendez as I held out my hand.

After he shook it he said. "Take Jr. Com. Teldat, his co-pilot and the rest of the pilots to the mess hall so they could have their twilight banquets," the Commodore said in his native tongue as he looked over at Jr. Com. Mendez. "Affirmative Commodore," Jr. Com. Mendez replied as he told me to wait until the rest of the pilots arrive.

"My craft needs refueling," I told them as we waited. I told the two officers where the fuel intake caps were located on my craft. "Not to worry Jr. Commodore I will personally show where the fuel enters.

"'PAT' remain here, the fuel tanker will arrive shortly. "Affirmative," she said. "After the tanks are filled, the caps replaced and the military citizens are away from the craft, lower the engine cover and then you can join us inside. "Affirmative sir," she said just as Commodore Colandro and Com. Santon and what was left of their squadrons arrived then we all walked toward the structure. As we walked away, I looked back and seen the Sot Bissalian Commodore take a closer look at my craft.

"First things first, where are the latrines located?" I asked as we entered the structure. "Down this hall a few metrics, as there is only one-latrine lady and gentlefolk have to share the same facilities," Jr. Com. Mendez said as we stopped in front of the huge latrine.

After everyone done his or her business and washed up we all met back in the hall. "I hope everyone is famished?" Jr. Com. Mendez asked as we walked to the entrance of the mess hall. "We sure are," Com. Santon said as we entered the cafeteria. I inhaled deeply as the spices and aromas of their ethnic fares tickled my fancy.

"This way," the Corstalian Jr. Commodore said as we all continued to the rear of the hall. There were a few air citizens waiting to serve us as we walked up. Jr. Com. Mendez went to grab trays and passed them out one at a time to the party of pilots. Just then a gorgeous female Sot Bissalian Sergeant smiled as she ladled beef, chili peppers, and beans on plates topped with shredded cheese and served with sides of corn bread.

After we each received our banquet we were asked what we wanted for refreshments? "Juice will be fine," we all said. "Many thanks for the refreshments," we said as she handed them out then we went to a long table and sat.

"When did the Tanglar Military bring your aircraft into circulation?" Jr. Com. Mendez asked me. "Affirmative when?" Com. Santon asked. I was getting tired of explaining everything about my ordeal and craft but I explained about it one more time.

"This might be hard to believe but 'PAT' and I come from the times yet to come. The tritton 2115 to be exact, and at that time the military just invented my craft. I am a test pilot and this aircraft is a prototype craft, I was to test and use on a secretive mission. A few p.a.r's ago I was flying through an electrical storm and my craft was struck by lightning as I was entering a Humanarian-made swirling wormhole and miraculously brought back to this time period; then the war broke out and we began to assist," I explained as we consumed our banquets.

"What is this Humanarian-made swirling wormhole?" Jr. Com. Mendez asked.

"Well I have a prototype third engine on my aircraft, which is called an Omagon 2115 Star Drive Engine, and connected to it is a wondrous component called an Electronic Flux Inducer. When this engine is activated golden modules and rod protrude from the exterior of my craft. My craft's Comodrone Electronics P-52 Hydrogenic Generator sends an electrical charge, which is combined with a Liquid Napricyte[2] compound and sent to the Electronic Flux Inducer."

"In turn the Electronic Flux Inducer converts that electronic charge to an Ionic charge that encompasses my craft electromagnetically going from each golden module then finally to the golden rod on the nose of my craft. The Ionic charge is then shot out directly in my crafts path creating a Humanarian-made swirling wormhole. I fly into this wormhole and my craft is able to fly at Star Drive speeds within ZarCedra's oxygenated resistant atmosphere and gravitational pull."

"Oxygenated resistant atmosphere within this wormhole means no oxygen. In order for me to breathe, my craft is equipped with tanks of compressed breathable oxygen that automatically releases into the cockpit as I fly through the wormhole, enabling me to breathe normally. 'PAT', my co-pilot doesn't require oxygen because she doesn't breathe." I told the flabbergasted Jr. Commodore.

As we continued eating, the remainder of Jr. Com. Mendez's squad entered the mess hall. They grabbed trays, received their banquets and came over to join our table. "Grand p.a.r sirs," they all said as they sat down. "What do you think of the war we are having with this alien race?" I asked the squad.

"I really don't like it, we are losing mates every p.a.r. Take the battle we just returned from, we lost ¾ of the squadron we went up with," Sgt. Gillerez responded. "That is truly a shame, another two p.a.r's and we'll receive the assistance we so desperately need and hopefully we can soon end this war. "What do you mean? "We will receive assistance from…"

Just then there was a message in Corstalish directed at Jr. Com. Mendez and myself. I had a little trouble making out the message. "Let us go Jr. Com. Teldat we are requested by the Commodore." I stood and began collecting my tray. "Leave it, it will be taken care of, let us go," Jr. Com. Mendez told me as we headed for the entry-way, down the hall then out of the structure.

As we got outside, 'PAT' joined us. "Is the craft secured?" I asked 'PAT'. "Affirmative it is," she said as we kept walking. "You have a grand view of the sea from this location," I said looking toward the coast as we were walking towards main headquarters. "Affirmative, and it looks a whole lot better when the sea faring transports are out of the harbor." The sun had set but the full moons shone enough illumination in the semi-darkness to see the harbor, and I could see lights on the sea faring transports and vessels anchored there.

When we finally arrived at main headquarters, we mounted the steps and entered. "We are to see the Commodore," Jr. Com. Mendez said in Corstalian, as we walked to the air citizen at the front desk. He picked up the PCD and chirped Commodore Monteyez. "Sir, Jr. Com. Mendez and party are now present. "Affirmative sir. He looked over at us. You may go right in," he said as he hung up.

Jr. Com. Mendez 'PAT' and I entered the Commodore's office; we stood at attention and saluted. "Close the entry-way and stand at ease," Commodore Monteyez told Jr. Com. Mendez as he returned our salutes. Jr. Com. Mendez did as he was asked then returned to his previous position as we all stood at ease.

"I just got off the PCD with Prime Minister Trembley and he had a lot to say about you," Commodore Monteyez said as he looked at me. "For instance, is it true that you are here from the times yet to come? "Affirmative sir, the tritton I come from is 2115. If you would like proof here are my military tags with my rank, name, serial digits, birthp.a.r and the tritton I entered the military," I said as I extracted the two metallic tags to show the two officers. "If more proof is needed you may ask 'PAT'."

"My rank was advanced from Major to Jr. Commodore after I arrived in this time, that's the only thing that you will find different on my tags. I also have a tattoo of a patriotic eagle on my shoulder that also has the tritton I entered the military. The craft I have in my possession is a prototype but a prototype from the tritton I am from, the Supersonic Dragon 228-D Spy Jet Stealth that is sitting outside."

"Affirmative, tell the Commodore about your aircraft; everything you told me in the mess hall," Jr. Com. Mendez said. "Ask about the firepower that his aircraft has," Jr. Com. Mendez told the Commodore.

"What are the types of firepower do you have on your aircraft? "My craft is equipped with a double-barreled Sareden Quantum Laser Cannons and two XTR-9000 Plasma Pulse Cannons. Additionally, it has Protonic Electromagnetic Cluster Missals and Neutronic Electromagnetic Cluster Torpedo's. My craft is also equipped with a Comodrone Electronics P-52 Hydrogenic Generator that keeps my Laser and Plasma Pulse cannons ammunition recharged at all times but I only have a maximum of fifteen Protonic EMC-Missals and ten EMC-Torpedo's at one time. After I expel them I must recharge them before my artillery can discharge more. As you seen, my craft is hover capable almost like the helijets, so I no longer have the need for a runway for liftoffs or landing."

"I also heard your airspeed is a lot faster than the aircraft we have now but by how much?" Jr. Com. Mendez inquired.

"What is the maximum air speed of the fighters you currently have? "Mach five," the Commodore answered. "My Supersonic Dragon 228-D Stealth Spy Jet excels to a maximum of Mach ten, then when I activate my Omagon 2115 Star Drive engine I go into Star Drive speed. Which activates my Electronic Flux Inducer, this device sends an Ionic charge that encompasses my craft electromagnetically going from each golden module then it travels to the golden rod at the front of my craft, it is then shot out directly in my path."

"The Ionic charge then creates a Humanarian-made swirling wormhole; I fly into this wormhole and access Star Drive speeds. Star Drive one is 10* faster than Mach ten, and Star Drive two is 20* faster than Mach ten, which is equivalent to Mach 200."

"My Gods that is some speed; may I ask how long it took you to arrive here from your point of origin?" Commodore Monteyez asked. "I left Dalarme, in the Cardola Territories at

Star Drive two and it took me thirty-seven secs to arrive here. "You've got to be jesting!" Commodore Monteyez and Jr. Com. Mendez both said in unison. "Negative that is the honest truth. "Affirmative it is," 'PAT' said.

"Can I ask what type of fuel these engines operate on?" Commodore Monteyez inquired. "My craft uses regular jet fuel for the main F405-F1D3 afterburning engines. My Star Drive engine however, uses a special radioactive chemical solution called Liquid Napricyte² SDC."

"You asked us for more fuel and we refueled your main tanks but we cannot offer you that type of fuel because I have never heard of that type of chemical solution before! "Oh, that is understood; all I required was the jet fuel, I have a sufficient supply of that chemical fuel on hand for the time being."

"Do you know what this alien race wants so bad that it is worth starting a war over?" Commodore Monteyez asked as he sat back in his chair. "The reason is because their planet is running out of energy and their sun is slowly on its way to going nova. Considering their Planet will eventually die, they are declaring war to take over ZarCedra as their new abode because our sun is still young and full of life, but."

"But what? "But we are supposed to receive assistance. "From who, if our whole planet is engaged in this war? "We are supposed to receive the assistance from the Protrerian High Command's archenemies known as the Antrerian Armada. Originally we lost this war even with their intervening but at that time we weren't here but we are now with a powerful prototype craft."

"To elaborate further, in the original war no one was able to defeat the huge Protrerian Energy Extractor Craft and they were easily able to defeat our forces; therefore, able to take over ZarCedra and control it under their reign. But right now in this time by defeating the four Protrerian Energy Extractor Craft we were able to get the upper hand in this war."

"Jr. Commodore Teldat, two transport craft just entered the stratosphere; by the rate of their descent they are on a course for the Cardola Territories." 'PAT' reported. "Transport craft? I said as I looked at her and scratched my head. "There was no transport craft reported this early in the original war.

"They were most likely deployed at this time, in retaliation to the destruction of the energy extractor craft and judging by the dimension of said transport craft, they are large enough to carry thousands of enemy soldiers each. "Affirmative; let's be on our way 'PAT'.

"My apologies gentlefolk but we must leave now. "By all means go. "Many thanks for the fuel and the banquet, muchly appreciated," I said as I saluted then 'PAT' and I headed for the entry-way. "Many thanks for all your assistance and insight of this war, and it was a pleasure to make both your acquaintances," the two officers said as we exited the office then main headquarters.

"Two additional transport crafts just entered ZarCedra's stratosphere," 'PAT' reported as we rose to the cockpit and entered.

I raised and secured the cockpit entry-way, inserted the electronic keycard then hopped in the pilot's seat as 'PAT' secured herself at her post. I removed my beret, put on the 'HUD' helmet and connected the safety belts. I activated the ignition sequence, I raised the face shield of the 'HUD' helmet then looked at my planet radar and seen the latter two transport craft were heading in the opposite direction of the first two transport craft. "By the rate of their descent their target area is Gergel on the Jroken Continent, 'PAT' stated.

I extended and locked the port wing in place as both wings lowered. My craft left the ground and as soon as the landing gear raised and the craft's wings leveled I increased speed and soon I was flying at Mach ten.

I pressed the finger touch pad that activated two-way communications. "Jr. Com. Teldat calling the Hemair Military Installation in Myfare. "Hemair Military Installation, go-ahead Jr. Com. Teldat."

"Two transport craft are descending somewhere in the Maccari desert. Most likely filled with thousands of enemy soldiers, by the rate of their descent I can now see they will attack Kelsar; contact the proper authorities in that territory to intercept ASAP. I am on my way to Gergel on the Jroken Continent; we also have incoming transport craft there, likely filled with ground troopers as well. "Affirmative sir, we now have them on radar; I will contact the Desert Snake Military Installation in Kelsar, Maccari, ASAP." The female voice answered. "Jr. Com. Teldat out. "Hemair Military Installation, out."

I raised the face shield of my 'HUD' helmet and checked my radar then activated the Omagon 2115 Star Drive Engine and the Electronic Flux Inducer. I lowered my face shield and when the swirling wormhole appeared, I flew into it and went to Star Drive one then Star Drive two.

Sixty-five secs later I pulled out of the swirling wormhole and decelerated over the Blacking Sand Dunes. I tapped the touch pad that activated two-way communications twice, so the channel would remain open. "Jr. Com. Teldat calling anyone in the vicinity who can patch me through to President Kishtofen."

"This is Michkavic Aviation, hold a mite," I heard a few secs later. Secs later I was in communications with the President of the Gergel Citizens. "What can I do for you Jr. Com. Teldat?"

"Grand p.a.r sir, this is Jr. Com. Teldat of the North Kor Bissal Military Coalition, Air Division. You may not remember me but I am here to inform you that there are two transport craft filled with Protrerian soldiers descending near Sankt Morsch. I suspect there are approximately one thousand alien soldiers per transport craft, have Gergelian ground troopers sent out to stop them from taking over your country. I am flying there now so there will be someone on hand when they approach the surface."

"Affirmative I remember you; you will have my digit # one military advisor and pilot, Maj. M. Malstrova from the Gergelian Military Coalition to be in contact with you shortly. "Affirmative sir, I will be over Sankt Morsch in forty-five secs, get moving on deploying the ground troops ASAP, and send additional aerial support as well. "Very well," the Gergelian President said then the radio went off and as it did I increased airspeed to Mach ten.

Secs later I slowed to 150 kps; I raised my face shield and checked my radar. "Jr. Commodore one of the crafts already landed and is in the process of deploying their army, and the other transport craft was in the process of landing," 'PAT' reported.

"Many thanks 'PAT'," I said as I went to engage the transport craft. When I was in range, I raised my shield and confronted the enemy craft with my SQ-laser cannons blazing. As I was in combat with the heavily armed transport craft, I heard a beep from my radar.

"Six waves of attack craft just entered ZarCedra's stratosphere. "Affirmative," I said just as I was hit. My shield absorbed the impact but shook my craft a few secs as sparks flew from the side control panels. I was starting to sweat as I kept firing my SQ-laser and Plasma Pulse cannons. I fired off Protonic EMC-Missals as one of the transport craft exploded in a grand ball of fire and crashed to the planet surface. I veered off and went after the other transport craft.

"Shield strength is down to eighty seven percent. "Affirmative," I acknowledged as I fired my starboard XTR-9000 Plasma Pulse Cannon and destroyed the last transport craft, just then the squads of attack craft entered range firing everything they had. I hovered in one position firing at everything that moved in the sky. The attack craft returned fire as my craft shook violently as it was hit.

"Shield strength down to fifty-six percent." Just then I saw the Gergelian Migs arrive to supply me with the backup I so desperately needed.

"Tanglarian, this is Maj. Malstrova we have come to assist you, I repeat we are here to assist. "I am Jr. Com. Teldat and I welcome you and your comrades to this air battle," I said still firing at the enemy.

Arrange for ground troopers to clean your countryside of these dirty rotten Protrerian land grabbers, I said as I continued to blast attack craft. "Affirmative," Maj. Malstrova said as he destroyed the attack craft aft of me, as it exploded in a ball of flames.

About an epock later there was only my craft, six Gergelian Migs and three alien attack craft remaining. One by one the enemy attack craft were destroyed, I raised my face shield, looked at my radar and seen it was finally clear.

"It was grand being in battle with you and I hope we could meet each other face to face," Maj. Malstrova informed me. "Hopefully some p.a.r, but right now I must return to Tanglar, have ground troopers to this location immediately to take care of the Protrerian High Command troopers that landed. "Affirmative, at once Jr. Commodore," Maj. Malstrova answered. "Adioso comrade and take care," I said as I turned my craft in the opposite direction and advanced speed. "Time to get back to Tanglar 'PAT'. "Affirmative," she said.

I increased speed to Mach ten; I checked my radar then lowered my face shield as I recharged my weapons and shield. I activated the Omagon 2115 Star Drive Engine, the remainder of the golden modules and rod extracted then the Electronic Flux Inducer supplied the Ionic charge to create the swirling wormhole. I entered and increased speed to Star Drive one then Star Drive two.

Seventy-two secs later I pulled out of the swirling wormhole and decelerated to Mach three. "'PAT', produce a map of the immediate area." Instantaneously a map of Nesbitia, Tanglar appeared on the lower portion of my face shield.

"A major electrical storm would ravage the vicinity east of St. Cerr's, Nesbitia at precisely 11: 30 twilight on 07.05," a radio broadcast reported as I surveyed the area.

"The storm will have (according to scans) all the characteristics of the storm that brought us to this time. Junior Commodore if you're inkling what I think you are inkling you have to remember there is a two epock time zone difference between the honorary regime of Placaden and the regime of Nesbitia," 'PAT' reported. "Affirmative, many thanks 'PAT'," I acknowledged.

'I wonder if Topanga would be willing to attempt to make it to the tritton 2115 with me. That is a big IF,' I thought as I flew my craft toward the honorary regime of Placaden.

"I wonder what all the possible changes to the 22nd centritton would be, if all our efforts here in the 21st centritton are a success. Just think 'PAT', how wonderful life would be if the Humanarian race were able to defeat these Protrerian High Command rebels; we would be permitted to live in total peace with the Antrerian race. Oh, I forgot you don't know the hellatious time the Protrerian High Command has put our race through for almost a centritton."

"On the contrary Jr. Commodore, Dr. Graham downloaded trillions of gigots of information into my core memory circuits when I was created; I know everything the Protrerian High Command has ever done to the Humanarian race in their centritton of power. "Then you probably have an idea how much being victorious in this war would mean to me? "Affirmative Jr. Commodore I do."

'If we are victorious in this war, and it looks really promising that we have a New Hope and if Topanga returns with me, she'll be the only female citizen I would ever want or need in my personal life,' I thought.

Before I knew it I was flying over the Honorary Regime of Placaden then I was flying over Cangla City, and the Grinshaw Military Facility. I slowed until I hovered over the military facility, after receiving permission to set down I raised the wings as the landing gear lowered then I slowly hovered down to the tarmac below. As soon as I was safely down I switched everything off, contracted and slid back the port wing. As the craft's engines wound down I removed the 'HUD' helmet then disconnected my safety belts. "'PAT' I just remembered something very important. "And what would that be Jr. Commodore?"

"I had a twilightmare last twilight and looking at it now, it is making sense. "Whatever do you mean sir? "What I mean is in my twilightmare, we were flying through an electrical storm and a bolt of lightning struck the craft as we were entering the wormhole. Instead of traveling through time as expected, the craft just exploded. "Oh my!" 'PAT' exclaimed.

"So I figured last twilight, if we ever attempted to return to the 22nd centritton we must locate the bolt of lightning with the exact voltage as the bolt that brought us to this time. "Affirmative, I will immediately commence calculating the exact voltage we would require so your twilightmare doesn't become reality. "Affirmative, many thanks 'PAT'," I said as I got out of the pilot's seat.

I removed my flight suit then put on my beret as I went over and removed the electronic keycard then pocketed it. I went and opened and lowered the main hatch platform then descended to the tarmac below.

It was pretty late but I hoped Sr. Com. Bancais' replacement was working late. I tapped the left wing of my com-link. "'PAT' you can now raise and seal the main hatch platform," I said as I continued on my way to main headquarters.

I walked into main headquarters, down the hall and up to the Commodore's secretarial assistant who was on duty. "Jr. Com. Teldat to see the Commanding Officer, if he/she is still present? "Affirmative, she is," the Lance Corporal said as he picked up the PCD and called the Sr. Commodore. "Ma'am, Jr. Com. Teldat is here and requests to see you. Affirmative ma'am," the Lance Corporal said. "You may enter. "Many thanks Lance Corporal," I said as I went to the office entry-way, removed my beret then knocked. "You may enter," I heard a sec later.

As I entered I saluted and stood at attention in front of the Sr. Commodore's desk. "Ma'am, I am Jr. Com. Teldat, I just returned from Gergel on the Jroken Continent and I have a verbal report for you. "At ease Jr. Commodore, I am Sr. Commodore Bieas, pleasant to meet you," she said as we shook hands. "Report Jr. Commodore. "Affirmative."

"Protrerian High Command ground troopers had probably landed in western Maccari; those two transport craft that landed have approximately total estimate of two thousand Protrerian soldiers. Sr. Commodore Bieas do you know if the Cardola Territories Military Forces had ground troopers sent to that location? "Affirmative, I was talking to President Torren a few mites ago and he informed me of the troopers of Protrerian High Command soldiers that landed in Maccari, and that he did send ground troopers to that location to intercept. "Grand, and by now ground troopers should have been sent to take care of the ground troops that landed in Gergel on the Jroken Continent."

"Affirmative is that all to report at this time Junior Commodore; if it is, I'd like to know how your aircraft is holding out and if you require anything? "The wing of my craft had been damaged when I was in a battle over Dalarme but since its repair, there has been nothing wrong. I will however, require more of the Liquid Napricyte[2] SDC soon as I depleted most of my supply; I only have $2^{3/4}$ vials remaining. "Affirmative, is there anything else you require at this time? "Nothing more than something to munch on, a hot shower and a grand twilight slumber won't cure. By the way, 07.05 is the BIG P.A.R."

"What do you mean by that? "What I mean is, on 07.05 sometime around mid-p.a.r our extraterrestrial assistance to fight this war will finally arrive. "Take a seat and explain. "Affirmative," I said as I sat. 'Here I go again,' I silently thought.

"I'm sure Sr. Com. Bancais filled you in on who I am and what tritton I am from? "Affirmative, he has. "Well then I will tell you how it has been going in my time up until the time I was transported to this time."

"ZarCedra was unlike it has been up to this time period, it was different because the Humanarian Race were no longer in control of our world. Because we originally lost this intergalactic war to the Protrerian High Command, so they were in charge. For the next seventy trittons the Humanarian Race lived a hard life under their command, then Protrerian's and Humanarian's started joining in matrimony and for the next few dectrittons we were almost acceptable in their eyes."

"But there was a side to us Humanarian's of ZarCedra that loathed the fact that they were in control of our planet. So that was when the Secret Humanarian ZarCedra Alliance secretly invented and constructed the Supersonic Dragon 228-D Spy Jet

Stealth. It was just supposed to be an advanced military aircraft with awesome Stealth mode and Star Drive speed capabilities. But everything changed when I was testing it. "What is your meaning?" I sat up straighter then continued.

"When I was returning to the military facility I was temporarily assigned to on Vertgren Isle, I flew through a major electrical storm and the lightening my craft was zapped with reacted with my craft's Omagon 2115 Star Drive engine and its radioactive chemical accelerant. Causing a rip in the time gamut, transporting my craft and I back in times elapsed. I am unsure there is a reason for this but I suspect it is to offer my assistance in this war with advanced technology, giving the Humanarian Race a second chance to be victorious in this war and change my times elapsed or your times yet to come."

"07.05.2015 is the p.a.r we will receive assistance from the Antrerian Armada who are extreme enemies of the Protrerian High command. We started changing times elapsed events when we were able to destroy the four Protrerian Energy Extractor Craft. Understand I wasn't here for the original battle so they triumphed, but since I am here now they were defeated and destroyed. What didn't happen in the time I am from was the deployment of ground troopers this early in the war and because the Energy Extractor Craft were defeated, I surmise they were deployed in retaliation."

"Do you know, what it is this Protrerian High Command wants so badly? "They first wanted our energy from our planet to save theirs. But since their sun is on a steady decline to going nova they plan to fight for control of ZarCedra. Instead of asking for assistance they simply attack our planet and try taking what they need and that is how the war started. Since the Antrerian Armada thought it a disgrace for them to disrupt our planet for their own gain, they would come to our aide. They will be here 07.05.2015 mid-p.a.r sometime."

"You mean you cannot tell me what time they will arrive? "Negative ma'am, through the course of times elapsed the precise time had become somewhat enigmatic; however, it is thought to be before 15 hundred epocks. That is all I know of this war, hopefully with their assistance we can once and for all be victorious in this war and the Humanarian Race will be able to stay in control of our own planet."

"This is part speculation and part truth according to the times elapsed archives I've studied in seminary. "Affirmative, it's getting late, go get something to calm your appetite then retire to your barracks. What you have advised me about 07.05, it should be quite aspiring. "Affirmative it should; have a grand twilight ma'am," I said as I stood, saluted, turned and left the Sr. Commodore's office.

"Have a grand twilight," I said as I put my beret back on and walked by the Lance Corporal; then I left main headquarters. I walked down the boulevard to the mess hall to grab my banquet then I took it to my quarters.

After I let myself in, everything was dark. "Illumination on," I said as the illumination in the front chamber illuminated and I removed my footwear and beret. 'Chad must be slumbering or not on the facility grounds yet,' I thought as I turned on the Intervision monitor to listen to the retro melodic composition then began to eat my toasty.

When I was through I checked the time and thought it was too late to call Topanga. 'I will call her in the morn,' I told myself.

I grabbed my jotter and ballpoint to jot in the events of this p.a.r. One and a half-epocks later I finished, I got myself a swill then went to the latrine to take a quick shower and get ready to slumber. When I was through, I turned everything off then went to my slumbering quarters, got into my twilight garments then crawled into my cot and drifted into a peaceful slumber.

****

In the middle of the twilight I started having a twilightmare; I was flying my craft over the landscape enjoying the scenery when I asked for the time and 12 hundred epocks flashed over and over, which I thought kind of strange because it never flashed that many times before. I thought nothing more about it and continued to fly, all of a sudden the sky turned black almost as if someone extinguished the sun.

I raised my face shield then glanced at my radar and seen multiple waves of Protrerian High Command attack craft. Then 'PAT' said the strangest thing.

"Jr. Com. Teldat we are outdigited and out armed we might as well give up and let them take the planet. "And let our whole time traveling ordeal be for nothing, I think not; we happened to come back in time for a reason and that reason is, to take back what we lost long ago so giving up is not an option." But before my craft got to them they branched out.

"By the rate of their descent they are going to hit planet capitals of industrialized countries around the planet, we can't save the planet Jr. Commodore so we shouldn't even try. "What?" I still couldn't believe my ears. "'PAT' why are you so determined to let them be victorious?"

I was unsure what happened next because at that time I awoke. "Whew what a twilightmare, why was 'PAT' so willing to give up considering she told me she knew what the Protrerian High Command put the Humanarian Race through." I couldn't even fathom the idea of letting them be victorious in this war.

I pressed the talk button on my timepiece. "The time is 04 hundred 37 epocks." I lay there awake for the next few mites wondering what the meaning of the twilightmare was? 'Why did the time of 12 hundred epocks keep flashing on my face shield? I hope this twilightmare was just that a meaningless dream,' I thought as I closed my eyes and slumbered once again.

P.A.R 10

As I finished in the latrine, the twilightmare I had troubled me but I got myself together. I walked through the front chamber; 'It sure is quiet either Chad is still slumbering or not back yet,' I said to myself as I went to his slumbering quarters entry-way and knocked. 'No answer,' so I opened the entry-way and peeked inside. 'His retiring unit hasn't been slumbered in; I guess he hasn't returned yet,' I thought as I closed the entry-way and walked into the front chamber.

'Time to go use the PCD and call Topanga maybe she's at her abode and wants to converse,' I thought as I left my quarters and went to the gribbit personal communication device, I checked my time piece and seen that it was 06 hundred 45 epochs. 'I hope she is there, I said to myself as I fished a quint gribbit from my pocket, deposited it then entered Topanga's digits. I waited patiently as it chirped a couple times then Cheryl answered. "Greetings.

"Grand morn grand looking is my immaculate Topanga around? "She is and she was just about to leave, you called just in time, here she is." A sec later I heard the angelic voice of my huni buni say "Greetings."

"Grand morn my Topanga."

"Grand morn Jero."

"So, where were you off to so early in the morn?"

"I have to be at work soon, I know we are supposed to stay off the boulevards and just stay at our abodes but I heard a lot of other citizens are leaving to go to work, why?"

"Just be careful! Oh the reason I asked is because there is something I would like to inquire of you."

"What is it?"

"I had a discussion with 'PAT', my onboard computer's avatar and she informed me there is going to be a major electrical storm off the coast of Nesbitia in the morrow twilight with all the characteristics of the storm that brought my craft and I to this time period. I was hoping to fly through it; in hopes I can get back to my own time."

"Aughh!" Topanga moaned.

"Don't be too upset, the reason I am calling is to ask you again if you wanted to accompany me? Like I said before it will be dangerous and I have no way of knowing if my attempt will be successful but I must try. If something goes wrong and I don't make it, my craft might be destroyed or I might go further back in time elapsed but if I do make it, I will hopefully be back in the time where I belong. If you do accompany me I'll have someone I love to make life more enjoyable."

"But if anything goes wrong we could be destroyed, Topanga said suddenly."

"Or end up in some other distant time in times elapsed, this is a chance I must take but you don't. Just think it over and tell me your answer when I call you later this p.a.r or in the morrow? But no matter what your response is Topanga, remember that I love you now and I always will."

"I love you too Jero and I will definitely ponder it."

"Remember my love; you are the only lady that makes me feel alive."

"Oh Jeroque many thanks for the kind words, you are very special to me as well."

"Ok huni I must go now, I'll call you later?"

"Ok, my adorable one."

"Say adioso to Cheryl for me and I hope you both have a grand p.a.r."

"Cheryl and I hope you have a terrific one as well and we both say adioso." Topanga said then we hung up.

****

After I hung up the PCD, I put my beret on then went down the hall and left the barracks. As I began walking up the boulevard I started inkling. 'Cheryl is a real exquisiteness and she's only a few trittons older than Chad. I think it best for a young whippersnapper like Chad, to have a grand lady in his life to keep him on the straight and narrow. "Affirmative," I said out loud. 'I will take that action,' I thought as I met up with Capt. Pane.

"Greetings sir," Capt. Pane said as I walked up to him. "How's it going?" I asked. "Pretty grand, say have you heard anything about my little brother? "Not yet but he might be with Fl. Sgt. Colthamner and LC Luxton, they should arrive sometime soon, if he is not don't worry too much we will locate him? "Affirmative sir," he answered as we walked to the mess hall.

We grabbed trays and stood in line and talked as we waited for our banquets. When we received them, we grabbed caffinated brew and silverware then went to a vacant table and sat.

"So what do you think of the progress of this war?" Capt. Pane asked. "It is progressing a lot easier and more rapidly than I read in my times elapsed archive; although the tremendous loss of life has diminished considerably, we are still losing quite a bit of grand air citizens. "Affirmative we are, that is very unfortunate," Capt. Pane said then took a sip of his caffinated brew.

At that time a few air citizens joined us. "Grand p.a.r, how are you? I am Sgt. Franchis Deforest; my associates are Capt. Gilliana Spencer and Master Sgt. Ryanaldo Hutchinson. "Greetings," they said with a smile and salute.

"Greetings, I'm Jr. Com. Teldat and this is Capt. Pane, grand to meet you," I said as we all shook hands. "Teldat, you are the pilot from the times yet to come with the exquisite aircraft, are you not? Capt. Spencer asked. "That is correct, ma'am; guilty as charged," I said with a smile. "Oh, I thought your rank was Major? "It was but when I fought in Brilain, my rank was advanced to Jr. Commodore," I said with a smile as I continued to consume my morn banquet. As we were talking and eating "PAT" cut in and reported.

"Jr. Com. Teldat, ten waves of interstellar craft just entered ZarCedra's stratosphere. I tapped my com-link and acknowledged. "I have to go," I said as I rose and put on my beret. "Grand luck and stay safe," Capt. Pane said as I darted for the entry-way. The first place I ran was to Sr. Com. Bieas' office; when I entered main headquarters', I hurried to the Sr. Commodore's office.

No one was at the reception desk so I knocked then entered the Commodore's office. "Ma'am, I just received word that ten waves of enemy attack craft just moments ago entered ZarCedra's stratosphere. "Affirmative Jr. Commodore, do you know where they are heading? I tapped the left wing of my communicator. "'PAT' can you tell by the rate of descent, where the enemy craft are heading. "A moment ma'am," I said as 'PAT' came back. "Jr. Commodore, by the rate of descent they will arrive in the sky above Taladen, in the Cardola Territories in approximately eight mites. "Affirmative many thanks 'PAT'," I acknowledged as I looked at the Sr. Commodore.

"Contact and advise the proper authorities. "Affirmative, Jr. Commodore," Sr. Commodore Bieas said as she grabbed the personal communication device and contacted the Lance Corporal who by now returned to his station. "LC Acernan, get me the Hemair Military Installation in Myfare, immediately. "Affirmative ma'am!" Secs later the Sr. Commodore heard; "Hemair Military, can I be of assistance?"

"Core citizen, this is Sr. Commodore Bieas of the Grinshaw Military Facility in the honorary regime of Placaden, Tanglar; let me talk to you CO immediately! "Affirmative ma'am, hold a mite," she said as Sr. Commodore Bieas was patched through.

"Commodore Greerbough here, go ahead Sr. Commodore Bieas. At that time Sr. Commodore Bieas activated the speaker. "Commodore it just came to my attention that ten waves of intergalactic enemy attack craft just entered ZarCedra's stratosphere and by the rate of descent they will attack Taladen in approximately six mites, can you contact and advise the appropriate authorities! "Affirmative Sr. Commodore, I'll also have fighters in the air immediately. "Affirmative Commodore, by this time you might have heard about the officer and his aircraft from the times yet to come, Jr. Com. Teldat?"

"Affirmative I have, that is all the chutzpa in Dek-kred have been talking about as of late, but I heard his rank was Major.

"His rank was recently advanced to Jr. Commodore. Well he'll be in Taladen to assist in mites so expect his arrival. "Affirmative Commodore Bieas, I have to go," Commodore Greerbough said as his line went dead.

"Well Jr. Commodore do you require anything before you depart? "My craft needs to refuel besides that I'm fit go. Oh there is one other thing; do you know where Sgt. Pane is, do you know if he is with Fl. Sgt. Colthamner and LC Luxton? "Affirmative, Sgt. Pane called earlier he is at the Kinkade Military facility in Dalarme. "Grand, his brother Capt. Pane was worrying about his wellbeing; if I have sufficient time this p.a.r, I'll go collect him."

"Grand Jr. Commodore, for now go to your aircraft and I'll send a fuel tanker at once then fly at Star Drive speed to Taladen. "Affirmative Sr. Commodore," I said as I saluted, turned and vacated her office. I ran to my craft, on my way I tapped my com-link. "'PAT', open the rear of the craft, it's going to get fuelled then we have to be in Taladen ASAP. "Affirmative Jr. Commodore. As she was doing that I got to my craft just as the fuel tanker arrived.

"How do you do airman," I said as the attendant got out of the tanker. I told him where the fuel caps were located and they need to be refilled immediately, double time. "Affirmative sir," he said as he went to work. As the Sergeant was refilling the craft, I went up to the cockpit and quickly put my flight suit on then went to check the levels of other important liquids inside the 'HUD' helmet. After I had, I went out to see how far along the Sergeant had gotten.

As I lowered to the tarmac, I saw the Sergeant lowering on his vehicles Automatic Mechanical Lift, by the time he lowered to the tarmac; his hose had already automatically rolled within his vehicle. "All through," I asked? "She's ready to depart when you are sir. "Many thanks Sergeant, muchly appreciated; now I must be off!" I said as I turned and got on the main hatch platform.

As I started to rise I tapped the left wing of my com-link. "'PAT, lower the tail portion of the craft. "Affirmative, Jr.

Commodore," she said as the tail portion of the aircraft lowered as I got to the cockpit.

I entered the cockpit and the main hatch platform closed then locked as I quickly put on my flight suit. Next, I hurried to the pilot's seat, connected my safety belts then put on the 'HUD' helmet. "Hi 'PAT'," I said as I smiled at her then activated the ignition and the craft roared to life as I toggled a few switches and activated touch pads as I activated my craft. Secs later I extended the port wing, had it slide and lock into place as both wings lowered and my craft left the tarmac. I rose to one thousand metrics, leveled the wings then rotated the craft southwest and advanced forward until my craft was at maximum mach.

I activated the 2115 Star Drive engine and the golden molecules and rod protruded from the exterior of the craft. At that time the ionic stream of energy flowed around my craft then shot out from the golden rod. It formed the swirling wormhole in my path and I guided the craft into it. I went to star drive one then two as the craft barrel rolled at star drive speed. Secs later I disengaged the star drive engine and I decelerated to Mach five as the golden rod and most of the golden modules lowered beneath the outer shell of my craft.

"'PAT', what is my current location?" I asked. A microsec later there was a map of Torxen on the bottom portion of my facemask with a red illuminator flashing above Dresnel. By the time I realized my exact position I was just entering the city limits of Taladen. "Jr. Commodore enemy attack crafts closing position. "I see them," I said as a swarm of attack craft left the fight they were having with other Kor Bissal fighters and came after me. I activated my crafts full-bodied shield in the nick of time just as my craft shook and sparks flew from the instrument panels.

"Direct hit, Jr. Commodore that brings shield strength down to eighty-nine percent," 'PAT' said as I fired my lasers and let off two EMC-Missiles in quick succession. Two of the five attack craft exploded as I continued firing my laser at the remaining craft dogging my craft. Two mites later I destroyed them and was on my way to the multiple clashes happening in front of me.

At that instance there were ten attack craft firing at my craft. My craft shook uncontrollably as I was hit but my shield saved my craft yet, again. "Shield strength down to sixty-seven percent," 'PAT' advised. At that time I decided it was high time to use my XTR-9000 Plasma Pulse Cannons. I accessed the menu in my HUD helmet and lowered them then accessed my targeting scanner. For the next epock and twenty mites we battled feverishly, after that time I looked at my radar and seen all enemy attack craft had been destroyed.

I'm not sure how many fighters were deployed from the Hemair Military Installation but there were ten ZarCedra aircraft that remained. As we flew back to the Hemair Military Installation, I charged my shield and all weapons and ammunition.

Once we arrived, the aircraft that were heavily damaged were the first to land then the rest followed. I scanned the area for the helijets and when I located them I nestled my craft down next to them. As I landed, I was in contact with the tower. "Tower, this is Jr. Com. Teldat, I request fuel; my craft is among the helijets.

"Affirmative, there will be a fuel tanker to your location immediately after that is complete you are ordered to Com. Rickard's office. "Affirmative ma'am, Jr. Com. Teldat out. "Tower out," the female air citizen said.

I looked at 'PAT'. "'PAT', raise the tail portion of the craft so the aircraft can be refueled before we go collect Sgt. Pane at the Kinkade Military facility in Dalarme. "At once Jr. Commodore," she said as she raised the rear portion of the craft. I contracted and had the port wing slide out of the way of the main hatch as I unbelted myself and went and withdrew the keycard then slipped it into my pocket.

I unsealed the main hatch, it opened then lowered to form the platform and I stepped on and lowered to the tarmac below. The first thing I did was check the tires for wear and tear. I went around my craft kicking each one to make sure they had the proper amount of air; then the fuel tanker arrived.

After I had told the airman where the fuel tanks were located, I asked. "Where would I find main headquarters? "Go straight up that way," he said as he pointed, turn right then carry on a couple boulevards; you can't miss HQ. "Affirmative, many thanks Sergeant," I said then I was off to see Com. Rickard. After walking a few mites, I came to the blue-green structure. The only lively thing that made the structure look patriotic was the Cardola Territory and Kor Bissal flags blowing in the gentle breeze.

I climbed the stairs then entered the structure and went to the front desk. "Jr. Com. Teldat to see Com. Rickard," I stated. "Affirmative Jr. Commodore you may enter, I was advised to let you to enter upon your arrival; right through that entry-way," the young man said as he pointed. "Affirmative airman, many thanks," I answered as I removed my beret then went and knocked on the entry-way.

"Enter," I was told so I went in; stood front and center in front of the Commander and saluted. "Jr. Com. Teldat, reporting as directed. "At ease Jr. Commodore," Com. Rickard said as he returned my salute. "Have a seat and tell me what went on in the skies above? The citizens of this city were lucky they were evacuated when they did or we'd have serious injuries with all the falling debris. "Affirmative, there would be," I stated as I sat and continued. "As I arrived in the sky above Taladen, I immediately began assisting the Cardola Territories fighters and continued until all enemy attack craft had been destroyed. "Jr. Commodore, could you tell me anything about this war? "All I know sir it is unlike the original war! "Explain airman!

"I'm sure you heard who I am and from whence I came, from your President "Factual, I heard a few things but I am interested in your exact words, what's different? "Well the first thing that happened that differentiated from my original time and right now, is in this time I am here and we were able to defeat the four Protrerian Energy Extractor craft. You see I was not here in the original war and the Energy Extractor craft were easily able to defeat ZarCedra's forces; but by me being here we were able to defeat them.

"One more thing in the morrow sometime around mid-p.a.r we are supposed to receive assistance from the Protrerian High

Commands arch enemies, the Antrerian race's armada. These two races of extraterrestrial beings have been mortal enemies for centrittons, the Antrerian race think it abominable for the Protrerian High Command to attack ZarCedra for their own gain so they will come to our aide. "You can't give a more definite time than in the morrow mid-p.a.r? Com. Rickard asked.

"Negative sir, over the course of times elapsed the precise time became somewhat enigmatic. Sir, there is a member of my squadron that is stuck in Dalarme, at the Kinkade Military Installation and I must retrieve. So if that is all, I must take my leave. "Affirmative, that is all at this time except get rest this twilight from what you say the morrow should be a doosy! "Affirmative sir," I said as I saluted then left the office.

As I left the structure, I tapped the left wing of my com-link. "'PAT', are you refueled and ready to depart? "Affirmative sir, the fuel tanker is just leaving as we speak. "Grand, lower the tail section of the craft and lower the main hatch platform, I'll be there directly," I said as I walked down the boulevard then turned a corner.

A few mites later I did a quick visual inspection on the under belly of my craft then I stepped on the main hatch platform and a few secs later the platform started to rise.

When I got to the top, I entered, then closed and sealed the main hatch platform then went and inserted the electronic keycard. I went and sat in the pilot's seat, connected my safety belts then activated the ignition sequence. As the engines roared to life, I put my 'HUD' helmet on; extended the port wing and it slid forward locking into place. The wings lowered and my craft left the ground. "PAT', what is the current time?" I asked as my craft rose to 1000 metrics. The time flashed on the upper portion of my visor. 14:35 epocks/mites. "'PAT', what would the ETA be to the Kinkade Military Installation in Dalarme at Mach 10? "25 mites," she answered. "Affirmative," I acknowledged as I turned my craft North East and increased airspeed to Mach 10.

As I flew I raised my face shield and 'PAT' & I appreciated the scenery, and in no time at all we enjoyed the red rock formations as we flew over Nek Partain and Krustain Territories.

As quick as they appeared, the red clay mountains disappeared and we were cruising comfortably over the coastline. 'I wonder just how much strength our alien foe has remaining up in the heavens?' I questioned myself as my craft cruised through the clouds.

"'PAT', with the oxygen remaining, if I were to go into stealth mode, how long could I venture away from ZarCedra? "We depleted one canister of oxygen so far; we have 72 epocks of compressed oxygen remaining. With my calculations we can use no more than 48 epocks of that oxygen and still have enough remaining to deal with the morrow's ordeal. "Affirmative, then that's what we'll do after we pick up Sgt. Pane."

"'PAT', what is our current location? I asked. "We are currently over the city of Jargon Vre, Jargon, at our current course and speed we'll be in Dalarme in approximately 7 mites. "Affirmative 'PAT', inform me at that time. "Affirmative, Jr. Commodore. I looked out the window at the watercraft on the water and citizens on the shore and it reminded me of creepy-crawlies scurrying about. 'It seems as if those citizens don't take this war seriously, they should not be out on the seashores and water,' I thought as we continued up the coast.

We flew the rest of the way in silence. "We are currently entering the city of Dalarme, Jr. Commodore; if you deviate course by 2° port side we'll be over the Kinkade Military Installation momentarily. "Affirmative 'PAT', I acknowledged as I adjusted my course direction while I decreased airspeed to 10 kps. At that time I contacted the tower; "Kinkade Military Installation, this is Jr. Com. Teldat and I've returned to retrieve the Tanglar pilot, Sgt. Pane, is there a place I can set down? "Affirmative, land in the helijet landing area. "Affirmative, contact Com. Magae and inform him that I am here to retrieve the Tanglar pilot, Sgt. Pane. "Affirmative Jr. Com. Teldat, I'll inform him directly. Affirmative air citizen, many thanks. Jr. Com. Teldat, out."

I stopped forward motion and hovered above the helijets, scanning the area. I raised the wings as the landing gear lowered then hovered down to the tarmac below. As the wheels touched down, I started tuning everything off and as my craft wound down I contracted the port wing. The wing slid back as I removed the 'HUD' helmet and disconnected my safety belts. I rose and went to retrieve my electronic keycard then opened and lowered the main hatch platform. "Adioso 'PAT', raise the main hatch platform when I step off," I said as I got to the tarmac. "Affirmative Jr. Commodore," 'PAT' answered as the main hatch platform started to rise.

I whistled a tune as I put my beret on then went to main headquarters to talk to Com. Magae. A couple mites later I came to the structure and climbed the stairs then entered the air-conditioned structure.

I went to the recruit at the front counter, "Jr. Com. Teldat to see Com. Magae," I said as I removed my beret. "Affirmative, just let me inform the Commander you're here," he said as he picked up his PCD and chirped the Commander. "Com. Magae, Jr. Com. Teldat is here and requests to see you. Affirmative sir, at once," he said then hung up. "You may enter sir," the young recruit said. "Many thanks," I replied as I went to the Commander's entry-way and knocked. "Enter," I was informed then went in.

I closed the entry-way behind me then stood at attention and saluted; "Grand p.a.r sir, I have returned to retrieve the Tanglar pilot, Sgt. Pane. "Affirmative Jr. Commodore, I already called him and told him to report here; he should be here momentarily. "Many thanks, Commander. "As we await his arrival, take a seat and tell me what you did this p.a.r? "Affirmative sir, this morn I was contacted by my craft's on-board super computer and informed of enemy attack craft on a course for Taladen, I went there and along with ZarCedra fighters from the Hemair Military Installation we took care of those extraterrestrial bastions!"

Just then the Com. Magae's PCD chirped. "Affirmative Corporal, send him in," then he hung up. "Sgt. Pane is now here," he said then asked. "What are your plans for the rest of the p.a.r?" Com. Magae asked as we heard a knock on the entry-way. "Enter," he said as young Sgt. Pane entered and saluted. "You called me sir? Sgt. Pane asked. "Affirmative I did airman, Jr. Com. Teldat is here to retrieve you, so you are now free to be off. "Grand," he said with a smile as he looked over at me.

"So, what are your plans for the remainder of this p.a.r?" Com. Magae asked again. "I do have a plan set out but I really feel that is up to Sgt. Pane. "And what is that?" Com. Magae and Sgt. Pane asked in unison. "Well, I was inkling of doing something I was informed my craft could do but I have never attempted. "What may that be and what does that have to do with Sgt. Pane?" Com. Magae asked.

"That is, my craft is able to break ZarCedra's atmosphere and I was planning to go in stealth mode to see what the strength is of our alien foe! I still plan to do that but if Sgt. Pane rejects that plan, I will first take him back to our military facility in the honorary regime of Placaden," I said looking at young Sgt. Pane.

"And what makes you thing I'll object?" Sgt. Pane inquired. "Because that has never been attempted and I thought you might not want to attempt it with me! "And reject that type of opportunity, I think not; it would be an honor to attempt it with you!" Sgt. Pane said with grand anticipation. "If it has never been attempted, what makes you think you'll be successful?" Com. Magae asked. "I was informed that it was theoretically possible by top scientific personnel when I was first given the craft to test in my timeline. "Besides everything Jr. Com. Teldat has said to date has been factual," Sgt. Pane said looking at Com. Magae.

"If you want to attempt it with me we should take our leave," I said as I stood and shook Com. Magae's hand. "Many thanks for the assistance you air citizens have given," Com. Magae said as he too stood and walked us to the entry-way. "My pleasure, glad we could assist," I said as we left the office.

Sgt. Pane and I left the structure then proceeded down the boulevard. "Many thanks for coming to get me, this is an ok military installation but it would be grand to get out of this city and back in the sky," Sgt. Pane said as he rubbed his hands together. "I know what you mean kid, I love being in the sky as well, I said as I tapped my com-link. "'PAT', open then lower the main hatch platform, Sgt. Pane and I will be there momentarily. "Affirmative Jr. Commodore."

When we arrived at my craft, we stepped on the main hatch platform and rose to the cockpit. As we entered, I went and inserted the electronic key card. 'PAT' retrieve the extra helmet from the rear closet and give it to Sgt. Pane," I said. "Here Sergeant put this on," 'PAT' said as I closed and secured the main hatch. "Many thanks," he replied as I went to the pilots seat. "Take a seat and buckle yourselves in," I said as I did the same then activated the aircraft, then extracted the port wing as it slid and locked into place.

I activated two-way communications and contacted the tower. "Tower, this is Jr. Com. Teldat requesting permission for lift off? "You are cleared Jr. Commodore. "Affirmative," I said as I pulled up on the flight stick and my craft left the tarmac and the landing gear automatically contracted. As the craft was rising I looked over at Sgt. Pane and seen the excitement on his face as he smiled and looked out the window. When the craft reached 5000 metrics, I activated stealth mode and the full-bodied shield activated as the craft disappeared. The red cockpit illuminator activated inside the cockpit as I pulled on the flight stick and the craft sharply turned upwards as we continued to rise.

By the time we reached the stratosphere I looked over at Sgt. Pane. "We can breathe thanks to the tanks of compressed oxygen equipped to the craft," I said as I stopped just as we broke the stratosphere then activated my radar. I raised my face shield and looked at it; all I could see was open space and the gentle illumination of distant stars.

"'PAT', scan the area as far as sensors will allow and inform me where the Protrerian High Command is or give me your best hypothesis for their location. "Scanning, wait a sec..." In the meantime I glanced at Sgt. Pane; he had a big grin on his face. "This is so cool," he said as he looked out the windows at ZarCedra below us. "You like being up here do you? I asked.

"Do I ever," he said. "So do I, you are very correct in saying this is so cool!"

"Jr. Commodore, scans came out negative of any interstellar craft in the immediate area surrounding ZarCedra. If I ventured an hypothesis, I would say they are either cloaked or located on the far side of the ZarCedra's 3rd moon. "Affirmative 'PAT', how long would it take if I flew to the 3rd moon at Star Drive two? "1650 secs or 27.5 mites," she said matter of factly. "Affirmative," I said as I increased speed then activated the Star Drive engine, moments later the wormhole appeared and I guided the craft into it. This time, as I flew through it, the craft flew straight and the wormhole walls were a different color, almost like it was an opaque blue color.

As we flew, I inquired, "PAT' is it because of the absence of external oxygen that the craft is traveling so smoothly? "Affirmative Jr. Commodore, without the presence of the gasses that make up breathable Oxygen, which are Oxygen and Hydrogen which causes grand resistance while flying through it. As you know those gasses are absent here in space so there is nothing to slow the craft and that is also the main reason we can travel to our destination in a shorter time. "Affirmative 'PAT', many thanks," I said as I enjoyed the flight through the wormhole.

At the precise time my craft exited the wormhole and we were positioned above ZarCedra's 3rd moon and immediately we went into stealth mode and my craft vanished. Almost instantaneously there was a beep then 'PAT' reported. "Jr. Commodore, I have detected a large fleet of spacecraft stationed above the dark side of ZarCedra's furthest moon. "Affirmative 'PAT', take us 150 Kiloms from their position then hold position. "Affirmative sir," she said as we traveled to the coordinates I had mentioned. 'I couldn't believe it, what we saw were enough huge spacecraft to dwarf ZarCedra's biggest city by twenty fold, at least,' I thought as I scanned port to starboard.

"I can't open fire on them in Stealth mode and if we became visible how long would we remain unscaved up here by ourselves even with the firepower my craft has?" I asked 'PAT' and Sgt. Pane. "I'm not sure but your craft has a grand size compared to the aircraft we have on ZarCedra but yet those spacecraft dwarf us in comparison. We should get back to ZarCedra pronto! You say the Antrerian Armada should arrive in the morrow?" Affirmative, I'm guessing sometime around 1500 epocks," I replied. "Ok, let's get back to ZarCedra and warn all we can to prepare for major air attacks," Sgt. Pane suggested anxiously!

"I believe you are correct but I'm first going to activate my craft's XT-165 DigiCam and take some cinematics of these crafts Sergeant," I said as I activated the DigiCam. I made sure I remained in Stealth mode as I flew around the huge ships. "Do what you must," Sgt. Pane said as we watched through its monitor.

Two mites later the lead ship altered course and turned directly in our path. Sgt. Pane's face turned white and hesitantly asked. "They can't see us could they? "I can't be positive but as far as I surmise we are still cloaked," I said as I looked at the glowing cloak touch pad as I turned the XT-165 DigiCam off then turned my craft towards ZarCedra and flew. "Watch Out," 'PAT' said just as the lead ship extracted what looked to be an electronic mesh net, which caught my craft like a Thrawl in a Thrawler citizen's net.

"Oh man, what are we going to do now? Sgt. Pane blurted out. I'm not sure; give me a sec to assess our predicament! I said as I raised my face shield. The first thing I did was take us out of stealth mode because it wasn't much use our enemy was easily able to detect our presence. "'PAT', what do you surmise our chances are of escaping this situation? I asked after a few secs.

"My apologies but looking at our predicament from an objected point of view I give us a 5% chance of escape. As her answer echoed in my head, I made certain the shield was still protecting us as I fired every weapon at the lead craft.

My fingers danced upon the finger touch pads of my flight stick, as I fired my SQ-Lasers, the Plasma Pulse Cannons, a volley of six Protonic EMC- Missiles just as the Protrerian mother ship blasted my craft with laser blasts of its own. As my craft shook a few secs it gave me an idea and I hoped with everything I had that it would succeed.

"'PAT', on my mark activate the star drive engine," I said as I lowered my face shield. I looked over at Sgt. Pane. "Hold on to something this might get a bit rough. "'PAT', target the ship at the base of the electronic mesh net," I said as I fired five of my craft's Neutronic EMC-Torpedo's and the remaining Protonic EMC-Missiles at the tremendous craft.

At the same instance I targeted the electronic mesh net with my craft's SQ-Laser but before I could fire, the electronic mesh net disintegrated as the Torpedo's contacted the huge ship and knocked out its power; just as other craft flew in our direction. At that time I yelled out "MARK," and we were able to escape the area at star drive speed.

Both Sgt. Pane and I let out a loud breath as we traveled toward ZarCedra then I quickly thanked the Gods in Godly paradise for our escape. "Apparently their technology is superior to our own, I'm not sure how but they obviously were able to detect us even though the craft was cloaked." Just then 'PAT' broke in our conversation and reported. "Jr. Com. Teldat do not forget it is with combined Humanarian and Protrerian technologies that this craft was created, given that fact wouldn't it stand to reason the Protrerian's could detect their own technology? "You are correct as usual 'PAT'", I said.

'PAT', Sgt. Pane and I discussed what we saw of the Protrerian High Command Stronghold as we flew towards ZarCedra. "They can't have many fighters remaining, look how many ZarCedra squadrons shot down," I said. "Nevertheless did you see the size of those ships in their fleet, they could have thousands more? "You are correct, they could have," I said just as my craft exited the wormhole and we halted position over ZarCedra.

"'PAT, scan the ozone layer of ZarCedra and locate the area where it is the least dense then give me the coordinates. "Affirmative Jr. Commodore, one moment," she said then went silent. "I still can't believe everything that happened, if you didn't record it, I don't think any one would believe our tale and the size of those ships," Sgt. Pane said. "You are correct Sergeant," I answered as 'PAT' cut in. "Location found, travel 200 Kiloms to the port side and there you will find it easiest to descend "Affirmative, many thanks 'PAT'," I said as I traveled to the predetermined location.

I turned the craft in its direction, and flew for a few secs then I guided the nose of the craft down. Darkness turned to illumination the further we traveled closer toward ZarCedra. As soon as we were through the ozone layer I turned the craft toward Tanglar and accelerated to Mach ten. "We have to report our finding to Sr. Commodore Bieas ASAP," I said as I looked over at 'PAT' and Sgt. Pane. "Affirmative, they both replied as we hurried towards the honorary regime of Placaden.

Mites later we flew over Cangla City then we hovered over the Grinshaw Military Facility a few secs. I then decreased speed to 20 kps as I made my way toward the helijets and I contacted the tower. "Tower this is Jr. Com. Teldat, am I cleared to set down? "Affirmative Jr. Commodore, you are," the air commuter transportation controller acknowledged. I hovered down to the vacant pads below then contracted and had the port wing slide as I started powering down the craft.

I disconnected my safety belts then removed the 'HUD' helmet as Sgt. Pane took off his helmet and released himself from his seat. I went to retrieve the keycard then quickly released and unlocked the main hatch platform. "'PAT', you are welcomed to join us if you so desire? "Affirmative sir." When the platform was opened the three of us stepped on and lowered to the tarmac below.

"PAT', raise and seal the main hatch platform. I said as we got to the tarmac. "Affirmative," she uttered and as it started rising we all ran toward main headquarters. Secs later we entered main headquarters and to Sr. Commodore Bieas' secretarial assistant. Gasping for breath. "Jr. Com. Teldat and party to see the Sr. Commodore immediately." I said. "You may enter," he replied as I turned and we ran to the Sr. Commodore's entry-way. I quickly knocked then flung the entry-way open and saluted as we got to her desk.

Sr. Commodore Bieas, we have an urgent oral report to report. "At ease and report Jr. Commodore," Sr.Com. Bieas said. "Ma'am, my cybernetic co-pilot 'PAT', Sgt. Pane and I decided to test my craft further and exit ZarCedra's boundaries and check to see where our alien foe is positioned, and their fleet is positioned over the North Eastern portion of ZarCedra's 3rd moon.

As my craft was cloaked I recorded digital cinematic footage of their massive fleet. Which consists of multiple huge and smaller crafts. We were unable to determine the digits of attack craft's they have remaining but by the size of their mother craft there could be many hundred or even thousands of attack craft still remaining inside. "Your craft was able to do that? You surely have an incredible aircraft," the Sr. Commodore said. "I do, but they were able to detect our presence; we were captured for a few mites in an electronic mesh net but with the fire power and speed of 'PAT' and my craft we were able to escape captivity." I said.

Just then Sgt. Pane jumped in the conversation. "Affirmative ma'am, Jr. Commodore Teldat has an unbelievable aircraft, by concentrating his arsenal of weapons on the lead mother ship and activating his star drive engine at the precise time we were able to get away unscaved. "What do you mean you were captured, how? "Well my craft was constructed using the combined technology of Humanarian and Protrerian. 'PAT', my cybernetic co-pilot and super computer informed us that it would be easy for them to detect their own technology on another craft, they surrounded my craft with a type of electronic mesh net; and we were captured."

"I see and understand," Sr. Com. Bieas said, and then asked. "Do you suppose they might still attack ZarCedra in the illumination remaining of this p.a.r? "Unknown ma'am. "We should remain on high military alert, at least for the time being," Sgt. Pane, bellowed. "It would stand to reason that we should remain on high military alert at least until in the morrow when our interstellar reinforcements arrive," 'PAT' stated.

"Your co-pilot is correct, for now go to your quarters, freshen up then have your banquet; Jr. Commodore keep your radar on in your craft and keep me informed if there are any enemy craft incoming," Sr. Commodore Bieas stated. "Affirmative ma'am," I said then we all saluted, turned and left the Sr. Commodore's office.

As we were walking up the boulevard I pressed the talk button of my timepiece. "18 hundred 35 epocks," it informed. "Well time to go to my quarters then head to the mess hall before the banquets are all gone," I said. "Affirmative," Sgt. Pane said as he walked away. "'PAT', return to the craft and scan the skies surrounding ZarCedra for any incoming enemy Protrerian attack craft and contact me immediately upon detection. "Affirmative sir, is that all?" 'PAT' asked. "It is for now. "Affirmative sir," she said then walked away.

I walked the rest of the way to my barracks whistling a tune and when I got to my structure I entered. I went to the retina scanner and had my retina scanned; after it had confirmed my identity, the entry-way to my quarters opened. I entered then went to the latrine; after I was through cleaning myself up I walked in the front chamber and removed my flight suit. I ran my fingers though my short cropped hair as my stomach reminded me it was time for my banquet as it let out a loud gurgling noise. "You will get fed soon," I said as I rubbed it. With that said I left my quarters then my barracks and walked towards the mess hall

A few mites later I entered the structure, went and grabbed a tray then proceeded to acquire my twilight banquet. As I was retrieving eating utensils I scanned our usual table and seen my consociates then walked towards them. "Grand p.a.r young citizens; how's everything going? I asked as I sat. "All right," they said. "You should hear what we did after Jr. Com. Teldat came to pick me up," Sgt. Pane said then took a bite of his banquet. "Wait until you hear this, you won't believe this but it's all factual," Sgt. Pane added. "What happened?" LC Luxton asked.

"Well I was informed when they introduced my craft to me that the craft could break ZarCedra's atmosphere and last 96 epocks in outer space with the tanks of compressed oxygen I have equipped on my craft. Since I haven't had the chance to test this theory for as long as I had the craft in my possession, so this mid-p.a.r I figured this was the perfect time to find out.

But first before I did I would ask Sgt. Pane if he wanted to attempt this feat with me or not? If not I would bring him back to the Grinshaw Military Facility and attempt breaking ZarCedra's orbit alone. But to my expectation, Sgt. Pane agreed to make this attempt with me," I said then took a few bites of my own banquet then took a swill and started again.

"So after I had collected Sgt. Pane we went up and broke the atmosphere. We went into Star Drive speed and to my surprise we traveled at Star Drive speed through the swirling wormhole without the twisted turning erratic flying I go through here within ZarCedra's atmosphere.

Anyway, we flew at Star Drive speed in stealth mode to ZarCedra's 3rd moon, where we discovered the Protrerian fleet. You won't believe what we discovered? "And what was that?" I was asked. "A fleet of ships large enough to house thousands of attack craft.

"Affirmative but with all the attack craft we destroyed over the course of this war we were unable to confirm they still had that many remaining," Sgt. Pane added.

"I flew closer taking digital surveillance, and this is where our circumstance takes a turn," I said then took a swill of my black caffinated brew. "How? Capt. Pane asked. "Well, the lead ship turned to face us even though we were in stealth mode and caught us in an electronic net that left us motionless. My craft's computerized avatar informed me that my craft Stealth mode was created with the combination of technology from ZarCedra and Protreria and it only stands to reason that the Protrerian's would be able to detect their own type of technology. I tried everything I could think of to break free but nothing seemed to work. Until I got the inkling to try all my weapons with the added activation of my craft's Star Drive engine at the precise time. My crafts Neutronic EMC-Torpedo's as well as its other weapons knocked out the power to the electronic mesh net and we were able to escape at star drive speed back to ZarCedra."

By that time everyone at the table had finished their twilight banquets so we all put our trays away then went out and those who puffed lit up when we got to the designated puffing area. "I still can't believe we got away," Sgt. Pane said then took a puff. "Affirmative the situation seemed futile for the first few mites but I am glad we were able to escape when we did or I do think we would not be here for the Antrerians arrival in the morrow," I said as I looked over at him. "Sounds like it will be an overwhelming p.a.r in the morrow, we should call it a twilight soon and get a grand twilights rest," LC Luxton said as he tossed his puff in the huge ashtray.

"Well, everyone have a grand twilight," I said as LC Luxton and I walked away. "Until in the morrow, you citizens have a grand twilight as well," Fl. Sgt. Colthamner said.

A few mites later we entered our barracks, I walked to the retina scanner and had my retina and voice scanned and the entry-way opened. We entered and I went to my slumbering quarters to jot in my jotter after I entered everything that happened during the p.a.r, I thought a hot shower would make me feel restored. So I got my shower supplies together and told Chad I was off to shower as I continued to the latrine.

****

After my shower, I got myself a swill then it was off to slumber. "Grand twilight Chad," I said then retired to my slumbering quarters and crawled into retiring unit. "Illumination off," I said as the illumination distinguished and I rolled over and closed my eyes.

P.A.R 11

"It's 07.05," I said aloud as I quickly sprung out of my retiring unit, as excited as a monk on the holiest p.a.r of the tritton. I quickly got dressed then made my retiring unit, then made my way to the latrine to get ready for this p.a.r. When I finished I walked through the front chamber and said, "Grand morn Chad. "Right now I have a PCD call to make; when you are ready to go for our morn banquet meet me in the hall. "Affirmative," Chad said as I tucked my beret under my shoulder loop as I exited our quarters.

As I was going to the personal communication device, I checked my timepiece and seen that it was 07 hundred 45 epocks. 'I wonder if Topanga is at her abode,' I thought as I fished a quint gribbit from my pocket, deposited it in the PCD then tapped her digits. I waited patiently as it chirped a couple times and then Cheryl answered. "Greetings."

"Grand morn grand looking is my exquisite Topanga around? "She is, and she was just ready to leave, you called just in time, here she is. "Greetings huni buni," I heard a sec later.

"Grand morn my exquisite Topanga."

"Grand morn Jero."

"So, where were you off to so early in the morn?"

"I have an appointment at Cangla City General Infirmary, why? "Because I would like to know if I can get your answer to the question I asked the p.a.r before this one?"

"I did talk to my abode mate about it but I want to talk with another consociate, if that is alright?" She asked.

"Of course it is huni buni, just let me know later this p.a.r. But no matter what your answer is Topanga, remember that the quixotic feelings I have for you will never whither."

"And my quixotic feelings for you will never whither as well Jero and I will definitely think about it, and we can talk later."

"All right huni buni, I will call again after the Antrerian Armada arrive and remember you are the only lady that makes me feel alive."

"Oh Jeroque many thanks for the kind words, you are very special to me as well."

"Ok huni I must go now, Chad is waiting for me, and I'll call you later to get your answer?"

"Ok, my darling."

"Say adioso to Cheryl for me & Chad and I hope you both have a grand p.a.r."

"Cheryl and I hope you and Chad have a terrific p.a.r as well and we both say adioso." Topanga said as we hung up.

*****

I turned around and started walking down the hallway just as Chad exited our quarters. "That was swift what did you and Topanga chat about? "Something of a personal nature that should not be repeated at this time but what I can say is she hopes we both have a terrific p.a.r," I said as we left the structure. I hope you said so long from me and I hope she also has a grand p.a.r? "Affirmative, I did."

As Chad and I walked up the boulevard, I put on my beret then pressed the left wing of my com-link. "'PAT,' monitor ZarCedra's stratosphere for enemy attack craft. Also inform me as soon as any Antrerian craft approached ZarCedra. "Affirmative, is there anything else? "Negative 'PAT', not at this time, that is all for now, Jr. Com. Teldat out. "'PAT', out."

As we neared the mess hall, we met up with Sgt. Pane and we all returned pleasantries as we continued walking. I contemplated whether or not to tell Sgt. Pane and LC Luxton about the twilightmare I had the other twilight. 'Might as well,' I thought as we all entered the mess hall.

We grabbed trays and waited in line. "There is something I want to discuss with you two," I told the pair. "Affirmative," they said as the line started moving and we were able receive our banquets, caffinated brew and silverware. After we found an empty table and sat, I took a sip of my black caffinated brew then removed my beret.

"What I want to discuss with you is the twilightmare I had a couple twilights ago. "Affirmative sir go ahead," they both said as we started on our morn banquet.

"In my twilightmare, I was flying over the landscape, I asked 'PAT' for the time and it appeared on my face shield but it kept flashing 12 hundred epocks over and over. A few secs later everything went dark as if someone turned off the sun, I looked at my radar and seen multiple waves of Protrerian attack craft. They branched off going to destroy the capital city of each industrialized country, that's when 'PAT' said the oddest thing to me. She said we were out digited and out armed and we might as well give up and allow them take over ZarCedra. I remember telling her we happened to come back in time for a reason and giving up was not an option."

"If you haven't told anyone, why have you trusted us with this information?" Sgt. Pane asked. "Because I thought you two could assist me in figuring out the meaning? "I'm flattered that you believe in us that much but I think you should ask the CO. "As do I," LC Luxton said. "I plan to, right after my morn banquet," I told them just as Fl. Sgt. Colthamner and a few other citizens sat down.

"Greetings, what's up?" She asked with a smile. "Not much," I said. "What do you mean not much, I think what you told us is something enough. "But that was just a twilightmare," I said as I looked at Fl. Sgt. Colthamner and all the other nearby air citizens.

"What I can decipher out of the twilightmare I had the other twilight is, this p.a.r at 12 hundred epocks we will experience intense air battles around ZarCedra a few epocks prior to the Antrerian Armada's arrival."

I finished my morn banquet and downed the last of my caffinated brew then looked at my associates. "If you citizens will excuse me I'm off to see what Sr. Commodore Bieas thinks of my twilightmare," I said as I gathered my tray. "GO!" they all exclaimed. I discarded my tray then started for the entry-way;

I took my beret from my shoulder loop and put it on as I left the mess hall.

I went to main headquarters, down the hall to the Sr. Commodore's secretarial assistant. "I have to see the Sr. Commodore immediately. "Affirmative Jr. Commodore, if it's that important you can go right in. "Many thanks," I said as I removed my beret and went to the Sr. Commodore's entry-way, knocked then entered.

I stopped in front of Sr. Com. Bieas's desk; stood at attention and saluted. "What can I do for you Jr. Commodore?" Sr. Com. Bieas asked as she returned my salute. "Ma'am, this p.a.r at precisely 12 hundred epocks about three epocks before the Antrerian Armada's arrival, I believe we will be hit hard by the Protrerian High Command. "Explain!" The Sr. Commodore ordered as she straightened in her chair.

"A couple twilights ago I had a twilightmare that this p.a.r at 12 hundred epocks Central Time, the Protrerian High Command will hit every capital city of each industrialized country around the planet. And the only thing my computer wanted me to do was give up saying we were out digited and out armed. I know this was only a twilightmare but over the last few trints I've learned there is some truth to my twilight slumber escapades."

"Sr. Com. Bancais told me to trust everything you say Jr. Com. Teldat," Sr. Com. Bieas stated. "Affirmative, if I am correct The Beige Palisades in Dek-kred, in the Cardola Territories will be the site of the first attack then about one hundred ninety nine other major cities around ZarCedra. "If you are correct I better warn the capitals of each continent about the air raids on their capital cities," Sr. Com. Bieas said as she picked up the PCD.

"Actually ma'am, it was just a twilightmare; I didn't think it was important enough to bring to your attention until I told a few air citizens about it and they suggested that I do talk to you. "Everything pertaining to this war is important enough to bring to my attention. "Affirmative ma'am."

"Is there anything else about this war I should know? I contemplated telling her of the storm that was going to happen this twilight but that had nothing to do with this war. "Negative, just warn the major continents of ZarCedra so they will be ready if the attack by the Protrerian High Command happens at 12 hundred epocks, Central Time. "You haven't given me much time!" Sr. Commodore Bieas exclaimed.

"Twenty-five waves of Protrerian attack craft just entered ZarCedra's stratosphere," 'PAT' broke in and reported. I tapped my com-link, "What is their rate of descent?" I asked. "By the degree of their descent, they are heading towards Tanglar and the Cardola Territories. Wait five waves have broken formation heading toward the East Coast of Sot Bissal. Five more waves also changed direction heading toward Brilain and five waves seem to heading towards Urik."

'Why are they so much earlier than predicted? Unless, this is just a prelude of what's going to arrive at 12 hundred epocks,' I thought to myself. "Sr. Commodore inform the President of the Cardola Territories also His Majesties Air Command in Craz, the leaders of Urik and Sot Bissal to dispatch squadrons immediately to intercept the incoming attack craft. "Affirmative at once," the Sr. Commodore said as she asked the Lance Corporal to get a hold of President Torren of the Cardola Territories immediately.

"If this is a prelude of what is to come at precisely mid-p.a.r, watch out because all hellatious will break loose, again. "Affirmative take to the air, I'll have your squadron meet you," she said as she pressed a button on her computer to sound the base alarm. As the alarm sounded, I turned and was about to run from the office. "Just hold on a sec Jr. Commodore," Sr. Com. Bieas said as she hung up her PCD. "Affirmative ma'am?" I asked as I stopped and turned around. "Grand luck and be safe up there," she replied as her PCD chirped. "Affirmative ma'am many thanks," I said as I ran out the entry-way then down the hall and out of the structure.

I ran toward my craft, as I neared it I pressed the wing of my com-link. "'PAT', lower the main hatch platform. "Affirmative." When I arrived I stood on the platform and rose to the cockpit, I entered and inserted my electronic keycard, activating the electrical system. I raised and closed the main hatch platform then removed my beret, put on my flight suit and hopped in the pilot's seat, placing the 'HUD' helmet upon my head as I extended the port wing.

"'PAT' what are the fuel levels in the two main & Star Drive engines also inform me of the water in the P-52 Hydrogenic generator?" I asked as I looked in her direction. "The tanks were refueled this morn, and the Omagon 2115 Star Drive Engine is at ¾ of a vile. As for the Hydrogenic generator it is currently sitting at ½ a tank of water," 'PAT' said. "Affirmative," I acknowledged as I activated the finger touch pad that activated two-way communications.

"Tower this is Jr. Com. "Time Star" Teldat, clear me for lift off immediately! "Affirmative, you are cleared. "Affirmative," I said as I raised my face shield and looked at the radar and saw that the enemy attack craft descend further towards Trigor. I pulled up on the flight stick and the craft started to ascend as I lowered the face shield. "'PAT', there is something I want to discuss with you later. "Affirmative Jr. Commodore."

At two hundred metrics I halted ascent, I leveled the wings as the landing gear raised then I waited a few secs until my entire squadron was airborne. Within secs there were a total of six squadrons all ordered to follow my lead. I took point and Sgt. Pane and LC Luxton took the starboard and port wing positions; the rest of the aircraft fell into formation behind as we flew away from the city.

We all flew at Mach 5 for a little while then we eased our speed as soon as we flew into Trigor, in the Cardola Territories. Immediately we engaged the enemy. I activated the shield as I accessed the menu inside of my 'HUD' helmet then accessed the targeting scanner and activated it. The face shield rose as the scanner protruded from my helmet and I started firing my SQ-Laser cannons as attack craft after attack craft exploded all around.

I had the XTR-9000 Plasma Pulse Cannons lower from the wings and destroyed all alien attack craft in the vicinity. I double tapped the finger touch pad that activated two-way communications and kept the channel open. "Sgt. 'Ace Flier' Pane, just look at all the fun Sr. Com. Bancais is missing out on," I said just as Ace Flyer destroyed the craft sneaking up on Fl. Sgt. Colthamner aircraft.

"Affirmative this is a blast, literally," Sgt. Pane said as attack craft disappeared from the sky! The laser blast of a renegade attack craft scraped my shield as I turned 45° and spent off a Protonic EMC-Missal. The missal missed its target but destroyed the attack craft aft of it. I fired my laser cannons and destroyed the craft I was after. "Grand shooting," LC 'Gunner' Luxton, said as he destroyed yet another pesky attack craft. All the while we were destroying attack craft, I noticed many ZarCedra fighters explode all around and fall from the sky. I looked down and seen blasts from the ground troopers as attack craft crashed to the planet below.

An epock later Sgt. Pane destroyed the last remaining attack craft. "Time to get back to Cangla City," I told the remaining pilots in my squadron as I disengaged the targeting scanner then lowered my face shield. I accessed the menu inside my 'HUD' helmet and had the two XTR-9000 Plasma Pulse cannons rise back into the wings. "Maj. Stringer calling Jr. Com. Teldat? "This is Jr. Com. Teldat, Major go ahead. "What's next on the agenda? We should return to the Grinshaw Military Facility and refuel, get everyone's ammunition restocked so we are all ready for the major attack I believe is coming at 12 hundred epocks."

"I have a gut feeling that is when all hellatious will break loose in capital cities around the planet. "Does Sr. Com. Bieas know of this? "Affirmative, I told her earlier this morn. "You say the Antrerian Armada will arrive here a few epocks after the Protrerian attack? "Affirmative, something like that," I answered. "Are you sure? "Not precisely but that is what I suspect," I said as we entered Cangla City and it started to rain.

"Aughh where did the sun disappear to?" Fl. Sgt. Colthamner asked. "Probably behind these big gray rain billows," Sgt. Pane said sarcastically. "Very amusing!" Fl. Sgt. Colthamner said as she and the remainder of the aircraft lowered their landing gear and started to descend.

What remained of the six squadrons that went up started to land as I raised my craft's wings, the landing gear lowered then set down as I contracted the port wing. I turned everything off as my craft wound down. "Jr. Com. Teldat whatever did you want to discuss with me?"

"About a twilightmare I had; I was flying over the landscape when 12 hundred epocks flashed numerous times on the view screen of my 'HUD' helmet. Just then everything went black as if someone turned off the sun, I raised the visor of the 'HUD' helmet, I looked at my radar and seen multiple waves of Protrerian attack craft descending toward ZarCedra. I went to engage the enemy and that's when you said the oddest things. "What was it I said Jr. Commodore?"

"You said we were out digited and out armed and we should just give up and let the Protrerian High Command be victorious in the war," I said just as I was ordered to report to Sr. Com. Bieas's office ASAP. "Affirmative," I responded.

"Not to worry Jr. Com. Teldat, I am determined to be victorious in this war as much as you are; I will never give up so wipe that thought from your mind. "Many thanks 'PAT', I will," I said as I removed the 'HUD' helmet then disconnected myself from the pilot's seat. I went and retrieved the electronic keycard then went and opened then lowered the main hatch platform as I put on my beret.

"See you later 'PAT', raise the main hatch platform after I step off and contact me as soon as enemy attack craft enter ZarCedra's stratosphere" I said as I descended to the tarmac. "Affirmative Jr. Commodore," 'PAT' said as I descended. Walking through the precipitation, I looked at my timepiece to discover it was 10 hundred 49 epocks.

A couple mites later I entered main headquarters and walked the ways to the Sr. Commodore's office. I walked up to LC Acernan and removed my beret. "Jr. Com. Teldat to see Sr. Commodore Bieas. "You may enter; Sr. Com. Bieas is expecting you Jr. Commodore. "Many thanks," I said as I turned and entered the office.

I saluted the Sr. Commodore. "You requested my presence ma'am? "Affirmative, close the entry-way," the Sr. Commodore said as she returned my salute. On my return, I stood at attention in front of the Sr. Commodore's desk. "At ease Jr. Commodore and have a seat."

"I warned the planet leaders of all industrialized continents, that capital cities will be attacked at approximately 12 hundred epocks central time, I said approximately because I was unsure what countries would be attacked first. "I am unsure as well but Kor and Sot Bissal, Urik, Brilain, and Zantara definitely would be among the continents attacked. Make sure the military coalitions of those continents are notified and appraised of what is to come. "Affirmative, as of right now almost everyone in power has knowledge of the ordeal and will be ready when the attack begins."

"As we speak, your aircraft is being serviced ready to fly at a moment's notice, so stay close to your aircraft. You say the Antrerian Armada will be here on ZarCedra sometime mid-p.a.r? "Affirmative ma'am, is that all? If it is I have just enough time to grab a caffinated brew? "Affirmative but come here when you are through and I will give you a list of air citizens that will be flying in your squadron. "Affirmative, I would like LC Luxton, Sgt. Pane and Fl. Sgt. Colthamner to remain in my squadron. "Affirmative dismissed." I stood up, saluted, turned and exited the office. I put my beret back on then continued out of main headquarters.

Outside it was still precipitating as I seen LC Luxton, Sgt. Pane and Fl. Sgt. Colthamner as they headed for the mess hall. "Wait up, there is something I would like to talk to you three about," I said as I ran toward them and the four of us entered the mess hall. "What is it? "I'll discuss it over caffinated brew."

We received our caffinated brews then went to a table and sat. "What would you like to discuss with us?" Sgt. Pane asked as he fixed his caffinated brew. I took a sip of my own brew. "I will be given a new squadron later, I told Sr. Com. Bieas that I wanted you three to remain in my squadron when the attack commences. "Affirmative sir."

"In the original war, a lot of grand citizens were killed defending ZarCedra but now with me here at this crucial time knowing important events, things have changed, many citizens have been saved and cities have been evacuated and ground troopers were called in to protect them. If everything goes as well as it has been going we should have this war wrapped up soon. "Affirmative, from what you were saying earlier about this war things are looking quite a bit better, especially for me," LC Luxton said with a smile.

I took another sip of my caffinated brew then sat up straight. "I am going to tell you three something of extreme importance, and you are only to reveal it if something goes wrong, that is a direct order. "Affirmative sir, what is it?" Fl. Sgt. Colthamner inquired. I lowered my voice a few decibels then started.

"'PAT' informed me that there will be a major electrical storm off the coast of Nesbitia, this twilight at 23 hundred 30 epocks having the same characteristics of the storm that brought me to this time. If we succeed this p.a.r and my craft is unscaved, I am going to fly through it in hopes I can return to my own time."

"Now if I make it back, you'll never hear from me again but if by chance something goes wrong, there's an automatic homing device equipped in my craft that will automatically activate if I crash. I read in my craft's instruction manual that my whole cockpit is an escape pod, if I need to eject; I eject the whole cockpit. "But your craft will be destroyed! Fl. Sgt. Colthamner said suddenly. "Let's hope that doesn't happen," I said as I smiled and winked at her.

We all drank our caffinated brews as I looked at my timepiece and seen that it was getting close to 11 hundred 30 epocks. "All most time to roc citizens, I will meet you up in the air," I said as I downed the remaining bit of caffinated brew in my cup. "Affirmative sir," they responded as we put our cups away then vacated the mess hall, as I replaced my beret on my head. "We are going to the latrine then go for a quick puff first," Sgt. Pane said. "Affirmative, don't take too long," I said as I made a pit stop at the latrine as well then went toward main headquarters to see Sr. Com. Bieas, as LC Luxton, Sgt. Pane and Fl. Sgt. Colthamner started towards the designated puffing area.

I entered main headquarters and went down the hall and up to LC Acernan. "Jr. Com. Teldat to see Sr. Com. Bieas. "Go right in Jr. Commodore, the Sr. Commodore informed me to let you in as soon as you returned. "Many thanks Lance Corporal," I said as I removed my beret and chirped the chime. "Enter," I was told.

As I went in, I closed the entry-way and saluted the Senior Commodore. "Stand at ease," Sr. Com. Bieas said as she returned my salute. "Here is a list of the air citizens that will be in your squadron," she said as she handed over the list. "You will be flight leader of the Potenza squadron as before and the three pilots you requested are among the pilot's on the list.

"Look it over and tell me if this is adequate?" I took the parchment and glanced at it. "This will be fine ma'am," I said as I handed it back to the Sr. Commodore.

"A few aircraft transporters from Urik and Tanzeer were doing maneuvers in the Sydoken Sea and were dispatched to Negra Parday a few p.a.r's ago; they should arrive this mid-p.a.r," Sr. Com. Bieas said. "Grand, I have a feeling we will need all the assistance we can get. But Urik and Tanzeer will most likely be attacked as well; I hope they didn't leave themselves shorthanded by dispatching those transporters here instead of requesting them back to their respective countries? "I'm sure they have enough defenses to protect themselves or they would have."

"Jr. Commodore, eighty waves of intergalactic attack craft just entered ZarCedra's stratosphere, now they are branching off. The first wave will arrive above the Cardola Territories in approximately five mites," 'PAT' reported. "Affirmative," I acknowledged as I saluted the Sr. Commodore.

"What did I say ma'am, the events of my twilightmare are coming true," I said as I looked out the window and the sunlight disappeared. "Let's just hope the remainder of my twilightmare doesn't come to pass. "Affirmative you were correct Jr. Commodore; your squadron will be sent up ASAP." At that moment Sr. Com. Bieas pressed a button on her computer to sound the base alarm.

I put my beret on as I ran out of the office, down the hall and out of the structure. I ran by the puffing area. "If you haven't noticed by twilight swallowing the p.a.r's illumination and by the wail of the base alarm we have multiple enemy craft incoming," I yelled as I passed.

As I neared my craft, 'PAT' had already lowered the main hatch platform. As soon as I arrived I went directly up to the cockpit and raised then secured the main hatch. I inserted the electronic keycard then jumped in the pilot's seat and buckled myself in. I removed my beret and put on the 'HUD' helmet as I looked at the radar and got a fix on the enemy's position. I activated ignition and the craft roared to life as I extended the port wing.

"Enemy attack craft at four thousand metrics and closing fast. "Affirmative," I acknowledged as I started to rise. Once I reached four hundred metrics, I leveled the wings as the landing gear raised then I lowered my face shield and accessed the menu. I wanted to make sure my artillery supply was recharged as I waited for the squadrons of military aircraft to leave the runways. As I rose, so did a digit of helijets rise to my altitude. I noticed as the fighters left the runways that LC Luxton, Sgt. Pane, Fl. Sgt. Colthamner and I had the only stealth aircraft the rest were G-14 and G-16 Striker Eagles.

I pressed the finger touch pad that activated two-way communications. "We have to fly into the Cardola Territories airspace to engage the enemy," I told the various squadrons. "Affirmative," they answered. "This is Jr. Com. 'Time Star' Teldat of the Potenza squadron and I will take lead, everyone fall in behind me," I said as we flew out of the city.

"Jr. Com. Teldat, come in? "Jr. Com. Teldat here go ahead. "Sir this is flight leader Maj. "Diamond" Gerwick of the Starblitz squadron, checking in. "This is Com. "Hoppy" Van Horn of the Hencentor squadron also here to assist. "I am Capt. "Chappy" Booker checking in as well. "This is Capt. "Skit" Blaneer of the Cortenza squadron ready for the enemy. "This is Maj. "Muffin" Greery of the Nerowitz squadron ready and willing to assist.

"Affirmative, fall in behind me; we're off to the Autobahn Military Installation in Negra Parday City. "The enemy would be in range in two mites fifteen secs," PAT' informed. "Affirmative; all ZarCedra military craft advance speed to maximum Mach," I commanded as I increased air speed.

We all flew at Mach 5 until we were off the coast of Negra Parday City where we engaged the enemy attack craft.

I activated my craft's shield in the nick of time just as I was struck on the port side. I spun around 70° and as I did I saw two Protrerian attack craft as they attacked Fl. Sgt. Colthamner's aircraft.

I quickly accessed the digital menu inside my 'HUD' helmet then accessed my targeting scanner and activated it. The face shield rose and the scanner protruded, I got one of the enemy attack craft in my sights and fired a Protonic EMC-Missal, a sec later upon impact it exploded in a grand blast of flames. With my lasers blasting I destroyed the attack craft aft of her. "Many thanks ever so much 'Time Star," Fl. Sgt. "Red" Colthamner said as she went after the endless supply of enemy attack craft.

"You are very welcome," I said as I stopped, rotated my craft 180° and with my craft's SQ-Lasers firing, I destroyed the three attack craft before me. I looked around and all the ally military aircraft were in skirmishes all around me.

"There are five attack craft on a direct course toward us," 'PAT' warned as I looked at my radar. "What is the shield strength," I asked as I glanced at 'PAT' just as my craft was struck and it shook violently? "79%, correction 70%, 'PAT' said after the aftershock subsided.

"Six more attack craft closing fast on the starboard side of our position," 'PAT' warned. "I see them," I said as I lowered the XTR-9000 Plasma Pulse Cannons and blasted them out of the sky. "Enemy craft directly before us," 'PAT' said as she fired off three consecutive EMC-Missals and destroyed them. "Many thanks 'PAT'. Two mites of extreme fighting later we received assistance from the Autobahn Military Installation below I swore every time we shot one attack craft, there were twenty more to take its place.

"We have additional ally fighters arriving from various aircraft transporters in the Oskretin Sea," 'PAT' reported. "This is Com. Hiromatsumoto, we are here to assist. "All assistance is muchly appreciated; fall in and engage the enemy." At that time I ordered Capt. "Skit" Blaneer and his squadron to fly to Dek-kred, Trebel to supply back up to save The Beige Palisades in that capital city. "Affirmative sir," he answered as he and his squadron veered off flying west.

Two and a half-epocks of heavy battle later 'PAT' sounded a buzzer. "Shield strength is down to 5%. "Affirmative," I said as I shot down the attack craft dogging Sgt. "Ace Flyer" Pane's aircraft. "Many thanks Time Star," 'Ace Flyer' said.

"Our extraterrestrial reinforcements just entered ZarCedra's stratosphere," 'PAT' reported. I raised my helmet's visor and glanced at my radar and saw unusual shaped craft descending towards ZarCedra then branched off going to various locations around the planet. "I count one hundred waves and there are additional craft following. "Affirmative, ha, ha, grand news 'PAT'," I acknowledged then pressed the finger touch pad that activated two-way communications. "Our extraterrestrial assistance have arrived," I told everyone. "It's about time," I heard.

A few secs later I seen the first sight of the blue, green and silver Antrerian Armada craft attack all Protrerian High Command attack craft.

At that moment I fell back to recharge the shield and all weapons and ammunition; all the while firing my lasers at any and all Protrerian High Command attack craft that flew by. I disengaged the targeting scanner and it disappeared back into the 'HUD' helmet and my face shield lowered.

"Flight Leader Kersh of the Antrerian Armada, informing all ZarCedra craft of our arrival. "Welcome and many thanks for coming to our aide; this is Jr. Com. Teldat. A Protrerian High Command Army had landed in the Kor Bissal desert region of Maccari in the Western part of the Cardola Territories. Also the Northern region of ZarCedra called Gergel on the Jroken Continent," I informed the Antrerian flight leader. **"Understood."**

Then he dispatched additional Antrerian attack craft to those locations. **"I also want to convey that our fleet engaged and destroyed the Protrerian stronghold positioned over the 3rd moon of ZarCedra.** "Many thanks to you and your fleet," I said as I continued to blast my craft's lasers at all stray Protrerian craft that flew by.

Twenty-five mites later all the Protrerian attack craft in the area were destroyed. I raised my face shield to check my radar and saw there were still enemy attack craft near the City of Dek-kred, Trebel. I informed the Antrerian flight leader and suggested we go lend assistance. **"Very well let us go. "**

"Our fighters are in drastic need of fuel," Sgt. Pane reported. "All of ours are," the rest of ZarCedra squadrons, reported. "Affirmative, descend to the Autobahn Military Installation below and get refueled then return to the Grinshaw Military facility. "Affirmative," Sgt. Pane acknowledged as all ZarCedra squadrons broke formation and flew down to Negra Parday City.

"Why is your craft unlike all the rest of ZarCedra craft?" Flight Leader Kersh inquired as the Antrerian Armada and I flew towards Dek-kred at Mach 7. "That is a very long story but this is the one and only Supersonic Dragon 228-D Spy Jet Stealth Craft in existence at the present time. **"Understood, but tell me what do the markings on the side of your craft mean?"** Flight Leader Kersh inquired. "Affirmative; N. Z. C. M. Co is the anagram meaning the North ZarCedra Military Coalition. S. H. Z. C. A. means Secret Humanarian ZarCedra Alliance. I am from another time in the times yet to come, and in my time we read in our times elapsed archive that we were defeated in this war by the Protrerian High Command, even with your kind assistance."

"In the times yet to come the planet of Protreria ran out of energy and the sun in your galaxy was going nova, which is why they are trying to take over ZarCedra. **"Agreed, it is known our sun is going nova, but we have digits of planet cycles remaining before that fateful happening,"** Fl. Leader Kersh said. "In the times yet to come your citizens secretly plan to settle here on ZarCedra."

"Tell me HUMANARIAN, how is it possible for you to travel back in times elapsed?" Flight Leader Kersh inquired. "Affirmative how; in my time we just managed to acquire Star Drive speed capability, and in order to reach and maintain Star Drive speed we needed a powerful engine called the Omagon 2115 Star Drive Engine. This engine uses a radioactive chemical solution called Liquid Napricyte² Star Drive Compound and a little invention called an Electronic Flux Inducer. This causes an Ionic charge to electromagnetically encompass my craft then shoot out in front of me creating a Humanarian-made swirling wormhole. I fly into this wormhole, which allows my craft to reach Star Drive speeds."

"One p.a.r I flew through a major electrical storm and was struck by a bolt of lightning just as I activated my Omagon 2115 Star Drive engine and was entering the swirling wormhole. The combination of grand amount of electricity and the radioactive Liquid Napricyte² compound of my Star Drive engine somehow caused me to travel in times elapsed. Personally, I think my craft and I were brought to this precise time to assist so ZarCedra would be the victors in this war this time."

"You have a grand imagination HUMANARIAN," Flight Leader Kersh said with a laugh. We eased our speed just as we flew into Dek-kred and seen ZarCedra military aircraft having a tough time, I activated my craft's shield as the partial Antrerian Armada and I joined in the battle. I accessed my targeting scanner and activated it. The face shield rose and the scanner protruded from my helmet. Attack craft after attack craft exploded all around including many Antrerian and ZarCedra military craft.

Twenty mites of fierce battle later not another Protrerian attack craft remained. "Flight leaded Kersh, return to Tanglar with me to meet my commanding officer, Sr. Commodore Bieas," I said as I disengaged the targeting scanner and my face shield lowered. "Agreed HUMANARIAN." At that time we changed direction and flew north toward Cangla City, as we flew we talked more about the new outcome of the war.

By the time we entered Tanglar air space, we caught up with my squadron and we all flew to Cangla City. A short time later as we entered Cangla City and when we were nearing the Grinshaw Military Facility, I activated two-way communications. "Tower, this is Jr. Com. Teldat, returning with what remained of the squadrons that were sent up. They are in desperate need of medical attention; I also have Flight Leader Kersh of the Antrerian Armada with me to see Sr. Com. Bieas."

We were all given permission to land and set down. After my craft was safely on the tarmac, I contracted the port wing then switched everything off. As my craft was whining down, I took off the 'HUD' helmet, disconnected my safety belts then went and ejected the electronic keycard. "PAT' you are welcomed to come with, I would like you to elaborate on my claim that we in fact come from the times yet to come," I said as I put the keycard in my pocket of my uniform then removed my flight suit and opened and lowered the main hatch platform.

"You are incredible 'PAT' and you fought commendably, I'm sure glad you are on our side. "Many thanks for the kind words Jr. Commodore, but Humanarian scientists created me who else's side would I be on? She said as we got to the tarmac. "That was just a rhetorical phrase 'PAT', learn how to take a compliment," I said as I put on my beret as we stepped off the main hatch platform. "'PAT', you can now close the main hatch platform. "Affirmative," she acknowledged as we went to the Antrerian craft.

As we arrived at the Antrerian Flight Leader's attack craft, we admired its complex construction and sheer exquisiteness. Its main hatch opened and at the same time an access ramp extended to the tarmac and Flight Leader Kersh and another Antrerian subordinate stepped out, they both stood about 3 metrics tall, both were lean and lanky. They had the same-ridged forehead and bluish-green skin color as the Antrerian citizens I met in my own time. The two looked like real official military officers dressed in military uniforms, and the laser pistols they had holstered on their hips, they looked professional, fearless and proud.

"Flight Leader Kersh, I'm honored to meet you; I am Jr. Com. Teldat," I said as I grabbed and shook the hand of the one with the most colored military rankings on his chest. "Many thanks for your assistance in this war. **Glad we could assist, you have a grand planet; it would be disgraceful to lose it to the likes of the Protrerian Magta,**" Flight Leader Kersh said. "Magta, that is a word I haven't heard before what does it mean? **"Magta is a small creature on our planet, it stands on two legs, has two wings, a beak, a tail and it barks. It was said as an insult toward all Protrerian High Command Citizens."**

"Before we go I would like you to meet my cybernetic co-pilot, her name is 'PAT' and she can affirm all that I tell you is factual. The letters P A T in her designation is an anagram standing for Prototype Advancements in Technology and her matrix of circuits are the brains of my craft. Ok, let us go meet Sr. Commodore Bieas," I said as we started walking towards main headquarters.

When we got there, Flight Leader Kersh and his subordinate had to stoop to fit through the main entrance because of their extreme height as air citizens stopped and watched us in disbelief. We walked the corridor and up to LC Acernan. "Jr. Com. Teldat and party to see Sr. Com. Bieas? "G-Go right in," LC Acernan stammered at the sight of the Antrerians. I went to the CO's entry-way and knocked then we waited until we were instructed to enter. I opened the entry-way and we stepped into the office. Again the Antrerian officers had to stoop in order to enter the office.

I saluted the senior officer as she sprung to her feet. "Sr. Com. Bieas this is the Antrerian Flight Leader, Kersh. Next to him we have," then I stopped in mid-sentence. "My apologies but I do not know your partner's name. **He is called First Sittar Meeg,**" Flight Leader Kersh said. "Glad to meet you both," Sr. Com. Bieas said as she extended her hand in consociateship. "I am eternally grateful for all the assistance the Antrerian Armada has given Humanarian kind."

"Our Armada wasn't going to interfere but the Protrerian High Command had no right to declare war on this planet. "Well you probably know their reasons but only if they would have asked for our assistance, we could have come to some agreement. You see we understand your two planets have been enemies for a long time but all the leaders of ZarCedra think it best to stay at peace, stay neutral in any conflict of other planets at least until we have a better space program set in place."

"I would also like to thank the Antrerian Armada for coming to our aide when you did, 'Sactumi'," I said as I bowed toward the Antrerian representatives.

"Sactumi? We have never been to this planet before, how is it that you know our language?" A surprised Flight Leader Kersh asked.

"Can I speak freely ma'am?" I asked as I looked at Sr. Com. Bieas. "Sure airman, speak at your discretion." I looked up at the Flight Leader and partner.

"Like I said earlier everything I convey can be verified by 'PAT' my cybernetic co-pilot. "That is correct, I've had gigots of information downloaded into my circuitry, I know everything the Protrerian's ever did when they attacked and did since taking over ZarCedra."

"I told you I am from the times yet to come, precisely one hundred trittons. At that time your abode planet of Antreria will be in danger as your sun is about to go nova. Therefore the leaders of your planet asked the Humanarian's of ZarCedra if they could settle on this planet. The Humanarian members secretly agreed because of the Antrerian Armada's assistance in this war; but because of your participation in this conflict your race had become grander enemies to the Protrerian High Command."

"Since in my time the Protrerian's had won this war they end up ruling ZarCedra. But because of your assistance we told your citizens to settle in the northern region of ZarCedra when they contacted us personally."

"Our citizens, settle in the north where it is frigid, that is hard to believe! The citizens of our planet like a warm climate, that is why we settle near the equator on our planet," Flight Leader Kersh said.

"Unfortunately we were no longer in charge of this planet, the Protrerian High Command was, and your race was banished from ZarCedra. Considering all the assistance your citizens gave us we secretly agreed to let your race settle here."

"To carry on, just before I was transported to this time, I was in contact with Administer Ambassador Kruni, the Antrerian officer in charge of settling your citizens on our planet. After I had talked to him he said Sactumi; he told me that was the Antrerian equivalent to our words many thanks."

"All right, we now know how Jr. Com. Teldat knows of your language but how is it you know ours?" Sr. Com. Bieas asked Flight leader Kersh. "**Your main language here on ZarCedra is English, English is the main interstellar language throughout all known galaxies, although; each individual race has their own languages. Amien'do sackuro crematz sackuro astrovietz, which means you are very welcome very much, in the main language of our planet.**"

"Do you know how long your race will be on this planet?" "**Unknown, but we will leave after we rid your planet of the Protrerian Magta.** "Before your citizens leave this planet, our Administration would like to talk over the idea of your race sharing this planet when the time of your planet's destruction is at hand," the Sr. Commodore said. "**Agreed,**" Flight Leader Kersh answered. Then again Sr. Com. Bieas took Flight Leader Kersh's hand and shook it.

"**Before we go, can I ask why your citizens grab hands and move them up and down?**" Flight Leader Kersh asked. "Affirmative, that is our way of greeting citizens and/or sealing a bargain. "**Understood, until the next time we meet adioso.**" Then he and First Sittar Meeg bowed then left the office.

"Pleasant fellows, even though they are very tall and they did have an unusual odor about them," Sr. Com. Bieas said after they vacated the office. "The Humanarian race was able to get used to the odor of the Protrerian High Command, I think it safe to say we will get used to the odor of the Antrerians."

"Ma'am, with the Antrerian Armada here this war should be wrapped up in the next few p.a.r's after they rid our planet of the

Protrerian ground troopers. "Affirmative," the Commodore said in agreement. "If that is all for now, I have a PCD call to make. "To whom? Sr. Com. Bieas asked. "To my lady, Topanga.

"Before you leave I have something for you," Sr. Com. Bieas said as she opened a drawer. "Here is a crest of your new rank to sew on your flight jacket." She retrieved the blue and yellow crest and handed it to me. "Sr. Com. Bancais asked me to give this to you and say many thanks for all your insight and assistance in this interstellar war. "Many thanks ma'am," I said as I looked at it.

It was an embroidered crest that read, Junior Commodore Teldat. "I was talking to Sr. Com. Bancais on the PCD and he asked me to tell you that everything was going ahead as predicted. "That's wonderful, but for now we must be going," I said as I put the crest in my pocket. 'PAT' and I both saluted the Sr. Commodore; we turned then left the office.

"I will be in my barracks if I'm needed," I told LC Acernan as we walked by. "Affirmative sir." We continued down the hall then walked out the main entrance. "If I am not needed any longer sir, I will return to the aircraft," 'PAT' said as we vacated the structure. "You are dismissed," I said as we parted company.

I walked down the boulevard over to my barracks when I saw Sgt. Pane and LC Luxton going to the designated puffing area. "Greetings citizens, talk to you later, right now I have a PCD call to make. Remember what we were talking about this morn with Fl. Sgt. Colthamner? "Affirmative sir, and if I don't see you again it's been grand knowing you. "You citizens also but I'm not planning to leave just yet," I said as I continued towards my barracks, then I detoured.

I decided first to go to my craft to retrieve my electronic flight manual so I changed directions and walked in its direction as I tapped the left wing of my com-link. "'PAT', I have returned to retrieve my craft's instruction manual; lower the main hatch platform," I said as I continued; when I got to it I stood on the platform and went to the cockpit.

"Greetings 'PAT'," I said as I entered and grabbed my electronic flight manual. "I will return later, raise, close and secure the main hatch platform after I get to the tarmac," I said as I stepped on, lowered then went in the direction of my barracks.

As I was walking, I noticed Sr. Com. Bieas driving by. "Excuse me ma'am," I hollered. Sr. Com. Bieas stopped and I walked to her "What can I do for Jr. Commodore. "Could you arrange for my craft to get refueled so I will be able to get airborne later? "Why? "Oh, I want to patrol the city to make sure everything is ok. "Affirmative I will make the necessary arrangements," she said as she returned my salute then drove away.

I tapped my com-link again. "Come in 'PAT'. "'PAT' here sir, go ahead. "The craft will be refueled shortly so open the engine cover. "Affirmative Jr. Commodore; is that all you require at this time? "Affirmative, Jr. Com. Teldat, out. "'PAT', out," she said as I continued to my barracks.

After I entered, I walked to the end of the hall to the gribbit PCD to call Topanga. I deposited a quint gribbit and entered her digits; a few chirps later I heard Topanga's lovely voice.

"Greetings."

"Greetings huni buni how is my lovey this mid-par?"

"Greetings Jeroque I am grand, how are you, I trust everything is grand?"

"Everything is wonderful. Did you make up your mind about accompanying me?" I asked in a cheerful voice.

"I have, and my answer is wherever you go I would be honored to accompany you. I know and understand the dangers but that doesn't matter as long as we are together."

"Are you absolutely sure?"

"Positive."

"How sweet, I will pick you up on top of your abode structure's gable at 20 hundred 45 epocks, oh I forgot at 8:45."

"I love you Jeroque, I hope this proves once and for all that you are the only citizen I would ever want to be with?"

"I love you too Topanga and affirmative, it does indeed."

"How was your mid-p.a.r?"

"Very rough, I saw a lot of action then I met the Flight Leader of the Antrerian Armada. He seems like a very gracious citizen even though there are a few differences between Antrerian and Humanarian citizens."

"What do you mean?"

"The Antrerian male stand up to three metrics tall, their skin color has a bluish-green pigmentation, their foreheads have a series of raised bones they also have a strong body odor. Don't get me wrong it isn't bad but it is strong. But you will hopefully witness this if everything goes well this twilight."

"Agreed," Topanga said with a very cute smile that I could only imagine.

"Did you talk over your decision with your abode mate?"

"I did, and she told me if I really loved you then do whatever I felt in my heart. She told me if I decide to accompany you, she was going to miss me terribly but if that's what I wanted then I should go for it before it was too late."

"Grand, tell Cheryl it was a pleasure to know her, it was unfortunate we didn't get to know each other better and that I said grand adioso. Oh I just thought of something."

"What is that Jero?"

"Is Cheryl seeing anyone in particular?"

"I don't think she is seeing anyone special, why are you inkling of asking her along as well?"

"Negative huni buni you are enough female for me, I was inkling about setting her up with my little buddy Chad. You said she was 28?"

"Correct, the same age as I."

"Would she ever consider seeing anyone younger than she? I believe Chad is about 23 trittons old."

"I don't know, let me ask her, hang on a mite?"

So in the interim I read the names scrawled on the wall one more time.

"Greetings Jeroque, negative she isn't seeing anyone and she agreed to socialize with a 23 tritton old."

"Grand. I will give Chad your digits and let him introduce himself to Cheryl. You want to know something about Chad?"

"Sure what is it?"

"In the time I am from Chad was a champion among citizens in this war but unfortunately he was killed; I told him and he was able to avoid bereavement. Now I would like to start him on a life with someone as grand as Cheryl so he could enjoy the new life he now has. I will give him Cheryl's digits after our twilight banquet."

"That is so gracious of you, I will tell Cheryl."

"I should go have my banquet soon so I will see you on the gable of your structure at 8:45."

"I will be there," she said then we both said grand-adioso for now.

*****

I hung the PCD up and went to my quarters and let myself in. Inside the chamber, I turned on the IV monitor and looked at my timepiece. It was 16 hundred 49 epocks. 'I have a few mites before chow, I should read my electronic manual in more detail,' I thought as I sat on the lounger.

"Greetings Jeroque, I am going to clean up before we go for our twilight banquet," Chad said as he entered our quarters then went to his slumbering quarters.

I accessed the manual and started reading, I read all about the craft's Stealth capabilities. I was especially intrigued how the Comodrone Electronics P-52 Hydrogenic generator twisted and reflected illumination in such a way that the entire craft would disappear from sight as well as radar.

I then read about the Omagon 2115 Star Drive engine and the Electronic Flux Inducer. I learnt that the compressed oxygen that was stored in the tanks was needed not only in the event I flew into the Humanarian-made wormhole, but also in the event I ever had to leave ZarCedra's atmosphere, which I found out the p.a.r before this one.

I then happened on the section that explained all about the ejection procedure. When the ejection handle was pulled the entire cockpit ejected. Apparently there was a plexialluminus outer shell encompassing the cockpit, so if ever the ejection handle were pulled the whole cockpit would disengage from the craft. It had a triple parachute that automatically deployed so I knew if it hit the planet it would land softly or if it ever landed in a body of water, the plexialluminus outer shell kept the cockpit waterproof. Also pontoons automatically protruded from the bottom of the cockpit so there was no danger of sinking.

"Hmm you learn something new every p.a.r," I said then turned off the electronic manual as I ran my fingers through my short-cropped hair. I put on my beret and waited for Chad.

When he was ready, I went and washed up then we left our quarters then the barracks, and walked up the boulevard towards the mess hall. As we were walking, we met up with Capt. Pane.

"How is everything going citizens? "Pretty grand, we both replied. "Glad to hear you got a promotion. Is it all right if I have another interview with you sometime? "Affirmative, anytime you want," I said as I thought, 'this interview would never happen because before long I'll be gone. "Capt. Pane are you going to the mess hall as well? "Affirmative I am, as you know my brother Sgt. Jasontri Pane likes it when I have my banquets with him. "Affirmative and I would like to say that is very gracious of you. "Well I would do almost anything for my little brother."

At that time the three of us entered the mess hall; we grabbed trays then stood in line and waited until we received our banquets. After we each got a caffinated brew and eating utensils we went to the table where Sgt. Pane and Fl. Sgt. Colthamner were sitting.

LC Luxton, Capt. Pane and I sat down as the two brothers started conversing. I took a sip of my caffinated brew then looked at the faces around the table. "How is everyone doing? I asked. "Grand now that the Antrerian Armada have arrived. Just as you predicted," Fl. Sgt. Colthamner said.

"Affirmative, they arrived not a mite too soon or too late," I said as I took a bite of my banquet. At that time LC Luxton tapped my leg under the table, so I leaned towards him. "Are you all set for this twilight? "Almost set. I will leave about

20 hundred 30 epocks for a routine examination of the city then go pick up Topanga and leave. I must be at the proper coordinates at precisely 23 hundred 30 epocks Nesbitia time," I whispered.

"What are you two discussing amongst yourselves?" Fl. Sgt. Colthamner asked. "Things pertaining to what we were discussing this morn and my after banquet plan. "And what might that be?" Capt. Pane asked. "Unfortunately that is privileged information and I say that matter is top secret, I will let your brother tell you later this twilight. "Affirmative." Then we all consumed our banquets in quiet conversation.

"Come join me for a puff?" Sgt. Pane asked when we were through with our banquets. "Affirmative," I said as a bunch of us rose, gathered our trays then disposed of them on the nearby cart. We all went outside and walked over to the designated puffing area.

Upon arriving Sgt. Pane took a puffer from his pack and offered it to me. "I have tried cigars but I haven't tried puffers. Might as well, I probably won't be able to where I would like to go." Sgt. Pane offered me a spark then sparked his own.

"It sure will be different around here once you leave. I sure wish I were going with you," Sgt. Pane said. "Be careful what you wish for, you never know it might just happen," I said remembering the wish I had made to change the times elapsed so the times yet to come would be worth wanting. I took a deep drag then started to cough. "Are you all right?" Fl. Sgt. Colthamner asked. "Affirmative," I answered as I quieted down.

"What a p.a.r, lucky for us the Antrerians arrived when they did. Because if they didn't I'm not sure we could have handled the Protrerian High Command with just your assistance Jr. Commodore," Sgt. Pane said. "Affirmative, but we were still truly blessed to have his assistance and we were able to prevail. Just think how much of a disappointment it would be to travel back in the time elapsed to change the times yet to come; and not be able to do anything that would change it," Fl. Sgt. Colthamner said. "Affirmative that would be a letdown for sure," I answered as I took another drag. After, I took the puffer out of my mouth and looked at it. 'Nichii Surge'; I wonder what the significance is for puffing these?' I asked myself as I put it back in my mouth and took another drag. When I finished the puffer, I butted it in the ash container. "I must be off," I told my consociates.

"Grand luck, be careful and take care of yourself," Fl. Sgt. Colthamner said as she embraced me." Affirmative don't do anything I would, Sgt. Pane said with a smile as he shook my hand. "What's all the commotion about?" Capt. Pane inquired as he came walking up. "Your brother will tell you after my craft leaves this military facility," I said as LC Luxton and I walked away.

A few mites later, we both entered our barracks; after I had my retina scanned and stated my rank and name, the entry-way slid open and we stepped inside. I took off my beret and turned on the Inter Vision monitor. "I'm sure going to miss listening to the melodic composition of this era after I leave, but the instrumental medleys are much livelier in my own time." I got a piece of parchment and a ballpoint then sat at the table to jot Sr. Com. Bieas a note. I jotted:

Sr. Commodore Bieas,
"It was grand to be here in this time and be of assistance in this war but I've heard there was going to be an electrical storm off the coast of Nesbitia, much like the one that brought me to this time. So I'm going to attempt to fly through it in hopes I can get back to my own time. I would like to say many thanks for everything but this is something I have to attempt.

Tell Sr. Com. Bancais it was a pleasure to know him and mention that the craft they produce would be very successful especially without the Protrerian High Command's influence. Also, tell him the portion of N. Z. C. M. Co they head can (also with the Protrerian's out of the depiction) set a standard of high security for the entire planet in trittons to come. In addition, tell all the air citizens of this military facility that it was a privilege and an honor to serve in this war with them.

I met a lot of citizens in this time that I will never forget. I must warn about the specifications that were taken of the Omagon 2115 Star Drive engine and Electronic Flux Inducer, they must surround both engines with an electronic buffer. To block any extra energy from reacting with the Liquid Napricyte[2] SDC, so the thing that happened to me will never happen to anyone else.

In addition, the golden modules and rod that are on my craft are a mixture of 30% goldane, 30% silvertrivane and 40% iron-cylium.

I feel honored that I was able to participate in the Grand War, and this time we were able to be victorious. All my best in your times yet to come and I wish you grand success in your military career, Grand adioso.

Your consociate,

Jr. Commodore Jeroque Teldat.

*****

I reread what I had written then folded the piece of parchment then on the next sheet of parchment I jotted Cheryl's name and PCD digits and handed it to Chad with implicit instructions. "Give this note to Sr. Commodore Bieas after I leave, and make sure she does everything I ask. On another, happier note; I hope you don't mind but I took the liberty of telling Topanga about you and that she should relay that information to her abode mate Cheryl."

"I told Topanga, and she no doubt told Cheryl that your life was taken during this war in my time but now in this time you were able to stay alive. I met Cheryl and she seems to be a wonderful attractive female citizen, I think you and her would make a terrific couple so I mentioned that I would give you her name and digits and you would call her for a social twilight get together, preferably this twilight after Topanga and I vacate the city. "Affirmative, so she is attractive?" Chad asked with a smile as he placed both pieces of parchments in his pocket.

"Affirmative, she is and she is 28 trittons old, I hope that is ok with you? "Sure, as long as she is attractive," Chad said as he raised his eyebrows a few times. "Maybe too attractive," I said with a smile as I got up and went to pack a bag, when I was through I looked at my timepiece. "It is time I set out to scan the area then pick up Topanga. "Affirmative take care buddy," he said as he shook my hand then saluted.

"Have a grand life because in my time your life was taken from you before you were able to accomplish anything," I said as I returned the salute. "Many thanks for everything buddy, especially for Cheryl's PCD digits and I promise I will call her this twilight," Chad said as he quickly embraced me and patted my back. "Glad I could be of assistance little buddy, this time make something of yourself," I said as I embraced him back then let go.

"You don't have to accompany me to see me off, I don't want to call attention to myself as I leave. "Affirmative," Chad said with a smile. I went and gathered a few more memento's and deposited them into my bag, zipped it saying "grand-adioso," as I went out the entry-way."

I stopped to see Sgt. Pane to say grand-adioso, one more time. "Grand adioso, I hope everything works in your favor and all your hard work in this time period works to your advantage in your own time period," he said as he saluted me for the last time. "Many thanks, tell Fl. Sgt. Colthamner I said grand-adioso and I hope you all have a grand life as well." I said as I returned the salute.

"The cockpit of my craft is equipped with a homing device; if by chance my craft is destroyed in my attempt to get back to the times yet to come, it may be picked up by radar, if my cockpit safely ejects from the craft," I told Sgt. Pane. "Wow, you do have one amazing aircraft. "Can you do me a favor? "Anything. "Tell Dr. Alexander I said grand-adioso and I hope he, his wife and offspring have a grand life as well. "Sure thing."

"Many thanks for all your assistance and take grand care of yourself, also you don't have to accompany me to my craft to see me off, I don't want to call attention to myself as I leave," I said as we shook hands. "Affirmative," he said, as I turned then proceeded to my craft.

As I neared it, I pressed the left wing of my com-link. "'PAT, are you fueled and ready to depart? "Affirmative Jr. Commodore, I'm ready whenever you are. "Grand, lower the main hatch platform, I will be there directly. "Affirmative.

She did and when I arrived I stepped on. As I was going up to the cockpit, I thrawled the electronic keycard from my pocket. When the main hatch platform got to the cockpit, I entered then put my duffel bag in a storage closet. I went and inserted the electronic keycard in its designated port turning the ignition system on as I removed my beret and put on my flight suit.

I went and sat in the pilots' seat and buckled myself in. 'PAT' what is the level of Liquid Napricyte^2 SDC in the Star Drive engine?" I asked as I put the 'HUD' helmet on. "The Liquid Napricyte^2 SDC is at 5/8 of a vile," 'PAT said as I fastened my safety belts then started the main engines. "'PAT', are you ready to go? "As you are aware Jr. Com. Teldat, I'm always ready. "I mean for our attempt to time travel? "Affirmative Jr. Commodore, I am whenever you are."

The sun was already starting to set as I pressed the finger touch pad that activated two-way communications. "Tower, this is Jr. Com. "Time Star" Teldat, am I cleared for lift off. "Affirmative sir, you are cleared." I slowly started hovering upwards as the landing gear raised, I switched on the XT-165 DigiCam to record the time I had visited, hopefully for the last time.

Once I was up to three hundred metrics I leveled the wings. "'PAT', what is the time." A microsec later it appeared inside my face shield. 20:27 epocks. "Grand many thanks 'PAT'," I said as I flew over the city and scanned it for anything out of the ordinary.

"I must remind you Jr. Commodore of the time difference between the honorary regime of Placaden and the time in the regime of Nesbitia. "Many thanks for the reminder 'PAT'."

I circled about ten mites then went in the direction of the boulevard Topanga lived. With 'PAT's directional assistance, it only took a sec to locate the boulevard she lived on then another sec to locate her abode structure.

I set my craft down on the helijet pad on the gable of the structure as I awaited her arrival. A few mites later the entry-way finally opened and Topanga stepped through accompanied by Cheryl. "'PAT', open and lower the main hatch platform for Topanga. "Affirmative," she said as she contracted the wing, opened then lowered the main hatch platform as I activated the P. A. "Cheryl it was a pleasure knowing you and I wish you a wonderful life and take care of my little buddy for me? Chad said he would call you this twilight. "Many thanks, I sure will, and you take care of my little buddy," she said as she hugged Topanga. "I certainly will with all my heart," I answered.

After their embrace, Topanga stepped on the main hatch platform carrying a blue duffel bag. She waved grand-adioso to her consociate and wished her all the best. "Adioso and I hope you both have a grand life," Cheryl said as the main hatch platform rose to the cockpit then Topanga quickly entered.

"Greetings Jeroque and 'PAT'. How are you?" Topanga asked as she put her bag down then came over to give me a kiss. "Greetings Topanga and welcome aboard," 'PAT' and I said. I had the face shield of the 'HUD' helmet down so Topanga kissed the face shield. When she pulled away from me she left a lipstick imprint on the side of the face shield. "Grand now that you are with me and we are leaving together. 'PAT' close and seal the main hatch then extend the wing. "Affirmative sir."

"Topanga, place your duffel bag in the narrow closet at the back then have a seat, buckle in and put on the helmet," I told her as I blew the air hooter at Cheryl then I hovered up to 500 metrics. Topanga did as she was asked then sat and put on her helmet.

"Jeroque I am now ready," Topanga told me as she finished connecting the buckles of her safety belt then looked out the window; waved grand adioso to her consociate as we lifted off. I pressed a button on the side of my 'HUD' helmet and a microphone extended from her helmet. I activated it so Topanga and I could converse.

We flew out of the city then I slowly increased speed until the craft was flying at Mach two. "We are high enough in the air, going slow enough that we can enjoy the view." She looked out the front window. "The city is absolutely breathtaking at this height. "Affirmative, it is."

A few mites later I turned the XT-165 DigiCam off then checked the radar. I saw my flight path was clear so I looked at 'PAT'. "'PAT' take the controls," I commanded as I raised my face shield and swiveled my chair to face Topanga. "I am very happy that you have decided to accompany me," I told Topanga as I squeezed her hand and kissed her succulent lips.

"After meeting you I'd accompany you anywhere. I love you Jeroque and there isn't anyone I'd rather be with," she said as she gave me an incredible smile. "Many thanks huni buni and I am honored that you agreed to return with me, and I love you too, ever so much." We looked deep into each other's eyes and our lips met in a quixotic kiss once again.

"I'm going to warn you now that the odds of us making it back to my exact time is about 70-30. "What do you mean? "Well, the first time my craft was struck by lightning, I traveled in times elapsed; I have to recreate the exact timing and the lightening must have the exact voltage, if not, I'm not that sure if we will travel in times yet to come. There is a bigger chance we will travel even further back in times elapsed or the God's realms forbid my craft explodes in the process."

Topanga looked at me with a troubled expression. "I guess we just have to pray hard and hope for the best," she said with a smile. My frown suddenly turned into a smile. "I was hoping you would want to chance it, many thanks huni buni."

"I really do hope this proves to you how much I care for you," Topanga said to me as she turned in her seat. "It does darling, it really does," I said as I pressed the finger touch pad on the side of my helmet and the face shield lowered as I took ahold of the flight stick. "Many thanks 'PAT'; hang on ladies," I said as I advance speed to Mach ten. "What speed are we flying at?" Topanga asked as she looked out a window. "We are cruising at Mach ten. We must be at the correct coordinates at precisely 11:30, which is 9:30 our time, factoring in the two epock time difference between the two regimes."

"I'm a little frightened," Topanga confessed. "I'd be telling falsities if I said I wasn't a little uneasy myself, but hopefully we will get through this all right; just think grand thoughts. "Ok," Topanga answered as I flew over the Rexiant Regime.

Topanga and I talked of X-rated thoughts of what we would do to each other when we got to where we were going through time and before we knew it we were almost at the Regime of Nesbitia. We had a little time to dawdle before the storm was close enough so I circled Tierney Cove and got Topanga, 'PAT' and myself ready for our big step through time we were hopefully about to take.

"In any time you are the only citizen I want to be with," Topanga said as she looked over at me with a quixotic gleam in her eyes. "Many thanks huni buni, and there isn't anybody else now that I want to be with but you," I whispered into the helmet's microphone.

Here comes the storm as the sky lit up with each flash of lightening. I maneuvered closer and the thunder grumbled even louder the closer I flew. "Remember I will always love you," I said as I increased speed back up to Mach ten and flew to the heart of the storm. I held my finger above the touch pad to activate the Omagon 2115 Star Drive Engine as I flew closer. With each flash of lightening 'PAT' tried to estimate the timing of the right size bolt with the correct voltage.

"Activate the Star Drive engine and Electronic Flux Inducer... now," 'PAT' said. I did and as the perfect bolt of lightning struck the craft as I entered the swirling wormhole then at that moment everything went black...

****

When I finally came to, my craft had exited the swirling wormhole, I was groggy and disorientated, it was still dark outside but the storm clouds cleared out of the way for the light of the triple moons to shine through. What was wet, stormy skies with the flashes of lightening all around was now clear, dry, starry skies.

"Did we make it?" Topanga asked also in a disorientated state. "Well the craft is still in the air and it in one piece but as for traveling through time to the correct p.a.r, I do not know. 'PAT' come in? "Affirmative Jr. Commodore, go ahead. "Do you know if we traveled to the correct time period? "Unknown sir, as what happened before, I was off-line. But according to star charts we are off course again, we are once again nearing the Northern Pole of the planet. "Understood," I said as I slowed my craft then turned 40°. "We certainly aren't in the right place we should be but as for being in the right time we'll know in a few mites," I told Topanga as I increased speed to Mach ten.

I pressed the finger touch pad and activated two-way communications. "Jr. Com. Teldat calling the Grinshaw Military Facility, come in? "Sgt. Kilpatrick here, how can I assist you Jr. Commodore?" I heard what sounded like a party in the background as I talked to the air commuter transportation controller.

"What's all the excitement I hear? "This p.a.r is the end of the five p.a.r's of ZarCedra's Independence Gala," he said as someone blew a noisemaker. "I called to inquire a few things? "Affirmative sir, you may commence. "Well for one thing, is N.Z.C.M.Co/S.H.Z.C.A operational? "Affirmative sir, N.Z.C.M.Co is but I'm not sure what SHZCA is? "Understood, Sergeant."

"Two, who is in control of ZarCedra? "By your rank in the military, why is it you don't know this?" I didn't really know how to answer the young Sergeant's question, so I just said; "I am curious. "Our President of ZarCedra is, President Kincaid. "Affirmative."

"Finally thrice, what is this p.a.r's date? "Are you serious sir? "Dead serious Sergeant. "This p.a.r is 07.05.2115, why? "I am curious, many thanks, out."

I tapped the right wing of my com-link and called Sr. Commodore Boone. "Sr. Commodore Boone come in? Still all I received was static. So using my 'HUD' helmets two-way communications again I called for Sr. Com. Boone. All of a sudden Sr. Com. Boone appeared on the communications monitor. "Affirmative may I assist you?"

"Sir this is Jr. Com. Teldat," I said as I raised my face shield. "Do I know you son? "Affirmative sir you do, or should. I am on my way to the Grinshaw Military Facility now we will talk soon, Jr. Com. Teldat, out."

"All right Topanga, we are in the right place and time," I said as I decelerated to Mach 2. "Grand, she said as she disconnected her safety belts and removed her helmet then came to give me a hug. I checked my radar and seen my flight path clear of obstruction, so I gave flight control to 'PAT' and turned to face Topanga.

"Welcome to the 22nd centritton my adorable one," I said as I took her hand and drew her to me as Topanga and I kissed intensely.

I looked at Topanga and winked and smiled. "I am going to advance speed so it would be advisable if you re-fasten your safety belts and replace your helmet." Topanga winked at me as she resettled and I relieved flight control from 'PAT', "'PAT' what would the ETA be at Star Drive one? "Eight mites," she replied without a moment's hesitation. "What about Star Drive 2? "Six secs," she answered without delay. "Affirmative," I answered.

"Topanga, I am going to restart the Star Drive Engine and we will arrive at the Grinshaw Military Facility momentarily. There you will meet Sr. Com. Boone; I'm not sure what he is like presently but before my little mishap of time travel, he was a great superior officer," I told Topanga as I spoke into the helmet mic. "All right let's get there," Topanga said with a smile. "Hold on tight sweetheart." I told her as I looked at the long-range radar.

Seeing my flight path clear I lowered the face shield as I advanced air speed to Mach 10. I pressed the touch pad that activated the Star Drive engine, the ionic charge encompassed the craft then shot out before us, and my craft flew into the swirling wormhole as my craft advanced to Star Drive one then Star Drive two.

As my craft barrel rolled through the wormhole I began whispering sweet nothings into Topanga's ears via the helmets mic and the time seemed to fly by. After six secs I pulled out of Star Drive speed and the wormhole to discover I was flying over the outskirts of Cangla City.

I decelerated all the way down to 25 kps as I got in touch with the tower at the Grinshaw Military Facility. "Tower, this is Jr. Com. Teldat, am I cleared to set down? "Affirmative set down next to the helijets. When we were safely on the tarmac, Topanga and I removed our helmets and disconnected our safety belts then Topanga was back in my arms.

"I'm really glad you are with me," I said as I squeezed Topanga and kissed her cheek. "I'm not sure how the times yet to come has progressed over the last centritton but I sure am glad you are with me so we can find out together," I said as I squeezed her hand then I removed my flight suit.

"After meeting and falling hopelessly in love with you anytime would be all right as long as we are together," Topanga said as she embraced me tight. "Let's go see Sr. Com. Boone and find out if this time is as good as I hoped it would be without Protrerian domination," I told Topanga as I tweaked her bottom. "All right," she said and I pocketed the electronic keycard as I opened and lowered the main hatch. I squeezed Topanga's hand as we stepped on the main hatch platform.

"'PAT' would you care to find out how the times yet to come has turned out? "Affirmative sir," she said as we all lowered to the tarmac.

It was pretty dark out, although the glow of the moons and the boulevard lights shone enough illumination so we could see as we stepped off. "'PAT', raise and close the main hatch platform. "At once Jr. Commodore," she said then we walked towards main headquarters.

"I know the base isn't much to look at right now because it is semi-dark but you will be able to see the whole base clearer in the morrow." I said as I kissed her hand. "Ok then let's go," Topanga said as she squeezed my hand and the three of us entered main headquarters.

A mite later we arrived at the front desk. "Jr. Com. Teldat and party to see Sr. Com. Boone," I said pretty loud to be heard over the excitement in the reception area. "The Sr. Commodore is expecting me." I said as I scanned the excitement all around. "Affirmative he is, the Sr. Commodore told me to let you go right in on your arrival," the Corporal happily stated. "Many thanks," I said as we walked to the Sr. Commodore's entry-way and chirped the entry-way chime.

After a moment the entry-way slid open. "Enter," Sr. Com. Boone commanded. As soon as we entered the office, the entry-way slid closed and the noise subsided, we stood at attention and I saluted the Sr. Commodore. "Stand at ease." Sr. Com. Boone said as he returned my salute.

"Sir, I am Jr. Com. Teldat, accompanied by my cybernetic co-pilot and this young lady is Topanga Shrenka." I stated as I introduced them. "Grand to make your acquaintance," Sr. Com. Boone said as he stood to shake our hands. "Now, you mentioned that we should know each other," Sr. Com. Boone said as he sat back in his chair. "Affirmative sir, and I have a doozey of a tale to tell you of the things that happened in the last eleven p.a.r's. "Affirmative Jr. Commodore, go ahead," Sr. Com. Boone said.

"Affirmative sir, well I am an instructor in the field of Aero Dynamics and a test pilot; since I am a test pilot you wanted me to test then use the secretly constructed prototype Supersonic Dragon 228-D Spy Jet Stealth, your top scientists had invented and constructed." Sr. Com. Boone looked at me inquisitively as he raised an eyebrow.

"I had schematics drawn up for a craft called the Supersonic Dragon but I had no reason to have it constructed. You say we had it constructed secretly, why was it constructed in secret?" Sr. Com. Boone inquired. "That was because at that time and for the last centritton we were under the reign of an extraterrestrial race, known as the Protrerian High Command."

"I know of them they are whom our ancestors fought with the assistance of the Antrerian Armada, but we were victorious in the Grand War that is why there is celebration now. The war lasted five p.a.r's, which is why we celebrate and have a five p.a.r gala." Sr. Com. Boone stated. "That is great now but in my original time line we were defeated in the Grand War, which is why we were under the reign of the Protrerian High Command."

"I don't follow, have a seat and start at the beginning," the bewildered Sr. Commodore said. "Affirmative," I answered as we sat. "Everything I say can be verified by 'PAT', my cybernetic co-pilot. Like I conveyed earlier your two top scientists improve the 228 line of the Stealth Craft and designate the name of this new craft the Supersonic Dragon 228-D Spy Jet Stealth. Apparently, I was handpicked to test and use this spy jet craft on a secret mission on Vertgren Isle. While on that mission, one p.a.r I flew through an electrical storm as I was ordered to return to my temporary base ASAP."

"One important addition made to my craft is that it has Star Drive speeds. It accelerates to its maximum regular airspeed of Mach ten then if I engage the Star Drive Engine this craft accelerates to Star Drive one then if I choose, Star Drive two. "How much faster is that than your fastest regular air speed?" Sr. Com. Boone inquired.

"Star Dive one is ten times the speed of Mach ten and Star Drive two is twenty times that speed or equivalent to Mach 200. "That is some airspeed airman; you say my two top scientists invent this craft?" Sr. Com. Boone asked as he let out a long whistle.

"That is correct sir but I think the idea of such an engine was borrowed from the Protrerian High Command."

"To continue, while I was flying through this electrical storm and as I was flying into a wormhole my craft was struck by lightning. What I think happened was the tremendous amount of electricity somehow came in contact with the chemical fuel of my Star Drive engine and flying in that wormhole caused a tear in the time gamut. That is what caused me to plummet 100 trittons in the·times elapsed."

"But personally I think this was the God's way of giving Humanarian kind a second chance at being victorious in the Grand War because, I arrived just before the start. Coincidentally the first p.a.r I was there I met and fell in love with Topanga," I said as I kissed her hand.

"You are from the times elapsed?" Sr. Com. Boone asked in surprise as he looked at Topanga. "Affirmative sir, I was born in the tritton 1987." Topanga told the flabbergasted Sr. Commodore.

"To continue, a few p.a.r's later we were attacked by the Protrerian High Command and that was the start of the Grand War. Since I was from this time period I knew in advance what was about to happen and with my assistance in that war we were able to do what originally was impossible. Any way I was talking to the flight leader of the Antrerian Armada and told him that in 100 trittons or solar cycles their sun was going to go nova. So I told them that ZarCedra was the closest M-Class planet they could settle on."

"Out of curiosity, what compelled you to tell them that?" Sr. Com. Boone asked. "Because of their assistance in defeating the Protrerian High Command. Besides that was the original secret mission I was on in the first place. They were settling on Vertgren Isle without alerting ZarCedra Force or the Protrerian High Command, per your orders." I told the Sr. Commodore.

"You must have one remarkable craft, with what you told me and to sway the outcome of the war, also in the way you told me; tell me more of your craft?" Sr. Com. Boone asked.

"Sir, the Supersonic Dragon 228-D Spy Jet Stealth is five times larger than any Stealth craft in times elapsed. It is equipped with Sareden Quantum laser cannons, twin XTR-9000 Plasma Pulse Cannons, Protonic Electromagnetic Cluster Missals and

Neutronic Electromagnetic Cluster Torpedo's, I have long-range radar and I told you of its Star Drive speeds."

"But what I haven't told you is that the wormhole that my craft goes into is without oxygen and for that reason there are tanks of compressed breathable oxygen equipped to my cockpit also in the event I ever need to leave ZarCedra's atmosphere, which we had. Another very important aspect of my craft is 'PAT'," I said looking at her.

"The letters P.A.T is an anagram standing for Prototype Advancements in Technology," Sr. Com. Boone stated. "That is correct sir, but how it that you know this? "I have the schematics for such a craft in my wall treasury vault except it doesn't have a star drive engine and we never had a reason to construct such a craft that is why it was never built. I should mention that I did think of putting a talking computer into my design but not a cybernetic co-pilot," Sr. Com. Boone added.

"But in my original time line you did have it constructed that is why I was on that secret mission in the first place. I in fact have that craft on the grounds if you would like me to taxi it into a hangar for an inspection?" I asked the excited Sr. Commodore.

"Affirmative Jr. Com. Teldat, hangar three is empty and should be large enough to hold your craft and later I have a digidisk letter addressed to you from a Sr. Com. G. Bancais, locked in my wall treasury vault I will retrieve for you. That digidisk letter is what allowed me to believe your tale."

"On the front of that envelope it says 'To only be opened by Jr. Com. Teldat'. That is why it has remained in the wall treasury vault unopened all this time, passed down from all previous Sr. Commodores who held this office for the last 100 trittons. You do know where hangar three is located, don't you Jr. Commodore? "Affirmative sir, I do."

Before I left the office I turned toward Topanga, "stay with Sr. Com. Boone and you can accompany him to the hangar I will be in. "All right," Topanga said. I saluted my Commanding Officer then 'PAT' and I turned and exited the office.

"So you are not in the military? "No sir I'm not; when Jeroque, I mean Jr. Com. Teldat and I met I was a manager at a Handiness Supply shop and when he and I met his rank was Major. During the Grand War his rank was advanced to Jr. Commodore for bravery in the heat of battle. "Understood; you have a cute accent Topanga where is it you come from?" Sr. Com. Boone asked. "I originally come from Oskesar, Mankuer," Topanga said with a smile. "Aughh, it's very cute" Sr. Com. Boone said with a smile.

He went to his wall treasury vault and entered his secretive digits on a keypad. The entry-way opened and the Sr. Commodore removed a clear bag, which contained a faded timeworn envelope.

"This computer digidisk letter was enigmatic to all the Sr. Commodore's that held this office for the last 100 trittons but written on the front was; this letter to only be opened by Jr. Com. Teldat signed Sr. Com. G. Bancais and the tritton 2015. Citizens through the trittons kind of figured this envelope was a hoax but we were told to keep it just in case. I think it's about time we go to hangar three to meet up with Jr. Com. Teldat, he should just be entering the hangar about now," Sr. Com. Boone told Topanga.

"Can I ask you a question? "Of coarse, what is it? "What made you leave your life in the times elapsed and accompany Jr. Com. Teldat to the times yet to come? "Well it was just the way he explained, if ZarCedra won the war against the Protrerian's, his mate in this time would cease to exist as the lady he fell in love with considering she was half Humanarian and half Protrerian. So if he ever made it back to this time he would personally be alone. He told me that if he had my love he would try to be victorious in the war and if he was ever able to somehow return to this precise time, would I consider returning with him?"

"What if it wasn't possible to make it back? Sr. Com. Boone inquired as they walked out in the semi-darkness. "I told him we would try or suffer the consequences together. "You must care for him a great deal," Sr. Com. Boone said. "I do, there isn't anything I wouldn't do for him." Just then they entered the illuminated hangar.

"Magnificent," Sr. Com. Boone said as soon as I exited the craft. "Here Jr. Commodore, this is for you," Sr. Com. Boone said as he handed me the plastic bag that contained the yellowish envelope containing the computerized digidisk letter. "We have been holding on to this for a very long time, I was curious to see if I would receive the opportunity to hand this to you. "Many thanks," I said as I accepted the plastic baggy.

"I know what the initials N. Z. C. M. Co means but can you tell me what the initials S. H. Z. C. A. stands for?" Sr. Com. Boone inquired. "Certainly sir, S. H. Z. C. A is the anagram for Secret Humanarian ZarCedra Alliance. After the Protrerian High Command allowed Humanarian's back into the military, a secret section of ZarCedra's force was integrated and S. H. Z. C. A was born. "I see," Sr. Com. Boone said.

"I will now show you the cockpit," I told the very impressed Senior Commodore. "Affirmative," he replied grinning from ear to ear. "Like I conveyed earlier, I had schematics of this craft drawn up but I never had the need to have it constructed and it would be great to see a working copy of my dream craft. "Well let's go," I said as the three of us walked to the lowered main hatch platform, stepped on and we rose to the cockpit.

As we entered the cockpit, Sr. Com. Boone let out a "whistle," as he seen the multi colored touch pads, gauges and monitors of the control panels. "Sr. Com. Boone if you will sit in the pilot's seat and try this on," I said as I held the 'HUD' (Heads up Display) helmet. "Affirmative," he said as he walked over and sat in the pilot's seat. Sr. Com. Boone took the 'HUD' helmet and placed it on his head.

"'PAT' activate the helmet and menu view screen," I said after Sr. Com. Boone had the sleek black helmet on. On the bottom portion of the face shield, Sr. Com. Boone accessed the menu and in an array of multi-colored lights, and a in a little while he seen everything the helmet had to show. The last thing he seen was the level s of fuel and Liquid Napricyte^2 Star Drive Compound in the Star Drive engine.

"I notice you are getting low on your Liquid Napricyte^2 compound, do you have any left?" Sr. Com. Boone asked as he took off the 'HUD' helmet. "I have just over two, 200 ml vials remaining sir but I have to ask you to have more made before I run out." I said as I took the helmet and set it aside.

"Me, I don't even know what Liquid Napricyte^2 Star Drive Compound looks like, how can I have it made? Not you personally, have your scientific personnel create it, I will give them a sample of the radioactive accelerant so they can break down the composition, I said as I was standing next to Topanga and she yawned.

"Getting fatigued sweetheart?" I asked in a hushed tone. "I sure am Jeroque, she said as she rubbed the sleeve of my uniform. "All right it's getting pretty late," I told her. "Senior Commodore, can we pick up where we left off in the morn? "Affirmative, you both had a tiring twilight," he said as he looked at us.

"Actually the whole p.a.r was pretty tiring, the Grand War may have ended a centritton ago for you but it in fact ended this p.a.r for me." Topanga went to get her bag as I disengaged the electronic keycard and almost everything in the cockpit went dark. "Here let me carry that for you," I said as I took the duffel bag from Topanga and swung it over my shoulder. "Grand twilight 'PAT'," I said then the three of us headed to the main hatch platform. "Grand twilight," 'PAT' replied as she returned to her alcove as we stepped on and lowered to the floor.

"Can I ask, what those golden modules are that is attached to your craft are for? They are not in my design. I was going to ask you when we entered the craft but I decided to wait. "They are necessary to assist my craft to create and enter the wormhole the craft needs to attain star drive speed. There are more modules beneath the frame of my craft; however, I will explain them in greater detail at a later time when I show you the Star Drive engine," I said as we stepped off the platform. I tapped the left wing of my com-link.

"'PAT', you can now raise the main hatch. "Follow me and I will show you two the barracks you can stay in," Sr. Com. Boone said. We followed the Sr. Commodore's direction a few blocks to a dark colored structure; we entered and went to quarters twelve.

"You both could reside here for the next few p.a.r's until a more permanent abode comes available." Sr. Com. Boone said as he popped a breath mint into his mouth. "Affirmative, many thanks sir," I said.

Sr. Com. Boone placed his chin on the chin rest as he looked into the retina scanner. "Sr. Com. Boone," he said as he entered a secretive code on a numeric keypad. Something new happened after that; a green button illuminated and a voice welcomed Sr. Com. Boone to the quarters.

"Now Jr. Com. Teldat look into the retina scanner and enter this code" he said as he whispered it into my ear. Press the record button, state your rank and name then let your lady state her name, your retina and voice patterns will be recorded then only you two can enter these premises. I was going to tell the Sr. Commodore I already know how to operate the retina scanner but I was too fatigued. So I let him go on.

I did everything the Sr. Commodore said. I entered the code then pressed and activated the record button while I peered into the retina scanner and said, "Jr. Commodore Teldat." After it scanned my retina Topanga did almost the same, but since not having a rank she said, "Topanga Shrenka. "Welcome Jr. Com. Teldat and Topanga Shrenka and I hope you both will be content with the accommodations," the scanner said. "Many thanks I'm sure we will be," I replied as the entry-way slid open and we walked in.

We didn't have to say illumination on when we entered the living quarters, the lights illuminated automatically as soon as it detected our presence. "Jr. Commodore, do you have anything else to wear besides what you have on? Sr. Com. Boone asked. "Negative sir, what I have on is all the apparelec I have. "Affirmative, I'll have my secretarial assistant bring you over a few uniforms and latrine supplies. "Many thanks sir."

"Looking at you, you take a large shirt and jacket; what size waist are you?" The Sr. Commodore asked. "91.4 centrics," I told him.

"Topanga, I see you have a duffel bag with you do you have everything you require? "Affirmative I do sir, many thanks for asking. "Affirmative, the Senior Commodore answered. "Jr. Com. Teldat I want to see you in my office in the morrow morn at 08 hundred epocks for a debriefing. "Affirmative sir," I said as I saluted the Sr. Commodore.

"One more thing, I'm not sure if you are aware or not but when you are ready to slumber just tell the sensory computer 'slumber mode' and your slumbering quarters table illumination will stay off until you tell it 'PAR mode'. Then the illumination will illuminate whenever a body is detected. You both have a great twilight and my secretarial assistant will be here directly with your supplies, I'll also try to keep the celebratory noise down but I can't promise anything, this being the last twilight of the gala," the Sr. Commodore said as he returned my salute. "Affirmative," I answered then he left our quarters.

Topanga and I looked throughout the quarters awhile. "I'm going to get ready to slumber," Topanga told me. "Affirmative, I'll just wait here in the front chamber and use the computer to access this digidisk letter that Sr. Com. Bancais recorded for me until Sr. Com. Boone's secretarial assistant arrives with my supplies," I told Topanga as I kissed her cheek.

I went into the front chamber and picked up the plastic baggy that contained the digidisk letter and opened it, withdrew the envelope and opened it, I took out the computer digidisk letter and powered on the computer. I inserted it in its slot and moments later I was staring into the face of Sr. Com. Bancais and he said:

****

"Jr. Com. Teldat, 12.01.2015

How are you and Topanga doing? You must have made it to your time of 2115 if you are watching this digidisk letter. I had to return to the Grinshaw Military Facility and Sgt. Pane informed me of the plans you made.

I first want to say many thanks for all your assistance when you were here. Now we have almost completed the schematics of the Hugo C-15 and when that is complete we will start on its construction. Well you will know if we were successful if you see them flying around in your time. I told Dr. Alexander to stop work on the star drive engine and Liquid Napricyte^2 Star Drive Compound; it is in my best judgment that we are not ready for that engine at this time.

Following this digidisk letter you will find a program consisting of the formula you have given us, so you can have more made up when you see fit. I sure do find this place a whole lot different now that you are gone, you were here only a short time but I give thanks for your assistance in the war. I hope everything in your time has changed for the better.

Sr. Com. Bieas informed me of the meeting with the Antrerian flight leader, too bad I wasn't here for that meeting so I could have met them as well. As of yet we haven't heard anything from them and I'm not sure we will. I hope you do in your time; I appreciate them giving us assistance when they did. I also heard they gave assistance in clearing up the Protrerian ground troopers that landed on our continents. There is planning in the works for an Independence Gala so when you get to your time don't be surprised if there is.

I have to go now so you take care of yourself and I most likely won't be alive when you get this digidisk letter but if you ever find yourself in my time again look me up. One additional thing I should tell you is that remember when constructing the Star Drive engine, to encase it with some sort of electronic buffer. So what happened to you does not happen to anyone else.

Take care of yourself and that pretty young lady Topanga, and I hope you two have a long life together, adioso.

Your Consociate Sr. Com. G. Bancais.

****

Just then there was a chime at the entry-way. "Enter," I said as I ejected the digidisk then replaced the disk in its envelope and baggy. The entryway slid open and a Corporal entered holding a big bag. "Corp. Lavine and it's an honor to make your acquaintance Jr. Commodore Teldat, sir. Here are the articles you requested," the young Corporal said as he handed me the bag and saluted then extended his free hand.

"Many thanks," I said as I shook his hand and retrieved the bag. "Is that all you require at this time? "Affirmative, Corporal it is. "Affirmative sir, have a grand twilight," he said as he saluted again, turned then vacated my quarters.

I powered off the Computer then left the front chamber and brought the bag to the latrine. As soon as my presence was detected in the latrine the illumination illuminated; I took the contents out of the bag and placed it on a shelf. I rummaged through the contents until I came across an electronic micromesh shaver.

"What no laser blade," I said to myself. "That too must have been invented by the Protrerian's," I said as I brought my uniforms to our slumbering quarters. I hung my uniforms then undressed, as I was doing that I looked over at Topanga slumbering on the retiring unit and thanked the God's realms that she came back to this time with me and of course that we were fortunate enough to make it back.

When I was finished I disrobed then crawled in beside Topanga and watched her angelic face as she slumbered, I rubbed her cheek and thought she must be really exhausted with the big p.a.r we had. I kissed her lips and looked at my timepiece and said, "Alarm time 06 hundred 30 epocks." A sec later it beeped then said, "Complete." I looked toward the table lamp, "slumber mode." I said and as the illumination extinguished, I cuddled Topanga and drifted off in a long overdue serene slumber.

The End